The Sacrificial Daughter

Daughter

Books by Janet Dawson

The Jeri Howard Series
Kindred Crimes
Till the Old Men Die
Take a Number
Don't Turn Your Back on the Ocean
Nobody's Child
A Credible Threat
Witness to Evil
Where the Bodies are Buried
A Killing at the Track
Bit Player
Cold Trail
Water Signs
The Devil Close Behind

The California Zephyr Series
Death Rides the Zephyr
Death Deals a Hand
The Ghost in Roomette Four
Death Above the Line

Other Fiction
What You Wish For
But Not Forgotten

Praise for
The Sacrificial Daughter

"In this suspenseful novel, Janet Dawson tackles one of the most serious problems facing us today: how to provide for an increasing population of aging citizens. Well-researched, with engaging characters and vivid settings, this is another winner for Dawson."

— MARCIA MULLER
Author of the Sharon McCone series and
Grandmaster, Mystery Writers of America

"Kay Dexter helps her clients navigate the changes and challenges that come with growing older—issues that can lead to discord in even the best of families. Can lead, in fact, to murder. Award-winning author Janet Dawson has crafted a fine tale of the high price one family pays for its greed, lies, and misplaced loyalties. *The Sacrificial Daughter* is a satisfying first entry in a promising new cozy mystery series, and Kay Dexter is a heroine you'll want to have on your side."

— MARGARET LUCKE
Author of the Jess Randolph series
and the Claire Scanlan Haunted House mystery series

The Sacrificial Daughter

Janet Dawson

Bodie Blue
Books

Alameda — Monterey

A Bodie Blue Books original

Sign up for the Bodie Blue Books newsletter at: www.janetdawson.com

ISBN: Paperback – 978-1-944153-14-4
         Ebook – 978-1-944153-15-1

Dedication

To all the elders, especially my mother,
Thelma Dawson, going strong in her nineties.
And to my brother, Roger Dawson,
who helps make that happen.

Contents

Chapter 1 1

Chapter 2 11

Chapter 3 20

Chapter 4 29

Chapter 5 33

Chapter 6 50

Chapter 7 58

Chapter 8 67

Chapter 9 74

Chapter 10 84

Chapter 11 94

Chapter 12 102

Chapter 13 112

Chapter 14 121

Chapter 15 131

Chapter 16 139

Chapter 17 151

Chapter 18 159

Chapter 19 172

Chapter 20.. 186

Chapter 21 195

Chapter 22..206

Chapter 23.. 215

Chapter 24..230

Chapter 25..244

Chapter 26..259

Chapter 27 265

Chapter 28.. 278

Chapter 29..284

The Sacrificial Daughter

Chapter 1

"I'M AT MY WIT'S END," Sheryl Garvin said.

I could see that.

She had the stretched-too-thin aura of someone who wasn't getting enough sleep. Her voice sounded tired. Her manicured fingertips played with the heavy gold chain around her neck. She had been fiddling constantly with the necklace ever since she arrived. The diamonds in her matched wedding set sparkled in a shaft of afternoon sun from the window.

Like me, Ms. Garvin was a woman in her fifties. She sat in a comfortable chair in my office, wearing tailored blue slacks and a matching jacket, the necklace set off by the scooped neck of her pale pink blouse. Her face was angular and sharp-featured, her short brown hair expertly cut and styled, with no sign of gray.

I had offered coffee at the start of the appointment, but Ms. Garvin declined. I took a sip from my mug and set it on the table to my right, next to the purple African violet, the ceramic bowl containing my business cards, and the folder I'd prepared for this prospective client.

"Tell me what's going on," I prompted.

"Last Thursday, she left the stove on. Again." She rubbed the chain between thumb and forefinger, as though it was some sort of talisman. "I've told Mother repeatedly not to use the stove, that she needs to use the microwave to heat food. Only the microwave. But she forgets. She put some eggs into a saucepan to boil. Of

1

course, she forgot them. The water boiled dry, the eggs exploded, and the smoke alarm went off. The fire department came. That's the second time she's done that this year. One of the neighbors called me and I got on a plane."

"You don't live nearby," I said.

She left off worrying the necklace as she shook her head. "No, Ms. Dexter, I don't. I live in Seattle. I have lots of commitments. Once again, I had to take time off to come down here and deal with Mother. The last time I made the trip was because she drove her car to the grocery store and got in an accident, a small one, just a fender-bender. I'm really concerned about her." She pressed her hands against her temples, as though attempting to push the feelings back into her head. "I try to visit every couple of months, but it's not enough. I know that." She sighed. "I insisted that she get one of those alert devices, but half the time she won't wear it. She leaves it hanging on a doorknob or on her dresser. I hired a caregiver to visit Mother several hours a week. The aide lasted two days. Mother fired her."

"I hear that a lot." My smile was meant to be reassuring, but it didn't relieve her tense expression. "How old is your mother?"

"Eighty-seven. She was fine until—" She stopped and thought for a moment, her fingers plucking at the chain again. "It's been a couple of years now that I started noticing Mother's memory loss. I realized it had been going on for a while before that. It was gradual, over several years. It's Alzheimer's, senile dementia, I guess."

I nodded. I'd had this conversation many times, with many different people. Regardless of who was sitting in the chair across from me, the feelings of frustration and helplessness were the same. "Memory loss and senile dementia can be caused by many things, some of them

2

physical. If you haven't already done so, I suggest that you and your mother visit her doctor."

"I'll see what I can do," Ms. Garvin said. "Mother hasn't had a check-up since her doctor died last year. I've suggested it, but she insists that she's fine. And she doesn't want to see anyone except the doctor she went to for so many years. I've told her several times that he died, but she forgets."

"When are you going back to Seattle?" I asked.

"As soon as reasonably possible. This latest incident with the fire department happened on Thursday. I took time off work and came down here. I do have some important obligations at work, things it will be difficult for me to get out of. And my husband—" Ms. Garvin frowned as she twisted the chain. "I had to back out of an event with his family this past weekend. My husband wasn't happy about that. It's Monday now. I really would like to get Mother settled and go back by the end of the week."

I could make that happen, I thought, if she decided to hire me. I had more questions, though. "Do you have any other family members who could help you deal with your mother's situation? Siblings, cousins?"

"I had an older brother. He died a long time ago." She paused. Her frown deepened. "My younger sister is out of the picture, has been for years. I'm not sure where she is. As far as I know, she hasn't been in contact with Mother. I do have a few cousins. But my mother was the youngest sibling in her family. All her brothers and sisters are dead. There aren't any relatives in the immediate area, no one I can call on for help, not on a regular basis. Besides, what relatives are left all have their own obligations, just like me."

"So, there's no one else," I said.

She shook her head and sighed again. "No. I'm it. I'm the one who has to take care of my mother. I hesitate to take the car away from her, but I don't want her to get into another accident. I plan to sign her up for Meals on Wheels deliveries. She hasn't been eating properly. If she's left to her own devices, she'd live on cottage cheese and crackers. Sometimes canned soup. Whatever is handy, but that sort of diet is not particularly nutritious. Certainly not enough fruits and vegetables. Her neighbor has been kind enough to buy groceries from time to time, but that's a temporary fix."

Her fingers moved once again to the gold chain. Then, realizing what she was doing, she folded her hands in her lap, attempting to keep them still. "I've suggested hiring a caregiver, several times. She says she doesn't want any strangers in her house. I've also brought up the subject of Mother moving to a senior apartment or an assisted living facility. But she won't consider any of those things. She could certainly afford it. Her financial situation is comfortable. She's lived in the same house for over fifty years. She wants to stay in her own home."

I nodded. "Most people do. And I find that forcing an elderly parent into a facility often backfires."

"Even if that elderly parent can't cope with living alone?" she shot back.

"It's a natural feeling," I said. "Most of us don't want to admit that we need help."

"Mother won't admit it, that's for sure," she said. "But I need help. Long-distance caregiving has got me completely frazzled. I'm not coping very well. That's why I'm here."

Her bag was on the floor near her feet. She leaned down and reached inside, pulling out a business card, bent at the corner. It bore the logo and name of my care management firm, with my name, Kay Dexter, and my contact information printed below that. "Someone gave me this card. She told me you're a care manager. Just what is that? And what could you do for me and my mother?"

I appreciated the referral. Word of mouth was how I got much of my business.

"A geriatric care manager plans and coordinates care of aging adults or others who have ongoing health issues. My firm specializes in assisting older people and their families with long-term care arrangements. Frequently our clients are people in situations like yours, an aging parent here in town, with family members living elsewhere. We also help people with physical or mental impairment, although the majority of my clients are older adults." I reached for the folder and handed it to her. "I've collected some information that will explain it in more detail."

"Thanks." She opened the folder and sifted through the papers and brochures.

I continued with my explanation. "What I can do to help you and your mother varies, depending on her needs, and yours. The first step is for me to assess your mother's situation. That will serve as a road map to guide us. I'll recommend services that will help improve her quality of life. And reduce your stress level."

She looked skeptical. "All of that sounds good, Ms. Dexter. But I'd like to hear some examples."

I nodded. "First, I'll look at your mother's housing situation, to see if she's a good candidate to stay in her own home. If that's possible, I can help make that happen, such as determining what kind of home care services she needs. I'll also monitor her at home and recommend adding things to help with her safety, such as grab bars at various locations in the house. The best choice may be that she stays in her home, helped by these modifications and caregivers. Those could be people like a home health aide, either one that visits or one that lives with her, or people to come in, help her bathe, buy groceries, cook simple meals. There are lots of possibilities. And if I feel she shouldn't stay in her home, I'll recommend appropriate facilities and help you evaluate and select where your mother should live."

"Good luck with that." She looked doubtful, fingers tweaking the gold chain. "What if she won't agree to a caregiver, or she won't go to an assisted living place?"

I smiled. "Let's take it one step at a time. I've had good results persuading people like your mother to act in their best interests. Sometimes the suggestion is better received if it comes from me, rather than a family member. If you like, I can assist you in monitoring her finances. I also help with medical management. That means going with your mother to doctors' appointments, helping you and your mother communicate with doctors, and if need be, making sure your mother is following her doctors' instructions and taking her prescribed medications."

She nodded, her expression moving from doubtful to thoughtful. "What are your qualifications and experience? And your references?"

"I'm happy to provide you with references," I said. "As for my qualifications, I have an MSW, a master's degree in social welfare, from the University of California in Berkeley. I've had additional training in gerontology, the study of aging. I have experience working in Alameda County, as a social worker for Adult Protective Services. Then I was a health care social worker for a hospital. I became interested in working with elderly people and worked as a geriatric care manager with a firm in Oakland. Several years ago, I moved here to Rocoso and started my own firm. I have two other care managers working with me. One has a lot of experience as a social worker, and the other is a registered nurse who has worked extensively with elderly people."

"Why here?" she asked. "After working in the Bay Area?"

"Aging parents, just like you. I know what it's like. I've been where you are, worrying about my parents. I moved back up here before my father died. After he was gone, I stayed, to be close to my mother, and to fill a need here in town."

She stared at the folder on her lap, then she looked up. "Okay. What I'm hearing sounds reasonable and workable. I'd like to move ahead. What's the first step?"

"Please fill out the preassessment form. It's the one on the right side of the folder," I said. "As you do that, you can describe your concerns in more detail. The information gives me an overview of the situation with your mother. Ordinarily, I would say take as much time as possible to answer the questions. But you're in town for just a few days, so it would be helpful if you'd fill out the form now. Then we'll set a time for the care-planning assessment. That involves a home visit with you and your mother, perhaps two visits. The home visit can take an hour or two. While I'm there, I'll take a look at her living situation, to see what issues she has around safety. And transportation. You said earlier your mother's still driving."

"Yes, but that needs to stop," she said. "She had several minor accidents. Her eyesight isn't as good as it used to be. I know her eye doctor mentioned cataracts, but he didn't think surgery was needed at the time. That was several years ago and I'm sure the diagnosis has changed. I don't know when her driver's license is up for renewal. I'll check that later."

"Good idea. If her driver's license needs to be renewed and she can't pass a test, that may make it easier to get her to stop driving. The physical therapy department at Rocoso Medical Center has a computerized driving simulation test that looks at things like reaction time. We could schedule your mother for a test, to see how she does, and then make a recommendation that she stop driving."

She nodded. "The suggestion comes from the medical people, not me nagging Mother to stop driving. I like that."

"Exactly," I said. "As for alternate transportation, we do have a senior ride program here in the county. I can provide information on that when I do the assessment. I will need a list of the medications she's taking, how much, and how often. If you decide to hire me as your mother's care manager, I will go with her to doctors' appointments to make sure we're all on the same page in terms of her medical issues and prescriptions. We'll also talk about your mother's meals and nutrition, as well as her legal and financial situation. I'll make recommendations based on my assessment, and you and I can work with your mother to make some decisions. We have a very good senior services system here in Rocoso, with lots of resources. We'll do what we can to keep your mother in her home. Having a caregiver is a good start. Together we might be able to persuade your mother to accept one. If she can't continue living in her own home, we can look at what alternatives might work for her, such as assisted living. Once the assessment is done and the recommendations are made, I'll monitor your mother regularly."

"Let's do it. As soon as possible. I'd like to hire you as Mother's care manager. Starting now."

"That's fine," I said with a nod, reaching for the appropriate paperwork. After those formalities were done, I stood and walked to my desk, where the calendar showed the week's appointments. Today was Monday. Did I have a two-hour block free in the next few days? Yes, another appointment had been rescheduled, leaving a slot open on Tuesday. "As for the assessment, I have time early tomorrow afternoon. Would one o'clock work for you?"

She looked up from the form she was filling out. "Yes, it would. Mother's name is Betty Garvin. She lives on Juniper Street." She gave me the house number.

I noted the appointment on the calendar, then picked up the mug and carried it to the small kitchenette in an alcove off the main office. I dumped the rest of the coffee into the sink, rinsed the mug, and set it to dry on a dish towel.

When I returned to my office, she had finished filling out the form. I looked it over and we discussed the additional information and records needed for the assessment visit and preparation of a written care plan. "Getting those documents shouldn't be a problem. I have power of attorney for Mother's financial and medical matters. I also have a lawyer here in town, John Fielding at the Guisewhite firm."

I nodded. "I know John. I've had dealings with him."

She stood to leave. The appointment had taken about forty minutes. I walked her out and shut the door. The front office window was open, letting in some air on this May afternoon. Sheryl Garvin stopped a few paces from my door, took her phone from her bag, and peered at it. She touched the phone's screen several times and raised it to her ear.

Unlike the more serious tone she'd used during our meeting, her voice on this end of the conversation was bantering and intimate. "I got your message. Of course, I want to see you." She laughed. "Not dinner, I'm afraid. A drink. Sure, I'll meet you there. Fifteen minutes." She ended the call and tucked the phone back in her bag, walking toward the street.

She had been my last appointment of the day and

while she was here in the office, I'd turned off the ringer on my cell phone, and the office phone had been forwarded to voice mail. I checked messages and email, responding to both. Then I leaned back in my chair and did a more careful and thorough read-through of the multi-paged preassessment form Sheryl Garvin had filled out, making notes on a lined pad.

Betty Garvin had lived in the same house for over fifty years. That meant Sheryl had attended Rocoso High School, as I had. At the time, it was the only high school in town. I didn't remember Sheryl at all, but that wasn't unusual. I was in my mid-fifties and I guessed Sheryl was a few years younger. Nor did I recall her younger sister. But I remembered her older brother. He had been a year ahead of me in high school. His name started with a G – George? Gary? No, Greg, that was it. He had played sports, football, but he hadn't been one of the outstanding players. After graduation from high school, he'd gone off to college. Then he died, a year or two later. By that time, I, too, had gone away to college, far from home and the Rocoso grapevine. I'd heard that he'd died in a car accident but had no details.

During her meeting with me, Sheryl Garvin looked frazzled. And I knew why. I saw it all the time. She was the only one available to look after her mother. Her brother was dead and she wasn't sure where her sister was.

Or so she said.

Something didn't feel right. It wasn't major, setting off alarm bells. Just a feeling I had, that gave me some reservations. The expression on Sheryl's face when she mentioned her sister hinted that there was more to the story than simply losing contact with her remaining sibling. There was estrangement there, something that ran deep and bitter.

Eventually, I'd find out what it was. I usually did.

Chapter 2

I GLANCED AT MY WATCH. Nearly five. Time to leave. I shut down the computer and reached for my purse and tote bag.

My office was on the grounds of the Rocoso Historical Museum, on Main Street in the downtown historic district. The large Italianate Victorian mansion had once been a bordello, back in the days when Rocoso was a rich and rowdy mining town, one of the jewels in Northern California's Mother Lode. The building in back had been converted from a stable, with four units carved out of the space. My stablemates, as we called ourselves, were an architect, an attorney, and an accountant. My firm had a large space, which had been divided into the main office and three smaller offices for my two associates and me.

I opened the front door and stepped out. My silver Prius was parked in the small lot off the alley. As I walked toward the lot, I saw my colleague Gwen Lewis getting out of her car. I'd known Gwen for years. Our paths had crossed frequently during our years as social workers in the Bay Area. An avid hiker and birder, she had moved to Rocoso four years ago, drawn by the lower cost of living and the outdoor recreation here. She had looked me up and I'd invited her to join forces with me and Carmen Castro, the RN who was the third member of the firm.

"Done for the day?" she asked now, running a hand through her short brown curls. "How did that appointment go?"

"We have a new client. I'm doing the assessment visit tomorrow."

"Good. I just got back from a client visit. I'm going to make some notes before I head home." She waved and headed for the office.

I had my keyring in hand, ready to unlock the Prius. Then I heard someone call to me. Dina Espinoza, director of the museum, had just left the building and was coming down the back steps.

Back when we were teenagers and best friends in high school, I was the bookworm, but Dina was never much interested in school. I was surprised when she wound up with a graduate degree in museum studies. And who would have thought that we'd both return to Rocoso? When we were kids, we'd talked about how much we wanted to get out of this little town in California's Sierra Nevada mountains, a place where it seemed that everyone knew us, our parents, and our business.

Life is full of twists, turns, and detours. For various reasons, Rocoso drew us back. I had never married, though I'd had two near-misses and several long-term relationships. Over the years I discovered that I was quite happy being single and on my own. As for my move back to the town where I grew up, there were several catalysts, my aging parents for one, and major changes in my work situation in the Bay Area.

Dina's story was somewhat different. Her first marriage hadn't lasted long and she had a son. Several years ago, she had rekindled a romance with Ed McGinty, whom she'd known in high school. Ed was now a widower with two adult children. At the same time they started dating, the historical society was recruiting a replacement for the director, who was planning to retire. The romance had turned into a happy second marriage, and Dina had left a position in Sacramento to run the museum in Rocoso.

"How goes planning for the fundraiser?" I asked. The

historical society's annual fundraiser was scheduled for this coming Saturday.

Dina pushed her wire-rimmed glasses up her nose and tweaked a strand of salt-and-pepper hair off her forehead. "Five days to go. I hope we'll be ready. All the decorations are ready to be transported to the high school gym Friday after school. Lorita Ma is still collecting donations for the silent auction. She has some great goodies. What are you going to wear?"

"My vintage dress. The same thing I wore last year." I found the 1890s evening gown in one of Rocoso's many antique stores. It had been an extravagant purchase, but once I saw it, I had to have the dress. It was deep blue silk with a bodice of gold and silver beads and white lace trim, in fairly good condition despite being more than a century old. I managed to remove a few spots on the skirt and an hour with a needle and thread repaired torn lace and added new beads. The dress set off my figure, which wasn't bad for a woman my age. I felt elegant each time I wore it.

"Wait till you see the dress I got. It's a knockout." Dina's cell phone rang. She pulled it from a pocket on the side of her purse and looked at the readout. "Sorry, I have to take this. It's the guy who's in charge of the food."

"I've got to go anyway. It's Monday. Tai chi class."

"Oh, right. I'll talk with you later." Dina turned, phone to her ear.

I unlocked my car and slid into the driver's seat, dumping my bags on the passenger seat. I started the engine and left the lot, turning onto Main Street.

Rocoso was a small city with a population of about 21,000. The county seat, it was the largest community in Rocoso County. Its business district and residential neighborhoods were spread out on either side of the river of the same name. Located in the northern Sierra Nevada, at an elevation of about 4,300 feet, it had once been a mining town. Millions of dollars in gold had been pulled from the rich gravel and sand bars along the Rocoso River, and its tributaries. There were still hopeful miners in the area, trying their hands at panning for the elusive flecks of ore.

These days, however, the money was in tourism. Rocoso was Spanish for "rocky." Upstream from town, the twisting, winding river had several sections of Class Five rapids, drawing rafting enthusiasts from all over the country. For those who liked to stay dry, the city was ringed with hiking trails, from easy to strenuous, and there were zip lines for the adventurous.

A historic narrow-gauge train took daily trips up the canyon from Rocoso to the old gold mining camp of Jermyn, forty-eight miles north, and at a higher elevation, more than 5,000 feet. Popular with railfans and tourists alike, the journey ran along the river most of the way. At times the rails were ten to twenty feet above the riverbank, then the route climbed over a ridge, with spectacular views of a deep gorge called the Narrows, where it was more than five hundred feet down to the river, a silver ribbon at the bottom. It was an all-day excursion, with the train taking about three and a half hours to reach Jermyn. Passengers had two hours to explore the Jermyn museum, gift shops, and restaurants before boarding the train for the return to Rocoso.

The town's name was reflected in many of the local establishments—a pizza parlor, a creamery, the local river rafting company, and various lodgings. Then there was Rocoso College, a four-year liberal arts college that granted undergraduate degrees in a variety of subjects.

I glanced down at the river as I drove across the Main Street bridge. In the summer there would be rafters idling in the stream, but I didn't see any today. It was May and the river, swollen with snowmelt, was too cold for any but the most dedicated rafters.

I heard the warning whistle before I saw the train. Steam puffed from the stack of the Rocoso & Jermyn Railroad locomotive, and the whistle sounded again. At the intersection, red lights flashed and bells clanged as the crossing arms lowered.

I braked, shifted into park, and turned off the car's engine as the train lumbered past. At this time of year, on a weekday, there were only three cars between the engine and the caboose, and one departure each day. As Memorial Day approached, and through the summer, tourists thronged the town. Two additional departures and more passenger cars would be added to the train. The annual railroad festival in late July brought thousands of attendees.

Once the train had passed, the crossing arms raised and traffic began moving again. I turned right off Main Street, heading into a residential area that was close enough to the tracks for residents to hear the train as the Rocoso & Jermyn locomotive pulled out of the station in the morning and returned to town in the late afternoon. My house on Dorado Drive overlooked the river. A park with a walking path edged the riverbank for several miles. On summer evenings, with my windows open, I could hear the constant noise as the river rushed by, splashing on rocks near the shore. The street was about twenty feet above the waterway, safe enough, but the Rocoso River had been known to flood in wet years. I remembered one such flood, the first year I'd lived here, when rain and snowmelt had pushed the river over its banks and into the street. The water hadn't reached my home, though it had covered the street, topped the curb, and soaked the front yard.

I share my home with three cats. My feline

companions are good company, although they can be needy and demanding. I had adopted them after a long weekend trip to the eastern Sierra ghost town of Bodie. Arriving home, I found a mother cat and two tiny kittens, sheltering in the flower bed in my backyard. When I spotted them, I got out the can opener and started feeding them. Lured by food and water, they had returned each evening. I caught the kittens two weeks later and named the male kitten Bodie, after the town. Clio was the female kitten. In Greek mythology, Clio is the muse of history. An appropriate name, since it was a historical tour of ghost towns that had led me to the other side of the mountains. It took another two months to persuade Mama Kitty, now called Lottie, to come inside. Lottie's name also had connections to that weekend trip. She was named after Lottie Johl, a famous resident of Bodie in its mining heyday.

I took the day's mail from the mailbox and unlocked the front door. The cats appeared, zeroing in on the food and water bowls set on a tray on the kitchen floor. "There's food in your bowl," I told them. Bodie didn't look convinced. I glanced through the mail, then left it on the kitchen counter and went to the bedroom. I changed out of my work clothes to a pair of khaki cropped pants and an olive-green T-shirt from last year's Rocoso Railfest. My ashy brown hair, streaked here and there with silver, was short, curling around my ears. It looked fine, I thought, glancing in the mirror.

My mother, Rose Dexter, also lived on Dorado Drive, several blocks away, in the house where my brother and I grew up. This afternoon she waited on her front porch, dressed in loose-fitting slacks and a roomy T-shirt, the wind ruffling her short white hair. She moved well for a woman who was nearing ninety. She had played tennis until a year ago, winning gold medals at the National

Senior Games. She reluctantly gave up the game she loved when she became concerned about her balance and the possibility of falling on the court. She had indeed fallen several months ago, stumbling in the backyard as she worked in her garden. Now she used a footed cane when she left the house.

Hand firmly on the wrought-iron railing, Mom stepped down from the porch and walked toward the car, wielding her cane with the other hand. She opened the passenger door and carefully levered herself into the seat, setting the cane on the floor near her feet.

"How was your day?" Mom asked.

"Busy. And yours?"

"I worked in the garden this afternoon, pulling weeds. Then I got tired. I read the rest of the afternoon. May have dozed off, too."

I smiled. Yes, Mom had been known to doze off while reading.

Mom fastened her seat belt. "Your brother called."

"What did he have to say?" I backed the car out of the driveway, shifted, and drove downtown as Mom relayed the gist of the conversation. My brother Robert was four years younger than me. He and his wife Brenda had three children, all grown and out on their own. Bob was in the Navy, a career that began when he joined the Navy Reserve Officers Training Corps while in college. He had been stationed all over the United States and in other countries as well. For the past four years, he'd been at Pearl Harbor and before that, three years at a command in Guam. Because of his career, his trips to Rocoso had been infrequent. He was in town when Dad died, six years ago. Since then he'd made two brief visits. I hoped he'd be able to take leave and come back for Mom's ninetieth birthday, since I was planning a party.

"He and Brenda are looking forward to their transfer

in the fall," Mom said. "He'll be at the Naval Station in San Diego. I hope they'll be able to visit more often."

"That would be nice. Maybe he'll retire from there. He's been in the Navy for nearly thirty years."

When we reached our destination, the Rocoso Community Center, I parked near the entrance. Mom and I walked toward the front door. I slowed my usual brisk walk to Mom's pace. Inside the center, we made our way to a large meeting room, where tables and chairs had been cleared away, stacked against the walls to leave plenty of space.

Marla Cates, the tai chi instructor, was dressed as usual in black yoga pants and a black T-shirt decorated with a yin-yang symbol that meant balance. She was tall and middle-aged, her salt-and-pepper hair a good match for her salty tongue. The late afternoon classes met four days a week, Mondays through Thursdays, and began with half an hour of qigong, the ancient Chinese moving meditation. Then Marla led the group through the tai chi form. I had practiced qigong and tai chi for years, ever since graduate school at the University of California in Berkeley. When I moved back to Rocoso, I was pleased to learn about these classes that fit with my work schedule. I persuaded Mom to join me, stressing that the practice was good for balance.

"As long as it's not yoga," she said at the time. "I might be able to get down on the floor but I'd have a heck of a time getting up."

I turned off the ringer on my phone and kicked off my shoes. Mom and I joined the group. Class attendees varied in numbers and ages, ranging from teens to people Mom's age, with a fair smattering of the middle-aged and students from the college. Today the group numbered eleven, including one newcomer. They stood in a wide circle and began the slow meditative qigong, with its deep breathing, slow movements, and stretches.

As I moved, I reviewed that day and thought about tomorrow's schedule. Then I pushed away all thoughts of work as I concentrated on stretching and deep breathing. After the qigong, we lined up and, with Marla's direction, began the tai chi form. By the time we moved into the first Single Whip, I was focused on the set and nothing else.

Once the group had completed the set, Marla split the class into beginners and more advanced practitioners. The advanced group did another tai chi set, while Marla worked with the beginners. Tonight, the class ran over its allotted hour. After we circled and did some final deep breathing, the class broke up.

I put on my shoes and checked my phone. There were two voice mails, both from the same client. I listened to them, hearing the urgency in my client's voice. I tucked the phone into my bag and turned to Mom, who was chatting with Marla.

"I'll drop you off at home. I have to deal with a situation."

Chapter 3

"THIS IS UNACCEPTABLE."

I stood with my hands on my hips in the middle of a private room at the Golden Acres rehabilitation and nursing facility on the east side of town. My job was to be my client's advocate, and I was feeling angry on her behalf.

"It's humiliating." Fran Lomax's face was indignant under her crown of short silver hair. She was in her early eighties, a retired librarian who had been one of Mom's frequent tennis partners. Fran still played tennis. But it hadn't been a mishap on the court that put her here. She'd slipped on the front steps of her house. The fall broke her leg. After surgery, she had been sent to Golden Acres for rehab until she regained enough strength to walk.

Right now, Fran's voice vibrated with anger, as it had in the two messages she'd left on my phone. She thumped her fist on the bed railing. "The staff took out my catheter yesterday. I was wary about that, I can tell you. I can't get out of bed and walk to the bathroom on my own, even with a walker. The doctor doesn't want me putting any weight on my leg until he gives the okay. This afternoon I had to go to the bathroom. I rang the call button and no one showed up to get me out of bed and to the toilet. I just couldn't hold it anymore. It's so humiliating, to wet the bed. The bedclothes are soaked. I'm lying here in my own pee, and still no one answers the call button."

"I'll deal with it. Give me a few minutes."

I did an about-face and left the room. The situation was humiliating for Fran. It would be for anyone, regardless of age or disability. Out in the hall, I looked for an aide but didn't see one. I kept walking, down the hall to the main office, which was in another wing. There I found the nursing home supervisor. Her jacket was draped over one arm and her bag was looped over the other. It looked like she was leaving for the day.

"Oh, Ms. Dexter. I didn't expect to see you this late in the day. Is there a problem?"

"There certainly is." My voice was steely as I explained the situation.

"Oh, no," the supervisor said. "I'm so sorry. One of our aides didn't show up. She's the person who's supposed to be on shift in that wing. I'll straighten this out."

"I'm sure you will." I followed the supervisor as she walked back to the wing where Fran's room was located. On the way, the supervisor flagged down an aide who was coming out of another room.

Back in Fran's room, I waited while the other two women changed the bedding and gave Fran a sponge bath. "I hope this doesn't happen again," I told her.

"It won't," the supervisor assured me.

But this was the second time it had happened to one of my clients. The earlier incident had occurred two months ago. At the time, I'd had a conversation with the owner of the nursing home. I planned to call him again, first thing tomorrow morning. This was his second strike, and a third would lead me to the next step, which was for me to file a complaint with the Licensing and Certification Division of the California Department of Public Health. I'd make sure the owner knew that.

I waited until the supervisor and the aide had gone, then turned to Fran. "Has the doctor given you any update on how much longer you'll be here?"

She sighed. "When I saw him this morning, he said another week or two. I can't wait to get out of this place. And I don't know whether it will be okay for me to play tennis again." She stopped and tightened her mouth.

I know Fran wondered if she should stop playing tennis. Like Mom, Fran loved the game and had played since she was a teenager. But she didn't want to run the risk of falling again. Up until this most recent incident, Fran had been active, both mentally and physically, radiating good health. It was ironic, then, that she should be sidelined by a freak accident, incurred while she was sweeping her front steps.

People like Mom and Dad, and Fran, are the reason I do what I do.

As I'd told Sheryl Garvin earlier that day, I had worked in this field for a long time. The work was interesting and satisfying, never dull, and sometimes stressful, especially in the days when I was with Adult Protective Services for Alameda County. As a health social worker, in several hospitals, I helped patients understand their diagnoses and make the necessary adjustments to lifestyle or housing, or changes in the medical care they would need. In other cases, I assisted patients who'd been discharged from the hospital to go home. Sometimes I worked with doctors and other health care professionals to give insights into how diseases and illnesses affect patients' mental and emotional health.

I worked with all sorts of people, of all ages. But I found myself increasingly drawn to working with elderly people. The old are sometimes forgotten and frequently marginalized in a society that celebrates youth. I found my voice as an advocate for the aged.

At the same time, my own family was going through what is experienced by so many families. My father had Alzheimer's disease. It is a slow and gradual deterioration that happens over a long period of years. In the decade before Dad's diagnosis, I noticed, as so many of us do, that he was forgetful. It got worse. He asked the same questions over and over. It was frustrating, until I realized that he didn't remember he had asked those questions, much less the answers. So, I just answered the questions. Dad was never the best patient, and it took some persuading and cajoling to get him in for an examination that revealed, in stark terms, his short-term memory loss. It was undeniable.

Except to Dad.

"Who says I have Alzheimer's?" he argued, argumentative to the last. That denial was in itself a symptom of the disease.

Alzheimer's is not the only kind of dementia but it's the one that gets much attention. It causes problems with memory, thinking, and behavior. Symptoms are slow to develop and they get worse over time, becoming severe enough to interfere with daily tasks. As for what causes it, researchers suspect that proteins called plaques and tangles build up inside the brain and kill nerve cells. When these cells die, that causes the symptoms of Alzheimer's, notably memory failure and personality changes. There are treatments, drugs that sometimes work, and sometimes don't. The drugs didn't help Dad's situation.

Alzheimer's would have eventually led to Dad's death. But the cause listed on his death certificate was liver cancer. In retrospect, the cancer was the quicker end. He went downhill fast after the diagnosis, that spring six years ago.

Dad went into hospice care in September of that year. He died two months later on a crisp November day, at home, in the hospital bed we'd set up in the family room at their house. We'd put the bed there so that he wouldn't feel isolated, shut away in a bedroom during those last months. When he passed away, I stood with my mother, my brother, and my sister-in-law, around the bed, our hands linked. I'd already told Dad that I loved him and it was okay for him to let go. We'd put music in the CD player, the great American songbook and the bluegrass tunes he'd loved. Sometimes the ability to hear music and the voices of loved ones is the last faculty to go.

I didn't cry, at least not much. I was too busy trying to hold things together, for Mom. My brother and his wife had flown in from Hawaii as soon as we knew the end was approaching. We made the phone calls to relatives and friends, decided on a date and time for the funeral, making arrangements with the church and the minister. Everyone brought food, a time-honored custom so that the family doesn't have to cook. My brother had to go back to Pearl Harbor, but I stayed, helping Mom with all the things you have to do when a spouse dies, like notifying Social Security, changing the title on the house and car, dealing with insurance.

I was here in Rocoso when Dad died, because I'd moved back the year before. My brother's Navy career kept him moving around between duty stations. That meant he was out of Rocoso and unavailable to help with Mom and Dad, except by phone and email. I was my family's sacrificial daughter.

The sacrificial daughter is a term describing the adult child who sacrifices her own time and resources to look after her parents, sometimes by choice, sometimes forced into it by family expectations. I say "her," because studies show that in most cases, the care of aging parents falls to the daughter. There are many reasons why the daughter winds up as the caregiver. One is the classic and long-held view that women are more nurturing and have more time to care for parents, as well as children. Traditionally men are more involved in their careers and leave the caregiving role to their sisters and wives. Even now, in the twenty-first century, it is frequently the daughters who shoulder the burden. But the sons are catching up.

In years past, the sacrificial daughter might be the one who never married, the spinster who never left home. But that model wasn't confined to history. There were many examples to hand, some in my own family. When I was a small child, my maternal grandmother took in her elderly father, caring for him until he died several years later. Then there's me.

I had made that choice willingly, after much soul-searching. Many of my clients don't have the same option. The role is imposed on them by circumstances.

My decision became easier when the universe provided a nudge. My work situation had changed. In the twenty-plus years since I'd gotten my master's degree, I had focused on geriatric social work at various East Bay hospitals, then I joined a large group practice in Oakland. After ten years, for a variety of reasons, the firm dissolved. I had the option of joining another practice. I'd had a couple of offers. Or I could strike off on my own. I liked the idea. I was thinking of looking for office space when I got that phone call from Dad.

Mom had been playing tennis when she fell and broke her arm. She was in the hospital, with surgery scheduled the following day. I quickly made the necessary arrangements on my end. Then I packed a bag and drove to Rocoso.

Mom came through the surgery just fine, with a plate and pins in her left arm. I stayed for a week, until she got out of the hospital and went to rehab for another week, returning when she got out of rehab.

Over the next few weeks, I made the hours-long drive back and forth between Oakland and Rocoso every weekend. I cooked, cleaned, and shepherded Mom to doctor's appointments and physical therapy. Dad seemed overwhelmed by the accident and its aftermath, and while

I was there in Rocoso I became increasingly concerned about him. He was always resistant to medical appointments. It took several tries to get him in for a test that finally showed the extent of his short-term memory loss. Not long after, Dad's cancer was diagnosed. As my long-distance caregiving stretched from weeks to months, I decided to leave the Bay Area and set up my practice in Rocoso.

In the Bay Area's overheated real estate market, my house in Oakland sold as soon as I put it on the market. I netted enough from the sale to pay cash for my house here in Rocoso, just two blocks from Mom and Dad. I banked the rest of the money, providing myself with a comfortable financial cushion. Then I signed a lease on the downtown office and asked Carmen Castro, the nurse I'd met during Dad's illness, if she wanted to work with me. She did. Gwen Lewis came along two years later, having retired from her job in the Bay Area.

I wasn't rich, but I was comfortable. I had plenty of clients and I didn't have to scramble to pay the bills. That allowed me to do pro bono work, volunteering my services at no charge to those who needed them. I worked closely with Rocoso County Social Services when their social workers identified elders who needed help. I also got referrals from the county's office of senior resources and in some instances, from local and county law enforcement.

Dad died a year after I made the move. I was glad I had that time with him. Being able to walk down the street to have dinner with Mom and Dad was a gift. I miss him still, the father who was funny and vital, who taught me how to ride a bicycle and built me a lemonade stand. I'm glad to have those memories.

Moving meant adjustments, of course. Rocoso was in the mountains and winter snow was something I hadn't experienced in a while. I missed hiking at Point Reyes and in the East Bay hills. But there was a network of county and city parks, many of them with hiking trails that wound up cool valleys with stands of pine and oak. The music of waves against coastal cliffs became the rush of water over rocks in the river or the many local creeks. In Oakland, where I'd lived before, it was never really dark. Here I can see the stars. And it's much quieter. No sirens, just the sound of the river across the street.

Rocoso didn't have the theaters and museums available to me in the Bay Area. Still, the college had both theater and music departments that produced plays and gave concerts. The local little theater, the River Playhouse, did five productions a year. The shows I had seen there were quite good, the performers talented. It was a surprise to learn that the woman who volunteered at the library had such a powerhouse voice that she nailed the role of Mama Rose in *Gypsy*.

Life in Rocoso had been good to me over the past few years, and I was content. My client list was growing and no crises were looming on the horizon.

When I got home, I fed the cats and opened the refrigerator, looking over the limited possibilities on the shelves. I really should have gone to the grocery store, but not all the items on today's to-do list had been checked off. I reached for a carton of cottage cheese and opened it, taking a sniff. No, that was going into the compost bin. I had two eggs left, plus a wedge of sharp cheddar and a bowl of leftover polenta. Scramble the eggs with the cheese and microwave the polenta, I thought. That would work.

The phone rang as I was taking the egg carton out of the fridge. I recognized the number on caller ID. "Saved by the bell," I told the cats as I reached for the phone.

"Had dinner?" Sam Jermyn asked.

27

"No. And the refrigerator's contents are not particularly inspiring. Make me an offer."

He chuckled. "The Gandy Dancer in fifteen minutes."

Chapter 4

BACK IN THE OLD DAYS, a gandy dancer was someone who worked on the railroad, laying rails and maintaining the tracks. In modern-day Rocoso, the Gandy Dancer was a pub with a large selection of locally brewed beer and excellent food. It was located on Main Street near the train station and museum.

Sam Jermyn was a rugged-looking man with a broad-shouldered, six-foot frame, who looked as though he could lay track. A prominent, straight nose dominated his face, with laugh lines around his wide mouth and deep blue eyes. His hair, light brown with touches of red, was always tousled. He had a habit of running his hands through it. Tonight, he wore black jeans and a blue T-shirt under his windbreaker.

His arms circled my waist. I leaned into him as he said hello and kissed me. He had a heavy beard and at the end of the day, the stubble had sprouted, tickling my cheek.

Sam released me and held open the door to the pub. Inside, the Gandy Dancer's walls were decorated with railroad memorabilia, from framed timetables and advertising brochures to conductors' badges, baggage tags, locomotive plates, and lanterns. Sonny Landreth's version of "Walkin' Blues" played on the sound system. The hostess, a young woman with braided blond hair and a Gandy Dancer T-shirt, looked up and smiled. "Hi, Professor Jermyn. Table for two?"

"Yes, thank you."

We followed her past the bar to a table with a varnished wooden top and ladderback chairs. She handed out menus and left.

"One of your students?" I opened the menu.

Sam was chair of the history department at Rocoso College. "Yes. She's a junior, focusing on American history."

"What are you drinking?" I asked.

Both of us turned to look up at the chalkboard on a nearby wall. It listed the pub's ever-changing beer offerings. He leaned back, studying it for a moment. "I like dark beer. I'll try the Blackguard Porter."

I pointed. "How can I resist something called Evil Twin Stout?"

When the server returned, we gave her our drink orders. I glanced at the chalkboard again, checking this evening's dinner specials, then regarded the menu again.

My usual choice was the Cobb salad, which was very good. Tonight, however, I felt like throwing caution, and calories, to the winds. When the server returned with our beers, I ordered a fried chicken sandwich with sweet potato fries. Sam opted for a Reuben sandwich, onion rings on the side. I took a sip of the stout. Excellent choice. Sam's porter was good, too.

Our entrees showed up a short time later. As we ate, we compared notes on our respective days, though the nature of my work meant that much of what I did was confidential. Sam told me about the latest news at the college, a proposal to bring the institution under the umbrella of the California State University system.

I reached for one of my fries. "Is the school large enough to be part of the statewide system? What's the current enrollment?"

Sam set down his messy sandwich and wiped his hands on a napkin. "Last I heard, it was around four thousand students. That's a much smaller enrollment than other schools in the Cal State system, such as

Sacramento State or Chico. But Cal State Monterey Bay has an enrollment of just over five thousand. A small campus joining the system isn't unheard of. Our current president has ambitious plans for the college, including offering graduate degrees."

"I know they offered you the president's job."

He grimaced, shook his head, and picked up his sandwich again. "They did. I turned it down. I'd rather teach. I have enough administrative stuff to deal with as it is."

We talked about the pros and cons of the proposal, with an easy give-and-take that stemmed from years of friendship. Our romantic relationship, however, was more recent.

Sam and I were the same age. We'd known each other in high school. We'd graduated the same year. But we came from different backgrounds and social circles.

My family was decidedly middle -class. Mom taught school and gave piano lessons in our living room. Dad worked for the Western Pacific Railroad, first as a fireman and then an engineer. He retired from the WP a few months before the railroad was sold to Union Pacific in 1983. But he hadn't retired from railroading. Dad signed on with the historic Rocoso & Jermyn Railroad and made several runs a week. When he wasn't in the cab of the locomotive, he volunteered at the museum.

Sam was a Jermyn, the rich kid whose family had business concerns all over the county and who helped found the college. Their name was on the old mining town upriver, as well as the railroad. They lived in a big house on the hill. Sam and his two younger sisters had left town after graduating from high school. The sisters hadn't come back, but Sam had. He'd gone to Stanford for his undergraduate degree, then switched to the University of California for his master's and doctorate. He had taught for many years at UC Davis. During that time, he married a fellow academic, a woman who taught English, and they had two children. The marriage broke up. His wife still taught at Davis, but Sam had moved on, first to Sacramento State and then to Rocoso. His kids were grown and on their own. His son and his wife had recently presented Sam with his first grandchild. Something was going on with his daughter, though. I knew that much and little else. Right now, he wasn't talking about it. I figured he would when he was ready.

Sam had come back to Rocoso for the same reason that I had, drawn by an obligation to look after his aging parents. His mother died of cancer not long after he returned. Then his father fell and broke his hip. That's how we'd met. Sam had contacted me for assistance in caring for his father, who had since died. After Sam's father died, our relationship had moved from professional to personal, a state of affairs that satisfied both of us.

"I'll trade you some fries for that last onion ring," I said now.

Sam grinned as he reached for his beer. "Be my guest."

Chapter 5

TUESDAY MORNING, I ARRIVED at the office early and started the coffee. Gwen, Carmen, and I usually had a check-in at the start of the day. By the time the coffee was ready, both of them had arrived. Coffee mugs in hand, we gathered around our small conference table.

Carmen, a woman in her mid-forties, was a small dynamo, just a few silver threads in her black hair and a seemingly unending store of energy. She shook her head and frowned as I described last night's situation with Fran Lomax at Golden Acres.

"I'm concerned because this is the second time something like this has happened," I said.

"Golden Acres is the worst of the nursing homes here in town," Carmen declared. "We should report them to the state. Now. Why wait?"

"They have a new manager coming on board next week," Gwen pointed out, taking a sip of coffee. "I think conditions will improve."

"I'm inclined to give them one more chance," I said. "I'm going to call the owner. No doubt he's already heard about it from the supervisor. At least I hope so. I want to know if he's discussed it with the new manager and whether he has a plan to correct the situation."

"Let me know what happens after you talk with the owner," Carmen said.

We discussed the nursing home a while longer, then moved on to other issues. Then all three of us left the office. Carmen and Gwen both had client appointments, and I had a meeting at the Rocoso Wellness Center. I was on an advisory committee for the Center, which had opened last year. It was the latest in the city's efforts to help homeless residents, with a focus on senior citizens. A lot of people living on the streets these days were fifty years old, or more. They'd worked all their lives and were falling through rips and tears in the safety net.

Being on the streets ages people fast. I'd seen those in their fifties who looked two decades older. That's why I viewed serving on the committee as one of my important outreach efforts.

Rocoso was not immune to the issues facing municipalities all over California, from rising housing costs to substance abuse and mental health issues. All of these could lead to people living on the streets, even here in the mountains, away from the urban landscapes of the Bay Area or Sacramento. Rocoso's terrain and its many parks gave homeless people places to pitch a tent or, for those living in their cars or RVs, places to park. The Center aimed to get people off the streets.

It was located on a three-acre parcel on the northeast side of town that had once held a strip mall and a small warehouse. The city council's decision to rezone the land and build the Center had been hotly debated and wound up on the ballot a couple of years ago, with the opposition proposing that the site be designated open space and turned into a park. The "yes" votes in the election outnumbered the "noes," and the city broke ground for the Center, which had opened last fall, just in time to get people off the streets before Rocoso was hit with a cold and snowy winter. Now there were fifty units of permanent supportive housing, a medical respite center, and an office providing resources and housing advocacy for people who were homeless or at risk of becoming homeless.

Many of Rocoso's citizens were retirees who had moved to town because housing cost less here. It was less expensive, but the problems of people and the places where they lived were similar, no matter the size of the town or the availability of services.

After my committee meeting, I called the owner of Golden Acres and told him my concerns. He assured me that he and the new manager had discussed the nursing home's problems. They would be making changes, he added. Fine, I said. I was willing to give the place one more chance. But I would be following up soon.

That done, I went on to a round of client appointments, taking one woman to the doctor, another shopping, and for a third, hiring additional caregivers. Several hours later, I had a quick lunch at my desk before my afternoon appointment with Sheryl and Betty Garvin. As I spooned yogurt from a container, I reviewed the preassessment form and the notes I'd taken the afternoon before, jotting a few thoughts in the margins. Then I left the office, giving myself plenty of time to arrive before one o'clock.

Betty Garvin lived on the south side of Rocoso, in an established neighborhood full of modest homes with well-tended yards. Mature oaks and tall pines shaded the lawns, as did the junipers that gave the street its name. The Garvin home was a one-story ranch-style house that looked as though it had been built sometime after World War II. The house and its neighbors backed onto an open meadow bisected by Wylie Creek, which meandered through town until it emptied into the river. Two doors down from the Garvin house was a pedestrian path that led from the street to the creek and the meadow beyond. Neighborhood children used it to get to the middle school on the other side of the creek.

The house, stucco and wood frame, was painted white with green trim. A blue Nissan sedan was parked in the single-car driveway on the right side of the house, in front of the closed garage door. A sidewalk led around to the backyard gate, where I glimpsed trash and recycling bins. On the left side of the front porch was a flower bed edged with large rocks, containing a pink rhododendron and two rose bushes, one covered with red blossoms, the other with yellow.

I parked my Prius at the curb, noticing the "For Sale" sign on the front lawn of the house next door. The front porch of the Garvin house held a bright orange ceramic pot holding an assortment of succulents. A yellow sign reading "Welcome" hung on the front door.

Sheryl opened the door as soon as I rang the doorbell. "Come in. Mom's in her bedroom. She's been napping. Wait here in the living room and I'll bring her in."

I stepped inside. On the left, a hallway led to the bedroom. To my right was a spacious living room with wall-to-wall carpet the color of wheat, and a sofa and a matching side chair upholstered in an olive-green fabric, both pieces of furniture brightened by throw pillows. On the other side of the sofa was a well-used tan recliner, its cushions showing some wear. An oval table with six chairs formed a dining area at the back of the living room, where a doorway led to the kitchen.

A nearby shelf held photos, including a family picture showing a much-younger Betty Garvin, her brown hair worn short and combed back from her face as she stood next to her husband, who had short blond hair and a square face. On either side were the three Garvin children. Greg, the eldest, was blond and broad-shouldered, his features reflecting those of his father. He appeared to be about sixteen in the photograph, and now that I saw the picture, I remembered him from high school. On his left was Sheryl, who must have been thirteen or fourteen at the time the photo was taken. With her short brown hair, she looked like her mother. The younger daughter, on Greg's right, looked about ten. She had long blond hair and a sulky expression on her face.

A bow-fronted oak china cabinet stood on the wall separating the dining area from the kitchen. The bottom shelves contained a set of china, cream-colored with gold rims and a pattern of pink flowers. The upper shelves held a sterling silver coffee and tea set, with coffee and teapots and a sugar bowl and creamer. It sat on a large rectangular tray. Each of the pieces had little floral details on the handles. A middle shelf held serving tongs and a small oval tray marred by a scratch, both of these in the same silver pattern. Next to these were matching silver bowls, about eight inches in diameter, each engraved with the initial G. At the other end of the shelf were several small collectibles, including a crystal vase, a porcelain teapot, and a carnival glass basket.

I turned away from the cabinet as Sheryl walked into the living room, followed by her mother. Betty Garvin seemed unsteady on her feet, though not all the time. A footed cane, similar to the one my mother used, was propped against the arm of a chair. But Mrs. Garvin didn't use it. Instead she "wall walked," her hands on either side of the hallway. When she reached the living room, she grabbed the back of a chair for support.

"Dexter, I know that name. Your father's name was Nolan. He worked on the trains, didn't he?" Betty Garvin's blue eyes sparkled behind her glasses and a smile wreathed her wrinkled face.

I smiled. "Yes, he did."

"I think my husband, Curtis, knew your father," Mrs. Garvin continued. "From the Chamber of Commerce or one of those organizations. Your mother's name is Rose and she plays tennis. I remember reading something about that in the paper, when she won a medal at a tournament."

"The National Senior Games." Mom won two gold medals that year, in women's doubles and mixed doubles. The *Rocoso Bugle* had given the story front-page coverage, with a color photo of my mother posing with her medals and her tennis racquet. "Mom doesn't play tennis anymore."

"I'm not surprised," Mrs. Garvin said. "We're all getting older. I think your mother's older than I am."

Sheryl gestured at the door leading to the kitchen. "Let's go to the family room. I've made some iced tea. Mother, use your cane, please."

"Oh, that thing is such a bother. But if I don't, you'll just fuss at me."

"I will." Sheryl handed the cane to her mother, who put it in her right hand and turned toward the kitchen, taking slow steps as Sheryl ushered her toward the kitchen. I lagged behind, observing that, bother or not, with the cane's support, the elderly woman moved with more confidence.

Inside the kitchen, a short hallway on the right led to the laundry room and garage. One wall held a pair of wooden mug racks, with pegs holding an assortment of ceramic mugs. It looked as though the mugs had been collected for years, bearing logos from Rocoso College and the University of California in Berkeley, as well as destinations such as Yosemite and the Grand Canyon. I saw the familiar image of the Rocoso & Jermyn Railroad hanging next to a floral mug with a legend reading "World's Best Grandma."

The family room was separated from the kitchen by a counter, furnished with a recliner and a sofa that had seen years of service. Next to the fireplace, a stand held a flat-screen TV and a DVD player, as well as a couple of DVDs—*Pillow Talk* with Doris Day and *The African*

Queen with Humphrey Bogart and Katharine Hepburn. Nearby was a stack of CDs, collections by Rosemary Clooney and Frank Sinatra visible on top. The table next to the recliner held several library books, all large print.

A sliding glass door led from the family room to a covered patio with a white wicker settee and a couple of matching chairs. A propane gas barbecue, lid closed and dusty, was to the right of the door. A hummingbird feeder, empty and streaked with grime, hung from a hook.

The patio was bordered on two sides by a flower bed containing succulents and rocks. The stones were both smooth and rough-edged, of varying sizes, some as big as grapefruits, looking as though they'd been picked from the riverbank or a hiking trail. Most of the rocks were granite, not surprising since the Sierra Nevada was comprised of that material. Planted between the rocks were several varieties of sedum, the low, spreading succulent frequently used as ground cover. The border also contained crassulas and aeoniums and the rosette-shaped succulent known as hen and chicks, so-called because it produced numerous babies.

A redwood fence, weathered to silver, surrounded the backyard. Overgrown camellias ranged on either side of the back gate, reached by a sidewalk that bisected the yard. On the left side, an oak tree shaded the back corner of the lot. An empty bird feeder hung from a branch. To the right of the sidewalk, near the back of the lot, was a square garden shed constructed of lumber, with several missing boards. In front of this were three wooden rectangles, raised planting beds that had once been used for a garden. Now the beds were overrun with weeds, some of them twining up the sides of the disused tomato cages.

"Are you the gardener?" I asked as Mrs. Garvin settled into the recliner.

"Call me Betty, dear. Yes, I like to garden. There's nothing like homegrown vegetables, especially tomatoes. My husband built those raised beds for me. And the garden shed. He was handy around the house, liked to build things. But he's gone now. I used to keep up with the garden. But it got to be too much for me. Last time I was pulling weeds and I lost my balance and fell. I didn't plant anything this year. I've got a fellow that comes to mow the lawn. I should have him pull out all those weeds and put in some ground cover, so it doesn't look so bad."

"I can arrange for that, Mother." Sheryl came into the family room from the kitchen, carrying tall glasses of iced tea for her mother and me. She returned to the kitchen to fetch her glass and sat down on one end of the sofa. I joined her.

"You do what you think best, dear," Betty told her.

"I will." Sheryl took a sip of her tea. She set the glass on a coaster. "Mother, I've been meaning to ask you something. What happened to the silver frame?"

Betty looked confused. "What silver frame?"

"The one that held that picture of you and Dad," Sheryl said. "I gave it to you for your fiftieth anniversary. Don't you remember?"

Her mother shook her head. "No, I don't. Picture frame, you say? Isn't it in the living room, with all the pictures?"

Sheryl frowned. "The photo is there. But not the silver frame. The picture is in a wooden frame now."

Betty looked confused. "I don't know anything about a frame."

"What about the brooch Aunt Millie gave you? The one with the sapphires?" Sheryl asked.

Betty smiled at her daughter. "Oh, I gave that to Ginny. She carried my groceries into the house."

Sheryl sighed. She turned the conversation to other

things. We talked for a while, then Betty dozed off. Sheryl took another swallow of iced tea. "She does that a lot. Falls asleep."

"Are there other things missing?" I asked. "Besides the brooch and the picture frame?"

"I'm afraid so." Sheryl rolled her eyes and her voice sharpened. "A gold brooch with three sapphires and she gives it to the twelve-year-old across the street. I'll have to talk with Ginny's mother and get the brooch back. When I realized the picture frame was gone, I looked in Mother's jewelry box. That's when I saw that the brooch was gone. I made a list. There's a locket missing. It's gold, heart-shaped, with a diamond in the middle. Dad gave it to Mother as a wedding present. Inside was a small black-and-white picture of the two of them. I can't find Mother's pearls, a necklace with matching earrings. And a couple of turquoise and silver pieces that belonged to Dad are gone. One was a belt buckle and the other a bolo tie. None of these things are hugely valuable in terms of money, but I suppose taken together, they would add up. Besides, they have a lot of sentimental value."

All the missing items were small and easily disposed of, I thought. Had someone been stealing from Betty Garvin? Or had the elderly woman simply given away the jewelry and the picture frame?

Sheryl echoed my thoughts. "I don't know if those things have been stolen or if Mother has handed them off to people, the way she did with that brooch. She also has a habit of keeping cash stashed in her sock drawer. She goes to the bank, cashes a check for a hundred dollars or so, and tucks the money into a sock. I've tried to break her of the habit, but no luck so far. I do take care of her finances, as much as I can. But sometimes it's hard from a distance."

I set down my glass. "Now that she's asleep, we

should go ahead with the assessment. I notice she has a cane but she doesn't use it. Unless you remind her."

"Nag her, you mean." Sheryl's voice had an exasperated note. "She doesn't like using the cane. It's the same situation with the alert device. Most of the time she leaves it on the dresser or the counter in the bathroom, or she hangs it on a doorknob. She's wearing it today, though. Probably because I'm here and I have been reminding her."

I had seen the oval medical alert device hanging from a thin chain around Betty's neck. "You should add me to the list of contacts with the alert company."

She assured me she would and led the way to the kitchen. "I took the knobs off the stove burners, since her using the stove is the reason for the latest incident. The kitchen was in a state when I got here. Mom can't see very well so she can't see that the counter is dirty. I've had to do battle with ants. Plus, she eats something then puts the leftovers in the refrigerator. The food goes bad but she doesn't pay attention to that, or she can't see the mold or smell that the milk is off. Last year she got a dose of food poisoning and she took something out of the medicine cabinet. It turned out to be a laxative. So, she got sick and was even more dehydrated. Her neighbor took her to the emergency room. Every time I come to visit her, I clean out the refrigerator and throw things away."

"I recommend clearing out all the nonessential medications." I looked at the large blue plastic pillbox on the counter. It had compartments for morning and evening medications for each day. Next to this was a lined pad with a list of the drugs, by name, dosage, and frequency, for each pill Betty Garvin was taking. I examined the list. Some of the medications were prescriptions, like those for high blood pressure, while others were over-the-counter drugs, like the low dosage aspirin tablet and a calcium supplement. "I'm concerned about accurate dosages for these medications. You told me your mother hasn't seen a doctor since last year, when her physician died."

"That's in the works," Sheryl said. "I made an appointment for her tomorrow morning, at ten o'clock, with another doctor in the same practice. You said you'd like to go with us to see the doctor. Are you available?"

I pulled out my phone and entered the appointment into my calendar. I'd have to juggle another commitment, but that was par for the course. I had to be flexible in this job. "I'll be there. We'll find out what the doctor says about her general physical condition as well as the memory loss. And we can make sure her prescriptions are up to date. What about the appointment to check her eyes?"

"I'm working on it," Sheryl said. "I'll let you know as soon as I set that up."

"Let's walk through the house and look at potential hazards." I pointed. "For example, that rug in front of the sink should be taken up. It's a trip hazard."

"Good idea." Sheryl bent down, picked up the rectangular rug, and tossed it into the laundry room. "As you see, the living room, dining room, and hallway are carpeted. So are all three bedrooms."

"Bathrooms first," I said.

Sheryl led the way down the hall. The first bathroom had grab bars in the bathtub and next to the toilet. We continued our inspection in the bathroom off the master bedroom. Grab bars had been installed here as well, next to the toilet and inside the shower stall.

"This is the bathroom Mother uses." Sheryl gestured at the medicine cabinet over the sink. "Every time I'm here, I clear out the cabinet and get rid of the over-the-counter stuff. I don't want a repeat of the laxative incident."

"Good." I gestured at the shower stall. "I recommend a shower chair and a handheld attachment, so she can sit while she takes a shower. A non-slip coating on the floor of the shower would help, instead of that bathmat. Those things can shift at the bottom of the stall. We don't want her to fall. The senior center has people who will install those things, and more grab bars, at no cost to you. I don't know if you'll be able to get that done before you leave. If not, make an appointment and I'll be here while it's done."

We worked our way through the bedrooms and walked back through the house to the kitchen. Betty was still asleep in the recliner, her head tilted to one side. "Does she use the fireplace?" I asked.

Sheryl shook her head. "Not anymore. I had all the wood removed. No matches, no fire starter. But it is a concern. She does like a fire in the winter. I suppose we won't have to deal with that for a while, since it's May." She pointed at the cordless phone on the table next to the recliner. "Sometimes Mother doesn't hang up the phone properly. When I call her, I get a busy signal. Then I'll call the neighbor and ask her to check on Mother. Once I even called the Rocoso Police Department and asked them to do a welfare check. Which they did. She was fine, but still, I worry."

"I know they're happy to do that. Definitely get your mother's hearing checked."

"I did that a year or so ago," Sheryl said. "She does have hearing loss but she refuses to get hearing aids. She says they cost too much."

I heard that a lot, too. It had taken me two years to convince my mother to get hearing aids.

"In that case, we can look into getting an amplifier for the phone. They don't cost all that much and it helps. So does having phones in every room."

I checked the preassessment form and my notes.

Yesterday Sheryl had told me Betty was still driving but had been in a couple of minor accidents. She suspected her mother's eyesight had deteriorated, possibly due to cataracts. I knew from my experiences that the decision to give up driving was, for many people, a difficult one. Being able to grab the car keys and go for a drive was often the last bit of independence left to a person, and for that reason, many of my clients were reluctant to give up driving. Some refused, although they couldn't see or hear well. I'd known family members to disable the vehicle or hide keys to prevent a client from driving.

"Yesterday I mentioned the senior shuttle," I said. "The cost is negligible and if your mother needs transportation to a doctor's appointment, for example, or a shopping trip, all she needs to do is call forty-eight hours before, to make a reservation."

We sat at the kitchen table and talked about finances. Betty was getting Social Security and Medicare, and a pension earned from teaching elementary school for over thirty years. According to Sheryl, there was also income from several CDs and annuities, as well as some property the Garvins owned. "Mom owns a duplex on the east side of town. We keep it rented out. A local real estate company handles that and takes a cut, about ten percent. The taxes take a bigger chunk. Still, she does get income. As for this house," she added, "Mom owns it outright. The mortgage was paid off years ago. I have power of attorney for financial and medical matters. My name is on the bank accounts, so I can write checks on those funds. There is enough money to make sure Mother is comfortable, whether she stays in her house or moves to assisted living."

"Based on what I've seen today, I think your mother is a good candidate for staying in her own home—if she has help." I took several brochures from my bag and fanned them out on the table. "These are local caregivers. Some of them are home health aides and others are like personal assistants, who will do laundry, grocery shopping, and drive your mother to appointments. We can also have someone clean your mother's house, a one-time deep cleaning. After that, you can also arrange light housekeeping on a schedule that works for you and your mother."

"That would be great." Sheryl took the brochures. "I'll look these over tonight."

"I'll work on my assessment later today and will bring it with me tomorrow morning when we meet at the doctor's office." I checked my watch and stood up. It was two-thirty now and I had a three o'clock appointment on the other side of town.

"Oh, I almost forgot." Sheryl got up and reached for a keyring on the kitchen counter. "Here's the key to the house. You'll need that."

"I certainly will." I took the key and added it to my client keyring.

Sheryl sat down again, a thoughtful look on her face. "Tell me, Kay, do you ever regret moving back to Rocoso?"

I leaned back in my chair. It was a question I had been asked before. "Sometimes I miss the Bay Area. I do like the slower pace here. I had good reasons. My parents needed me and I'm glad I had the time with my father before he died."

Sheryl looked as though she was turning this over in her mind, then she gave her head a little shake. She walked with me to the front door. As I left the house, a van from a staging company was parked in the driveway of the house next door, the one with the "For Sale" sign. I recognized the real estate agent, Arlette Simmons, who was getting out of her car, parked at the curb. Arlette waved with one hand, her other hand holding her cell phone to her ear as she headed for the front door of the house that she was selling.

I got into my car. As I drove away, I thought about Sheryl's question. Was she considering a move back to Rocoso? My client had a husband and a job in Seattle. At least that's what she'd told me.

BETTY'S DOCTOR'S APPOINTMENT was the following day, at a practice near the Rocoso Medical Center. Betty Garvin and her daughter arrived at the same time I did. My assessment report was in an envelope and I handed this to Sheryl after she had settled Betty into a chair. As it happened, the woman next to Betty was an old friend and the two women began chatting. Sheryl walked to the reception desk and checked in. Then she took a seat next to me and opened the envelope, reading through my assessment. "This all looks good," she said. "I feel so relieved to have you on board to help with Mother."

A nurse came through the door leading to the back of the office and called Betty's name. The three of us went through to the examining room. Dr. Everett was new in town but I'd met him before, in conjunction with another client. I sat in as he examined Betty and spoke with all three of us. Betty had hypertension, high cholesterol, and hyperthyroidism. Betty's former doctor, the one who had died, had prescribed medications for all of these. Now Dr. Everett ordered a complete blood workup as well as some other tests, adding that he'd know more when he got the results from the lab. That would be later today. He would adjust her prescriptions accordingly.

"I looked through those brochures you left with me," Sheryl said, as we waited outside the lab. "I think for caregivers, let's go with Louise Beltran."

"She's very good," I said. "I think you'll be happy with

her. If you'd like me to, I will call and see when she's available."

"The sooner the better."

"As far as cleaning and groceries, I recommend Bea Lovell. She has a company called the Helping Bee. For a start, I'll have her do a thorough housecleaning, then laundry and groceries on a regular basis."

Sheryl nodded. "That's fine. I set Mother up with Meals on Wheels. They'll deliver five days a week."

"Good. The local Meals on Wheels people have a great operation. The food is nutritious and I think it tastes good."

"By the way, I got the sapphire brooch back," Sheryl said. "I talked with Mrs. Cavalieri across the street and explained that it's valuable. Of course, she insisted that her daughter return it."

"Good. I'm glad that's sorted out. Have you found any of the other missing jewelry?"

Sheryl shook her head. "No luck. I'll keep looking and hope those pieces turn up. It's possible Mother gave them to other people. Maybe she'll tell me something, or I'll find them when I look through the house."

"I have a client who has started giving away her jewelry and other collectibles," I said. "She's made a list of which things go to her children and other relatives, and she's giving them the option of taking those items now or after she dies. I have another client who has been sticking notes on furniture saying who it goes to."

Sheryl frowned. "I don't want to think about that now. I hope I don't have to deal with Mother's estate for a long time yet. As for her physical condition, I guess we'll have a clearer picture after these tests."

I understood Sheryl's reluctance, but it was advisable to prepare for the death of an elderly parent. It would happen eventually, and sometimes sooner than the family would like. I'd had my share of clients who had died suddenly. One never knew when a heart attack, aneurysm, or accident would strike.

Chapter 6

I SWAYED TO THE MUSIC, the dark blue silk of my vintage dress swishing around my hips. The Rocky Rhythm Trackers, dressed like the miners who once panned for gold on the river, were playing "Swing, Swing, Swing."

The historical society fundraiser was called "After the Gold Rush." On this Saturday night in May, the high school gymnasium had been transformed into a street scene from old Rocoso, the prosperous town that had evolved from the mining camp and became an important stop on the Western Pacific Railroad. At one end of the room was a replica of the train station, with a half-size version of the Rocoso & Jermyn Railroad's Locomotive Number One constructed of cardboard, chicken wire, and papier -mâché. Number One was the locomotive Dad drove during his years as a volunteer engineer.

Dina stood at the front of the ersatz locomotive, resplendent in a low-cut red-and-gold dress that hugged her curves and fell to mid-calf, with red leather high-button shoes visible below the hem. Her dark hair was caught up in an elaborate twist on the top of her head, set off with rhinestones, scarlet ribbons, and feathers. She was supposed to be a madam, not surprising, given that the historical museum was located in a former bordello. She looked out of character, though, as she consulted a small tablet computer, no doubt directing the ongoing fundraiser she and her army of volunteers had put together.

Dina's husband, Ed McGinty, who owned the Rocky River Rafting Company, wore the uniform and hat of a

Western Pacific conductor, complete with a pocket watch. He took a swig from a bottle of beer and laughed as he talked with another man dressed as an engineer. All around me, my fellow townspeople were dressed as railroaders, miners, shopkeepers, saloon girls, farmers, and mountain men.

I waved at my colleagues, who stood together on the other side of the room. Gwen Lewis was garbed as actress Lotta Crabtree, who was born in New York City but grew up in the California gold mining towns, working as a child performer before her family moved to San Francisco and Lotta became a star. Gwen wore a russet-colored wig topped with a feathered hat and a voluminous floral-patterned dress. Carmen and her husband, Rafe, were gold miners, in matching pants and shirts, with worn wide-brimmed hats on their head, decorated with tiny picks, shovels, and gold pans. Marie Devorno, the architect who had an office near mine, wore a Gibson Girl costume and an enormous hat festooned with flowers and feathers.

I had eschewed a hat. My short brown hair was threaded with enough silver to complement the beads decorating my dress. I was also wearing comfortable, low-heeled shoes. I'd given up heels a long time ago. I valued my feet more than authenticity.

Someone called my name. I turned to see Benny Ma, a local attorney, dressed as a laborer in grubby denim pants and thick-soled boots. He had a beer in one hand and several sticks of what I hoped was fake dynamite protruding from his pocket. "What's with the explosives?"

Benny laughed. "I am my great-grandpa several times back. He came over from China in the eighteen-sixties with all those other Cantonese to build the transcontinental railroad. He blasted the tunnels above Donner Lake, then he stuck around and tried his hand at gold mining. That's how he wound up in this part of the Sierra."

Benny was a decade younger than me. He too had left Rocoso to go to college, first at Sacramento State, then law school at UC Berkeley. He'd practiced law in Sacramento for a few years, then set up shop in his hometown.

Dina left off looking at her tablet and joined us. "Hey, Benny, you were going to look through those old photos, the ones your aunt found in that trunk. Is there anything you can donate to the museum that tells the story of the Ma family in Rocoso?"

"Oh, yeah. That trunk." Benny took a swallow of beer. "It was in the attic of my grandmother's house on Auburn Street, and it was full of pictures. The oldest one I found was a daguerreotype. The date written on the back is eighteen ninety-five, which is around the time the house was built."

"I want to do a whole section on the Chinese experience in the Sierra," Dina said. "I'm sure your family photos will be an important part of the display."

"We had our own version of the Anti-Coolie League up here," Benny said. "Though it wasn't as bad as what they went through in San Francisco. My daughter Winnie, the one that's going to school at Berkeley, has done a whole lot of research on the subject, and the family. She's majoring in history. The two of you should get together when she's home from school."

Dina looked thoughtful. "Maybe I could figure out a way to make her a summer intern. Let me recuperate from the fundraiser, and then I'll call you and set up a time to look at those pictures."

"You know where to find me." Benny scanned the room and spotted his wife Lorita, the volunteer who had collected all the items for the silent auction. These were on tables at one side of the gym. Lorita waved at him to join her, so he excused himself and threaded his way through the crowd.

"I also want to restore that old Buddhist temple on Tenth Street," Dina said. "Maybe we'll bring in enough money tonight to at least think about it. Where's Sam?"

"He went in search of liquid refreshment." I pointed at the bar, which was on the other side of the train station replica. Then I spotted him, walking toward us, carrying a glass of wine in each hand. His hair was unruly, as usual. His shoulders filled out the black frock coat he wore with black trousers, his torso set off by a vivid red silk vest. A deck of cards peeked from his breast pocket.

He stopped and held out a glass. "Chardonnay for you, merlot for me."

"Thanks." I took the glass.

Dina looked Sam up and down. "You look quite rakish."

He grinned at her. "So do you. Want to play a few hands of seven-card stud after the party?"

"Poker is not my game. I lose all the time. Talk to Ed." Dina waved at her husband.

"The last time I played poker with your husband, he took twenty bucks off me," Sam said. As the band swung into "Nice and Easy," he turned to me. "Let's dance."

We set our glasses on a nearby table and I stepped into his arms. He was a good dancer. Finding Sam had been a stroke of luck, *lagniappe*, as they would say down in New Orleans. Marriage and children weren't in the hand life had dealt me—and I was fine with that. Sam wasn't interested in matrimony, either. I enjoyed our middle-aged romance. Being with Sam was nice and easy, just like the song.

The song ended and the band took a break. We retrieved our wine and headed for the buffet table, filling our plates with hors d'oeuvres. Then we made our way around the room to the small round table where Mom sat, sipping from a glass of sparkling water. She wore a simple pale-blue dress with a matching hat. Draped over one shoulder was a white muslin banner with black letters, reading "Votes for Women."

"May I taste your wine?" she asked.

"I'd be glad to get you a glass," Sam told her.

"No, I just want a sip."

"Sure, Mom. This is a chardonnay. Sam has a merlot."

"Chardonnay." Mom reached for my glass. "Nice. But if I have more than a sip, I'll fall asleep." She handed back the glass and took a skewer of satay chicken from my plate.

"Hello, Kay." The newcomer was Arlette Simmons, the real estate agent. She wore a 1920s flapper ensemble in beaded green and gold, complete with a green beaded headband that sparkled against her red hair.

"Hi, Arlette." I nibbled on a cracker covered with goat cheese. "You must be busy. I see your real estate signs all over town."

Arlette took a sip from her wineglass. "It's May. That's when people buy and sell houses. I'll be hopping until the fall. That's the way the real estate business is. I just took on that house on Juniper Street, where you saw me with the guy from the staging company. It's a nice little two-bedroom, small, but it would be a perfect starter home or retirement home. The kitchen has been updated and it has new carpet. I've already had lots of lookers. Including the woman whose mother owns the house next door."

"Sheryl Garvin?" That was a surprise.

"Yes, she came over to talk with me after you left," Arlette said. "I remember her from high school. She was a class ahead of me. Anyway, when she looked at the house, she seemed interested. I told her it won't be on the market long. She'll need to make up her mind very soon if she's going to make an offer."

That must be why Sheryl had asked me about my own decision to move back to Rocoso.

Arlette turned to Sam, who was downing a stuffed mushroom. "You're the local history expert. I'm interested in finding out what's going on with that old hot springs property on Lost Woman Creek, the one with the hotel that burned down."

The land Arlette was talking about was located upriver, midway between Rocoso and Jermyn. Lost Woman Creek, which emptied into the river, was full of natural hot springs. The area's indigenous tribes, most of them from the Maidu nation, had used the springs for generations before white settlers had moved into the area.

Sam wiped his fingers on a napkin. "The land and the hotel were owned by the Maysfield family and then the Waldron family. The Waldrons are long-time residents of the county. They had stores in Rocoso and Jermyn but mostly they settled in Appleton, downriver from here. They owned that big apple farm, still do, I think. Ruby Waldron died a few months back and her husband has been gone several years. I'm sure someone in the Waldron family owns the Lost Woman Creek property now."

"Waldron's Apple Farm," Mom said. "We used to go down there every year in the fall. They grow so many different varieties of apples."

I took a sip of my wine. "I've hiked the fire trail up at the creek. There's a section where it looks down on the old hotel." Like many others who visited the area, I'd also made my way down the hill to the ruins, to soak in the warm pools that lined that section of the creek. "I've seen photos of the resort. It was a beautiful building in its day."

Sam nodded. "A showplace. The hotel was built in

the eighteen-nineties. It burned down twice, once before World War One, and again in the nineteen-forties, right after World War Two. The Waldrons rebuilt the hotel after the first fire but didn't after the second. I'm not sure why, but it may have had something to do with their finances. The fact that the hotel burned down doesn't mean no one is using the hot springs. You can hike down to the creek from the fire trail. It's private property and it's posted, but as we know, everyone ignores those signs. Why are you interested in the hotel?"

Arlette took another sip of wine. "I've heard rumors that someone plans to develop the place. Rebuild the hotel and have a hot springs resort, with a spa and a restaurant. That would mean an increase in property values for adjoining parcels. And there's more to the parcel than just the area where the hotel was. Several acres, at least, all of which could be redeveloped. Condos maybe."

I made a face. "More condos? Couldn't we just have open space?"

"You're talking to the wrong person," Arlette said, raising her glass. "I'm a real estate agent, remember. Anyway, I'll have to do some research to see which of the Waldron heirs owns the property now. They must be the ones who are making the plans I've heard about."

The band reappeared and took their positions, swinging into "San Antonio Rose." Sam and I moved out to the crowded dance floor and stayed as the band played several other songs in its repertoire, leaning heavily on the Great American Songbook, with excursions into country and western. When we returned to the table, Mom was still there, talking with Dina and Ed.

Dina had unbuttoned both of her red leather shoes and now she removed them, massaging first one foot, then another. "My feet are killing me. I shouldn't have worn these shoes."

"I warned you." Ed chuckled and raised his beer bottle to his lips.

"But they look so good with the dress," Dina said, adjusting the low neckline that grazed the tops of her breasts.

"The dress looks good because you're wearing it." Ed leaned over and his lips brushed her forehead.

"How's it going?" I asked.

"Great," Dina said. "The turnout is bigger than last year. It looks like the silent auction is going to net us a lot of money."

"What will you do with it?" Sam asked.

"Create more exhibits." Dina relieved her husband of his beer bottle and took a swallow. "I'd really like to have more on the Native American population that lived here before the Gold Rush. I've been reaching out to the Maidu who are still in the area. They do wonderful basketwork."

"And restore the Buddhist temple," I added.

"At the top of my list," Dina said.

Chapter 7

SAM WAS STILL ASLEEP. He lay on his back, his head tilted to one side, his hair tousled as usual. During the night, the down comforter had slipped down, revealing his chest, furred with fine curly hair, mostly light brown, with some gray as well. He had a scar on his left shoulder and upper arm, the result of a motorcycle accident when he was in college. He wasn't conventionally handsome, but he had a way about him. A sense of humor, an easy grace. Being with him felt comfortable but never boring.

I reached out and traced the scar with my fingers. He stirred and then settled again. I pushed back the comforter and stood up, reaching for the cotton robe I'd tossed onto a nearby chair. I slipped it on and tied the belt. At the foot of the bed, all three cats roused themselves, stretching. Then they jumped off the bed and raced to the kitchen, anticipating their morning chow. I started the coffee first. As it went through its cycle, I put the dirty cat bowls in the sink to soak and dished up cat food in a set of clean bowls. When I set them on the floor, the cats lined up to eat.

As the coffee maker sputtered, I glanced at a postcard I'd tossed into a basket on the counter separating the kitchen from the dining room. A local bluegrass group was giving a free concert at the county park, which had an open-air theater. I like most kinds of music, including bluegrass. I'd thought about going, which must be why I'd kept the card. Now I pulled it out and propped it up against the basket.

The coffee was ready. I poured two mugs and added milk to mine. I took a sip. Dark roast, a good way to start the day.

I carried both mugs back to the bedroom. Sam was awake now, stretching his arms over his head. "Is that for me?" he asked with a grin.

"No, I thought I'd drink both cups myself."

He laughed. I handed over one of the mugs and got back into bed, settling back against the pillows, cradling my coffee with both hands. "You need a shave."

He rubbed a hand over his chin. "Always do. More gray than brown these days."

I sipped coffee, then set the mug on the end table. I shifted position, facing him, and rubbed my hand on his cheek. "I like it."

A slow smile spread across his face. He set his mug on the floor next to the bed and leaned in for a coffee-flavored kiss. He tugged at the robe's belt. Then he slipped his hand inside, his fingers making my skin tingle as he cupped my breast.

I slipped out of the robe and put my arms around him.

Also a good way to start the day.

MUCH LATER, WHILE SAM was in the shower, I dressed and went back to the kitchen for more coffee. Then I opened the back door and stepped out onto the deck. It was a fine spring day, with a blue sky and a hint of clouds at the higher elevations. I heard the river, full now with the spring snowmelt, rushing over rocks on its way through town. I sat down in one of the patio chairs and sipped coffee, looking at the raised planting beds I built when I first bought the house. Time to think about the vegetable garden and to look at seed catalogs before paying a visit to the local nursery. After several years of persistent drought, there had been more precipitation this year, which meant a bumper crop of weeds to eradicate. That lilac in the corner of the yard was drooping at one side. It needed tying back.

The kitchen door opened and Sam came outside, carrying his coffee mug. He'd dressed in worn jeans and a T-shirt, his feet bare. He kept a few clothes and toiletries here. He'd also brought a change of clothes with him when he picked me up last night to go to the fundraiser. Our costumes were hanging in my closet.

He kissed me and sat down, stretching out his legs.

"How about waffles for breakfast?"

He nodded. "As long as you have plenty of butter and maple syrup."

"Of course. What's the point of eating waffles if you don't have lots of those?"

He put a hand on my arm as I started to get up. "No need to hurry. Let's sit and enjoy our coffee first. Eventually, I need to go home and work on all that stuff I have to do at the end of the semester. Finals start next week and the research papers are coming in. I have a stack of those to grade."

"There's a free concert tonight at the county park," I said, remembering the postcard. "I was thinking about going."

He cocked his head to one side. "Who's playing?"

"It's that bluegrass group, the one we saw a few months ago at the club here in town. We both liked them. Are you really going to spend the whole day grading research papers?"

He smiled. "I could be persuaded."

"I could pack a picnic supper."

"What time is the concert?"

"Seven. I'll bring food, you bring wine?"

"Okay, I'll pick you up at five-thirty."

I finished the last of my coffee and stood up.

"Another cup?"

"Still working on this one."

I went back to the kitchen and poured the last of the coffee into my mug. Then I started another pot. A phone pinged, signaling an incoming message. My phone was in the bedroom and so was Sam's. I retrieved both and went back out to the deck.

"You have a message." I handed off his phone as I sat down, mug in hand.

"It's from Cory," he said. He opened the message and smiled. "Pictures of Hannah." He scrolled through the images and then handed the phone to me.

His son, Cory, worked for the California State Water Resources Board and lived in Sacramento. He and his wife had become parents earlier this year, and Sam enjoyed his new role of grandfather. Hannah was a pretty baby, with blond hair and a plump smiling face. I couldn't tell whether she looked like either of her parents, as I'd only met them twice.

"I'll go for a visit when the semester is over," Sam said now. "Babies grow up so fast. She's changed every time Cory sends a picture."

"How's Stella?" He hadn't mentioned his daughter in a while.

He frowned. "I don't know what's going on with her."

Over the course of our relationship, he had hinted about his daughter's problems. She was the younger of his two children, now in her mid-twenties, and had been a concern since high school. Stella had been in trouble several times, most recently into drugs and alcohol, which led to a stint in rehab. After she got out of the program, she seemed unable to keep a job for very long. Right now she was living in Davis with Sam's ex-wife. Other than offering a sympathetic ear when Sam did want to talk about it, which wasn't often, I stayed out of it.

"Do you ever regret it?" he asked now, setting aside his phone. "Not getting married? Not having kids?"

I took my time answering. These were questions I'd considered many times in the past. Women are programmed to think we should get married and have babies. Everywhere I go most people are paired up. It gets old after a while. When we had our high school reunion a few years ago, I was one of a handful of people who'd never been married or had children. It means I can't relate to some of the issues married people and parents face, but I try. It also means I don't have anyone in my bed on a regular basis, except cats. But the relationship Sam and I had developed over the past eighteen months was good, solving the need for companionship, physical and otherwise.

"I used to want that very much," I said finally. "A baby. A little girl. Up until I was in my mid-thirties. At one point I thought quite seriously about just having a baby, whether I was married or not."

"Lots of women do," Sam said, sipping his coffee.

I nodded. "My career was important to me, though. I kept thinking of all the compromises I'd have to make if I had a baby without anyone else involved to support me. Eventually, as I got older, it just didn't seem to be as much of an issue. So, I would say at this stage of my life, I don't regret it." I paused. "Any particular reason for your question?"

He thought about it, then shrugged. "Just wondering. Roads not taken, and all that. There was a time I thought I'd never get married and have children. I like the single life. And then, well, I met Elaine, we fell in love, had the family. Then we fell out of love and split up, which seemed to be for the best. All those changes."

"Life sometimes leads us in directions we hadn't anticipated." I raised my mug. The coffee was lukewarm.

"I'm going to get a warmup and start breakfast."

"I'll set the table," he said as we stood up.

We went inside. I pulled a well-used cookbook from a shelf in the kitchen and stirred up my tried-and-true waffle recipe.

After breakfast, Sam cleaned up the dishes and utensils, then left for home, bearing the garment bag that held his costume. I poured the last mugful of coffee and took the Sunday newspaper out to the deck to read. That done, I went back inside and worked on a long-neglected project, reorganizing the walk-in closet off the living room. I was putting things back on the shelves when Dina called. "Ed and I are going to that bluegrass concert at the park this evening. Want to come with us?"

"As it happens, Sam and I are going. I'm packing a picnic and he's driving."

"Swing by the rafting company and we'll ride with you," Dina suggested. "That way we only have one car to park."

"Sounds like a plan. Sam's picking me up at five-thirty, so we'll see you shortly after." We sorted out the menu, then I called Sam to update him on the evening's plans.

"In that case, I'll come by earlier. And bring more wine. I'll be ready for a break from grading papers."

I had made it to the grocery store a few days ago, where I'd bought a roasted chicken. I had a lot left. Now I took the meat off the bone and chopped it, making a batch of chicken salad sandwiches for the evening's alfresco supper. I also had salami and several different kinds of cheese to round out my supper offerings. A search through the pantry netted an unopened bag of tortilla chips and a jar of salsa. I got out my padded cooler picnic bag, which had glasses, cutlery, and plates for four people, and left it on the counter, ready to fill when Sam arrived.

Rocky River Rafting was located on the river, just north of the city limits. The one-story main building was surrounded by a gravel parking lot for customers and staff. A gradual slope led down to a line of sturdy metal sheds where the rafts were stored when not in use, transporting white water enthusiasts down the rapids on the upper Rocoso River, that stretch between Jermyn and Rocoso. On the south side of the building were two vans and two Jeep Wranglers. Both the vans had trailers hitched to the rear, ready to transport rafts and rafters up the canyon to a location near Jermyn, where rafters put in for their trips down the river. There were several such spots along the river, places where people could put in and take out rafts.

All four vehicles were blue with the distinctive rafting company logo painted on the doors. Ed McGinty was definitely into branding—the logo could be found on T-shirts and ball caps worn by Ed and his employees, as well as lots of people around town. He sold the shirts and caps inside the building, along with packs, blankets, and other kinds of rafting gear.

Sam parked his Honda Accord near the entrance to the building and we both got out of the car. We were dressed somewhat alike, in jeans and shirts, with plenty of warm layers, such as the fleece vest I wore. I knew from experience that outdoor concerts here in the mountains could be cold at night, no matter how sunny it was during the day.

Nearby, a couple of the rafting company's employees were cleaning out one of the Jeeps. The vehicle's passenger-side door was open and a stocky young woman in her twenties, her blond hair caught back with a red bandanna, scooped up an armful of gear and carried it to the nearest storage shed. Another woman was at the back of the Jeep, the rear hatch door open, as she leaned in and gathered items into a green plastic crate. She straightened and carried the crate to the shed. Her shoulder-length brown hair was decorated with several bright streaks of color—red, green, blue, and purple.

"Ed and Dina must be inside. I'll check." Sam, hands stuck in the pockets of his jacket, headed for the front door.

"I'll look out back." I walked past the Jeep and the storage sheds, heading for the river. I spotted Dina, standing near the water's edge, where a log had been shaped into a bench.

She waved at me. "Look, there's a green heron in that tree."

I quickened my step. I frequently saw great blue herons and both snowy and great egrets along the river. But the smaller herons, such as the black-crowned night heron and the green heron, were harder to spot. The larger birds stood like sentinels in the marshes on this stretch of the river, while the smaller birds, with their hunched backs, were concealed in the shallows or in branches of trees. And the green heron's coloration often made it hard to see.

When I reached the bench, Dina pointed at an oak tree. The heron, short and squat, perched on a lower branch that stretched over the river. The bird had a velvety green back and a dark chestnut body over its yellow legs. I took out my phone and pressed the icon that opened the camera, using my fingers to increase the size of the image. After I snapped off several shots, the heron took wing. But it didn't fly far. It swooped over an old car decorated with patches of rust and landed on the roof of the storage shed where the two employees were working. Now I could see the bird's colors even better, as well as the long dagger-like bill. I snapped off several more pictures.

I heard someone call my name and turned, tucking

my phone in my pocket. Sam and Ed were walking toward us. Ed carried a wicker picnic basket. He detoured briefly and spoke to the two employees at the storage shed. Then he joined us.

"I've got ham sandwiches and a big green salad," Dina said, relieving Ed of the picnic basket. "And I hope everyone likes brownies."

"Who doesn't?" I said.

We loaded the provisions into Sam's car and left, heading north toward the park and the concert.

Chapter 8

ON MONDAY MORNING, Gwen, Carmen and I had our usual check-in over the first pot of coffee. Then I headed for my office, hoping for some quiet time to deal with paperwork, phone calls, and emails before beginning my daily round of appointments and client visits. My calendar promised a routine week. No emergencies, I hoped, but there was always that possibility.

The phone rang. I spent the next half hour dealing with a frustrated client, the client's health care provider, and a company that provided oxygen equipment. We went back and forth via phone and email about a referral for a portable oxygen concentrator. So much for my paperwork.

I headed out the door for my first client visit of the day. As it happened, that visit also involved an oxygen concentrator. Marina Davis was on oxygen after a bout with pneumonia last winter. She had finally gotten used to the tubing with the cannula that had to be inserted into her nostrils to deliver a continuous supply of oxygen. The concentrator lived in her guest bedroom, providing a low and ever-present hum. The biggest danger for Marina was the tubing that led from the concentrator to the cannula. It was a hundred feet long, enabling her to move from room to room in her house, but early on, she was forever getting her feet and legs tangled in the tubing. Fortunately, she hadn't fallen. While I was there, I checked the settings on the concentrator to make sure she was getting the two liters of oxygen per minute that her doctor had prescribed. Everything was in order with the machine. Earlier this year, during a brief power failure caused by a particularly harsh snowstorm, she had to switch to her portable concentrator. I checked Marina's medications and called her doctor to reorder one of the prescriptions. I was perspiring by the time I left the house, not from exertion but from the interior temperature. Like many of my elderly clients, Marina kept her house warm because she was cold all the time. Troubled with arthritis after an active lifetime, she complained that cold made her joints ache.

Several appointments later, I returned to my office, bearing a sack from the nearby deli. Carmen was just leaving. Sometimes my colleagues and I were like the proverbial ships passing in the night. I sat down at my desk and unwrapped my sandwich, turkey on whole wheat.

While I ate, I reviewed the Garvin file. Betty, Sheryl, and I had gone to the doctor on Wednesday of last week, and after viewing the results of Betty's lab tests, Dr. Everett had adjusted her medications and recommended that she reduce her salt intake. I'd contacted Meals on Wheels to request that future deliveries to Betty include salt-free food. On Thursday, we'd seen an ophthalmologist. Betty's cataracts had worsened and surgery was recommended. The first of these operations was set for June. Sheryl planned to return to Rocoso in June for Betty's cataract surgery.

Lunch over, I returned several phone calls, then left the office. I drove to Juniper Street and parked in front of the Garvin house. Louise Beltran's Subaru was in the driveway. Louise was a Rocoso native who had been a caregiver for more than twenty years, first working for other firms, then forming her own company with several employees.

Louise greeted me at the front door. "I helped Mrs. Garvin take a shower and get dressed. She has told me, twice already, that her daughter is overreacting and she doesn't need a caregiver."

Betty's reaction was common. Many of my clients felt they were managing well on their own, despite evidence to the contrary.

"I'll talk with her."

"She's in the family room. She ate her Meals on Wheels lunch, not all of it, though. She said it was bland and there was too much food."

I nodded. "She's getting the salt-free entree. On her own, she has been eating erratically, things like cottage cheese and crackers, not a lot of fruits or vegetables. The full meal must seem like a lot."

The meals delivered by the local volunteers were nutritious, based on a diet of 1800 calories per day. They were packaged on a tray and included three ounces of protein, a vegetable, a starch, bread and butter, a salad, and dessert, as well as something to drink, such as milk or juice.

"I put the rest of the food in the refrigerator, in case she wants some later," Louise said. "Bea Lovell phoned and said she'd be over soon with groceries. Mrs. Garvin's daughter set it up so Bea will shop once a week and keep the kitchen stocked with basics."

I headed for the family room. Betty was in the recliner, dressed in green slacks with a flowered blouse. She held a hardcover book on her lap. "Sheryl got me books from the library. Big print, easier for me to see. This one's by Dick Francis. It's good so far."

"Louise says that you got your Meals on Wheels lunch."

Betty wrinkled her nose. "I did. It was chicken. It tasted all right, but it didn't have much flavor. I goosed it up with salt and pepper. Before you say anything, I know I'm supposed to cut back on salt. Sheryl and the doctor already gave me that lecture. I know I'm getting the salt-free meals but things taste so bland without it."

"I understand. There are several spice blends that add flavor to the meals without salt. I'll mention that to Bea Lovell. She's buying your groceries now."

"A lot of fuss and expense." Betty's face took on a stubborn look. "I don't need all this looking after. Yes, I set the saucepan on fire and the fire department came. Sheryl didn't have to come all the way from Seattle to check on me. It's a tempest in a teapot. You girls are making too much of it."

"Sheryl is concerned about you," I said. "She wants to make sure you're well and people are looking after you. You'll have plenty of company, because I am going to check on you, along with Louise and Bea. You won't be alone all the time."

"All these people to wait on one old woman." Betty sighed. "I do sometimes get lonely by myself. You're nice, and so are Louise and Bea. I worry about the expense. I don't want to outlive my money. Sheryl keeps track of things. She says I should use my money to make myself comfortable." Betty leaned toward the side table, as though looking for something. Then she stuck one hand in the pocket of her slacks, pulled out something, and held it out. "Here, I want to give you this."

I leaned forward and examined the object. It was a gold ring with a small dark red stone, probably a garnet. "Why do you want to give that to me?"

"Because you're such a nice lady."

"I appreciate that. It's a lovely ring, but I don't really need it."

Betty frowned. "Someone has to pay you for coming over to check on me."

"Sheryl is taking care of that."

"Does she write checks for you?" Betty asked. "Sheryl

70

says I'm not supposed to write checks, that she'll do it for me. The checks are in that front bedroom, the one my husband used as an office after the kids were grown up and gone."

"I'm going to put the ring in your jewelry box."

Betty nodded. "Yes, you go ahead and do that." She went back to reading her book.

I went into the kitchen. Louise was pouring out glasses of iced tea. "Want some?"

"Sure. I'll be back in a minute."

I walked into the living room, intending to head back to Betty's bedroom. Then I glanced at the china cabinet. I should have seen the silver coffee and tea set on the top shelf. It was there, but it wasn't complete. The coffee and teapots stood on the rectangular tray, but the sugar and creamer were gone. I looked at the middle shelf. The smaller tray and silver tongs were missing, along with the matching pair of silver bowls.

"Is something wrong?" Louise asked from the kitchen.

I pointed at the china cabinet. "When I was here last week, there was more silver in this cabinet. Several pieces are gone."

Louise joined me in the living room and peered at the shelves. "I didn't notice them when I was here before. But I wasn't looking. Ms. Garvin did tell me about the missing jewelry. She said if I find any of those pieces, I should let her know."

The doorbell rang and Louise went to open the front door. Bea Lovell bustled into the living room, bearing a blue canvas bag filled with groceries. "Hi. I'm here with provisions. This is just basics, from the list that her daughter gave me."

"When are you due to clean the house?" I asked.

"This afternoon," Bea said.

"Some things are missing from the china cabinet."

Bea nodded. "Mrs. Garvin's daughter alerted me to the missing jewelry. I'll keep an eye out while I clean house and let you know if any of the stuff turns up."

"These are larger items." I described them, wondering if Betty had moved them herself. I walked back to the family room.

Betty looked up from her book. "I thought you'd left."

"Not yet. I have a question about that silver set in your china cabinet. And the two silver bowls."

Betty thought for a moment. "Oh, yes. I got the silver set for my twenty-fifth wedding anniversary. That's the silver anniversary, you know. And those bowls belonged to my mother-in-law. I got them when she died. She collected all sorts of pretties."

"Did you take them out of the cabinet?"

"No, they're on the shelf."

"They aren't there now," I said.

The elderly woman looked confused. "But they should be. Maybe Sheryl moved them. You call her and ask her what she did with them."

"Thanks, I will."

I stepped into the kitchen, where Bea and Louise were unloading the groceries from the bags. "I heard," Louise said.

"I'll take a quick look through the house before I leave," I said.

The first bedroom off the hallway had been used as an office and a guest room, containing a single bed and nightstand as well as a desk and filing cabinet. I saw no sign of the missing silver. The next bedroom was larger and contained a queen-sized bed. No luck there. I walked down the hall to the master bedroom, where I returned the gold and garnet ring to Betty's jewelry box, which sat atop the dresser. I turned around and found one of the silver bowls on the nightstand next to Betty's bed, a few pretzels at the bottom. I carried it to the kitchen. "Here's one of the bowls. I didn't see any of the other silver." I found a storage bag in a drawer and dumped in the pretzels. Then I rinsed and dried the bowl and returned it to the china cabinet.

"We'll keep looking for the stuff that's missing," Louise said.

Thanks." My phone chimed, a reminder for my next appointment. I said good-bye and left the Garvin house.

Chapter 9

"MY SON'S ALWAYS AFTER me to go see him in Carson City." Dolly Halstrom's blue eyes twinkled behind the lenses of her bifocals.

"Why don't you visit him?" I already knew the answer.

"Oh, if I go, he'll put me in a nursing home." She laughed, a wicked chuckle. "The only way I'm leaving this house is when they carry me out."

Dolly was ninety-five. She planned on making it to a hundred, preferably here in her comfortable home. She lived alone in this one-story, wood-framed bungalow that she and her late husband bought when they moved to Rocoso. Martin Halstrom had used his GI benefits to study engineering at the University of California in Berkeley. After graduation, he got a job working for the county and Dolly found employment with the school district, working in administrative jobs. It was here in this house that they had raised their two children.

Her husband had loved gardening, growing roses in the beds at the front of the house, and vegetables in several raised beds in the backyard. When he died fourteen years ago, the garden had become a problem, Dolly had no particular love for digging in the dirt, as she called it. She kept up with the yard and garden for a while, because it was Martin's garden. But in the past few years, she had neither the stamina nor the inclination. After fussing about the weeds for a time, she'd hired a yard service to look after the lawn and roses and the raised beds had been planted with ground cover and succulents.

"I have to keep up the house," Dolly always said. "I

want something to leave to my family."

Her children would have been quite happy to sell the house and move their mother to a senior apartment or an assisted living facility. Both had tried to persuade her to do just that, or to move closer to them, either to Carson City, where her son, Peter, worked for the Nevada Gaming Commission, or to Bakersfield, at the southern end of California's Central Valley, where her daughter, Nanette, taught at a local college.

But Dolly wasn't having any of that. She was staying put. And she was quite happy living alone, she said. Though she wasn't completely alone. She was assisted by regular visits from a team of caregivers, a visiting nurse—and me.

Dolly's house on Cameron Street had been built in the 1940s and it had many architectural touches that reminded me of my grandmother's home, such as hardwood floors and glass-fronted built-in shelves on either side of the fireplace. At Dolly's house, the mantel was decorated with framed photographs of her family, including lots of grandchildren, and some great-grandchildren.

Dolly reminded me a lot of my mother. Mom, too, was determined to stay in her own home.

Dolly had been a quilter in years past. The evidence was all over her living room, from the brightly colored "Sunbonnet Sue" quilt hanging from a rack at one end of the living room to the smaller lap quilt draped over the back of the chair where I sat. She no longer sewed, though. She had arthritis in her hands and arms and admitted that her eyesight wasn't as good as it used to be. She'd had cataract surgery, but thankfully there was no evidence of macular degeneration. Hearing aids and glasses were part of her ensemble. Even while seated, I loomed over her. At one time, Dolly might have been taller than five feet, but age and osteoporosis had taken a toll.

I had been working as Dolly's care manager for two years now. On this Monday afternoon, her regular caregiver had already left for the day. Now I sat on the sofa opposite Dolly and we talked. With all my clients, social interaction was as important as seeing to their physical and emotional needs.

Dolly brought me up to date on her family. One of her granddaughters was graduating from the University of California at Davis later this month, and Dolly was planning to go to the ceremony. "My son's going to drive over and pick me up. Then we'll meet everyone in Davis. It should be a lot of fun." Dolly stopped and yawned. "I'm sorry, I'm feeling drowsy."

"Did you sleep all right last night?" Many of my elderly clients were often troubled by insomnia or interrupted sleep.

Dolly shrugged. "Some. I woke up early and couldn't get back to sleep. Goodness, my skin is so dry these days." Dolly ran one hand over her forearm, where veins traced blue lines under papery-thin skin wrinkled with age and scattered with brown age spots. She also had thin skin that would bruise or bleed if she hit her arms or legs against something. She yawned again. "I feel like I'm getting a headache."

"Are you drinking enough water?" I sat forward, alert to a potential problem. Drowsiness, dry skin, and headache were all symptoms of dehydration, and Dolly frequently didn't drink enough water.

"I had some water with my lunch." Dolly got Meals on Wheels deliveries. In addition to getting a good, nutritious meal, MOW had the added benefit of having the delivery person touch base with elderly clients on a regular basis. Since many seniors like Dolly didn't drive anymore, the interaction with another real person was an additional benefit.

"That was a couple of hours ago. I think you should drink some more water." I went to the kitchen and filled a glass with water from the tap. A blue glass fruit bowl on the kitchen table contained several apples and bananas.

"Dolly, do you want a banana?" There was no answer. "Dolly?"

I heard a thump. I set the glass on the counter and hurried to the living room. Dolly was on the floor in front of the chair where she'd been sitting. Her walker was nearby, the book she'd been reading next to the front wheels. Had Dolly tried to get up?

I knelt and felt the pulse at her neck. It was rapid, and the skin was cool and dry.

The white console on the nearby table beeped and I heard a voice. "Mrs. Halstrom?" The alert device Dolly wore around her neck was extremely sensitive, intended to trigger a response if Dolly fell. At first, Dolly had objected to the alert device because, as she put it, the damn thing went off every time she sneezed. The console connected to a dispatcher from the alert company, who said again, "Mrs. Halstrom?"

I leaned toward the console. "This is her care manager, Ms. Dexter. Mrs. Halstrom passed out. Please send the paramedics and call her son and daughter. They're on the list."

"Will do," the dispatcher said.

The list had been provided by Dolly's family when they convinced her to get the alert device. As Dolly's care manager, I was on the list, along with her son, daughter, and one of her granddaughters. I also had the Halstrom family contacts in my cell phone.

Peter Halstrom answered on the first ring. "Kay, I just got the call from the alert company. They called you, too?"

"I'm here visiting her. I went into the kitchen and that's when she fainted. I think she's dehydrated."

On the other end of the line, he sighed. "Yeah, that's happened before. She just doesn't drink enough water. Listen, I know the alert company called my sister. Would you please call my daughter? She's the one who lives the closest. I'll drive over as soon as I can."

"Yes, I'll do that. The ambulance is coming. I hear the siren now."

After disconnecting, I scrolled through the contacts and found the number for Peter's daughter in Loomis, a small town in the Sierra foothills northeast of Sacramento. If need be, she could be in Rocoso in a couple of hours. There was no answer, so I left a message.

The siren was very loud now, then it stopped. I met the paramedics at the front door and watched as they checked Dolly, then loaded her onto a gurney and took her out to the ambulance. I locked the house and followed. At the Rocoso Medical Center, I stayed in the emergency room lobby while Dolly was seen and then checked into the hospital. Dolly was indeed dehydrated and the staff was giving her fluids. While in the waiting room, I'd received a couple of phone calls. Dolly's granddaughter was on the road, heading up to Rocoso, and Peter planned to drive in from Carson City this evening.

DOLLY WAS MY LAST client visit of the day. Once I returned to the office, I planned on getting to the paperwork that always seemed to accumulate on my desk. Instead, I crossed the courtyard to the Rococo History Museum. Inside, I walked past a display case containing a basket made by an artist from the Rocoso Valley band of Maidu, the indigenous people who had populated this area for centuries. As Dina had pointed out at the fundraiser, the

Maidu were renowned for their basketry skills, and the large basket in the center of the display, with a geometric black design circling the honey-colored bowl woven of willow strips, was an excellent example.

Dina had an office at the back of the first floor. Her fingers skimmed over her computer keyboard and she frowned at the monitor. She looked up and smiled when she saw me. "What brings you to my bailiwick this afternoon?"

"I need to do some research in the library."

Dina got up and stepped around her desk. "What are you looking for? I'll point you in the right direction."

"Any information you have on Lost Woman Creek and the old hot springs resort."

"That's a popular topic. We've had several people in here over the last month or so, looking up information. Most recently Marie Devorno, the architect who has the office near yours."

"Really? Interesting. I'm curious because people were talking about the property at the fundraiser on Saturday night. Arlette Simmons says she's heard rumors about plans to rebuild the hotel and reopen the hot springs."

"There's a lot of speculation about what's going to happen to the land." Dina shut her office door. "I've heard the rumor about the hotel, and another one about leveling the ruins and building condos. I'd hate to see that happen. The hotel site has some historical significance. My local Sierra Club contacts tell me they'd like to convince the county to take it over and turn it into a park. Who knows? Anything can happen."

We walked through the main display gallery to a staircase that descended to the building's basement. Back in the days when the historical society building had been a bordello, the basement had been a dark, dank hole used for storage and a coal cellar. The addition of several ground-level windows and a well-designed remodel had turned it into a comfortable, light-filled space. Pale yellow walls held framed prints and photographs from the historical society's collection, and the beige carpet warmed the room and muffled sound. Several pine tables with chairs were arrayed in front of a counter, with two computer stations on one wall. Behind the counter were bookshelves and filing cabinets. Sandy, one of the museum's staff, was helping two young women who looked like college students. She waved at us as we walked past the main counter to a bank of filing cabinets arrayed against the back wall.

Dina pulled out a file drawer and removed several folders. "We haven't digitized this stuff yet. That's another item on my ever-growing long-term wish list. You'll have to dig through the folders. The information is mostly in chronological order. When you're done looking through the files, put them in that wooden tray over there. Sandy will refile them."

"Thanks."

"Are you going to Grace McCann's funeral tomorrow?" Dina asked. "It's at ten o'clock, graveside services at the cemetery."

"Yes. I thought I'd pay my respects." I shook my head. "It's really sad."

She nodded. "It is indeed. I'll see you there." She turned and headed up the stairs.

I carried the files to one of the tables and sat down, opening a folder. It contained the transcription of an oral history dating from the 1950s, in which a Maidu woman told the story of how Lost Woman Creek got its name. The tale was familiar to me, a story commonly told about the decimation of the California tribes. The native people were hunters and gatherers who had lived on the bounty of the land for hundreds of years. The influx of white settlers, first the Spanish Californios and then the rush of gold seekers from all over the world, killed natives by the thousands, by violence and disease. Surviving natives were enslaved, forced to labor on the missions, or farms. In some cases, the natives were hunted for sport.

In the early years of the Gold Rush era, a young woman from the local Maidu band had gone out to gather acorns, a staple of the native diet. She disappeared, perhaps kidnapped or killed by gold miners or soldiers. She was never seen again, at least not in the flesh, said the old woman who told the tale. Whatever her fate, the lost woman's ghost was said to haunt the banks of the creek.

Another folder contained yellowed paper, both newspaper clippings and typewritten pages, that told the history of the area where the creek flowed into the river. There had been a gold strike on the creek in the 1850s, and a mining camp appeared overnight, abandoned a few years later after the gold ran out. Another gold strike came in the 1870s, then waned. Settlers logged the slopes on either side of the creek. Farms appeared, the earliest and largest property owned by the Maysfield family. Then came a village called Creekside, with a general store and blacksmith shop serving the needs of the community. Later came a school and a post office, both gone, along with most of what made Creekside a community. There were few residents now, and the village was mostly foundations and derelict buildings.

Lost Woman Creek was known for the natural hot springs that fed into the creek, with pools, mostly shallow but some deep, tucked in various places on both sides of the stream. Both the Maidu and the gold miners had bathed in the springs, and later settlers had also relaxed in the warm water. Henry Maysfield built the hotel in 1893, a two-story building with wings and a huge lobby, with a restaurant and ballroom at the back. Cottages dotted the back garden, where a stone path led to a bathhouse with changing rooms and a rectangular pool constructed of the local rock. From here, stone steps descended to the creek itself.

Another folder contained a map that was nearly a hundred years old. My fingers traced the route of the creek as it meandered to its confluence with the Rocoso River, then lingered at the clearing about a mile from the main highway. When my brother and I were growing up, Dad had loved taking the family for drives through the mountain byways on Sunday afternoons, a picnic lunch in the trunk. I remembered turning off the highway onto the county road to Creekside. From the village, a fire trail led through a meadow to the site where the hotel once stood, the ruins silent and shrouded as the forest reclaimed the lawn in front of the main building and the paths that led to the cottages and ballroom.

I leafed through a folder full of black-and-white photographs. Many of these had been slipped into clear sheet protectors because the photos were torn at the corners or weathered by time. As I examined the images of another era, I wished I had a time machine so I could go back and visit Creekside Hot Springs Hotel. Pictures showed men and women in Edwardian dress, strolling in the gardens or posing on the creek banks. Other photos showed the flappers of the Twenties, women with their hair bobbed, and their skirts short as they danced the Charleston in the hotel ballroom. Here was a shot taken in winter, with snow on the ground and people in swimsuits, stretched out in the warm pools.

Hemlines dipped again in the 1930s, and the women in the pictures wore their hair in the marcel waves that were popular at the time. Some of their male companions looked like gangsters. I fingered a photo that showed a dark-haired man posing on the running board of a Packard. Indeed, Dina had once told me that bootleggers and speakeasies were in evidence up and down the Rocoso Valley during Prohibition.

The hotel had closed during World War II and opened again in 1946. I found a few photos of the post-war era, then a collection of shots showing the aftermath of the fire in the autumn of 1948 that had leveled the cottages and seriously damaged the main building.

What had caused the fire? A few clippings from the *Rocoso Bugle* mentioned that initially the investigators had looked at the possibility of arson, but a later article told me the cause had been laid to faulty wiring. I wondered why the owners hadn't rebuilt. Maybe they didn't have the money or the will.

The will, I thought as I looked at my watch. I still hadn't satisfied my curiosity as to who had inherited the property from the late Ruby Waldron. A trip to the county courthouse would answer that question, if the will had been filed. Not that it was any concern of mine. I'd spent enough time on this local history excursion. I closed the file I'd been looking through, gathered up the folders, and took them to the counter.

Chapter 10

A BREEZE RUFFLED THE leaves of a nearby oak tree. Somewhere above me, a rhythmic tapping signaled the presence of a woodpecker. Tall ponderosa pines, their crowns pointing high into a blue sky painted with clouds, ranged along the other side of the wrought iron fence surrounding the Rocoso cemetery, where generations of residents were buried.

Dina and I stood near a white marble headstone decorated with a carving of a lamb. The lamb meant innocence, a symbol indicating the grave was that of a child. The lamb also figured in other symbols, that of the sacrificial lamb, a person or animal sacrificed for the common good. It was a short step from a sacrificial lamb to a sacrificial daughter.

Sacrifice didn't always involve death, but in Grace McCann's case, it had. The woman being buried this Tuesday morning was the classic case of the sacrificial daughter, an unmarried daughter who had given up her own life to care for her aging parents.

The minister took his place near the casket, flanked by Grace's out-of-town cousins. It was just after ten o'clock on a sunny morning in May and we were waiting for the services to begin. I counted about twenty people grouped around the McCann family plot.

Dina spoke in a low voice. "She wore herself out looking after her folks. I can't believe she's gone. She wasn't even sixty yet."

"It's sobering when people we went to high school with start dying," I said. "Grace wouldn't accept any help, from her cousins or her friends. All she would say is that they were her parents and her responsibility."

"I get that. But still . . ." Dina's voice trailed off.

A woman from Grace's church began to sing "His Eye Is on the Sparrow" in a wavering soprano that hit a flat note on the second stanza. Grace would have hated that. She loved to sing, priding herself on her perfect pitch. She had often been the soloist with the Rocoso High School chorus and she'd played the leads when the theater department did musicals. Grace went on to major in music in college, getting a teaching credential at the same time she harbored a desire to be a performer. But that didn't happen. After a brief marriage that ended in divorce, she moved back to Rocoso, buying a condo near her parents' home. She took a job teaching music at one of the local middle schools.

Mrs. McCann had Alzheimer's. Her deterioration was gradual and inexorable. It got to the point where she couldn't be left alone because she'd wander off. Looking after his wife became too much for Mr. McCann. He'd been diagnosed with cancer. Grace sold her condo and moved in with her parents. Her mother had died last year, followed by her father's death six weeks ago.

I had tried several times over the past few years to convince Grace to get some help. Stress was the number one problem affecting caregivers. That's why they needed respite.

But Grace always smiled and said, "I can manage." She had, up to a point.

In the end, though, caring for her parents had taken its toll on her health. A week after her father's funeral, she had a stroke that put her in the hospital. She appeared to be recovering. Then, last week, a second stroke took Grace's life.

The graveside service over, the mourners walked away from the plot, heading for cars parked along the narrow lanes inside the cemetery. "Are you going over to the house?" Dina asked.

I pulled my keyring from my shoulder bag. "I don't know any of Grace's cousins that well. Besides, I have client appointments."

I headed for my car. It was just past eleven. A glance at my phone showed several messages. I sat in the car for a few minutes, checking voice mail and email. One of the voice mail messages was from Bea Lovell. "Call me when you get a chance. It's about Betty Garvin."

I returned the call. "What's up?"

"A couple of things. Yesterday afternoon, while I cleaned Betty Garvin's house, I looked for the missing jewelry and the things from the china cabinet, but I didn't find anything. After I was finished cleaning, Betty tried to give me a gold bracelet. She said it was to pay for housecleaning. I told her she didn't need to pay me because her daughter has arranged for all that. She insisted, though. I finally took the bracelet and put it in her jewelry box."

"Thanks for letting me know. Betty may have given that missing jewelry to someone. I'm heading over there now."

I needed coffee first. I left the cemetery and, a few blocks away, pulled to the curb near a coffee shop. I carried my stainless-steel thermal mug inside and asked the woman behind the counter to fill it with French roast. After a restorative sip, I put the lid on the mug and went outside. I drove across town to Betty Garvin's house. There was no answer when I rang the doorbell. I used the key Sheryl had given me to open the front door. The faint lemony smell of furniture polish lingered in the living room, left over from Bea's cleaning session the day before.

"Betty?" I walked through the living room to the kitchen, carrying my coffee mug. Betty was in the family room, dozing in the recliner. The book she'd been reading had fallen to the floor. The remains of that morning's Meals on Wheels delivery were strewn across the kitchen table. The meatloaf entree had come with a side of green beans, a green salad, and a roll, with a slice of lemon cake for dessert. Betty had eaten half of the meal, leaving the rest on the tray on which it had been delivered. Crumbs were scattered all over the table. A paper napkin was balled up next to the tray, along with a spoon and a glass with an inch or so of milk at the bottom. Salt and pepper shakers were near the tray, meaning that Betty had used them on her salt-free meal. I needed to discuss that with Sheryl. There was no point in having salt-free meals delivered if Betty was going to use salt anyway.

I set my mug on the counter, covered the leftovers, and put them in the refrigerator. The spoon and glass went into the dishwasher. I grabbed a dishcloth and wiped crumbs off the table.

In the family room, Betty came awake with a start. "Who's that? Sheryl? Tamara?"

"It's Kay."

Who was Tamara? I wondered.

I hung the dishcloth over the kitchen faucet and retrieved my mug. In the family room, I picked up the book Betty had been reading, a large print Mary Stewart novel, and put it on the side table. I took a seat on the sofa. Betty had seemed energetic yesterday, but today she looked confused, as though going through photos in her head, trying to remember who I was. Then she nodded, looking relieved.

"Kay," Betty said. "You're Rose's daughter. You were here yesterday."

"That's right. How are you feeling today?"

"So-so. I didn't sleep well last night. But I've been dozing off and on all morning. I ate some of that meatloaf that came from Meals on Wheels. It was okay. Not as good as the meatloaf I used to make. Needed salt."

"I'm sure your meatloaf was wonderful." I took another sip of coffee. Then the doorbell rang.

When I opened the front door, a girl stood on the porch, dressed in a short denim skirt and a hot pink blouse that hugged her body. She appeared to be about twelve years old. Middle-schoolers looked a good deal more grown-up than they had when I was younger.

The girl tossed back a lock of dark brown hair. "I'm Ginny Cavalieri. I live across the street. I'm on my lunch break from school."

"I'm Kay. I visit Mrs. Garvin to make sure she's all right."

The girl nodded. "I know. My mom told me. You look after Mrs. Garvin because she's old and can't look after herself."

"I'm one of the people who is helping out. Can I help you with something, Ginny?"

Ginny made a face. "Mrs. Garvin gave me a fancy pin a couple of weeks ago, and I gave it back. I didn't know those blue stones were really sapphires, honest, or I wouldn't have taken it. I was out in the front yard and she came home from the store and I helped her carry her groceries. So she gave it to me."

"Thanks for returning the pin."

"Well, Mrs. Garvin gave me something else." Ginny held out her hand. In her palm was the gold ring with the dark red stone, the same ring Betty had tried to give me. "She was out in the yard this morning when I was leaving for school, looking for her newspaper. That boy who delivers it had thrown it in the flower bed. I got the paper and gave it to her. She had this ring in her pocket and she gave it to me. I said my mother wouldn't like it and tried to give it back, but Mrs. Garvin wouldn't take no for an answer. I stuck it in my backpack and went to school. I came home for lunch and saw your car and I figured I'd better bring the ring to you."

"Thanks, Ginny. I appreciate it."

As the girl crossed the street to her house, I shut the door and went back to the family room to talk with Betty. She seemed confused and didn't recall giving the ring to Ginny. I put the ring in the jewelry box, thinking it was more and more likely that Betty had given away the missing items.

AT THE ROCOSO MEDICAL CENTER, I parked near the main entrance, checked messages, and returned a phone call. Then I went inside the hospital, heading for the bank of elevators on the other side of the lobby.

Dolly Halstrom was in a third-floor room. Her adult children were in a small waiting room just past the nurses' station. Peter Halstrom, a short man with thinning blond hair, had arrived from Carson City late last night. His sister, Nan Spies, had driven up from Bakersfield, arriving this morning.

"How is she?" I asked.

"Better," Peter said. "They've been giving her fluids and she's getting some rest. The doctor wants to keep her one more night. Then she'll be released and we'll take her home."

Nan ran a hand through her graying hair. "She can't go home, Peter. She needs to be in assisted living, or she needs round-the-clock caregivers."

Her brother sighed. "Sis, there's no way we're going to force Mom to do anything she doesn't want to do. What do you think, Kay?"

I was well aware that the two siblings didn't agree when it came to their mother. But my job was to make recommendations and let them decide.

"I think it's a decision all three of you will have to make. Forcing Dolly to give up her home isn't a good idea. I've seen people who went unwillingly into assisted living or a nursing home and it didn't work out well." During my long tenure as a care manager, I'd encountered many such cases. The elderly person had simply given up, sometimes deteriorating rapidly. "I would urge you to discuss it with her again and see if you can come to some sort of agreement or compromise."

Nan gave an exasperated sigh, as though she'd been hoping that I would back up her opinion. I smiled and left them conferring in the waiting room. Dolly's room was across the hall. She looked perky and in good spirits. She was saying good-bye to her granddaughter, who then left the room.

"You can tell Peter and Nan I am not going into a nursing home," Dolly declared. "I don't care what they say. I'm not senile, I've still got all my smarts. I'll just have more caregivers."

"That's up to you. You'll need to discuss that with Peter and Nan. And please understand that they are concerned about you. Let me know what I can do to help." I stayed a few minutes longer. Out in the hallway, I saw the Halstrom siblings and Dolly's granddaughter, all talking intently. They didn't notice as I walked past and punched the button on the elevator.

It was a question that came up frequently. Can Mom or Dad continue living at home? Sometimes people adapted well to senior living facilities, happy to have someone else take over things like meal preparation and cleaning, glad of the social interaction such places provided. Others, like Dolly, were fiercely determined to age in place in their homes.

My next client visit was to a man who'd made his own decision. Earl Wendell was in his nineties. The retired attorney had lived in a one-story ranch-style house on the west side of Rocoso for decades, sharing it with his wife, who had died five years ago. Since her death, he had resisted the suggestions of his son and daughter that it might be time to consider a senior apartment or an assisted living facility. Over the past year, however, he had changed his mind.

Both of Earl's adult children lived in other cities, and the family had requested my assistance with the transition. Bea Lovell and her staff were assisting as well, helping Earl sort through a lifetime of possessions, determining what to take with him, and what to do with the rest of his belongings. Earl's living room was full of cardboard cartons, boxes labeled with the names of his son, daughter, and grandchildren. Other boxes had labels that read "Move," "Donate" and "Sell." The furniture, which included several heavy oak pieces, was similarly tagged.

"I'm glad you made the decision, you alone, not anyone making it for you," I told him.

Earl chuckled. His small brown-and-white dog, Jojo, was curled up on his lap, and he scratched the dog's ears. "I told my son last year that he wasn't going to force me into some place I didn't want to go. I figured I'd stay here until I died and they carried me out, feet first. He said he'd try to convince me. He didn't. I convinced myself. Tripped over my own feet in the kitchen and broke my ankle. If that's not a convincer, I don't know what is. It healed up all right, but I'm on a walker now." He nodded toward the four-wheeled walker, with a basket and a seat, that was parked next to his chair. "I finally had to admit this house is too much for me. Can't keep up with the cleaning, much less the yard."

Earl scratched Jojo's ears and the dog gave a contented snuffle. "They take pets. That's the most important thing for me. I dote on this mutt. My wife and I got him when he was a pup, about ten years ago. I'll be fine once I settle in. I've got a good-sized living room with a kitchenette, a bedroom, and a bathroom with a shower." He waved at the boxes around him. "I'm moving in a few days, taking some of the furniture with me. What my kids and grandkids don't want, we'll donate or have an estate sale. I've given up driving. That was hard. I like the independence of getting in my car and going places. But I'd just gotten out of that cast and my driver's license was up for renewal. So was the car insurance and registration. I figure for all three of those things to come due at the same time, that was a sign." He flashed a conspiratorial smile. "One of my grandsons is going to start college here in Rocoso in the fall. I told him I'd give him my car, with the stipulation that he has to give his old grandpa a ride now and then."

"That sounds like a good trade to me. In the meantime, when you need to go anywhere, The Pines has a shuttle. Plus there's the senior ride program."

In fact, on the way over here I'd seen one of the blue shuttles, operated by Rocoso Senior Services, parked outside a nearby grocery store, disgorging elderly shoppers.

Earl nodded. "Right. That shuttle goes to the grocery store a couple of times a week and takes people to doctor's appointments, the senior center, that sort of thing. There's a group of people I play bridge with at the senior center and I sure want to continue with that."

It was nearly three when I unlocked my car and slid into the driver's seat. I always checked messages between appointments and now I did it again, seeing that I had several email messages and voice mails. There was nothing urgent in the emails. The voice mails were a different story. Louise Beltran had called twice in the space of half an hour, each time leaving a terse message asking me to call.

Louise answered on the first ring. "When I got to Betty Garvin's house this afternoon, she told me to leave. Said my services are no longer needed and I should just get out."

"Betty told you that?"

"No, the daughter. At least she said she was the daughter. But she's not the one I met last week."

Uh- oh. I recalled the premonition I had when Sheryl Garvin told me that her younger sister was completely out of the picture.

Not completely out, from the look of things.

Chapter 11

THE JEEP WRANGLER IN Betty Garvin's driveway had California plates. Its dark green body was dented and scratched, covered with dust. Bug splatters decorated the windshield. When I rang the doorbell, I heard a dog barking inside the house, then a voice, indistinct, as someone approached.

The woman who opened the door was short, her slender frame encased in tight faded jeans and a sleeveless tie-dyed T-shirt. A sunflower tattoo, bright yellow with a long green stem, was visible on her right shoulder. Lines crinkled at the edges of her pale blue eyes and on either side of her small snub nose. Straight blond hair fell past her shoulders, long crystal earrings tangled in the strands. Her feet were bare. At her ankles was a small dog with long, light-brown fur, probably Chihuahua and something else, barking for all it was worth.

"Hush, Mitzi." The woman's voice was as sharp as the angular features on her face. The dog stopped barking and growled, fixing me with a malevolent stare. "Can I help you?"

"I'm Kay Dexter. You must be Hallie. I'm here to see Betty."

The woman narrowed her eyes. "Yeah, I'm Hallie Garvin. What do you want to see my mother about?"

"I'm her care manager."

Hallie looked mystified. "What the hell is a care manager?"

"I look in on Betty several times a week, to make sure she's all right, that she's eating properly and taking her medications. I also oversee the work of the caregivers who visit her."

Hallie put her hands on her hips, a pugnacious look on her face. "That woman called you, huh? After I told her to leave. Care manager? I'll bet this is something my sister cooked up. She hired you, didn't she? Yeah, that fits. Sheryl outsources everything. She doesn't want to interrupt her perfect upper-middle-class life with the big-shot husband in Seattle and she feels guilty about ignoring Mom, so she hires you to do the work. Well, my mother doesn't need to be managed by you or anyone else. I'm here now, and I can look after her just fine."

Complications. I would have to tread carefully. This could be a minefield, one salted with differing views and opinions from two sisters who evidently didn't like each other, much less agree on how their mother should be looked after. I'd encountered such disputes before. In fact, on at least two other occasions, I'd seen disagreements that wound up in court, with siblings suing each other over the disposition of a parent's estate. That didn't usually happen with an argument about the parent's care, though. At least I hadn't had one of those—yet.

I smiled. "I understand. You're staying with your mother, then?"

There was a note of defiance in Hallie's voice. "Yes, I am. Not that it's any of your business. I'll stay as long as she needs help."

Given my assessment of Betty's needs, that could be permanent. "May I come in? I'm here already and I'd like to check in with your mother. It's a routine visit, of course. I drop by several times a week."

Hallie glared, looking as though she was going to shut the door. "Routine, my ass. You just want to check up on me and report back to my sister."

I kept my voice reasonable and pleasant. "It's true that I'll call your sister. After all, she hired me. While I'm here I'd like to see your mother and talk with you."

Hallie snorted with derision. Then she shrugged and opened it wider. "Okay. Come in. You can see for yourself. Mom's fine. Be sure to tell my sister that."

"Thanks." When I stepped into the entry hall, Mitzi left off growling and sniffed my shoes.

"What's your name again?"

"Kay Dexter. I grew up here in Rocoso. Your mother knows mine. I was in high school with your older brother. He was a year ahead of me."

"Greg? Well, he's dead and gone, a long time now."

"An accident, I believe."

Hallie's mouth twisted. "Yeah. It happened when he was in college at Sac State. One night he figured he could get across a railroad crossing before the train did. He figured wrong." She shut the front door and waved toward the back of the house. "Mom's in the family room."

As we went through the living room, I caught a faint whiff of a familiar substance—marijuana. Sure enough, there was an ashtray on the coffee table, with several hand-rolled butts visible among the ash.

I followed Hallie through the kitchen to the family room. Betty was in the recliner where she'd been sitting when I was here earlier this afternoon. She had the large print novel in her lap, but she had dozed off, her head tilted to one side and her glasses sliding down her nose. She came awake with a start.

"Mom, there's someone here to see you," Hallie said.

Betty straightened and pushed her glasses up her nose. "Is it Louise? She comes in the afternoon to check on me. Oh, it's Kay. I know your mother. And your father, Nolan. Such a nice man. He worked on the railroad. They're both gone now, your father and my husband. How is your mother?"

"She's fine. She keeps busy."

Betty nodded. "She likes to work in her garden. Roses. Rose grows roses."

"She does enjoy her garden."

"It's nice of you to come visit me," Betty said, evidently not remembering that I'd been here a few hours earlier. "That nice lady from Meals on Wheels came by this morning. She brought me something to have for lunch. I ate part of that. It was meatloaf today. Not as good as the meatloaf I used to make, of course."

"It didn't look very appetizing either." Hallie turned to me. "There's not much in the fridge. Does your care manager gig include grocery shopping?"

"A woman named Bea Lovell will shop for groceries regularly. She did that yesterday, although she only got a few staples. Your mother gets a Meals on Wheels delivery every day during the week."

"A few staples are too few," Hallie said. "We need more food in the house. I've made a grocery list. And there's no knobs for the damn stove burners."

"Your sister took them off. Your mother has a habit of putting something on to cook and then forgetting it. There have been a couple of small fires."

Hallie frowned and swore under her breath. "Well, I'm here now and I need to be able to cook. That's got to be fixed."

"When did you get here? Sometime this afternoon?"

"About an hour ago. We drove from Arcata, up in Humboldt County. That's where I live. I left early this morning. I called Mom last night and she wasn't making much sense. I decided to come and check on her."

Sheryl had told me she didn't know where her sister lived, but Betty did. And Hallie had said "we." Who was the other person?

The answer to that question was the tall, broad-shouldered man who walked into the kitchen. His graying hair was tied back into a ponytail. He wore sandals, a pair of baggy denim shorts, and a roomy T-shirt with the team logo of the Humboldt State Jacks. Tattoos ran up and down both arms. He yawned and scratched his bristly chin. "I'm gonna make a beer run. Need anything else while I'm out?"

"We definitely need groceries," Hallie told him. She stepped over to the counter and picked up a sheet of paper covered with penciled words. "Here's the list. Pick up anything else you want."

"Okay." The man yawned again and surveyed the list.

"First thing you gotta do, though, is go to the hardware store and get some knobs for that stove. Otherwise, you're not getting any home cooking."

"Copy that, too." He peered at the stove. "Shouldn't be too hard to fix." Now he looked up, as though seeing me for the first time. His pale blue eyes were kind, wreathed in laugh lines. "Hi. Who are you?"

"I'm Kay, here to visit Mrs. Garvin. And you?"

"Lanny Fitzpatrick. I'm a friend of Hal's." He folded the grocery list and stuck it in his pocket, then pulled out a set of keys. "Okay, I'm off. See you ladies later." He headed through the living room and the front door slammed as he left the house. A moment later, the Jeep's engine roared to life.

"Lanny came along to keep me company." Hallie walked back into the family room, with the dog at her heels. She sat down on the chair near her mother and the dog jumped into her lap. She leaned over, ruffling the long brown fur.

Betty shifted in the recliner, a puzzled expression on her face. "Where's Tamara?"

Hallie looked startled. "Tamara's not here."

"But she was." Betty frowned. "I thought I saw her. She must have gone away. When is she coming back?"

Hallie shook her head. "You're mistaken, Mom. Maybe you had a dream. Tamara's not here. She hasn't been here."

Tamara again. I waited for Hallie to explain who Tamara was, but no information was forthcoming. I glanced at Betty's blue plastic pillbox on the counter. "Betty, I want to check and make sure you took your medicine today." That was one of Louise's duties, but Hallie had told Louise to leave as soon as she'd arrived.

"As long as you're here, I want to talk to you about that." Hallie tapped the cover of the book she'd moved out of the chair. I read the title: *The Herbalist's Way: The Art and Practice of Healing with Plant Medicines.* "It looks to me like Mom is taking a lot of drugs, and I don't like it. I don't hold with all that stuff."

"I went with your mother and sister to see the doctor last week. She had a complete blood workup as well as other tests, and she's taking meds for high blood pressure, high cholesterol, and hyperthyroidism. All the prescriptions are up to date as far as the dosage and frequency."

Hallie shook her head, unconvinced. "Doctors and pharmaceutical companies, yeah, right. I take anything the medical establishment says with a grain of salt, that's for sure. They're more interested in making money than they are in people's health. For all I know, she's over-medicated and that's why she's so confused. I'm going to start Mom on some herbal supplements and phase out all that crap she's been taking. Her high blood pressure, for example. First thing is to cut the amount of sodium in her diet. Then some other things. Hibiscus is good, so is hawthorn. And something I've been reading about called cat's claw."

Hallie was like a steamroller, barreling down the road and flattening everything in its path. I kept my expression, and voice, neutral. "Cutting salt intake is a good idea for all of us. The Meals on Wheels entrees she's been getting are salt-free. I would recommend that you go slowly in changing any of Betty's medications."

She got that prickly look again. "I know what's best for my mother. Better than some doctor who's only out to make money. I'll have her off that Big Pharma crap in no time. I brought a lot of herbs with me. That's what I do back in Arcata. I work in an herb shop with holistic remedies. Is there a place like that in Rocoso?"

"I think so. This is a college town, after all, just like Arcata."

"That's good. I plan to stay for a while and I might need to resupply my stash."

"So, you're staying indefinitely?"

"As long as my mother needs me." Hallie moved the dog off her lap and stood up. "I'm sure you've seen all you need to see and you're going to call my sister the minute you get out of here. I'll walk you to the door."

I said good-bye to Betty and walked with Hallie to the front door. I was being kicked out. Just as well, since I had another appointment in twenty minutes. Betty was all right for now, but I was concerned about Hallie's vow to dispense with her mother's medications. Holistic or not, Betty's medical conditions needed proper treatment.

I drove away from the house, turned the corner at the next intersection, and parked at the curb. Sheryl answered her cell phone on the third ring.

"It's Kay. I just visited your mother's house. Your sister is there."

"Son of a bitch." Sheryl sputtered with rage. She went into a rant, her words salty and profane.

I broke in, stating the obvious. "You and your sister are estranged."

"Estranged doesn't even cover it. When did she show

up?"

"About an hour ago, she told me. She has someone with her, a man named Lanny. And a little dog called Mitzi."

"Son of a bitch. I am going to pack a bag and drive to Sea-Tac. I'll be on the first available flight to Sacramento, rent a car and drive to Rocoso. I'll call you as soon as I get to town."

"I'll talk with you then. By the way, who's Tamara?"

But Sheryl had already ended the call.

Chapter 12

SHERYL CALLED TUESDAY NIGHT to tell me she'd arrived in Rocoso. She had checked into a local inn. "I won't stay with Mother, because I can't stand to be around my sister. But I want to go over there as soon as possible and have it out with her."

"You and I should talk first."

"Tomorrow morning," Sheryl said.

"See you then."

The next morning, I had a quick breakfast of fruit and yogurt. I left a message for Gwen and Carmen on the office line, telling them I wouldn't be in right away, due to a situation. They would understand my missing our usual check-in. At times, we'd all had to deal with situations. That done, I headed out the front door, keys and bag in hand.

Years ago, the Redd House belonged to Marcus Redd, who'd struck it rich mining gold. He had built the Queen Anne Victorian mansion on the edge of downtown, where its lawn and garden sloped down to the banks of the Rocoso River. His family line had not survived, nor had his fortune. After the last member of the Redd family died thirty years ago, the house fell into a state of decline. Eventually, it was turned into a rundown boarding house inhabited by students from the college. Five years ago, a fire broke out in one of the upstairs rooms and it spread, damaging the house so much that the owners evicted the tenants and then abandoned the house. Deemed a derelict eyesore, it was slated for demolition.

But Dina and the Rocoso Historical Society had other ideas. A middle-aged couple, Joe and Caroline Daltry, had money and dreams of owning a bed and breakfast inn. Aided by the historical society's old photos, donations, and low-interest loans from the bank, the Daltrys had purchased the house and spent more than a year rehabbing the place, restoring it to its former glory.

In keeping with its name, the exterior of the Redd House was painted dark red, with white trim on the porch and windows. I went up the steps and opened the brass-festooned front door, entering the inn's spacious foyer. Directly ahead, a wide staircase with a polished wood banister led to the second floor. The living room, full of antique furniture, was on the right. Most of the guests sat around the big oval table in the dining room on the left, eating breakfast. Beyond the big table was an open door leading to the kitchen. I saw Caroline Daltry at a counter, removing muffins from a tin and putting them into a cloth-lined basket.

Sheryl was at the end of the table closest to the foyer, pushing a wedge of quiche around her plate. When she saw me, she set down the fork, excused herself, and pushed back her chair.

"Don't rush on my account."

"I've had all I want." Sheryl stepped out of the dining room. We went down the hallway past the stairs, out the back door to the inn's garden. The sidewalk was lined with roses, a colorful array in varying shades of red, pink, and yellow. The sun was out and this day in mid-May promised to be pleasant, warm with a hint of a breeze. We sat on a white wrought iron bench. Sheryl didn't speak, instead staring down the slope to the river.

I broke the silence. "When you first came to my office, you told me you didn't know where Hallie was living."

Sheryl frowned, her mouth tight. "I didn't. That's the truth. She's moved around quite a bit. For several years she was up in the mountains—Mariposa and later Sonora. After that, she migrated over to the coast—Monterey, Santa Cruz, Half Moon Bay. Then Sonoma County, up at Bodega Bay. Last I heard, she was in Mendocino."

"Hallie told me she lives in Arcata. She called your mother the night before last and thought Betty sounded confused. So she drove to Rocoso yesterday." I paused. "You said your sister was out of the picture. It's important that I know the whole story, particularly since she is now very much in the picture."

I wondered what else Sheryl was leaving out. However, this wasn't the first time a client hadn't been open with me, and probably wouldn't be the last. Betty was my focus. Doing what was best for her was the most important task. I was ready to help Sheryl work this out, now that Hallie was on the scene.

Sheryl sighed. "I haven't had much communication with Hallie over the years. For a variety of reasons, we're not on good terms."

"It appears she's communicating with your mother."

Sheryl's tone would have withered the nearby rosebuds. "Oh, Hallie drops in and out of Mother's life. When it suits her, she shows up and goes through her concerned daughter song-and-dance. Usually it's when she needs money. But as far as taking any long-term responsibility for Mother or her care, forget it. I'm the one who has that on my shoulders."

"I believe your sister is planning to stay a while." Hallie had said as much, during yesterday's conversation. "She told Louise to leave."

Sheryl swore. "I'm the one who hired Louise. Hallie can't just come in and fire her."

"Given your mother's condition, I do think your mother needs regular caregiving. If Hallie is going to stay—"

"She's not!" Sheryl looked indignant.

"We'll have to straighten this out, then. Perhaps if you, Hallie, and I sit down and talk about it, reasonably."

Sheryl looked at me as though I'd taken leave of my senses. "Reasonable? Hallie? Not a chance. If you want to try to reason with my sister, be my guest."

I fixed her with a look, feeling like a schoolmarm disciplining a recalcitrant student. "Reasonable would be greatly preferred. I don't want to upset your mother. We need to get past whatever is going on between you and your sister and look at what we can do for your mother."

Sheryl's mouth tightened. "I'll be on my best behavior. I can't make any promises for Hallie. She doesn't have any best behavior." She got to her feet with the martyred expression of someone who was facing a firing squad. "Let's go on to Mother's house. I'd just as soon get this over with. I assume you have commitments this morning, so we'd better take two cars. My rental car is parked in the lot."

I did have commitments. My first appointment this morning was at ten. It was after nine now. "By the way, who's Tamara?"

Sheryl turned. "Hallie's daughter. Why?"

"Your mother mentioned her yesterday. She seemed to think Tamara had visited her."

"Mother is imagining things," Sheryl said. "Tamara lives in Oakland. And to my knowledge, she hasn't visited Mother in months. Like Hallie, she's in and out. Mostly out."

Sheryl seemed very sure of that, but I wondered. She'd been equally adamant when she said her sister was completely out of the picture.

What had happened between the two sisters? Did the breach go all the way back to childhood? Or was it something that had developed as they grew into adolescence and adulthood? There had to be a reason for the estrangement between them. In my years as a care manager, I had brokered peace treaties between relatives, and I could do it again. But I needed more information about what appeared to be bitter and long-standing enmity between the Garvin sisters. This situation would not be easily resolved. But Sheryl didn't want to talk about it, at least not right now.

Sheryl had rented a gray Nissan. I followed her as she drove to her mother's house on Juniper Street. When we arrived, the dark green Jeep, washed since I'd last seen it, was in the driveway. We parked our cars at the curb. Sheryl used her key to open the front door. Mitzi, the little dog, burst into the entry hall, barking furiously. Sheryl stopped short and glared down at the dog, as though willing the chihuahua to disappear. Then Hallie appeared in the doorway between the living room and kitchen, wearing a short-sleeved shirt over a pair of khaki shorts.

"Well, that didn't take long." Hallie glared at her sister, then she did an about-face and returned to the kitchen.

Sheryl stalked through the living room, the dog at her heels. I followed. In the kitchen, Hallie stood at the stove. Betty and Lanny sat at the round table, which was set with three places. A bowl of fresh fruit salad, with bananas, apples, and berries, was in the middle of the table, along with a butter dish and a bottle of maple syrup.

"This is Lanny," Hallie said. "He's a friend of mine. Lanny, this is my sister, Sheryl."

Lanny looked up from his breakfast with an easy smile. "Hi, Sheryl, nice to meet you."

Sheryl glared at him and said nothing. Lanny shrugged and turned to Betty. "Like I was saying, I'll paint the kitchen. Pale yellow, maybe. What do you think of that? It would brighten things up. And I'm definitely

gonna replace the light fixture." He pointed upward with his fork. "We need more light in here, especially at night."

"Yellow would be nice." Betty cut a small piece from her pancake. "I've always liked yellow. It's so cheerful. And it would go with the flowers on the curtains."

Lanny nodded. "Great. I'll get the paint and the other stuff I need and start doing the prep work." With his fork, he chased the last bite of his pancake around his plate, sopping up butter and syrup. He looked up at Hallie. "Pancakes are good, babe. Got any more?"

"Sure do." Hallie lifted a skillet from the stove, which sported new handles. There were three browned pancakes in the skillet and she gave two to Lanny. "Want another pancake, Mom?"

Betty smiled at her younger daughter. "Thanks, but I'm still working on this one." Then she beamed at Sheryl. "Hi, honey. Have you had breakfast? Your sister made us some delicious pancakes."

Sheryl's voice was abrupt and cold. "I've had breakfast, thank you."

"I just made a fresh pot of coffee. Help yourselves." Hallie waved the spatula toward the coffee maker on the counter. She put the third pancake on her plate and set the skillet back on the stove. Then she sat down and reached for the butter and syrup.

Sheryl frowned. "We have to talk."

"I agree. However, I'm going to finish breakfast first." Hallie buttered her pancake and poured syrup over it. She cut a generous piece with her fork and conveyed it to her mouth.

"I want to discuss this now."

Hallie sighed. "Oh, for God's sake. You never did have any patience. Get yourself some coffee. You, too, Ms. Dexter. I will join you on the patio in five minutes."

I took two mugs from the rack on the wall near the

refrigerator, pouring coffee into both. "Do you take anything in yours?" Sheryl shook her head. I opened the refrigerator, took out a carton of milk, and poured a splash into my mug. I set the carton back on the shelf and handed the mug of black coffee to Sheryl. The sliding glass door that led from the family room to the backyard was open. I herded Sheryl that way, out onto the patio, where she perched on one of the white wicker chairs surrounding the table. She took a swallow of coffee and grimaced, setting the mug on the table. I wasn't sure whether it was in response to the strength of the coffee, or her sister.

"Passive-aggressive. She was—and is—passive-aggressive." Sheryl's voice tightened, aggrieved, as years of tamped-down resentment teased cracks in her façade. "Hallie was the baby, of course. My parents thought she could do no wrong. They never saw her for the manipulative little bitch she really is. Same with my brother, Greg. He was the oldest, and the boy. So he was perfect, until —" She stopped, some memory flickering over her face, then she continued. "And me, the middle child. Always caught in the middle. Greg's dead and Hallie's been off doing her own thing for years. It's always been left to me, all the heavy lifting of looking after my parents."

I sipped her coffee. "The sacrificial daughter."

Sheryl frowned and narrowed her eyes. "What does that mean?"

"It means the adult child who is a caregiver for aging parents, usually the daughter."

"I see. Yes, that makes sense. I'm one of those, all right."

The patio door opened and Hallie came out to join us. "How's the coffee?"

"It's too strong," Sheryl said.

Hallie bristled. "Nothing ever suits you, does it?"

"I didn't come here to talk about your coffee-making skills."

"No, I don't imagine you did." Hallie folded her arms over her chest.

"What are you doing here?" Sheryl demanded.

"I'm here to look after Mom."

Sheryl gave a short, derisive laugh. "I doubt that. You're after something."

"You always expect the worst from me," Hallie said.

"In all these years, you've given me no reason to expect anything better."

"That says more about you than it does me." Hallie tilted her head upward and gave her sister an appraising look.

"Don't throw that new-age, touchy-feely crap at me," Sheryl snapped. "What is it? You need money? You're tired of roughing it in Arcata? You need a place to live? Or maybe you've already gone through the money Aunt Ruby left you and you need access to Mother's bank account."

"Like I'd have a chance in hell of getting access to Mom's money," Hallie snapped. "You've got that locked up tight. Power of attorney this and that, your name on every single account, so you can write checks and make investments. For your information, no, I do not need money. As for the money Aunt Ruby left me, it's in a CD. And I'm not here looking for a place to live. I have a nice place in Arcata. My visit is motivated by concern for Mom."

"Bullshit." Sheryl got to her feet. She was taller than Hallie and she leaned over, facing her sister. "You're up to something. You always are."

"I guess you could pay me to go away." A bitter smile played around Hallie's lips.

"You conniving little —"

"Tight-assed, tight-fisted bitch." Hallie leaned forward and spat the words at her sister.

Now the two were talking at once, their voices raised into shrieks. Alarmed, I tried to pull Sheryl away from the fray. "This isn't helping."

Sheryl backed away from Hallie, bumping into the table. The coffee mug went flying, crashing to bits on the patio. The screen door opened and Betty came out, crying, "Stop it, stop it!" The dog was at Betty's heels, barks adding to the cacophony.

Now Lanny came out to the patio. For a big man, he moved fast. He grabbed Hallie by her arms. "Okay, that's enough." He propelled her into the house. The dog followed them, growling and yapping.

I discovered I'd been holding my breath and released it in a sigh. How quickly the conversation between the two sisters devolved into battle. Blows might have been exchanged if Lanny hadn't intervened.

"Why?" Betty cried, tears running down her face as she appealed to Sheryl. "Why are you and your sister always at each other's throats? I hate it. Why can't you get along? I won't be around forever and you'll only have each other."

Sheryl shook herself like a dog flinging off water, then looked contrite as she took Betty in her arms. "I'm sorry, Mother. I'm sorry I let her get to me. It's just that she always pushes my buttons."

Betty sobbed and wiped away tears. I steered her toward one of the patio chairs.

The door leading to the kitchen opened again and Lanny came out. "I think you'd better leave now."

Sheryl glared at him. "Who the hell are you to tell me to leave my mother's house?"

Lanny shrugged. "I'm just saying it looks to me like the two of you gals need to cool off. Your mom's crying and that can't be good for her blood pressure. Right? I got Hallie stashed in the bedroom, but she won't stay there long."

"I think that would be a good idea," I said. "I'd hate to upset your mother even more. A time-out would be helpful. Besides, I have to leave for an appointment."

"Fine," Sheryl said. "Come on, Mother. Let's go into the living room. How would you like to go for a ride this morning? We could go up the canyon and look at the scenery. Maybe stop at Lost Woman Creek. You'd like that, wouldn't you?"

"That would be nice, honey. Get out and get some fresh air." Betty got to her feet and took Sheryl's arm. Together mother and daughter crossed the patio to the door. Betty went inside the house. Sheryl turned and spoke to Lanny. "I'm staying at the Redd House. It's a bed and breakfast downtown. My mother has my cell phone number. Tell Hallie this isn't over, not by a long shot." She didn't wait for a response. She walked into the house.

I knelt and picked up the fragments of the coffee mug, then straightened.

Lanny held out his hands. "I'll take care of that."

"Thanks." I deposited the pieces in his big hands.

"Sorry things went south like that," he said. "I'll bet you've seen worse, in your line of work."

"I have. But it's always unpleasant when it happens."

"I'll see if I can smooth down Hal's feathers."

"Why is she here?"

"As far as I know, she's here to look after her mom," Lanny said. "I just came along for the ride. I figure as long as I'm here, I'll do some odd jobs to keep busy. Right now, I'm gonna clean up the breakfast dishes."

Chapter 13

AFTER THE EMOTIONS ON display at Betty's house, I hoped the rest of the day would be routine. When I returned to the office, Gwen wasn't there, off to a client meeting. And Carmen was headed out the door, for the same reason. "Did you take care of your situation?"

I shook my head. "It could get worse. I'll update you and Gwen later."

There was a pot of coffee in the kitchenette. I poured myself a cup and went to my office to get ready for a meeting with a prospective client. Later that morning, I visited another client in her home, then went to the nursing home to see Fran Lomax. She was in good spirits. Her mobility was improving and the doctor had told her that she'd be able to go home soon. From there, I went to the hospital to check on Dolly Halstrom. She was going to be released that afternoon. Her son had arranged for more caregivers, as Dolly was fiercely determined to return home.

After that, I stopped to see another client who lived in a neighborhood near the college. I called Sam to see if he was available for lunch. He was. We met at a deli on a street bordering the campus, where we shared a turkey sandwich and a salad at a corner table.

I speared a tomato with my fork. "Do you remember Greg Garvin? He was a year ahead of us in high school."

Sam had just taken a bite of his sandwich. He chewed the mouthful and washed it down with a sip of coffee. "I do remember him. He played football. I was not a sports kind of guy, so we didn't move in the same circles."

"Typical jock?" I poked at the salad with my fork.

"Not really. Well, on the surface, maybe. But looking back on it, there was something about him. Can't put my finger on it, though. I know he died a couple of years after he graduated. Some kind of accident in college." He nodded. "I remember now. His car got hit by a train at a railroad crossing."

"His sister said he was trying to get across the tracks ahead of the train. Something my father the railroader always warned me about. Trains move faster than you think."

"And they don't stop on a dime," Sam added, shaking his head.

IN THE MIDDLE OF the afternoon, I went back to the Redd House. Sheryl was on the bench at the back of the inn, looking out at the river and working her way through a bottle of chardonnay. She saluted me with her glass. "If you'd like some wine, I'm sure you could get a glass in the kitchen. I have half a bottle left. I think."

I sat down. "I'll pass. How are you this afternoon?"

Sheryl lifted her glass, swirling the wine, and took a sip. "Frustrated. As you no doubt can guess from the amount of wine I've consumed."

"Did you take your mother for a drive?"

"Yes. We went up the canyon, as far as Lost Woman Creek. Then we had lunch here in town and I took her home. And left her to the grasping ministrations of my sister, her boyfriend, and the damn barking dog." Sheryl reached for the wine bottle, which was on the ground next to the bench, and topped off her glass, lowering the level in the bottle even more. "Cheers. Or not."

As Sheryl raised the glass to her lips, I noticed her gold wedding band was gone. Maybe this was the time to ask a question I'd been thinking about since Saturday night.

"Arlette Simmons, the real estate agent who's listed the house next to your mother, mentioned that you'd inquired about buying that house."

"Did she? Talkative of her." Sheryl took another sip of wine. "Yes, I asked about the house. I wondered what the listing price is. Though I'm probably more interested in a condo. No yard work."

"Are you thinking of moving back to Rocoso?"

"Why not? You did it." Sheryl looked out at the river. "Yes, I'm moving back. I'm leaving my husband. The marriage is over. It's been running on empty for years. I had a feeling it wouldn't last after my son went off to college, and I was right. I've been planning my escape for several months now. Ethan will be twenty this summer. He's in his second year of school at UC Berkeley. When I move here, I'll be closer to Ethan and we can see each other more often. And I'll be with Mom, who obviously needs to have me around. That was my plan, anyway."

"Then Hallie showed up."

"Yes. And I doubt her reasons are altruistic. My sister is a mercenary little bitch who has spent her whole life looking after number one. She used to help herself to my toys when we were kids. When we were teenagers, it was my clothes and jewelry. Then she upped her game and stole the man I was going to marry."

That explained it. Or some of it. Sheryl was holding a grudge and had been for a long time.

"Justin Brownlow," Sheryl said, as though the name tasted bad. "We met during our second year in college, at Chico State. We dated for a year. After a while, it got more serious and we talked about marriage. Then I made the mistake of bringing him home to meet my family." She paused and drank from her glass.

"Next thing I knew, Justin was putting on the brakes,

saying he wasn't ready to get married. Turns out he was screwing my little sister, who instead of going to college was waiting tables at a bar here in town. And Justin was coming up here every chance he got. She got pregnant. Justin wound up getting married after all. To Hallie. Not that the marriage lasted. They split up when Tamara was in grade school." She took another sip of wine. "After Justin threw me over for Hallie, I transferred to UC Berkeley and got a degree from the Haas School of Business. I got a job offer in Seattle, so I went north. I was working as the business manager of Richard's law firm. That's how we met. And that's how it ends. Back here in Rocoso."

"About Tamara," I said. "Hallie's daughter, your niece. Your mother has mentioned her a couple of times."

"In what context?" Sheryl reached for the wine bottle, then thought better of it and set it back on the ground.

"When I went to the house yesterday, after Hallie arrived, Betty asked where Tamara was. The way she phrased it made me think that Tamara had been there recently."

"I doubt it. I think she does visit from time to time. She's twenty-five, older than my son, and she lives in Oakland, as far as I know. And the only reason I know that is because Ethan sees her now and then." Sheryl looked at her glass as though she'd lost her appetite for chardonnay. She set it on the ground next to the bottle. "You know, I think I'd better go lie down in my room."

Sheryl got to her feet, a bit unsteady, and took a step toward the inn. Then she turned. "Oh, the glass and the bottle."

"I'll get those." I leaned down and retrieved the items.

Sheryl walked slowly toward the inn. When she

reached the back steps, she grasped the railing and carefully mounted the steps to the porch. I followed her into the house and left the bottle and glass in the kitchen. As I left the Redd House, Sheryl was slowly making her way up the stairs.

I SPENT THE REST of the afternoon in my office, where I had a brief check-in with Gwen and Carmen, then did paperwork. I finished an assessment report for a client, printed it out, and put it into the file. I had an hour or so until tai chi class. I shut down the computer and printer and left the office. I walked toward my car, then I heard a sound, a door slamming. I turned and looked back toward the building and was surprised to see Sheryl Garvin coming out of the office next to mine. Sheryl hadn't seen me. Head down, she walked briskly toward the street and disappeared from view. She didn't look much the worse for wear after her bout with that bottle of chardonnay.

The office she'd just left belonged to Marie Devorno, the architect. Given what Sheryl had told me earlier this afternoon about her plans to move back to Rocoso, I wondered if she had been looking at houses and condos each time she'd been here in town, and whether she'd found a property she wanted to buy. A fixer-upper, maybe. Marie did both kinds of work, residential and commercial, and it made sense to talk with an architect before embarking on any major remodeling.

I shrugged and unlocked my car. At home, I changed into my workout clothes, then fed my demanding cats. At Mom's house, I parked in the driveway. My parents had purchased the place early in their marriage and this was where my brother and I grew up. Built in the early 1950s, it was a one-story wood-framed house with three bedrooms and a big backyard where we always planted a vegetable garden. The house had always been painted pale yellow with dark blue trim, a color combination that my mother liked.

A porch swing hung on the right side of the front door. Whenever I saw that swing, I remembered my childhood summers, when I rode my blue bicycle down to the library and pedaled home with a stack of books tucked into the basket. Then I'd sit here on this porch swing, my bare feet tucked under me, reading through my library haul. Sometimes I'd just gaze at the river, down the slope on the other side of the street.

I knocked before opening the front door with a key. There was no sign of Mom in the living room, furnished with a comfortable sofa and several chairs. Family photos decorated the walls and table surfaces. Mom's favorite wingback chair was angled close to the flat-screen television set, and a table next to it held several books and magazines, as well as the TV remote. Lulu, her cat, had pulled a blue -and -green crocheted afghan from the back of the sofa and bunched it into a cozy nest. The cat was curled up into a ball, her paws over her nose. Her fur was a patchwork of white, gray, black, and brown.

"Mom, I'm here. Are you ready for tai chi class?"

"Just putting on my shoes," she called from the back of the house. "I'll be right out. Would you feed Lulu?"

"Sure. C'mon, kitty. Time for dinner." Lulu unwound herself and stretched, then she jumped down from the sofa and ambled in front of me, twitching her tail. In the kitchen, she walked to her water and food bowls, which sat on the floor at the end of the counter. There was a dishtowel spread underneath the bowls to catch bits of food, since Lulu seemed to think things tasted better if they were dropped on the floor first. I opened the refrigerator and took out a can of cat food, removed the lid, and spooned some into the bowl. The cat began eating.

I leaned down and scratched her between the ears. "You don't look as though you've missed any meals."

"What's that?" Mom came into the kitchen, wearing the same loose-fitting slacks and shirt she usually wore to tai chi class.

"I'm talking to your fat cat." I replaced the lid on the cat food can and set it back in the refrigerator.

"She's not fat, she's just fluffy." Mom reached into the fridge, took out her stainless-steel water bottle, and shut the door.

I chuckled. "Fluffy, is it? Okay, if you say so."

We walked through the living room to the front door, where Mom grabbed the footed cane she used when she left the house. Outside, we went down the front steps to my car. As she got into the passenger seat and fastened her seat belt, Mom said, "I see Sheryl Garvin is back in town. Her sister, Hallie, too."

"How did you know that?" I shouldn't be surprised. Mom seemed to be tuned into some wavelength where she knew everyone in town, and what was going on. I latched my seat belt and started the car, backing out of the drive.

Mom flashed an impish smile. "I know things. And I see things." When I gave her a look, she continued. "My neighbor Carla saw Sheryl downtown. Evidently, she's staying at the Redd House and not at her mother's house. Which is where Hallie is staying. With some fella, or so the story goes. Which doesn't surprise me at all. Sheryl and Hallie never did get along."

I stopped at an intersection and waited for a car to pass before turning right. I was curious to find out what Mom knew about the Garvins. "Did you and Dad know the family?"

"Curtis and Betty? We did, though not well. Your father and I were a few years older than they were. Your father never did have much use for Curtis. He drank too much. And when he was in his cups, he wasn't very pleasant to be around. Loud and argumentative. He was really conservative politically and he didn't like it when people disagreed with him. He was controlling, always bossing Betty and the kids around."

Mom might call that controlling, but in my experience, such behavior could be considered abuse. It was emotional rather than physical but abuse all the same.

I found a parking space in the community center lot and switched off the ignition as I released the latch on my seat belt. I got out of the car and went around to help Mom from the passenger seat. She used her cane and the car door to get to her feet, pausing a moment to steady herself. Then she took my arm and we walked to the front door.

"The Garvins had a son named Greg. He was a year ahead of me in high school."

"That's right. He died in a car accident. That was after you went away to college." Mom paused as I opened the door and ushered her through. "Sheryl was the steady one in that family, reliable and serious. Now the younger daughter, Hallie, she was the wild one."

I could believe that, after meeting her and hearing what Sheryl had to say about her sister. But was Sheryl all that reliable? She'd kept the truth from me before, when she'd told me that Hallie was out of their mother's life. It made me wonder what else she'd neglected to tell me.

Inside, Mom and I made our way to the room where the tai chi class was held. We said hello to our classmates, then joined the circle. Marla Cates began the session, leading us in breathing exercises. I felt the day's stress slowly ebb, as it did every evening when I did a few qigong exercises followed by a tai chi set. It was moving meditation, a way to smooth out the wrinkles that collected during the day.

As we made our way through the exercises, I managed to smooth the Garvins and their problems from my mind. The problems of Sheryl, Hallie, and Betty would wait till another day, when I was fresh and ready to tackle the situation.

Chapter 14

THE NEXT MORNING, HALLIE answered the door at the Garvin house. She was barefoot, in a red tank top and denim shorts, a pair of soil-stained gardening gloves stuck into the front pocket of the shorts. Her barking dog was at her feet. Both of them looked at me with suspicion.

"Why are you here?" Hallie demanded, brushing a strand of blond hair away from her face.

"I'm here to visit Betty. Until things are sorted out between you and your sister, visiting your mother is part of my job. Besides, I think she's gotten used to me."

"I don't know that anything to do with Sheryl will be sorted out. My sister has always been wrapped too tightly. The slightest thing sets her off. She's wound up so tight she's gonna have a heart attack one of these days. Me, I'm more relaxed. Go with the flow, that's me." Hallie opened the screen door. "Mom is out back. Hush, Mitzi," she added, as the long-haired chihuahua growled.

Hallie led the way through the house and out the patio door. Betty sat at one end of the white wicker settee, holding a glass of iced tea. She had a photo album open on her lap, with snapshots in plastic sleeves and others tucked between the pages. Mitzi scampered past me and jumped up, wagging her tail as she settled in next to Betty.

As the gardening gloves implied, Hallie had been doing yard work. An assortment of house plants, which had lately been inside the house, were arrayed on the patio, next to a large bag of potting soil and several clay pots. One of the house plants lay on its side and I could see that it was root-bound, with roots pushing through the holes on the bottom of the pot and gaining purchase in a crack. An old trowel with a wooden handle, the metal of the blade dulled with rust and dirt, had been thrust into one of the pots.

"Kay, how nice to see you." Betty set her glass on the end table. "Hallie, honey, get Kay some tea."

"Sure thing," Hallie raised her voice and called, "Hey, Lanny, want something to drink?"

Lanny was out in the yard, trimming and shaping the camellias that grew along the back fence. Branches with glossy leaves filled the nearby green plastic recycling bin. He wore sturdy work gloves, his right hand wielding garden clippers. The sleeveless shirt he wore over his khaki shorts showed off his tattooed arms. He paused now and wiped his forehead with the back of his hand.

"Yeah," he called. "Some of that iced tea. Lots of ice. I'm working up a sweat."

"Sure thing." Hallie turned and went back into the house.

I looked out at the backyard, noticing the changes. The hummingbird feeder that I'd seen on my earlier visit had been washed and filled with sugar water. An Anna's hummingbird swooped in, wings beating as it stuck a tiny beak into the feeder. In the back-left corner of the yard, the bird feeder hanging from the oak tree had been filled with seed and was getting a lot of attention from chestnut-backed chickadees and white-crowned sparrows. I heard a familiar tapping and looked up, spotting an acorn woodpecker on one of the higher branches. The raised beds to the right of the sidewalk had been cleaned, the tomato cages removed, the weeds pulled, the soil turned over. Bags of potting soil and compost were stacked at one side of the wooden garden shed, next to a shovel and a rake.

Betty turned the pages of the photo album and pointed. "There's my husband, Curtis."

I leaned closer and looked at the photo, its colors faded. It showed a thickset man with a florid face and a pugnacious expression. I recalled what my mother had told me last night, that Curtis Garvin drank too much and was controlling. Betty turned another page and one of the loose photos fell onto the patio. I picked it up. It showed an older woman, tall and broad-shouldered, with short gray hair and a round face. Wearing a blue dress, she stood next to a man of similar height and a young woman wearing a cap and gown. I handed the picture to Betty.

"Oh, that's my niece Tish and her husband, Dan, with their youngest when she graduated from college." She tucked the photo back between the album's pages.

Hallie returned from the house, carrying two tall plastic tumblers brimful of ice and tea. She gave one to me, then took a step and stumbled as her foot encountered one of the rocks bordering the patio. She swore as tea sloshed out of the glass. "Damn, damn, damn. Stubbed my toe. Hurts like a son of a bitch." She glared down at the border. "These rocks are an accident waiting to happen."

Lanny crossed the yard to join us on the patio, sweat glistening on his arms. He took a glass from Hallie and tilted back his head, gulping down the tea. Then he examined the rocks. "I can move them if you like. Get them out of the way and plant more succulents."

"Now, Hallie," Betty said, "don't be tampering with that. You know your father made that border." She glanced at me. "Curtis used to bring rocks home from the river and the creeks around here."

Hallie rolled her eyes and pursed her mouth, as though she'd heard the story many times before and didn't care to hear it one more time. I suspected Hallie's memories of her father were less than fond, especially after what my mother had told me the night before.

"Yeah," Hallie said now, "and Dad built that garden shed that's falling down. That doesn't mean we have to enshrine the damn thing."

"That oak tree is too close to the back fence," Lanny said, taking another swallow of his iced tea. "The roots are doing a number on the fence posts."

Hallie grinned. "Hey, that tree is how I used to sneak out. Dad kept the back gate locked, so I'd climb the tree and get over the fence that way. Or through some loose boards on the fence, behind that shed."

Betty laughed. "So that's how you got out. You were a wild one. You used to have me tearing my hair." She patted the place next to her on the settee. "But you're a good daughter. Sit down and give me a hug." Hallie chuckled and sat down, leaning in as Betty hugged her.

On the surface, it looked as though Betty and Hallie had a good relationship. Their interactions, those that I'd observed, were less formal than those between Sheryl and her mother. But I was mindful of Sheryl's comment that Hallie frequently showed up to visit Betty when she needed money. Though Hallie had said something yesterday about her job at an herbal shop, and money she'd inherited being stashed in a CD.

I stepped out into the yard, walking toward the back gate, which was open. Reaching the gate, I looked out at Wylie Creek, about twenty feet away. The creek wound through an open meadow the size of a football field, with walking paths on either side. To my left, a few houses down, was the pedestrian path that led from Juniper Street to the creek, joining the path on this side of the stream. Here a small footbridge arched over the creek. To the right, on the other side of the meadow, was Wylie Middle School. Classes were over for the afternoon and kids were walking home along the creek. As a group of girls reached the bottom of the bridge, I saw that one of them was Ginny, the girl who lived across the street.

I glanced to my left again, looking to see how long the drop was from the oak tree to the path. A good five feet, at least. Yes, I could see the teenaged Hallie, climbing the fence and the tree, using it as a means to get out at night.

Lanny came up behind me and leaned over, examining the gate. "Got a couple of screws missing from this faceplate," he said, jiggling the handle, which was quite loose. "And the bolt on this lock won't move. Could be jammed or rusted. I gotta fix that. Don't want anybody getting into the yard. Guess that means another trip to the hardware store."

"I thought Curtis liked to build things," I said. "That's what Betty told me. I should think there would be tools and hardware in the garage."

"At one time," Lanny said. "When he died, though, she gave away most of that stuff. I found a hammer and some screwdrivers, that's about it. And a coffee can full of rusted nails and screws." He bent again, peering at the faceplate and the handle. "I don't think any of those screws are going to fit, so I'll have to buy some." He straightened, one hand on the small of his back. "Things have gone to pot around here, in terms of home repairs, that is. I'll do what I can while I'm here."

"I thought you and Hallie were staying indefinitely."

Lanny shrugged. "Hallie might. But I got a business in Arcata. I need to get back to it pretty soon. That Jeep out there is mine. I drove Hallie down. She'll be using Betty's car from now on. It's old but it's in pretty good shape."

"The car's still here, then?"

"Yeah. It's in the garage. Why do you ask?"

"Sheryl talked about getting rid of it, because she didn't want Betty driving."

"I don't want Betty driving either," Lanny said. "She's

a sweet lady. Reminds me of my own mom. But these days, she's got no business behind the wheel of a car." He shut the gate and returned to the camellia, pruning a straggly branch.

I walked back to the patio, in time to hear Hallie say, "Now, Mom, I want you to think about what we discussed."

"I will," Betty said. "But I don't think we need to make a decision right now. We should talk with your sister."

Hallie made an exasperated sound. "Sheryl's a pain in the ass, Mom. I don't have to talk with her. I know what she's going to say."

"She's involved, too. No matter what you say."

Hallie looked up, as though she'd just realized I was standing there. "We'll talk about this later."

Family business? Was it about Betty's situation and her care? I hoped the two sisters could come to a truce of some sort, long enough to work with me concerning Betty.

"Where is Tamara?" Betty asked.

Hallie shrugged. "As far as I know, Tamara's in Oakland. I haven't seen her and she hasn't called me in ages. That's just the way she is. She's more into texting these days. Aren't they all? I did text her, to let her know I was in town."

Betty looked perplexed. "But she was here. I saw her, I'm sure of it."

Hallie gently stroked her mother's arm. "I think maybe you're mixed up, Mom. Tamara's not here. I'll text her again and see if we can get her up for a visit. She's got a job, though, so it would have to be on a weekend." Betty nodded, as though Hallie's answer was sufficient. Hallie leaned back on the settee and looked up at me. "Tamara's my daughter. She's all grown up and lives in Oakland. She does come up to Rocoso, though. She likes to raft and a friend of hers works for one of the rafting outfits here."

I said good-bye and headed for the front door. This was the second time Betty had mentioned Tamara. She talked as though she'd seen her granddaughter there at the house. Were these the ramblings of a confused old woman? Or had Tamara actually paid a visit to her grandmother?

I HADN'T TALKED WITH Sheryl since yesterday. This morning, my phone call had gone straight to voice mail. I hoped to hear from her soon. The dispute over Betty's care needed to be resolved, though the toxic relationship between the sisters made that difficult.

After visiting another client, I went back to my office. I unlocked the mailbox near my door and removed the contents. Inside, I sorted out the mail. A professional newsletter, a magazine. Some envelopes were addressed individually to me, Gwen or Carmen, others to the firm itself. Several of those contained checks, payments from clients. I tucked the checks into my bag. My stomach growled. No wonder. It was nearly one o'clock, a long time since that bowl of oatmeal I'd had for breakfast. First, I would deposit the checks into the firm's business account. Then I'd find a place to have lunch.

Rocoso National Bank was two blocks away. I walked along the west side of Main Street, enjoying the sunny spring weather. What did I want for lunch? Noodles from the Thai restaurant I had just passed? Or maybe I'd go to the Marigold Cafe, which was near the bank. The cafe had a menu I liked. I heard a train whistle in the distance as the Rocoso & Jermyn locomotive pulled out of the train station farther down Main Street, heading out for its midday run. The window of a nearby watch repair shop held a poster for the upcoming Rail Festival, held each year in July.

I neared the intersection. The bank was on the other side of the cross street. The two-story building dated to the nineteenth century, with shallow steps fanning out from the double glass doors that angled across the building's corner. I walked past a quilt shop and side-stepped a pair of women who were chatting. Then I saw Sheryl coming out of the bank. She carried a large folder, the kind with a flap and a stretchy band to keep it shut. She must be running errands, I thought. Perhaps that was why she hadn't returned my call.

She paused and tucked the folder under her arm, scanning the intersection, as though she was looking for someone. Suddenly she looked alarmed. Had she seen me? Why would that disturb her? No, it wasn't me who'd caught her attention. It was a man who was jaywalking across Main Street, dodging through a gap in the traffic. And she wasn't happy to see him. She turned quickly and went back into the bank, standing just inside the glass doors, peering out.

Curious, I examined the man, who was now stepping onto the curb in front of the bank. He turned and crossed the side street, walking toward me. I had never seen him before. He was in his fifties, I guessed, close to my age. His round face showed some middle-aged jowls and wore a preoccupied frown. He wore brown slacks and a beige sports shirt that didn't disguise how age had thickened his waist. His dark brown hair was cut short and heavily threaded with gray.

After he passed me, I looked back at Sheryl. She'd exited the bank again and was now staring at the man's back, as though shooting daggers at him. She came down the steps and turned to her right. I crossed the street, heading toward her. She stopped a few doors down from the bank, outside the Marigold Cafe, the place I'd been planning to have lunch. A white awning decorated with stylized yellow and orange marigolds sheltered a portion of the sidewalk. Small bistro tables were set up on either side of the front door. Sheryl looked at the menu displayed in the cafe's window. Then she glanced up and smiled.

The man was about six feet tall, with a muscular frame dressed in a pair of faded blue jeans and a purple shirt. His blond hair was long enough to be pulled back into a short ponytail. He put his arm around Sheryl's shoulder, then leaned down and kissed her on the cheek.

I recognized him immediately. Alex Delattre was an artist. He also taught at the college. Sam knew him and had introduced us at a reception last year. Delattre lived in the little town of Lakeview, up at Osprey Lake, and he painted vibrant landscapes. At the Rocoso & Jermyn train station, his impression of a steam locomotive high above the gorge called the Narrows hung on one wall of the gift shop. Another of his paintings, a scene of old Rocoso during its mining camp days, hung in the historical museum. The local bookstore, Pages, had one of his smaller paintings, showing an owl in a tree. I particularly liked one that was on display at a gallery over on Second Street. With bold strokes in blue, purple, and green, the painting showed an osprey on the hunt at the lake, the raptor rising from the water with a silvery trout in its talons.

Alex Delattre knew Sheryl Garvin, well enough to greet her with a kiss. A friendly kiss, or something else? After all, she'd told me she was leaving her husband and moving back to town. She wanted to be near her mother, she told me. And closer to Berkeley, where her son was going to school. Was there another reason, a romance with Delattre?

Now I remembered the phone call Sheryl had returned after leaving my office last week. Her voice had a quality of intimacy as she spoke with the person on the other end of the line, arranging to meet whoever it was for a drink. Was the other person Delattre?

Last year, when I'd met the artist at that reception, I'd looked him up on the Internet, interested in his art. That's how I knew he was in his forties, a few years younger than Sheryl. They were both middle-aged adults, so what did the age difference matter? Besides, it was none of my business.

Sheryl and Delattre, arms linked, entered the cafe. I wouldn't be going to the Marigold Cafe for lunch after all. I went into the bank to deposit the checks.

Chapter 15

MY LAST APPOINTMENT WAS a follow-up visit to Earl Wendell, whose son, Darren, was in town to help his father move into his new senior apartment. Bea Lovell opened the front door, motioning me into the hallway. "I'm here to finish packing up the kitchen. Darren is out running an errand. Earl's in the living room."

The living room was now empty of furniture, except for a pair of armchairs covered in faded blue upholstery. Earl sat in one of these, his walker nearby, his little dog, Jojo, in his lap. As Bea headed back to the kitchen, I sat down in the other chair and held out my hand to the dog. The little mutt was normally quite friendly, but today he looked anxious, spooked by the missing furniture and the cardboard cartons stacked along the walls. He whined and Earl stroked the dog's ears, reassuring him. "It's okay, little guy. I'm here." The dog whined again and snuggled deeper into Earl's arms.

Earl looked around the room. "It feels strange to see the house empty like this. My wife and I bought the place over sixty years ago, when our kids were teenagers. I have a lot of memories. Accumulated a lot of things, too," he added with a chuckle. He swept his hand around, indicating the room that had been full of furniture a few days ago. "My daughter took the dining room table, the china cabinet, and her mother's china. Royal Doulton. My wife wanted her to have it. My son is taking the silver and a few pieces of furniture he'd asked for. Years ago, my wife and I made a list of things and who they would go to, or things that our son and daughter indicated that they'd like to have. I'm glad we did that. Saved a lot of arguing."

"I know what you mean." I had seen too many families squabbling over who would get their parents' possessions, to the point of one sibling refusing to speak to another. All for the sake of a piece of furniture or jewelry. In some cases, it had been the in-laws who argued, rather than the sons or daughters. I thought of one former client whose daughter and son still weren't speaking, four years after their mother had died.

"The movers came this morning and took my things over to The Pines. When my son gets back from the bank, we'll head over there and get me settled into my new place. I hope Jojo can adjust." Earl rubbed the dog's ears again. The pooch wagged his tail, reassured.

"Jojo wants to be wherever you are. I'll visit the two of you later in the week. I want to see your home."

The front door opened and Darren Wendell entered. He was in his mid-sixties, older than me by about ten years. As he greeted me, Bea came out of the kitchen, carrying a small cardboard box. She set it on the floor in the hallway, with the other boxes.

Darren turned to his father. "You ready to go, Pop?"

"I am." Earl set the dog down on the floor and reached for his walker, using it for support as he stood. Jojo stayed close to the old man's legs, whining softly, his ears up and his tail wagging. Bea had Jojo's leash. She knelt and fastened it to the dog's collar.

Bea straightened and hugged Earl. "I'll visit you. If you and Jojo need anything, you just call me."

Bea and I walked out of the house with Earl and Darren, Bea holding the dog's leash. Darren helped his father into his car and fastened Earl's seat belt. He picked up Jojo and deposited the dog on his father's lap. Earl took hold of Jojo's collar while his son loaded the walker into the backseat.

When father and son had gone, I went back inside

with Bea. "Packing up this house must have been a big job."

"It certainly was." Bea pointed at the sealed boxes in the hall. "This is the last of the kitchen and dining room stuff. Most of it went to Earl's family or got donated, but these things go to an antique store. The dealer was interested in serving pieces and kitchen doodads."

"Kitchen stuff is collectible. I have a friend who has a lot of glass food storage containers from the fifties."

"People collect all sorts of things," Bea said. "When Mom or Dad dies, the families call me to help them get rid of the stuff. I've seen it all, from soap dishes to shot glasses to salt and pepper shakers." She glanced at her watch. "I'll have to deal with these boxes later. I have another appointment. Sally, one of my helpers, was going to take these boxes to the antique store, but she's got a sick kid and couldn't come help today."

"I have some time in my schedule. I'll take the boxes. Which antique store?"

Bea looked relieved. "Thanks, you're a lifesaver. It's Riverside Antiques. The dealer's name is Joanne Parker. I'll help load the stuff into your car."

Riverside Antiques was in Rocoso's antiques row, one of a dozen stores ranged along several blocks of North Main Street. I parked in the lot at the side of the building, which had once been a grocery store. Now it was an antique mall where various dealers had booths. Inside, the main counter was a rectangle, with jewelry cases at one end and two cash registers at the other. Two women staffed the counter. One was talking on the phone, while another rang up a purchase for a customer. While I waited, I looked at the jewelry displayed in the case.

The woman who'd been talking on the phone ended the call and stepped over to join me. "May I help you?"

"I'm delivering some boxes to Joanne Parker.

They're in the trunk of my car."

"Joanne's not here right now," the woman said. "But I'll have someone get the boxes and put them in our storage area."

"Thanks. I'm parked in the lot."

The woman picked up the phone and said, "Marty, it's Coral. Could you help unload some boxes?"

I went out to my car. There was an entrance at the side of the building, back by the alley. An older man came out the side door, wheeling a dolly. By the time he reached me, I'd opened the trunk. The man lifted the three large boxes onto the dolly. "I'll carry the small one," I said.

I shut the trunk and followed him back to the side entrance, into a storeroom. I set the small box on a counter while he unloaded the other boxes. He pointed at a door that led into the antique mall. "Coral at the front counter will give you a receipt for these, and she'll call Joanne to let her know the stuff is here."

I thanked him and walked into the mall, past two women who were examining a slat-backed rocking chair in one of the back booths. I headed up the aisle, glancing at the booths. One person's junk, another person's treasures. There was one booth devoted to railroad memorabilia, and another had a large collection of Depression glass. A nearby case held an assortment of compacts and vanity purses.

In the next booth, a small mahogany bookcase caught my eye. I stopped to look at the price tag. Reasonable. It would look good in the hall. I'd consider it.

I turned and glanced at the glass display case on the booth's back wall. What was that? I moved closer to the case. On the top shelf, I saw a sterling silver sugar and creamer. They looked exactly like the ones I'd seen in the china cabinet at Betty's house, right down to the floral detail on the handles. It could be a coincidence, I thought.

I stepped back and looked at the other items in the display case. On the middle shelf were several pieces of sterling silver flatware—serving spoons and forks, a carving knife, a pie and cake server, a large ladle. They matched, the handles in a Rococo style, with an ornate scroll design and fleur-de-lis accents, the small card next to them reading "Gorham Sterling Silver, Chantilly Pattern." In another case, I saw more silver, an oval tray with serving tongs. The smooth surface of the tray was scratched. And there, on the bottom shelf, a sterling silver bowl engraved with the letter G. No, this couldn't be a coincidence. I took out my phone and snapped a few pictures of the items that had caught my attention. Then I looked around for the booth number and headed up the aisle to the main counter.

"Did Marty get those boxes unloaded for you?" Coral asked.

"Yes, he said you could give me a receipt."

"Sure, I'll take care of that now." Coral wrote out the receipt and handed it to me.

"Thanks. I would like to look at a couple of things in a case in booth number twenty-four."

"I'll get the key and meet you there."

I walked back to the booth and waited. A moment later, Coral joined me, jingling a keyring in her hand. "Which case is it?"

I pointed and the woman unlocked the case. She slid open the glass door and I reached in, picking up the silver bowl. It was the twin of the one I'd found the other day on Betty's nightstand.

"Whose booth is this?" I asked.

Coral frowned. "Meg Duran. Is there a problem?"

"I'm not sure." I handed the bowl to her and she set it back on the shelf. "But I would like to talk with her about some of the items in this case." I pointed at each one of them in turn. "The bowl, the sugar and creamer, and the tray and tongs."

"I'll call her." Coral locked the case. We walked back to the main register. She went behind the counter and reached for the phone.

I stepped away from the counter while she called the other dealer, walking back to the jewelry display. I took out my phone and called Sheryl, but the call went straight to voice mail. I left a message. Then I looked at the jewelry under the glass in front of me, thinking about the jewelry that had gone missing from Betty's house, just like the silver items. Had Betty given those pieces away, as she had the sapphire brooch and the garnet ring? Or had the items wound up here, or at another antique store?

Coral walked over to the display case. "Meg is on her way."

"Thanks. I appreciate your calling her."

Meg Duran arrived about ten minutes later. She appeared to be in her forties, slim and well-dressed in matching green linen separates, her shoulder-length dark hair combed back from her face. She stepped behind the counter and conferred with Coral, then she came over to the jewelry counter, carrying the bowl. "I'm Meg. Coral said you had a question about some of the things in my booth. How can I help?"

"I'd like to know where you got them. And when."

Meg Duran gave me a wary stare. "May I ask why?"

I took out a business card and handed it to her. "I'm a geriatric care manager here in town. Several items are missing from the home of one of my clients, including a bowl that looks very much like this one. The other items are a sugar and creamer set and a tray with tongs."

She hesitated and frowned. "You think these belong to your client?"

"I do. There's a matching silver bowl at her house,

engraved with the letter G."

Meg Duran looked at the bowl, her fingers tracing the engraving on the side. "I bought those things from someone. I paid cash for them. I had no reason to think it was anything other than a legitimate transaction."

"Who sold them to you?"

"I can't tell you that." She shook her head. "Not just on your say-so. Your client should come into the store and take a look. Then we'll see."

"I'll take that up with her." If these items had been taken from Betty's house, how would I prove it? That would be tricky, considering Betty's state and her pattern of giving things to people.

I left the antique store and called Sheryl's cell phone again. This time Sheryl answered. "I'm on my way over to Mother's house to talk with Hallie."

"Does Hallie know you're coming?" I asked.

"I don't have to announce myself or ask my sister for permission to visit Mother," Sheryl snapped, her tone aggrieved.

"That's not what I meant." I was afraid another scene would ensue between the two sisters. "May I come over?"

"Why? To referee?"

"There's something I'd like to discuss with both of you." And if I had to referee, so be it. Besides, Hallie should be made aware that valuable items had disappeared from the house.

"Fine. I'll see you then," Sheryl said, ending the call.

I drove across town to the Garvin house on Juniper Street. Sheryl's rental car was parked in the driveway. The Jeep was nowhere in sight. As I went up the walk, I heard Mitzi barking. The screen door was closed, but the front door was open. I knocked and called out. "Sheryl? Are you there?" Mitzi appeared from the back of the house, barking furiously. I opened the screen door, careful not to step on the little dog.

She snapped at my heels as I walked through the living room and entered the kitchen, where the table held a half-gallon can of yellow paint and a smaller container of Spackle, along with an aluminum paint tray, several brushes, and a package of sandpaper.

Then I turned toward the family room and saw Betty, slumped against the back of her recliner. At first, I thought she was asleep. But no, her face was ashen, her breathing rapid and shallow. She moaned and then one hand came up, clutching at her chest. I rushed to her. Her heartbeat was rapid and her skin, cold and clammy, had a gray tinge. A heart attack? But she was also showing signs of shock. What had happened? And where was Sheryl?

I covered Betty with a cotton throw from the back of the recliner, then eased her into a prone position, using a cushion to elevate her feet. My cell phone was in my hand. I pressed the buttons for 911. When I straightened, I realized the sliding glass door leading out to the patio was open, and so was the screen. Mitzi was outside now, on the patio, barking, a frantic, frenzied sound.

I took a step toward the patio door. Then I stopped, feeling as though all the air had been sucked from my lungs.

Chapter 16

HALLIE LAY ON THE patio, arms outstretched, eyes closed. A crimson gash stained the blond hair at her left temple.

Sheryl was on her knees, her back to me as she leaned over her sister. Then she turned and saw me, her face stunned and white.

I rushed to Hallie and knelt, avoiding the blood on the pavement near her head. Her eyes fluttered and opened wide. She stared at me, but I had the feeling she wasn't seeing me. A long sibilant sound escaped from her lips. She said a word, but I couldn't make it out. Then her eyes closed again. I touched her neck, feeling a weak, erratic pulse. She took a long shuddering breath and expelled it. The faint heartbeat stopped.

She's dead, I thought in disbelief. I willed the pulse to start again. It didn't.

The dog had stopped barking, whining instead as she nudged Hallie's arm with her muzzle. I heard a voice coming from the cell phone in my hand, the 911 dispatcher. I scrambled to my feet, raising the phone.

"I need an ambulance. One person dead, one person in shock, possible heart attack."

I gave the dispatcher the address. By the time I ended the call, I heard sirens in the distance. I stuck the phone in my pocket and turned to Sheryl. "Tell me what happened."

Sheryl opened her mouth, but nothing came out. Then she gasped and stood, struggling for control. "I don't know. I found her—" She took a deep breath and let it out. "I found her like this. I came in the front door and heard the dog, yapping like crazy. I called out and no one answered. When I came out to the patio, she was lying here." She shook herself. "Mother! Oh, my God, where's Mother? When I came in, she was in the recliner, asleep."

"She's not asleep. She passed out. It could be a heart attack. She seems to be in shock. The paramedics are on their way."

Sheryl darted into the family room. I followed. As Sheryl knelt beside the recliner, smoothing Betty's hair, I checked Betty's pulse again. Her heartbeat was rapid and her skin still cool to the touch. The cotton throw I'd tossed over her wasn't enough. I snatched the crocheted afghan from the sofa and doubled it, spreading it over the old woman.

I went back outside and looked down at Hallie's body. What had happened here?

It looked as though she'd been repotting plants, as she had been when I was here yesterday. A pothos and a philodendron both looked root-bound. Next to these was an assortment of empty pots. Near Hallie's feet was a cracked clay pot holding a multi-colored coleus. The pot lay on its side, as though it had been knocked over. A pair of gardening gloves, stained with dirt, lay on top of the bag of potting soil. I didn't see the trowel she'd been using the day before. Where was it?

I took a closer look at the bloody gash on Hallie's head. Mingled with blood and strands of blond hair, I saw dirt. Was the trowel now a murder weapon?

I straightened and looked at one of the columns that held up the patio roof, seeing tiny drops of blood splattered on the wooden support. Hallie must have been standing when she was struck on the head. I stared at the back fence and saw that the gate was ajar. I stepped off the patio and headed back there to take a closer look. Between the gate and the fence, there was a gap of about six inches.

The faceplate around the handle was still loose, missing screws. Lanny hadn't gotten around to making the repairs he'd talked about yesterday. Now blood smeared the rusted metal handle.

Whoever struck Hallie had come this way. It would be easy to get rid of the murder weapon by tossing it into the creek.

I heard voices and peered through the gap between the gate and the fence. I saw kids, now released from their day at the middle school on the far side of the meadow. Four girls were on the other side of the creek, dawdling and talking as they headed for the bridge. One of them stood out, wearing a bright pink shirt. It was Ginny, the neighbor girl.

I wanted to go outside and look at the creek, to see if the trowel was there. But I couldn't touch the gate. With the smear of blood on the handle, it was now part of the crime scene. Besides, the sirens were getting closer. I headed back to the house.

Sheryl still knelt next to Betty, talking in low soothing tones. I couldn't make out what she was saying. Her hands brushed Betty's face and shoulder. I didn't see anything on those hands, no dirt, no blood, nothing to indicate that she'd touched Hallie.

But I couldn't stop the thought from entering my head. Was it Sheryl? Had Sheryl gotten into another screaming argument with her sister, one that escalated into violence? And had Betty seen what happened?

The sirens, deafening now, stopped outside on the street, I headed for the front door. The dog was at my heels as I greeted the first responders from the Rocoso Fire Department.

"Out back, in the family room." As the first man moved to open the screen door, Mitzi barked, charging forward. I reached down and scooped up the dog. "I'm shutting this dog in the bathroom."

The paramedics opened the door, maneuvering a gurney into the living room. I carried Mitzi down the hall. She nipped at my hands. Then she twisted around and bit my forearm. Fortunately, the sharp little teeth didn't break the skin, but they left red marks. In the bathroom, I shut the door with my foot and released the dog. Mitzi growled and shied away, hiding behind the toilet. I picked up an empty glass next to the sink, filled it with water, and set it on the floor. Then I let myself out of the bathroom and headed for the living room. A Rocoso Police Department cruiser pulled up to the curb. Two uniformed officers got out and approached the house. I knew one of the officers, a woman named Anne Borokas.

"What happened, Kay?" Anne asked. "Has there been an accident? Is this one of your clients?"

I shook my head. "The dead woman's name is Hallie Garvin. She was still alive when I got here and died a moment later. The paramedics are in the family room, seeing to Hallie's mother, Betty Garvin. She's my client and she's in shock. Sheryl Garvin, Hallie's sister, was out on the patio with her sister when I arrived. It looks as though Hallie was struck in the head. I think she was repotting plants, at least she was yesterday when I was here. Today I saw gardening gloves and pots, but not the trowel she was using yesterday. The back gate is open and there's blood smeared on the handle."

Anne frowned. "Suspicious death and a crime scene. That ups the ante. We haven't had a murder since last year, just the usual assaults and property crimes. Anything else I should know?"

"Hallie and a friend were staying here with her mother. The man's name is Lanny Fitzpatrick. They both live in Arcata and they drove here in Lanny's Jeep. It's not outside. I assume Lanny is driving it. He must be out running errands."

"Okay. I'm calling the sheriff's office for reinforcements. They're the ones who have the resources to deal with a homicide." Anne headed for the back of the house, cell phone in hand.

The Rocoso County Sheriff's Department had a Criminal Investigation Division, and the city used its services when it came to serious crimes. The department employed a pathologist who acted as the medical examiner for the whole county. I had met the pathologist once, when I had arrived at a house to find that my elderly client had died.

I went outside. Neighbors clustered in groups on the sidewalks and in yards on both sides of the street, talking among themselves as they looked at the police and fire vehicles parked in front of Betty's house. I spotted Ginny, in her pink shirt, standing with several other girls. Then a Jeep sped up Juniper Street and screeched to a halt at the curb. Lanny Fitzpatrick got out, dressed as he had been the day before, in baggy shorts and his Humboldt State T-shirt. He carried a brown paper sack clutched in one big hand. He rushed toward the house, stopping suddenly as a uniformed Rocoso police officer barred his way. "You can't go in there, sir."

"But I'm staying here. I'm a guest. What the hell's going on?" Lanny saw me. "Kay, what's going on? Did something happen to Betty?"

I walked over to him and put my hand on his arm. "I'm sorry, Lanny. Hallie is dead."

His face crumpled and tears flooded his pale blue eyes. "Oh, no. How can that be? What happened? I was only gone for an hour or so."

A car and a van arrived and parked at the curb. A man in a business suit got out of the car and walked toward me. Riley Hamilton, my cousin, was a detective with the sheriff's office and he headed up the criminal investigation division. The people getting out of the van were members of his team and included a photographer and a couple of crime scene investigators.

"Kay, Officer Borokas," Riley said. He looked at Lanny's stricken face. "And who's this?"

"Lanny Fitzpatrick," I said. "He's a friend of Hallie Garvin, the dead woman. They've been staying here with Betty Garvin, my client, who is Hallie's mother."

"Riley Hamilton, with the sheriff's office. I'll be investigating what happened here. We'll need a statement from you, Mr. Fitzpatrick. For the time being, please wait in the living room. Kay, same for you."

I steered Lanny to the front door. Inside, we sat on the living room sofa, watching as Riley and others on the investigation team headed for the back of the house. Lanny looked at the sack in his hand, stamped with the logo of McWhirter's Hardware on South Main. He set the bag on the coffee table. "I was at the hardware store, to get the stuff I need to fix that back gate. Batteries, too. And a ballcock for the toilet in the master bathroom." He tilted his head to one side, listening to Mitzi's muffled barks. "Where's the dog? Is she all right?"

"She's upset. I shut her in the bathroom. She bit me." I showed him the red marks on my arm.

A smile flitted briefly over his face. "She's a feisty little critter, that's for sure. Hallie loves that dog." He shook his head. "What happened?"

I hesitated, reluctant to voice my suspicions about Sheryl. Finally, I said, "It looks like Hallie was hit on the head."

Lanny stared at me, as though wrapping his mind around what I'd just said. "Sheryl. That's her rental car outside. She's here? And Betty? Is she okay?"

"Betty was in the family room. She's had a bad

shock."

"Where was Sheryl?" he asked.

"On the patio. With Hallie."

"Shit," he said. Then he clamped his lips together. We sat in silence. A few minutes later, the paramedics maneuvered a gurney through the kitchen, into the living room. Betty Garvin was strapped in place, an oxygen mask over her face. Lanny looked stricken at the sight.

"How is she?" I asked.

"Shock. And probably a heart attack," one of the paramedics said. They carried Betty out of the house, heading for the ambulance. Sheryl followed, her hand clutching her bag and keys.

Riley was close behind her. "Ms. Garvin, we need to ask some questions."

Sheryl whirled to face him. "Can't we do this later? I have to go to the hospital, to be with my mother."

"We need to do it now," Riley told her. "Please come with me, back to the family room." He held out his hand, his gaze brooking no argument. Sheryl's mouth tightened. She stepped past him and walked toward the back of the house.

Lanny frowned as Riley followed Sheryl out of the room. "Do they think Sheryl . . .?" His voice trailed off.

"I don't know, Lanny. That's for the police to determine."

He rubbed his hand over his face. "I know Hallie didn't get along with her sister. She used to give me an earful about that. But the cops, they can't think Sheryl had anything to do with this."

"I don't know."

Anything was possible. I considered the blood on the back gate. That telltale smear seemed to indicate that an intruder, perhaps a killer, had gone through that gate. Or was it a red herring? To deflect the police's attention?

There was certainly bad blood between the two sisters and the estrangement went back years. I figured there was more to this than what Sheryl told me. Perhaps Lanny knew something. But I didn't want to ask those questions now.

The minutes stretched. The medical examiner arrived. An older man with a bald spot, he nodded at me and followed one of the investigators back through the house. Mitzi barked for a while, then settled down to an occasional whine. At one point I heard Sheryl's voice, loud and indignant, coming from the family room, and Riley's lower voice in counterpoint. But I couldn't make out what they were saying.

Finally, Sheryl stalked through the living room, scrubbing her hands with a tissue. She shoved the tissue into her pocket and glanced at me, without a word. Instead, she gripped the strap of her shoulder bag. Betty's blue plastic medicine container stuck out of the top. Sheryl went out the front door.

Riley followed her at a slower pace. "Mr. Fitzpatrick, I'd like to take your statement now."

"I can go outside," I said.

Lanny reached for my hand. "I'd rather you stay. I'm okay with you being here. I got nothing to hide. Besides, you're a friendly face. I don't know anyone else here, except Betty."

"If that's all right with Detective Hamilton."

Riley nodded and sat down in one of the chairs. He took out a pen and notebook. Lanny gave his full name as Lanford Michael Fitzpatrick. He was fifty-four years old and owned a small business in Arcata. He told Riley his address and cell phone number, adding, "That's the only phone I've got. Don't have a landline."

"What is your relationship with Hallie Garvin?" Riley asked.

"She was my girlfriend." Lanny's blue eyes were tinged with sadness. "We lived together in Arcata. Nearly three years. We talked about getting married but—" He stopped and took a deep breath, his hands clenching. "Never got around to any kind of wedding ceremony."

"When did you arrive in Rocoso? And why?"

Lanny took another breath before answering. "We got here Tuesday. Hallie called Betty, her mom, on Monday. I didn't talk to Betty, but Hallie said her mom sounded confused, like she wasn't making any sense. She was worried and she wanted to come down here and check on Betty. So, we packed up my Jeep and left Arcata early Tuesday morning. I'm not sure what time we got here, but it was after noon."

"How long were you planning to stay?" Riley asked.

"It was kinda open-ended," Lanny said. "Hallie decided to stay longer, to look after Betty. Me, I was looking at going home in a few days."

Riley nodded as he wrote in his notebook. "You weren't here when this happened?" When Lanny shook his head, he went on. "What time did you leave? And where did you go?"

Lanny shrugged. "I'm not sure what time I left. We'd had lunch. I guess it was an hour or so after that. Maybe one, or one-thirty. Betty was reading, in her recliner in the family room. Hallie was out on the patio, messing around with some plants, putting them in bigger pots. I went to the hardware store on the main drag." He pointed at the paper sack on the coffee table. "The toilet in the master bathroom is running. I got a ballcock so's I can fix it. And I got some hardware, so's I can fix the back gate. The faceplate's loose and the lock is jammed, rusted out, I think." He stopped. "Wait. Hallie texted me while I was out, told me to get some double-A batteries."

"May I see the text?" Riley asked.

"Sure thing." Lanny pulled his phone from his pocket. He opened the list of text messages, then handed the phone to Riley.

Riley looked at the time stamp on the text. Hallie was alive at the time she sent it, so that should narrow down the time frame of the attack that led to her death. There should also be a time stamp on the receipt from the hardware store. Riley handed the phone back to Lanny, then he leaned forward and reached for the sack on the coffee table. He opened it, examined the receipt, and returned it to the bag. "So, you've been fixing things around the house?"

"Yeah. Doing handyman stuff," Lanny said. "First thing was, I had to put some knobs on the stove. Sheryl took them off, because Betty's been using the stove and forgetting to turn it off. I fixed that so we could cook. I replaced a screen on one of the windows, in the front bedroom. Went around replacing light bulbs that had burned out. I was getting ready to paint the kitchen, already got the supplies I needed. Yesterday I did some work in the garden. That's when I noticed the gate. It's been closed, but when I looked at it yesterday, I saw that the faceplate is loose, missing a couple of screws. Plus, that gate's supposed to lock, but it doesn't. The bolt won't move. I decided I'd better fix it so's nobody can get in the back way. There's open space back there, along that creek, and there's a school down the way. Hallie told me that's the way she used to go to school, out the back, and along the creek bank."

"The gate was open today," Riley said.

"You're thinking somebody got in? Damn it." Lanny struck his fist against the palm of his other hand. "I should have gone to the hardware store yesterday instead of putting it off. But I got sidetracked, doing yard work. By the time I finished with that, I was beat. I figured it would keep till today."

"We'd like your fingerprints, Mr. Fitzpatrick," Riley said. "Yours too, Kay. For comparison purposes."

Lanny looked startled at this. Then he nodded. "I guess that makes sense. My prints are all over this place."

Riley stood and led the way to the kitchen, where one of the technicians fingerprinted both of us. I went first, then Lanny. I glanced out the kitchen window and saw another tech at the back gate. From this angle, I couldn't see Hallie's body, still out on the patio.

I turned. Riley was talking to Lanny, handing him a card. "My address and phone number are there. I may want to talk with you again, so I'd prefer that you stay in town for the time being."

Lanny spread his hands wide. "I'm not going anywhere, not until you guys get to the bottom of this. I was staying here, with Hallie. But that doesn't feel right now. I can't stay in this house. I'll take Hallie's dog and find a place. Somewhere close, and pet friendly."

"The Pinewood Motel on the south end of Main Street," I said. "That would be a good place. It has kitchenettes and will take dogs. I know the owners. Mention my name. In fact—" I pulled one of my business cards from her purse. "Take my card. It's got my cell phone number on it. Call or text if you need anything."

"Thanks, I'll do that." Lanny looked at Riley. "Hallie and I were staying in the second bedroom. I'll pack up my stuff now."

Riley nodded. "Since Ms. Garvin's things are in the bedroom as well, I'd like to have an officer with you while you pack."

"Sure thing. I understand."

Riley gestured to one of the nearby officers, who accompanied Lanny down the hall to the bedroom. They came out a few minutes later, Lanny carrying a gray nylon duffel bag and a soft-sided pet carrier. He set both of these on the floor in the living room and told the officer he was going to the kitchen to get the dog's food and dishes, which he put in a canvas shopping bag. Then he unzipped the pet carrier. He went to the main bathroom and opened the door. Mitzi shot out of the bathroom, barking and whining. Lanny leaned down and picked up the little dog, cradling her against his broad chest. Then he put Mitzi in the carrier and zipped it shut.

When Lanny had gone, Riley turned to me. "Okay. Tell me how you fit into all of this."

Chapter 17

"I'M BETTY GARVIN'S CARE manager," I said. "Her daughter Sheryl hired me a week ago Monday. She came down from Seattle, where she lives, to look in on her mother. She made an appointment with me at my office. The next day, I met with Sheryl and Betty here at the house, to do my usual assessment, of Betty and her living circumstances."

"But you didn't meet with Hallie Garvin?" Riley asked.

I shook my head. "According to Sheryl, she's the long-distance caregiver with all the responsibility. She told me Hallie was out of the picture, that she didn't even know where her sister lived."

"Ah." He nodded, a thoughtful look on his face. "Go on."

"We set up a plan, involving caregiver visits by Louise Beltran and her staff and additional help from Bea Lovell. I went with Betty and Sheryl to doctors' appointments, on Wednesday and Thursday, so I could get up-to-date information on Betty's condition. Sheryl went back to Seattle on Friday. I thought everything was settled. Then Hallie showed up on Tuesday, two days ago."

"So, Hallie wasn't out of the picture after all. I take it the two sisters didn't get along."

I wasn't sure how much detail I should give Riley about the antagonistic relationship between the two sisters. I didn't want to breach client confidentiality. On the other hand, Hallie was dead—murdered. Finding her killer was the first priority. The details of their enmity were sure to come out as Riley investigated.

"No, they did not. My impression is that the rift between them goes back years, to childhood. Hallie married the man Sheryl was engaged to, which led to a lot of bitterness on Sheryl's part. At least that's what she told me." I stopped as another thought came to me. "Hallie's divorced but she has a daughter from that marriage. Her name's Tamara Brownlow. Hallie said she lives in Oakland."

"We found Hallie's cell phone in her pocket," Riley said. "We'll check that for a phone number for Ms. Brownlow. Tell me more about the sisters. So, they were rivals as kids and adults, especially after Hallie made off with Sheryl's guy. Any other reasons?"

"The usual reasons I encounter in my line of work," I said. "They disagreed on how to care for their mother. Betty has several health issues, including a heart condition, cataracts, and memory loss. She does need monitoring. There was an incident a few weeks ago, when Betty used the stove and left the burners on, prompting a visit from the fire department. Betty takes several medications prescribed by her doctor. When Hallie arrived, she told me she distrusted conventional medicine. She wanted to dispense with her mother's prescriptions and get Betty started on natural remedies." I paused. "Sheryl told me the only time her sister showed up to visit their mother was when Hallie needed money. I don't know how accurate that is. Hallie mentioned a job, so she was employed. She also said she had money in the bank. Money seems to be one of the issues between the two sisters, or access to Betty's assets. Sheryl has power of attorney. Her name is on all of Betty's accounts. Hallie made a remark about Sheryl having control of Betty's money. It was clear she resented that."

"Money's always an issue," he said. "Tell me more about what happened when Hallie showed up on

Tuesday."

"Louise Beltran was here on one of her scheduled visits. Hallie fired her on the spot. Louise called me. I came over here to check out the situation. Hallie told me the same story that Lanny told you. She'd talked with her mother on Monday night. Betty seemed confused and Hallie was concerned. She and Lanny drove down here on Tuesday. Betty was fine on Tuesday, happy to see Hallie. I left and I called Sheryl. She was furious. She told me she was coming to Rocoso as soon as possible. She arrived late Tuesday night. I met with her Wednesday at the Redd House, where she's staying. Then we came over here. Sheryl and Hallie had a heated argument, sniping at each other verbally. Lanny and I had to intervene, and Betty was in tears."

"I'll be having another conversation with Mr. Fitzpatrick," Riley said. "To get his version of that event."

That made sense, I thought. The only questions he'd asked Lanny earlier related to his whereabouts this afternoon.

"Do you think Sheryl could have killed her sister?"

I knew Riley would ask me that question. I played back the scene of Hallie and Sheryl out on the patio, screaming at each other. They could have come to blows if Lanny hadn't separated them. But murder?

"I honestly don't know," I said. "It's possible. My experience as a social worker tells me that anything is possible. But as far as I know, Sheryl arrived here shortly before I did. I don't know where she was before that."

Riley nodded and I knew he would have someone check on Sheryl's movements. "Why did you come over here today? One of your regular visits?"

"No, something related to another matter. Things are missing from the house. Valuables, like jewelry and silver. One of them is a silver bowl engraved with a G. There's another one like it in that china cabinet." I pointed, then went on with the story. "The first time I was here, both the bowls were in the cabinet, along with a full coffee and tea set, the kind with pots and a sugar bowl and cream pitcher. There was also a silver tray and some tongs. A few days later, the sugar and creamer set was gone. So were the tongs, the tray, and the bowls."

"Stolen?" he asked.

"At the time, I thought they might have been misplaced. Or that Betty could have given them away. You see, a few days ago, Betty tried to give me a ring. Later she offered the same ring to Bea Lovell. To pay us back for being so nice, she said. She's also been giving jewelry to the neighbor girl, Ginny, who lives across the street. I found one of the bowls in Betty's bedroom. I didn't find the other items until this afternoon. I was running an errand for another client, taking boxes to a dealer at the Riverside antique mall on North Main. While I was there, I spotted the missing silver in another dealer's stall. I talked with the woman who rents the stall. Her name is Meg Duran. She says she bought them and paid cash, but she wouldn't say who sold those things to her."

"So, it looks like the silver was stolen and sold for some quick cash."

"That's what I think," I said. "Betty certainly didn't take those things over to the antique mall. She didn't even know they were gone."

"Could Hallie have taken the silver? Or Lanny Fitzpatrick? Or the girl who lives across the street?"

I shook my head. "I don't think so. I noticed the silver was missing the day before they showed up. It must be someone with access to the house, but I can't imagine Louise or Bea would take anything. They are licensed and bonded and quite reputable. I can see Betty letting someone in, if she knows them. As for Ginny, she returned the jewelry Betty gave her. And the dealer wouldn't buy things from a kid."

"Unless the kid's working with an adult," Riley said. "Look, I'll send someone over to talk with the dealer. But my priority is Hallie Garvin's death, not the thefts. What happened after you left the antique mall?"

"I called Sheryl, to let her know I'd found the missing silver, though I didn't tell her that over the phone. I just said there was something we needed to discuss. She told me she was on her way over here and asked me to meet her."

Riley nodded, as though processing this. "Come out to the family room and tell me what you saw."

I followed him through the house, steeling myself for the sight of Hallie's body as I glanced out at the patio. The medical examiner knelt near the body, a pair of blue gloves covering his hands and forearms. He looked up and spoke to one of the detectives. I heard a few words. "Sharp trauma . . . Metal . . . There's a laceration here . . . Right-handed."

The trowel, I thought.

"Kay," Riley prompted. "What did you see when you got here?"

I looked away from the body and the medical examiner. "When I got here the front door was open, not the screen. The dog was barking like crazy. I came through the house. I found Betty lying in the recliner. She was pale, breathing rapidly. I went over to her, covered her with a blanket. I had just called 911 when I looked out on the patio and saw Hallie. Sheryl was beside her. I went outside, knelt by Hallie. She was still alive. She opened her eyes, looked right at me, but I had the feeling she wasn't seeing me."

"Did Hallie say anything?"

"She made a sound, like a hiss. Maybe she was trying

to form a word, to say something. I can't be sure. Then she stopped breathing. At that point, I heard the 911 dispatcher on my cell phone and gave her the details. Sheryl and I went to the house to check on Betty. Then I came back out to the patio for another look. It looked like she'd been repotting plants, just as Lanny said. That's what she was doing when I was here yesterday. I saw the garden gloves, but no trowel. The back gate was open a bit. I went to investigate and saw blood on the handle. I thought that must be the way—" I stopped and looked at Riley. "The trowel Hallie was using yesterday was metal, with a wooden handle."

He nodded and asked, "What's your take on this guy Fitzpatrick?"

"A nice guy, fond of Hallie and Betty. He seems quite broken up about Hallie's death."

A woman in plainclothes, a badge clipped to her jacket, came through the back gate, carrying an evidence bag. She walked toward the house, crossing the patio, and entered the family room. When she saw Riley, she held out the bag.

"What have you got?" Riley asked.

"A trowel. Whoever tossed it was aiming at the creek, but this didn't make it into the water. Landed on the bank instead."

Riley turned to me, holding the bag open so I could see what was inside. "Is this the trowel you saw yesterday?"

I stared at the object. Wooden handle, rusted metal blade, although some of the red-brown stains could be blood rather than oxidation. I nodded. "It looks like the same one."

Riley glanced at the detective. "Get it to the lab. Maybe we'll get some prints."

She nodded and left, heading for the front of the

house.

It was murder, then. I turned that thought over in my mind.

Then I looked at Riley. "After I called 911, I saw that the gate was open and walked out to check. That's when I saw blood on the handle. Then I heard voices. Four girls were walking on the path on the other side of the creek. I figured they were coming home from the middle school. Riley, one of them is the neighbor girl, Ginny, that Betty gave jewelry to. I saw her later, out in her front yard, when the paramedics rolled up. She has dark hair and she's wearing a bright pink shirt. She and her friends may have seen someone going in or out of that gate."

"We'll certainly ask, when we do our knocks and talks. We'll start with the people outside, especially that girl, then go up and down the street."

Another detective loomed near the patio door. "The ME wants to talk to you."

Riley nodded. "I'll be right there. You can go now, Kay. I know where to find you if I have more questions."

I glanced out at the patio as he walked outside to meet with the medical examiner, who was on his feet now, gesturing as he talked with Riley.

When I left the house, people were still gathered on the sidewalks on both sides of the street. Anne Borokas and the other Rocoso city officer were talking to one group, while two of the county deputies were interviewing others. While I had been inside, Arlette Simmons had arrived, parking her car in the driveway of the house next door. She stood near the "For Sale" sign and when she saw me, she hurried across the lawn. "What's going on, Kay?"

"Betty Garvin had a heart attack." That much was true, but I wasn't going to say anything else.

Arlette looked skeptical. "With this kind of response? Come on, it's got to be more than that."

"Sorry." I waved my hand and walked to my car, glancing across the street, where Ginny stood with her friends. She caught my eye and it looked as though she wanted to say something. Then her mother called to her and she turned away.

Chapter 18

I FINISHED MY BREAKFAST and downed the last of my morning coffee, then put the dishes in the dishwasher. I had called Sheryl several times, both last night and again this morning. My calls had gone straight to voice mail. I wanted to talk with her, to find out about Betty's condition, and to discuss other things. I checked the time. My first appointment this Friday morning wasn't until ten o'clock. I had time to stop at the Redd House on my way to the office.

As I climbed the steps to the inn's front porch, the door opened and Sheryl came out, carrying the car key fob in her hand. The dark circles under her eyes told of a sleepless night and she looked as though she was holding herself together with an effort.

"How's Betty?" I asked. "I called and left several messages."

Sheryl's mouth tightened, then she nodded. "Yes, I got your voice mails. But things have been overwhelming. And I was so tired last night." She sighed. "Mother is doing as well as can be expected. The heart attack was minor, according to the doctor, but I'm worried about her. They kept her overnight. I don't know how long she'll be there. I'll find out this morning when I meet with the doctor. As for me, rough night, not much sleep. After I left the house, I went straight to the hospital and stayed late. When I got back here, I fell into bed but tossed and turned. I'm on my way to Mother's house now, to get a few things for her, a bed jacket and some toiletries. If she's going to be in the hospital for a few days, I want her to have her own things."

"You go straight to the hospital. I'll get those things from your mother's house. I have time before my first appointment."

"Thank you." Sheryl looked relieved. "I appreciate that. I want to get to the hospital as soon as possible and spend time with Mother before I go see Detective Hamilton at the sheriff's office. I'm supposed to be there at ten. He told me not to leave town. He suspects me of having something to do with Hallie's death. Which is ridiculous. I thought it was an accident. Hallie must have tripped over one of those rocks. Surely, she fell and hit her head. That rock border around the patio has been a trip hazard for years. Besides, I got there a few minutes before you did."

Sheryl didn't know about the trowel, found on the creek bank. And it wasn't my place to tell her. "Hallie was still alive when I got there. Did she say anything?"

Sheryl shook her head. "She made sounds, like she was trying to talk. Nothing that I could make out. I was shocked to see her lying there."

"Even though your mother was in the family room, she must have seen or heard something. She's a witness."

"And it triggered her heart attack." Sheryl's mouth tightened. "I've told the detective that Mother can't be interviewed just yet. And the doctor agrees with me. As for myself, it would be a good idea to have an attorney with me when I talk with Detective Hamilton. I'll contact John Fielding, the attorney who helped with Mother's will. Although his area is wills, trusts, and probate, I'm sure he can recommend someone."

"Just in case, I know a lawyer named Benjamin Ma. He's local and his office is downtown, not far from here." I took out my phone and went into my contacts.

Sheryl pulled a pen and a receipt from her purse and jotted down the number. "Thanks. I'll call him. Now, the bed jacket will be in the top left drawer of Mother's dresser. The toiletries are in the bathroom. I took Mother's medications with me yesterday."

I nodded, remembering the medicine box she'd stuffed into her bag. We walked toward the parking lot.

"Have you called Tamara, Hallie's daughter?"

"Not me. I don't have her number. I'll leave that to the police." Sheryl hit the button that unlocked the car and opened the door. "I called my husband and son last night, to tell them the news. I told my son not to come. He's got finals coming up at UC Berkeley." She paused, an odd expression on her face. "As for my husband, I don't know whether he will show up or not. Or whether I care."

That, I thought, spoke volumes about the state of Sheryl's marriage.

Sheryl got into the car and fastened the seat belt. She looked up at me. "What was it you wanted to talk with me about? Yesterday afternoon, when you called, you said there was something you wanted to discuss. That's why you came over to Mother's house."

What I'd wanted to talk about was the missing silver from Betty's house and how it wound up at the antique mall. That mystery paled beside Hallie's murder. It would keep for the time being.

"I'll tell you later." I watched as Sheryl drove away. Then I got into my car. I called the office and Gwen answered. "I won't be in until later."

"Is this about the murder?" she asked. "It's all over town. You know how it is."

"Yes, I do. I'll update you later. Is Carmen there?"

"At the hospital, visiting a client. I'll see you whenever you get here."

Ending the call, I started the car and headed for the Garvin house. As I drove, I asked myself the same question that Riley had asked me the day before. Would

Sheryl kill her sister? I had only Sheryl's word that she'd arrived at the house shortly before me. And Sheryl had taken liberties with the truth before. The two sisters didn't get along, and that was putting it mildly. Since Hallie arrived in Rocoso, they'd already had a nasty altercation. They would have come to blows if Lanny hadn't intervened.

But murder? Had their quarrel escalated into physical violence, with Hallie dead as a result?

Betty was the key. She must have seen what happened. But she wasn't in any condition to tell what she'd seen.

At Betty's house, I unlocked the front door and went to the master bedroom. The cotton bed jacket was where Sheryl had told me it would be. I put it into a shopping bag I'd brought from my car. In the bathroom, I scooped up toiletries and added them to the bag. I was back in the living room when the doorbell rang.

The woman on the porch was tall and broad-shouldered, dressed in faded jeans and a red-and-blue plaid blouse. Short, iron-gray hair swept back from her round, snub-nosed face. I was sure I'd seen her face before. Then I remembered. Earlier in the week, Betty had pointed out this face in a photograph, identifying the woman as her niece.

The woman's bright blue eyes narrowed. "Who are you?"

"Kay Dexter. I'm Mrs. Garvin's geriatric care manager."

"I'm Tish Lehigh, Betty's niece. I live in Appleton. I heard about Hallie this morning and drove up as soon as I could. Where is Betty?"

I motioned her into the house. "She's in the hospital. She went into shock yesterday afternoon and had a minor heart attack. I don't know when she's coming home. I came over to collect a few things to make her stay more comfortable."

Tish Lehigh walked to the middle of the living room and stood, hands on hips, giving me a thoughtful once-over. "So, you're the geriatric care manager. I've heard about you, setting up shop here in Rocoso. Sheryl hired you. I'm sure it wasn't Hallie. I know how hard it can be, with an elderly parent. Mom was older than Betty. My brothers helped, but it was left to me to take care of her until she died. Before that, it was my dad that needed looking after. What with Sheryl living up in Seattle, I guess she figured she needed extra help." She paused, a look on her face that was half-sympathetic and half-annoyed. "You know, I told Sheryl last year I would be happy to come over a few times a week, to check on Betty. It's not far. I can be here in less than an hour. But Sheryl said, oh, no, she didn't need any help. Just like her, of course."

More lies and half-truths. According to Sheryl, no family members lived near Rocoso. Yet Appleton was thirty miles downriver. She'd also said she had no relatives who could help her with her mother's care. Here was Tish, her cousin, claiming that wasn't true.

"Yes, Sheryl did hire me."

"Interesting that Sheryl didn't call, to let me know she was in town, or that Hallie was dead. I shouldn't be surprised, though. She rarely communicates with me or anyone else in the family. I heard about this from my neighbor's son, who works for the sheriff's department. He called me this morning. Didn't come right out and say it, but he implied Sheryl might be a suspect in Hallie's murder. Is that true?"

"I'll tell you what I know, Ms. Lehigh."

"Call me Tish, and I'll call you Kay. No reason to stand on formalities." Tish sat down on the sofa, settling in with the air of someone who was ready for a long talk.

I took the nearby chair. "I was supposed to meet Sheryl here yesterday afternoon. When I arrived, I found Betty passed out in her recliner and Sheryl outside, on the patio, with Hallie." I fought down a shudder as I recalled Hallie, stretched out on the concrete, blood pooling around her head. "Hallie was alive when I got here, then she died. I called 911 and told them to send an ambulance as well, since Betty looked terrible."

"Good lord," Tish said. "What was Hallie doing here? She hardly ever comes around."

"She arrived earlier this week, with a friend and her dog. She moved in, said she was going to stay as long as Betty needed her."

Tish gave a derisive snort. "I wonder what prompted this sudden interest in Betty's welfare. Though I can guess. Dollar signs. Hallie's all about the money. She always was. I'll bet Sheryl was fit to be tied when Hallie showed up."

"I called her to let her know. She came down from Seattle later that day. May I ask you some questions, Tish?"

Tish smiled. "I've been asking my share, so sure, ask away. I'll answer, within reason."

"Can you tell me why Sheryl and Hallie were at odds? My observation is that it goes deep and it's been going on a long time."

Tish measured me with a look, as though wondering how much to reveal. Then she sighed. "Let me count the ways. A lot of it has to do with money. But you're right, it goes back farther than that. Those two have been at each other's throats as long as I can remember."

"Tell me about money first. When Sheryl hired me a few weeks ago, she told me her mother's finances are comfortable, as she put it. This house looks like a typical middle-class home, nothing special. But I gather Betty's assets are more substantial than Sheryl led me to believe."

"More than this house and what's in the bank," Tish said. "Betty owns a dozen or more rental houses around Rocoso, enough to provide her with a steady income."

That was a lot more than the rental properties that Sheryl had mentioned when we talked.

"There's some good jewelry that was passed down in the family," Tish continued. "That should be in a safe deposit box at Rocoso National Bank. And there's the land up at Lost Woman Creek. My mother left it to Betty."

I leaned forward as the tumblers clicked into place. "Lost Woman Creek? Your mother was Ruby Waldron?"

"That's right." Tish smiled. "Mom was the oldest and Betty was the baby of the family. It was my great-grandfather, Henry Maysfield, who built the hot springs hotel up at the creek. Mom married Fred Waldron, whose family owned the apple farm, and most of Appleton."

The small town of Appleton was located in the lower Rocoso Valley, where the canyon widened into rolling hills and green meadows. Apple orchards surrounded the community and fruit stands popped up along the highway when the fruit harvest began in the late summer and early fall. The Waldrons, as Tish said, owned much of the property in and around Appleton. I understood the family to be quite wealthy.

"Your mother left the land to Betty," I said. "There's a lot of speculation around town about the Lost Woman Creek property and what will happen to it. Why did your mother leave the land to Betty, and not a member of your immediate family?"

"My brothers had the same reaction, I can tell you," Tish said. "They're being greedy and I told them so. We got a big estate from the Waldron side of the family. Before she died, Mom told me why she did it that way.

165

Originally her father was going to split the land between all four of his children. There were two Maysfield boys. One of them died in World War Two, and the other in Korea. That left the two sisters. Grandpa Maysfield liked my father, a lot. But he never had any use for Curtis, Betty's husband."

"Why?"

"You never met Curtis. He died seven years ago. And good riddance," Tish said, acid etching her voice. "He was a piece of work, a real son of a bitch. My mother never liked him, not one bit."

That fit with what my mother told me about Curtis. "I grew up in Rocoso. I left town after college and moved back a few years ago. My father worked for the railroad and my mother knows Betty. She remembers Curtis and told me a little bit about him."

"She probably didn't have much good to say about him, either. Anyway, Curtis riled Grandpa Maysfield one time too many. Grandpa changed his will and left the Lost Woman Creek property, all of it, to Mom. Curtis was pissed off about that, I can tell you. Mom always thought that was wrong. She said the land should have been divided between her and Betty. At one point she was going to deed half of it to Betty. But she didn't like Curtis any more than Grandpa did, and she didn't want him to get his hands on the property. By the time Curtis kicked the bucket, Mom changed her mind about deeding the property. Instead, she left it to Betty in her will."

Sheryl and Hallie were fighting over Betty's assets. This was another familiar story in my line of work. I'd seen bitter arguments about who was going to get what in the family estate. Contention happened even when the departed parent had left explicit instructions. Sometimes bickering led to outright battles, with siblings and their spouses estranged, sometimes for years, sometimes for good. But that wasn't the only reason the two Garvin sisters were at odds.

"You said the quarrel between the sisters goes back a long time."

"To Greg," Tish said. "And even before."

"The car accident?"

"It was no accident. Greg killed himself."

I took a moment to digest this. I'd always heard Greg Garvin's death described as an accident, his car struck by a locomotive when he tried to speed through a crossing. That's the way Hallie told it, just a few days ago.

"Suicide by train." Tish's eyes flashed with anger as she spoke. "Greg and I were the same age. We were close. And I mean close enough for Greg to tell me he was gay. I knew all through high school he was different. In the closet, until he went off to Sac State. Then he came out of the closet, but not to his parents. Somehow, they found out. Betty was okay with it, but Curtis, as you can imagine, was not." She grimaced. "I don't know what was said during that confrontation, but I can just guess. Not long after, Greg drove his car onto those train tracks." She glanced at the photos on the living room shelf.

I followed the direction of Tish's gaze and saw the photograph I'd noticed on my first visit to the house, the one that showed Greg Garvin. It had been taken a long time ago, and he looked so young. "Back to Greg, you said, or even before."

Tish nodded. "Those two sisters were always fighting, even when they were kids. Lord knows, my brothers and I were always getting into it, but it was different with Sheryl and Hallie. Truth be told, I think Curtis used to play them against each other. Sheryl was the classic good girl, always trying to please, and Hallie was the rebel. That played into Hallie marrying Justin Brownlow. He was Sheryl's college boyfriend. Sheryl

167

brought him home one weekend and Hallie zeroed in on him. Next thing I heard, Hallie was pregnant and Justin married her. Sheryl didn't have much use for Hallie before that, but after Hallie stole her fella, it got even worse."

"What can you tell me about Hallie's marriage?"

"Just that it didn't last," Tish said. "Mom said it wouldn't, and she was right. Hallie left the guy when Tamara was in grade school. She's been moving around ever since, doing this and that. Betty told me she was living up in Humboldt County."

"How often did Hallie come to visit Betty?"

"Not sure. When the spirit moved her, I guess. Last time I saw her was about a year ago. Sheryl continued being the good girl. She's got durable power of attorney for Aunt Betty and she's a signatory on all of Betty's accounts. Hallie hated that. Last year, she accused Sheryl of moving money from Betty's account to her own. Sheryl still has an account at the bank here, so Hallie's theory was that it would be easy for Sheryl to help herself to Betty's money. Not that I think she's been doing that. But Hallie sure believed it. I figure Hallie would like to have some say-so about Betty's assets and Sheryl's attitude about that is, hell no."

"This has been very helpful," I said. "I've been trying to understand how the family dynamics work."

"When it comes to the Garvin family, just call it dysfunctional." Tish stood up. "I guess I'll head over to the hospital to see Betty and Sheryl."

I checked my watch, then looked at the bag containing the bed jacket and toiletries. "Since you're going to the hospital, would you mind taking these for Betty? That's why I came over here, to fetch them so Sheryl wouldn't have to. I have an appointment in half an hour and I don't want to cut it too close."

"Not a problem." Tish got to her feet and reached for

the bag.

We left the house and I locked the door. As Tish drove away in her silver SUV, Ginny Cavalieri came out of the house across the street, carrying a backpack. She was heading for school this morning, like the other teenagers I saw walking toward the path that led back to the meadow. Instead of heading that way, she crossed the street to where I stood. "Is Mrs. Garvin okay?"

"She had a mild heart attack. The doctors are keeping her in the hospital until they're sure she can come home."

"I'm glad to hear she's all right. She's a nice old lady."

"She is."

Ginny hesitated, then said, "I hear Mrs. Garvin's daughter died, the one that was staying with her. That's why the police were here yesterday."

"That's true. Ginny, I saw you and some friends yesterday afternoon, in the meadow behind Mrs. Garvin's house."

"That's right. We were walking home from school. We always go that way."

"It was about the same time Mrs. Garvin's daughter died. I mentioned that to the detectives. Did anyone talk with you?"

"Yes. A man came to my house yesterday and talked with me and my mother. I think he said his name was Hamilton."

Good. My cousin Riley had followed up on my information. "If you don't mind my asking, what did you tell him?"

"He asked if me and my friends saw anything. I did see somebody come out the back gate."

"A man or a woman?"

"I couldn't tell for sure," Ginny said. "I wasn't that close to Mrs. Garvin's house. My friends and I were talking, not paying attention to whatever was going on over there. I happened to look in that direction and saw somebody come out the gate, wearing jeans and a T-shirt."

"Blue jeans?"

"Yeah. And a blue shirt. And dark hair. That's what I told the detective. I think he was going to talk to my friends, to see if they saw anything."

I digested this, thinking about the trowel and wondering if Ginny had seen the person, presumably the killer, toss the murder weapon toward the creek. "Did you see the person make any kind of a gesture?"

"Well . . ." Ginny drew out the word. "The detective asked if I saw that person throw anything. But I didn't. I guess I was looking away. I better go. I need to get to school and I don't want to be late."

Ginny moved away, in the direction of the path that led between the houses back to the meadow and the nearby middle school. Just then, a car came down the street. The car was a hatchback, somewhat beat up, with rust stains marring the beige paint job. It slowed as it went past and I caught a glimpse of the driver, a woman, looking out at us. Or the Garvin house. No doubt the woman was curious about what had happened here. As Gwen had remarked earlier, the news of Hallie's murder was all over town.

I spent the rest of the morning visiting clients and doing paperwork in my office. I had a quick lunch, then took time out to go to the hospital, to check on Betty. As I entered the hospital lobby, I saw Tish Lehigh step off the elevator, walking toward me.

"Hello again," she said. "I was just upstairs with Betty. She's kind of out of it, though. In and out, really. I'll be back tomorrow. I did talk with Sheryl. She had to leave for an appointment with someone at the sheriff's office. I sure hope they can get this straightened out."

"So do I. What room is Betty in?"

"Third floor, west wing, room 307." I crossed the lobby to the elevators. When I got to the third floor, I stepped into the corridor and saw Carmen at the nurses' station. As a registered nurse, she had at one time worked here at the medical center and I was sure she knew many of the nurses. She spotted me and turned from the counter as I joined her.

"Hi," she said. "I'm here to visit one of my clients. Mrs. Liu. Remember her?"

"Oh, yes. I hope she didn't fall again."

Carmen sighed. "I'm afraid she did. Cracked some ribs. I have a meeting with her son and daughter later today."

"I'm here to see Betty Garvin," I said. "She had a heart attack."

"I heard about that. And the murder. Well, I've got to get going. See you later at the office."

She headed for the elevator and I continued down the corridor until I located room 307. I stopped when I heard voices. Someone was inside with Betty. Was it one of the nurses? No, it was someone else. Someone who wasn't talking like a nurse. I stepped into the room and saw a woman leaning over Betty's bed.

"You must be Tamara," I said.

Chapter 19

SHE TURNED TOWARD ME with a frown. "Who're you?"

Though she hadn't confirmed her identity, I was sure this was Tamara. There were echoes of Hallie in Tamara's face, which had the same shape, light blue eyes and fair skin, and snub nose. Her hair was the same sandy blond as Hallie's, but where Hallie's hair had been long and straight, her daughter's was short and tousled, curling around her ears and at the nape of her neck. Tamara was taller than her mother, by four or five inches. Perhaps the height was a legacy from her father. Her lean, well-muscled body was tanned, showing evidence of outdoor activities. She wore khaki cargo pants with lots of pockets, worn with a blue Rocky River Rafting Company T-shirt.

She also looked familiar. Had I seen a photograph of her at Betty's house? That was probably it.

Tamara radiated tension. I wondered why. Of course, her mother's death and her grandmother's heart attack were stressful. But something else was going on. I was sure of it.

I reviewed what I'd just seen. Tamara had been leaning over her grandmother's prone form. It was a one-sided conversation and Tamara had been doing all the talking. The only words I'd heard were "Think about it."

Think about what? And what did it mean? Just a few words, in and of themselves innocuous. Surely the words and meaning were completely innocent, a granddaughter expressing love and concern for her grandmother. But Tamara's face and body language said otherwise.

So did Betty's. Her eyes were closed, as though she

was asleep. But her face didn't look natural. In addition to her squeezed-shut eyes, her mouth was compressed into a tight line.

Whatever Tamara was saying to her grandmother, I was sure Betty didn't want to hear it.

I composed my face. "I'm Kay Dexter, your grandmother's care manager."

Tamara smoothed the frown from her face and toyed with a strand of hair. "What does a care manager do?"

"I oversee your grandmother's care."

"I thought my mother was doing that. I mean, that's why she was here, right?"

"She arrived recently, that's true. I've been working with your grandmother a bit longer than that."

Tamara fiddled with a silver ring she wore on her left hand. "I'm glad Grandma is okay. I don't get up here to visit her as often as I should."

"Where do you live?"

"The Bay Area." Tamara moved away from the bed.

"I used to live in the Bay Area," I said. "In Oakland, near College Avenue."

"I've got a place in North Oakland." She relaxed, her guarded expression easing into a tentative smile.

Both of us turned as someone else entered the room. Sheryl, her face drawn and tired, stopped and surveyed the scene.

"Tamara. When did you get here?"

It was clear from the chill in Sheryl's voice that the relationship between aunt and niece was strained. Somehow that didn't surprise me.

"This morning," Tamara said. "The cops called last night, to tell me Mom was dead. Did you kill her?"

Sheryl winced, then her expression hardened. "Don't be ridiculous."

"What am I supposed to think?" Tamara shot back.

"You and Mom never got along. Every time you're together it ends up in a shouting match. Then Mom gets conked over the head and you're there, watching her bleed out. She's dead. Why shouldn't I think you killed her?"

"This isn't the place to have this conversation." I needed to keep things from going downhill any faster than they already were. "Perhaps we'd better step out of Betty's room."

Sheryl's voice dropped from chilly to icy. "I don't intend to have this conversation at all. I'm here to see Mother." She walked toward the bed, ignoring us.

"I'll talk with you later, Sheryl." I walked out to the hallway.

Tamara followed me, flashing a crooked smile as she fiddled with her hair.

"Do you really think your aunt had something to do with your mother's death?" I asked.

Tamara shrugged. "Maybe. Hell, I don't know what to think. Aunt Sheryl and Mom have been at each other's throats as long as I can remember. Sure as hell makes for some tense family get-togethers. I gather it has something to do with my father preferring Mom to Sheryl. Believe me, Sheryl's such a tight-assed bitch I'm not surprised." She laughed. "That's what I call her. Sheryl the Bitch. Anyway, Mom's marriage didn't last. Dad bailed out when I was nine."

We stood in the small waiting room just this side of the nurses' station. The elevator doors opened and several people stepped out. One of them was a young man in his early twenties, dressed casually in faded jeans and a white T-shirt sporting the logo of the University of California in Berkeley. He was tall and lean, with dark hair and eyes, a tiny cleft in his chin. His pace quickened as he walked toward us.

"Hey, Ethan." Tamara gave him a quick hug. "Kay,

this is my cousin Ethan Gillette."

"You're Sheryl's son. I'm Kay Dexter, your grandmother's care manager."

He shook my hand. "Yeah, Mom told me she hired you to help. Where is Grandma?"

Tamara pointed. "Down the hall, to the left. Sheryl's with her now."

"Good. I need to talk with her, after everything that's happened." Ethan hesitated. "I'm sorry about your mom."

"Yeah, well, shit happens." Tamara's mouth twisted down into a frown. She blinked her eyes rapidly and looked down at the floor.

Ethan put his arms around her and she leaned into him. Then he released her. "Call me if you want to talk. You got my number."

Tamara nodded. "Sure. I'll do that."

Ethan excused himself and walked down the hall toward Betty's room.

"He seems like a nice young man," I said.

"He is." Tamara's crooked smile was back. "Hard to believe, with Sheryl and Richard as parents. Talk about a couple of cold fish. I don't know how the hell they got together."

"I understand Ethan's in school in Berkeley."

Tamara nodded. "Yeah. It keeps him busy. We get together now and then. Well, I gotta go." She walked away, toward the elevator, and pushed the down button. The elevator door opened and Tamara stepped inside. As the door shut, my phone vibrated. I moved into the small waiting area and took the call. A prospective client wanted to reschedule an appointment. We settled on a new day and time, then I ended the call.

I stood for a moment, thinking. I was sure I'd seen Tamara before, and recently. Was it because she was wearing a T-shirt from the rafting company? But it seemed that every other person in town had one of those.

Then it came to me. The woman in the rust-stained hatchback who had driven by the Garvin house when I was talking with Ginny this morning. Tamara had been at the wheel. She must have left the Bay Area very early this morning to have arrived in Rocoso by mid-morning. And I supposed it was natural for her to drive by Betty's house. But it would have made more sense for her to go directly to the sheriff's office, to get more details about her mother's death, even more so than coming to the hospital to visit Betty.

I kept going back to the scene in Betty's room, with Tamara leaning over her grandmother's bed. Her body language had seemed off, menacing rather than comforting.

Perhaps I was reading too much into it. But if I was right, Tamara was threatening my client. I needed to find out why.

The elevator door opened again. Lanny Fitzpatrick walked out, wearing khakis and a green T-shirt, sandals on his feet. He carried a cheery flower arrangement of yellow and white daisies with pink carnations, festooned with multi-colored ribbons. When he saw me, he detoured in my direction. "Hi, Kay. How's Betty?"

"I think she's all right, considering. It was a heart attack, apparently triggered by shock."

"Is Sheryl here?"

"Yes. She's in the room, with her son."

"I better not go in right now," Lanny said. "Too many visitors. I don't want to crowd things. Besides, Sheryl doesn't have much use for me. Didn't have much use for Hallie, either, truth be told."

"Can you give me some background on that?"

Lanny shrugged. "I can tell you what I know."

"I'd appreciate it. I have some time in my schedule,

and they make a decent latte in that coffee shop downstairs."

Lanny left Betty's flowers at the nurses' station. We took the elevator down to the first floor. We stepped into the lobby, then Lanny turned and held open the elevator door, waiting as an elderly woman moved slowly into the car, using a wheeled walker with her portable oxygen concentrator tucked into the basket on the front. The coffee shop was located in the front section of the cafeteria, both reached through a wide door at the rear of the lobby.

We queued up behind a nurse wearing pink scrubs and a woman with a small child in tow. When our turn came, I ordered a latte. Lanny opted for plain coffee. Once we had our drinks, Lanny stopped at a counter and added sugar and cream to his cup. Then we found a table in a corner.

"Glad to hear Betty is doing all right," Lanny said. "I like her. She reminds me of my mom, who's been gone a while." He sipped his coffee. "I'm staying at that motel you suggested. Thanks for the recommendation. Nice place, nice people. The lady that owns it, she's gonna look in on the dog. I'm debating whether to stay in town until the funeral, or head to Arcata and then come back. I guess they can't have any kind of service until they release the body to the family. Any idea when that might happen?"

I warmed my hands on my coffee cup. "The autopsy happens twenty-four to forty-eight hours after the body is found. It's Friday, so that means today or tomorrow. With a homicide, I would imagine the pathologist would work on a Saturday. After that, the body will be released and the funeral arrangements can be made. You and Hallie were together for several years, right?"

He nodded. "Lived together three years. We talked about getting married but never did get much past talking.

Both of us had been married and divorced, with all the baggage that entails. I guess we were happy with things the way they were. Never figured on either of us dying. Truth be told, I thought if one of us was going to die, I'd be the first one. I'm gonna miss her." He sighed and stared down at his coffee cup. "I guess the funeral arrangements are up to the next of kin. Which would be Tamara, Sheryl, and Betty."

I nodded. "That's right. Tamara was here at the hospital, about half an hour ago."

"I figured the cops would get in touch with her." Lanny took a sip of coffee, his expression neutral.

I wondered what he thought about Hallie's daughter. I'd ask him, at some point, but first I wanted to find out more about the strained relationship between the two sisters. "How long had you known Hallie?"

"I met her four years ago. She had just moved to Arcata and got a job at an herb shop. A mutual friend introduced us. We hit it off, started seeing each other. Then she moved in with me."

"You told Detective Hamilton you were a businessman in Arcata."

"Yeah. I got a farm east of town."

"What do you grow?" As soon as the words were out of my mouth, I knew the answer. "Of course. Marijuana." Arcata was in Humboldt County which, along with Mendocino and Trinity Counties, formed Northern California's Emerald Triangle, where marijuana was the prime agricultural crop. I recalled the whiff of pot I smelled at Betty's house, the ashtray full of smoked-down butts.

He smiled. "Yeah, I'm one of those mom-and-pop growers they talk about. I moved up there about twenty years ago, after my divorce. Bought some land, built myself a cabin, and started a small operation. I do all right, grow some good weed. Anyway, Hallie moved in and she helps . . . helped with my operation. She had a good head for business, had some great ideas about marketing and other products we could sell, like cannabis cream for aches and pains. We were already working the medical marijuana market. Now that pot's been legalized for recreational use, it's a whole different business. I'm waiting to see what shakes out with permits and regulations. From what I can tell, it's different county by county."

I sipped my latte, getting back to the question that was uppermost in my mind. "What do you know about the relationship between Hallie and Sheryl?"

"All I know is what Hallie told me. Secondhand. I never met Sheryl until this week."

"What did she tell you?"

"They didn't get along, never did. Classic case of two sisters butting heads from the time they were little kids. I guess the brother, Greg, used to make them toe the line when they were little. Then he died, and there wasn't anyone to get between them when they had a pissing contest, which to hear Hallie tell it was frequently. The guy Hallie was married to, Tamara's father, I guess he was dating Sheryl, engaged to her, even. Then he decided he preferred Hallie. She says Sheryl never got over that. Been angry with Hallie ever since."

That jibed with what Sheryl had told me. But there was more, according to Cousin Tish. "That was long in the past, over twenty years ago. What about recently?"

Lanny took another swallow of his coffee, as though composing the words in his head. "Sheryl has this pattern. She moves in, takes over, and bosses everyone around. She took over with Betty. Hallie really resented that. She thought Sheryl was trying to cut her out."

"Out of what?"

"Decisions. Like looking after Betty, for one thing. Hiring you to oversee things. Hallie was really mad that Sheryl didn't consult her. I mean, she could have picked up the phone, called Hallie and said, look, we need to figure out some caregiving stuff for Mom. But no, Sheryl just barreled into town and hired you, without giving Hallie a chance to give her input. When Hallie found out about that, she was hot to get down here and stick her oar in."

This sounded like other situations I'd encountered, with adult children of elderly parents who needed care and couldn't agree on what should be done. "Sheryl told me Hallie was out of the picture, not involved with Betty at all."

Lanny gave an exasperated snort. "That's not true. Hallie called her mom once a week or so. And she drove down every few months. This is typical of Sheryl, from what I can see. That's what she does. She just takes over and stomps on anyone who gets in her way. Sheryl's got durable power of attorney for Betty, for health care and financial stuff. She figures that gives her the right to do whatever she wants."

That confirmed what Tish had said this morning. Tish also said that Hallie had accused Sheryl of siphoning money from Betty's accounts to her own.

I took a sip of my latte. "Money is an issue, then. It sounds like Hallie was concerned about being cut out of Betty's assets as well as decisions about Betty's care."

"I guess you could put it that way," he said slowly. "From what Hallie told me, it's a good-sized estate, with money in the bank and some property. She once told me she had her suspicions that maybe Sheryl was helping herself to Betty's money. But I don't know. That might have just been Hallie taking shots at her sister. But yeah, where there's money, there's always a bone of contention.

It's not like Hallie was waiting for her mom to die so she could get her share. I don't want you to think that. But she was irritated with Sheryl for acting like Hallie wasn't even part of the family. Then there's this one property in particular. Betty inherited this big piece of land from her sister that died. A place called Lost Woman Creek. Hallie said it would be a perfect place to grow weed, and I agree. We drove up there and took a look. Great terrain, plenty of water."

"Of course, Betty owns the land," I said. "She is the one who decides what to do with it."

"That's right. Hallie told me Betty's will leaves everything to her and Sheryl, equal shares. Hallie was going to suggest that Betty deed the land to the sisters now. But that wouldn't work, because they both have different ideas about what to do with the land. Sheryl wants to rebuild that hot springs resort, turn it into a hotel and condos."

"And she wouldn't want a marijuana farm next door to a resort."

"You got that right." Lanny shook his head. "You wouldn't want any kind of agricultural enterprise next to a fancy resort. Unless it's a winery, maybe. But pot? No, I don't think so. Besides, marijuana needs lots of water. So does wine, for that matter. These days in California, water's a big issue. Anyway, Hallie told me Sheryl's not interested in dividing the land. She's after the whole parcel."

Based on the local interest in the land up at Lost Woman Creek, that property must be worth millions. Betty Garvin's assets were quite valuable. Control of those assets certainly gave Sheryl a motive for murdering her sister. Though Tamara would presumably inherit her mother's share.

"Did Hallie have a will?"

Lanny frowned. "I don't know. I don't recall her ever going to see a lawyer. But she could have one of those wills where you write it out yourself."

"Holographic." I nodded. "Yes, handwritten wills are legal in California. They don't have to be witnessed, but they do need to be signed and dated."

"That's good to know," Lanny said. "I need to do something like that, too. I don't know if Hallie had one of those wills, but when I get back to Arcata, I'll look through her papers. I know she had a life insurance policy. She named Tamara and me as beneficiaries, on that and on her bank account."

"Code stroke, ER. Code stroke, ER," a voice announced from the hospital public address system. A woman in blue scrubs, queued up for coffee, did an about-face and headed out the door.

Sheryl and Ethan walked into the coffee shop. Lanny stood to greet them. "How's Betty?"

"She's doing well," Sheryl said, her voice polite. "Thank you for your flowers. This is my son, Ethan Gillette."

The big man extended his hand. "Lanny Fitzpatrick, a friend of your Aunt Hallie."

I glanced at Sheryl. "Have you heard anything about the autopsy?"

"Not yet," she said. "Detective Hamilton told me the body should be released this weekend, Monday at the latest. Then we can plan the funeral."

Lanny cleared his throat. "Hallie told me she wanted to be cremated."

Sheryl's politeness slipped a bit as she turned her gaze on him. "I don't know that for sure. In any case, the family will make that decision. Hallie will be buried in the family plot with my father and brother, of course."

Lanny didn't say anything. But the look he gave me

said clearly that he thought this was another example of Sheryl taking over and telling everyone what to do. In this case, I thought he had a point.

So did Ethan. "That should be Tamara's decision. She's Hallie's daughter."

"What about Justin Brownlow?" I asked.

Sheryl frowned, taken aback. "What about him?"

"He's Hallie's ex-husband."

She waved a dismissive hand. "He's out of the picture."

That's what she'd told me about Hallie, I thought. It wasn't true then. Was it true now?

"Ex or no," I said, "he should be notified of her death. Do you know where he is?"

"He lives in Sacramento. He works for Caltrans," Ethan added, using the common term for the California Department of Transportation.

"How do you know that?" Sheryl asked.

Ethan shrugged. "Tamara told me. She's in touch with him. I think she even sees him now and then."

"That surprises me," Sheryl said. "After he and Hallie divorced, I thought he kept his distance and didn't have much to do with Tamara. I know from Hallie's complaints that he was fairly inconsistent with child support. Another reason, I suppose, that Hallie was always asking Mom and Dad for money."

"I'll ask Tamara if she's called him," Ethan said.

"Time for that once we've scheduled the funeral," Sheryl said. Then her face closed up as a man walked into the coffee shop. "How did he know we were here?"

"I texted him." Ethan smiled at the newcomer. "Hi, Dad."

So this was Sheryl's husband. The one she was planning to leave.

Richard Gillette was probably ten years older than

his wife. He had a thin ascetic face, sparse gray hair, and a way of tightening his mouth when he disapproved of something. That's why I thought he disapproved of me, and of Lanny. Tamara had referred to Sheryl and Richard as a couple of cold fish. Now, looking at Richard's pursed mouth and pale blue eyes, I found myself agreeing.

Sheryl had said earlier that she wasn't sure whether her husband would come to Rocoso and had added that she wasn't sure she cared. But here he was, telling her he'd flown from Seattle to Sacramento early this morning and rented a car for the drive up the canyon.

He turned to his son. "Shouldn't you be in Berkeley? Classes are over and finals are coming up."

"Next week is review week," Ethan said. "Finals start the week after that. I've got all my stuff with me, so I can study here."

Richard gave his son a curt nod, then addressed Sheryl. "I went to the place you're staying but they don't have any rooms."

"Then I guess you'll have to stay somewhere else," she told him. "Ethan and I will be staying at Mother's house."

The implication was that he wasn't welcome there, either. Richard quickly masked his annoyance. The brief exchange between husband, wife, and son said a lot about the family dynamic.

It was past time for me to leave. It felt awkward here in the coffee shop. I still hadn't discussed Betty's silver, the items that I'd seen at the antique store. But now was not the time, especially as Richard drew Sheryl to one side for a private conversation.

I stood. "I have an appointment. I'd better go. Sheryl, I'll talk with you later." She gave me a distracted wave.

Lanny got to his feet as well. "Guess I'll head back to the motel. I'll walk out with you."

We deposited our empty coffee containers in a nearby trash can. As we started for the door leading from the coffee shop to the hospital lobby, Ethan caught up with us. "Mr. Fitzpatrick? I know you and Aunt Hallie were close. In spite of what Mom said, I think you should have a say about the funeral, along with Tamara. If Aunt Hallie wanted to be cremated, that's what we should do. I'll talk with Mom and Tamara and get back to you. Have you got a cell phone?"

"I do." Lanny pulled out his phone. He and Ethan traded numbers. "I'd really appreciate whatever you can do. But I understand if the family . . ." His voice trailed off. "It's just that since Hallie and I were together a few years, I kinda feel like I'm family."

After Ethan had rejoined his parents in the coffee shop, Lanny and I walked out of the hospital lobby, heading for the parking lot. "Is it possible Hallie wrote down her wishes, about being cremated?"

Lanny paused near the back bumper of the Jeep. "She might have. I will go up to Arcata now. That way, I can go through Hallie's stuff, to see if she's got a will or anything that says something about what she wanted, like we were talking about earlier. I'll take the dog back with me and leave it with a friend for the time being." He sighed. "In the end, though, it doesn't matter if she's cremated or planted in the ground. Just so Hallie gets a good send-off."

Chapter 20

SAM GRINNED AT ME, with a wicked gleam in those deep blue eyes. He raised his hand and cupped my chin, leaning toward me. "You have chocolate in the corner of your mouth."

"Are you offering to lick it off?"

He chuckled. "Is that an invitation?"

"Not here, not now."

We were at the Rocoso Farmers' Market, at a food stand selling crepes. I grabbed a paper napkin and eliminated the telltale evidence of the chocolate crepe I had just consumed.

"I hope it was good," Sam said.

"Melted dark chocolate. What's not to like?"

"I must confess I had one earlier, with Nutella."

"I like my chocolate plain, unadulterated with nut products." My hands were sticky from the crepe. I wiped them, balled up the napkin, and dropped it into the blue - and -white canvas tote bag I'd brought with me.

The farmers' market was held on Saturday mornings and Tuesday afternoons. The city shut down a one-block section of a downtown street and vendors from all over the county set up stalls and sold their wares. The market ran from early spring until late autumn, whenever the snow began to fall.

I had arrived early, parking my car down the street from the market. As I entered the row of vendors, I was enticed by the smells coming from the food stands, selling everything from *pupusas* to *empanadas* to crepes. The crepes won out. I bought one and ate it. Then Sam showed up, dressed in faded jeans and a Rocoso College T-shirt, and obligingly pointed out the chocolate residue.

We left the food stand and strolled together, looking at the locally grown fruits and vegetables that were arrayed on tables, along with eggs, honey, jams and jellies, baked goods, flowers, and all sorts of crafts. Some stalls sold prepared food.

Much of Rocoso County was located in the Sierra Nevada mountains, but the county's well-watered valleys and microclimates were perfect for agriculture. In some parts of the county, such as the south river valley and the meadows and hills around Appleton, apples were the big cash crop, and in recent years, wine grapes. County viticulture produced excellent red wine grapes used in the production of pinot noir, like that produced at the Riverbend Winery, located south of Rocoso, where the river curved. The same rich soil in other parts of the county, such as the little town of Starfield, was great for the cultivation of blueberries and for wildflowers, a key element in Starfield Valley Honey. At Pellgrove, in the western section of the county, peach and apricot orchards thrived and the crops included cherries and berries. Out near Camacho, farmers grew hops that went into the production of local beers at several craft breweries located in Rocoso.

Sam stopped at a stand and pulled several muslin produce bags from his canvas tote. He picked up a head of broccoli and examined it, then tucked it into a bag. He added zucchini, onions, lettuce, and a head of garlic, then dug out his wallet as the vendor totaled up his purchases.

"Am I going to see that broccoli tonight at dinner?" I asked as we strolled to the next booth. We had tickets for a concert at the college and Sam was cooking.

"You are. I'm going with my tried-and-true." His specialty was roast chicken, the exterior rubbed with butter, herbs, and spices, the bird's cavity stuffed with more herbs, garlic cloves, and a whole lemon, pierced so the juice dripped and flavored the chicken during cooking. I had promised to bring dessert. I'm always in the mood for chocolate, so I had baked a moist, dark chocolate cake, using a recipe handed down from Mom. I had yet to frost the cake, so that was on my to-do list this afternoon.

Before going home, however, I was going to the Garvin house to talk with Sheryl. I had called her before leaving the house this morning and she agreed to meet with me. We needed to talk about the missing items that had turned up in the antique store.

I stopped, my eye caught by the display of artichokes, asparagus, and spring peas, each a different shade of green. Dad had been fond of asparagus, but it wasn't one of my favorites. I loved artichokes, though. I bought two, plus what I call the reliables— carrots, celery, onions, potatoes, and a bunch of spinach. The first apricots of the season were here, pale gold with a rosy blush. And strawberries, my favorite. It was still too early for cherries, but one of the vendors had blueberries. I couldn't resist those.

Across the way, Sam was at another stall, picking out a few Yukon Gold potatoes. He told me he was going to roast them along with the chicken. "Dinner is at six," Sam told me.

"See you then." He leaned toward me again, examining my face. "Hmmm. No chocolate. Guess I'll have to settle for a kiss." He followed through, his lips warm on mine. Then he headed up the street. I watched him go, admiring the rear view of a well-built man in a pair of jeans.

I stopped at another stall. Did I have any cucumbers at home in the refrigerator?

I looked up and saw Tamara. She was a few yards

away from me, in front of a stall selling hummus and pita chips. But it didn't look as though she was making a purchase. She stood with her back to the seller's table, scanning the crowd. She must be waiting for someone.

A man walked past me and joined Tamara at the stall. His round face looked puffy. He was dressed in jeans and a gray polo shirt that showed a protruding abdomen. His brown hair was streaked with gray. From this angle, he was in profile. I saw him say something to her. Then I realized I'd seen him before. Thursday, on Main Street, when Sheryl had crossed the street to avoid him.

Who was he, I wondered, to cause such a reaction from Sheryl? And to now get such a dismissive look from Tamara?

But Tamara didn't move away. She looked out at the passersby. I lowered my head and selected a few cucumbers, paying the vendor. When I looked back at Tamara and the man, they were face to face. I couldn't hear what they were saying, but their body language told me they were arguing.

I turned away from the vegetable stall just as Tamara moved from the other stall, heading my direction, with the man a step behind her. Meeting her was unavoidable. She looked startled to see me.

"Hi, Tamara." I glanced at the man. When an introduction wasn't forthcoming, I said, "Hello, I'm Kay Dexter."

Tamara didn't say anything, but the man favored me with a slight smile and broke the awkward silence. "Justin Brownlow."

"Ah, you're Tamara's father." I looked him over. He was the same age as Sheryl. They'd been at school together at California State University in Chico, engaged to be married—before Hallie came between them.

"Yeah. I heard about Hallie. Just drove up from

Sacramento this morning. That's where I live."

Sacramento, I thought. Well, yes, he certainly could have made the drive from the state capital this morning. I could see him coming to town today, to support his daughter now that her mother had been killed. But he'd been in town on Thursday, the day Hallie died. Why? He and Hallie were long-divorced and the story I'd heard from others was that he wasn't a big part of his daughter's life.

"Look, I have to go," Tamara said now. "I promised I'd meet Crystal."

She walked off. I noticed that she wasn't carrying a bag. She hadn't bought anything at the farmers' market. Had she come here just to meet her father?

I turned to Justin Brownlow, making awkward conversation in the hope of finding out more about the relationship between father and daughter. "Just so you know, I'm Betty Garvin's care manager. Are you here for Hallie's funeral?"

He shrugged. "Yeah, whenever that might be. I haven't heard anything from Sheryl about when that's gonna happen. I thought, well, Tamara needs my support. I'll come up to Rocoso and see what I can do."

"Has Tamara said anything about the funeral? I mean, she's Hallie's daughter. I would think she'd have some ideas about the service. Were she and her mother close?"

He took his time answering. "Close? Sometimes. Sometimes not. When Tamara was a teenager, she and her mother didn't get along half the time. They could both be prickly, you know what I mean. With Hallie dying like this— I mean, murdered? Hell. I don't think Tamara wants to talk about it right now." Now Justin checked his wristwatch. "Looks like my parking meter's about to run out. Nice meeting you, Ms. Dexter." Justin turned and made his escape.

Eager to get away from me and my questions? I wondered.

It was time I left, too. I carried my farmers' market purchases to the lot where I'd left my car and stashed them in the trunk. Then I drove to the Garvin house on Juniper Street. Sheryl's rental car was in the driveway. At the curb was a blue Toyota. The UC Berkeley student parking permit visible on the dashboard told me this was Ethan Gillette's car.

Sheryl opened the front door and ushered me into the living room. She waved me toward a chair and took a seat on the sofa.

"Detective Hamilton called," she said. "The medical examiner finished the autopsy so the body has been released. I've made arrangements with a local funeral home to pick up the body. Scheduling the funeral depends on several things. Mother getting out of the hospital, of course. And the availability of the church. Not that the family was particularly religious, but Mother liked to go to services at a church near her house. I want to honor her wishes."

"What about Hallie's wishes?" I asked. She looked blank. "Lanny said Hallie wanted to be cremated."

Sheryl leaned back, her mouth tightening. "I don't know that for sure. It's just his opinion. Besides, none of the family has ever been cremated, to my knowledge."

Her attitude made me wonder if she simply didn't like the idea of cremation. Not uncommon. Or was this another example of Sheryl taking charge and doing things her way?

"Hallie and Lanny were together for several years and they'd even talked about marriage. Hallie may very well have discussed her wishes with him. It would be good if you would consider his feelings."

She looked unconvinced. "That's what Ethan says. I'll give it some thought."

"What about Tamara? Does she have any preferences regarding her mother's funeral?"

"I haven't spoken with her. That exchange you witnessed at the hospital is the extent of my communication with Tamara." She sighed. "Naturally if she has an opinion about her mother's funeral, I'll accommodate it—up to a point. But obviously, she doesn't care for me. And frankly, the feeling is mutual. She's in town. I assume she'll turn up here, eventually."

"I saw Tamara this morning, at the farmers' market. She was with her father."

Sheryl's hands, which had been resting in her lap, now twisted together. "Justin? He's in town, then? I suppose Tamara must have called him. I certainly didn't. I haven't seen him in years."

A lie, again. My client had a way of sidestepping the truth or ignoring it altogether. She had seen Justin on Thursday, on Main Street, when she'd taken steps to avoid being seen by him. Why? And why had Justin claimed he arrived in town this morning? It was possible he had, but he'd been here two days earlier.

It seemed that every topic I'd raised with Sheryl was a sore point. I was about to raise another. "Have the detectives talked with Betty yet?"

"Certainly not." Sheryl frowned. "I don't want her disturbed. She's upset about Hallie's death. I won't have her badgered by the police. Besides, she couldn't possibly help their investigation. She didn't see anything. She was in the family room when— When it happened."

"You don't know that for sure," I said. "She may have seen something. As close as the family room is to the patio, she could very well have heard Hallie talking with whoever killed her."

Sheryl shook her head. "Mother is too frail right now. I've spoken to her new doctor and he agrees with me. He's keeping the police at bay."

For now, I thought. But knowing how dogged Riley could be in investigating a case, he wouldn't be kept at bay for long. In some ways, having Betty in the hospital made it easier for the Garvin family to avoid talking about the murder, and about the killer. Once she was released from the hospital, however, that would change.

Sheryl shifted in her chair, signaling that she was ready to move to another topic. "When you called, you said this had something to do with the things that are missing from the house."

"It does." I settled into the chair. Ethan emerged from the middle bedroom and came up the hall. He greeted me with a pleasant smile. After he'd gone into the kitchen, I continued. "I saw some of the missing items on Thursday. That's why I wanted to talk that afternoon. But when I got here—"

Finding Hallie's body had pushed every other priority out of my mind.

"Yes, Hallie," Sheryl said. "But tell me now. Where did you see those things?"

"At an antique mall here in town." I took out my phone and located the photos I'd taken a few days earlier. "I was there on another matter and happened to see these items in one of the display cases. I took pictures."

I handed Sheryl my phone. She frowned as she examined the images of the silver sugar and creamer, the oval tray with the scratch on the surface, and the silver bowl engraved with a G. As she did so, her face clouded. "That's Mother's bowl, all right. So is the tray with the scratch. And those serving pieces. That's a pattern called Chantilly. Mother has the same silver pattern. How did they get there? Did you talk with the dealer?"

"Yes. She says she bought them from someone. But she wouldn't say who."

Handing back my phone, Sheryl looked indignant. "How dare she? These things were stolen. I've half a mind to go over to that store right now. But—" She stopped, a sour expression on her face. "I have too much going on right now. What with Mother and Hallie. We need an inventory. To find out what else is missing, now that it's clear someone has been stealing from Mother. I'll put Ethan to work on that."

"And I'll email these photos to you." I pressed a few icons and did just that.

Chapter 16
Priest Hole

Badersley Compton, Sunday 2nd September, 1666:
mid-afternoon

"Artemas! But we saw you ride off!"Gabriel gasped. The Cavalier sniggered in response.

"Yes you did: that was clever of me, don't you think? I, um, get these ideas occasionally. Inspiration and improvisation, they say, they are the signs of true genius."

"Who says?" Ben's voice was mocking. Artemas hesitated for a moment and then just shrugged.

"Well, I do anyway. Actually, boy, I am not being entirely truthful with you. Morris here spotted you hiding in the ditch and I decided to let you do the work for us. That was the improvisation bit."

"Go on - and the inspiration part?"

"Well that was you, dear boy: it was inspired of you discovering that priest hole. Still, I guess that makes you half a genius," Artemas smiled.

"Whilst I guess it makes you a total-"

Ben's intended insult was cut off by Artemas. "Watch your language boy! Have you no respect for your elders and betters?"

"Betters?"

"Indeed. In fact I only have your true interest at heart, Benjamin. The Master wants to know more about you. He knows you have talents to read the words that others cannot: that you have the power. He and I can teach you how to use that power if you want it?"

This took Ben by surprise and although he still glared at the man, his interest must have shown on his face because Artemas' eyebrows went up and he smiled, "Ah, I see that you do."

Gabriel frowned and with a small shake of his head, turned to look at Ben, but the Cavalier just laughed. "I also see that Gabriel does not approve. Perhaps the meek fool does not appreciate what he has found. The Master knew who you were: who your great ancestor was. 'Imagine, the blood of the man who imprisoned me,' he said to me just this morning, 'how potent that would be. How perfect the partnership between me, Dantalion, and the descendant of Cornelius. There is nothing we might not accomplish together. Rulers of this and every world: just imagine that!'"

Ben said nothing, but he did imagine and in his mind's eye he saw himself wielding the sort of powers his ancestors must have done, countless millennia before: powers that could defeat demons and dominate men. It was a temptation and he could see that Artemas knew it.

"Enough of this!" Gabriel said breaking the moment. "So then, Artemas, you want the journal. Well here it is," he pointed at the book on the table. Are you sure you want it?"

"Well, that was the general idea."

"You will take it back and use it to free your master and then you will rule through him. It is as simple as that?"

college. That house had been sold to the college after Sam's parents died. It was now home to several research institutes.

In the living room, I examined the stacks of books piled on the tables on either end of the sofa. That usually gave me a clue as to what Sam was working on. Two of the books were by Walter Noble Burns—*The Saga of Billy the Kid* and *The Robin Hood of El Dorado: The Life and Adventures of Joaquin Murrieta, the Celebrated California Bandit*. Next was a book by Mark J. Dworkin, titled *American Mythmaker: Walter Noble Burns and the Legends of Billy the Kid, Wyatt Earp and Joaquin Murrieta*. And here was a copy of *Bad Company*, by Joseph Henry Jackson. I had read that one. It was about outlaws in California.

I left off studying the books and walked over to the round oak table in the dining room, separated from the kitchen by a counter. The polished wood tabletop held a pair of dark blue placemats with matching cloth napkins, set with plates and cutlery. We'd already started on the wine, a buttery chardonnay from a local vineyard. I picked up my glass and watched Sam in the kitchen, transferring the roast chicken to a small oval platter. It smelled wonderful, redolent with garlic, lemon, and spices. Carving knife in hand, Sam sliced into the chicken.

"You're researching outlaws." I reached for the bowls on the counter, one containing steamed broccoli and the other roasted potatoes, and set them on the table.

"California outlaws, specifically Joaquin Murrieta." He carried the platter to the table.

We sat down. I unfolded my napkin, then helped myself to a slice of roast chicken. "Joaquin is a subject that has been extensively mined. Like Billy the Kid."

Murrieta's legendary exploits were an inextricable part of Gold Rush folklore. Had he actually existed? That had been called into question by writers and historians ever since the middle of the nineteenth century.

"I know. Joaquin and Billy. The lore around both of them is fascinating." He served himself broccoli and potatoes. "Billy the Kid actually existed. The Lincoln County War is fact. Both the war and Billy's actions, during and after, were extensively reported, given the time frame, from 1878 to 1881. With Joaquin in the 1850s, we have a lot of fantastic stories. Some could be true and others are pure fiction. But I'm enjoying my research. As always, I hope I'll have something new to say."

"Have you found anything interesting?" I added a spoonful of potatoes to my plate.

Sam reached for his wineglass. "I have. Joaquin never made it to Rocoso County. Neither did Black Bart, as far as I know. But we had our own homegrown outlaw."

I looked up from my plate. "Really? Tell me more."

"His name was Grant. Or maybe Geraint. Which caught my eye, because the name Geraint comes from Welsh folklore. Some of my family tree originates in south Wales, so I've heard the name before. I was doing research at the historical society and I started seeing this name in various primary sources, such as letters and newspaper articles." Sam speared broccoli and waved his fork. "The first Gold Rush in this area was in the early 1850s, then another one came along about twenty years later, in 1871. Jermyn and Rocoso boomed for ten years or so, then went into a long, slow decline. That story is repeated all over the west, with lots of variations in the length of times of the booms and the busts. Ten years was a good run, before the gold played out. And the Rocoso outlaw was active in the mid-1870s."

He grinned and reached for his glass. "Must have been some lively times. Geraint robbed the bank in Jermyn, the one owned by my esteemed great-great-grandfather. I don't know if the outlaw operated alone or if he had a gang, but as the story goes, he had a hideout somewhere near Lost Woman Creek."

I laughed. "What fun. Maybe he's a long-lost relative. I hope you can find out more about him."

"So do I. I'll keep looking. As with any kind of historical research, it's a matter of separating the legend from the fact, and that can be difficult."

We talked about other things while we finished our dinner and wine, then I served slices of the chocolate cake I'd brought with me. I asked about his family and he talked about his son readily enough, but again, he didn't mention his daughter.

Finally, I gave into my curiosity. "How is Stella?"

He took his time answering. "I don't know. She's moved out of Elaine's house."

"When did that happen?"

"A couple of weeks ago. She and her mother had a fight. Stella packed her bags and left. Elaine has no idea where she is. She hasn't contacted Cory, either. She usually stays in touch with him." He sighed. "I hope she's not back into drugs, but it's possible."

I didn't know what to say about Sam's wayward daughter. All I could do was listen, when he wanted to talk about her, which wasn't often.

Tonight was typical. He hadn't said much and now he changed the subject. "We'd better get going. Don't want to be late." He got up from the table and carried his plate to the kitchen. I joined him. Between the two of us, we soon had dishes, glasses, and cutlery in the dishwasher and the leftovers stowed in the refrigerator.

We were going to the end-of-semester concert at Rocoso College. The college orchestra was playing one of my favorites, George Gershwin's *Rhapsody in Blue*, followed by Leonard Bernstein's *Symphonic Dances from*

West Side Story. Rounding out the evening was another Gershwin classic, *An American in Paris*.

I wore black slacks and a gauzy shirt, with swirls of red, pink, and orange. I slipped on my shoes, which I'd removed when I got to Sam's house, and reached for my black chenille jacket. Sam hated ties, so he wore a lightweight crew-neck sweater with his gray slacks and jacket. Sam drove his Honda. As we parked and got out, a car honked at us. Esther Lapine, a retired nurse who was a friend of my mother, was at the wheel, with Mom in the passenger seat. Esther parked in a nearby space and the four of us walked together to Bellweather Hall, the performance space adjacent to the college's music building. It was named after an alum who had made a fortune in the tech industry and had given back to the college with a large donation, specifically to build the hall. The college was on a hill overlooking the city, and the building, several years old, was a centerpiece. There was a patio with tables and chairs outside the hall's main entrance.

Sam gestured in the direction of the entrance, where wide doors opened onto the lobby bar. "Would you ladies like something to drink?"

Both Mom and Esther shook their heads.

"I'll have a glass of pinot noir," I said. "You know the one I like, from Riverbend."

As Sam headed toward the bar, I scanned the crowd and saw Riley Hamilton and his wife Darlene, each holding a glass. Their youngest daughter, Belinda, was a junior at the college, majoring in music, and she played the oboe in the orchestra. They crossed the patio and joined us. We chatted for a few minutes, catching up on family. Riley and Darlene had two other children, Melanie, who was attending California Polytechnic University in San Luis Obispo, and Steven, a grad student at UCLA. Sam returned bearing a pair of glasses, one filled with white wine and the other with red.

"Thanks." I took the glass and sipped, enjoying the rich taste of the pinot noir. Then I leaned toward Riley. Ever since my conversation with Lanny Fitzpatrick at the hospital on Friday, I'd been thinking about what he and Hallie had planned to do with the land Betty Garvin had inherited at Lost Woman Creek—assuming that they had been able to get Betty's okay to move forward. "I have a question."

Riley quirked his eyebrows and gave me his cop look. "If it's about the Garvin investigation, you know I can't talk about that."

"It has to do with growing marijuana."

Now he looked amused. "Are you thinking of adding some pot to your vegetable garden?"

"No. But I'm sure a lot of people have, since marijuana is legal for recreational use."

California voters had legalized medical marijuana back in 1996, with the passage of state proposition 215. Medical pot was sold in dispensaries, located in the larger municipalities, like Rocoso and Appleton. In 2016, the state's voters had taken the big step of legalizing the recreational use of marijuana. Over the past few years, implementation had led to some fits, starts, and growing pains as everyone adjusted to the new reality.

"What's your question?" Riley asked.

"It relates to marijuana growers. Here in the county, we grow all sorts of things. With legalization, it looks to me like we're now at the point where pot is just one more agricultural crop."

Beside me, Sam nodded. "Apples to blueberries to wine grapes. Now marijuana is part of the mix."

Riley flashed a rueful smile. "That's true. Look, we've always had pot farmers in the county. A few acres here and there, mostly up in the hills where it was hard for law enforcement to find the grows. And let's face it, enforcement of state and federal laws has been sporadic. Don't ask, don't tell, that's the way the county supervisors looked at it. The sheriff's department took its lead from that. After the medical marijuana initiative was approved in the nineties, it didn't take a crystal ball to figure out that eventually the state would legalize recreational use. Now the supervisors are the ones who are making laws affecting growers and pot sales."

I sipped my wine. "Let's set aside the people who have a couple of plants in their garden, for their personal use. How many commercial pot growers would you estimate we have in the county? And how many are legal?"

"The county has a population of fifty-one thousand, give or take." Riley swirled the wine in his glass. "I hear the sheriff's department and the county planning department estimate that we have as many as sixteen hundred commercial marijuana growers in Rocoso County."

My eyes widened. "I had no idea."

He nodded. "Most people don't. I'd bet more than half of those growers are illegal, meaning that they're not adhering to the provisions of the state law. Most of the illegal growers have taken steps to get legal. They applied for commercial growing licenses and they're paying taxes. They've even formed the Rocoso Cannabis Alliance. They join the local organizations like the Rotary and they get involved in schools and community organizations. And they give money to local charities."

"I can second that," Darlene said. "I'm on several boards, including the Friends of the Library and the River Playhouse. The Cannabis Alliance has made several large donations over the past year."

Esther sniffed with disapproval, and Mom joined her

in that opinion. "They're outlaws trying to become respectable. Like bootleggers back in the Depression, going into legitimate businesses."

Mom had voted against the recreational use initiative, but I had voted for it. The city of Rocoso tended to be more liberal than other, more rural areas of the county. Older residents had been opposed, while younger people went into the affirmative column. County statistics showed that the legalization vote had reflected those demographics.

There was an obvious historical parallel and Mom had just referred to it. "They're not outlaws any more, Mom," I said. "Prohibition didn't stem the urge to drink, or the liquor trade. It made things worse and led to more crime. Same thing with marijuana. The laws against it didn't make most people stop smoking pot. I've always thought we should legalize marijuana and tax it, which we are doing."

"I agree with you about Prohibition." Sam took a sip of his wine. "We had stills and bootleggers here in the county all through the twenties and thirties. And the crime that went with it. There was a bootlegger in Pellgrove who was responsible for several murders. As for the current situation, the Cannabis Alliance commissioned a study from UC Davis, where I used to teach. The results show that legal cannabis cultivation contributes over three million dollars to the local economy. That's on a par with other agricultural pursuits here in the county, such as timber, cattle, wine, apples, and other crops. The study says the financial contribution from cannabis is sure to increase. That's the positive. The negative is outlined in an environmental impact report from UC Berkeley talking about the negative effects such as degradation of habitat, increased water use, traffic, things like that."

"I'm just coming at it from a law enforcement perspective," Riley said. "The legal growers are trying to be good citizens. And they would like it if the county would get rid of the illegal growers."

"Less competition?" Darlene asked.

"That's not the only reason," Riley said. "There's a prevailing belief that the illegal growers are responsible for most of the problems, like crime, noise, and environmental damage."

"That's painting things with a broad brush," Sam said. "Of course, we at the college also hear that our students are responsible for most of the crime and noise in town, and that's not true. I'm not sure that the pot growers are the ones causing most of the environmental damage."

"That's a big one, though," Riley said. "That and water use. Marijuana is a very thirsty crop, and when we've had a drought for several years, it just puts a strain on resources. Land use issues, like not wanting to have pot farms on marginal land that would be better left alone. We've had lots of problems with illegal grows and pollution. Illegal growers use all sorts of pesticides and poisons, indiscriminately. They don't care about anything but their crops. And they're encroaching on public land, like the state park up by Starfield. We found out about that one because the growers had diverted a creek and they were polluting the watershed. That was having a bad effect on a legitimate fruit grower farther downstream. Something similar happened last year near Camacho, where the growers rerouted a stream. In both cases, the pot growers were also killing a lot of wildlife. We did a joint operation with the state and cleaned out those two farms, but there are still a lot of illegal grows all over the county. I don't think all the growers are going to embrace legality and line up to get permits. Because that costs them money and it means they have to toe the line in terms of regulations. Legalizing pot isn't going to make the problems go away."

I took another sip of wine. "Maybe it will mitigate the problems. I know we have our own homegrown pot farmers. Are you aware of growers looking to move into the county? Any land that's considered up for grabs?"

Riley nodded. "I heard a grower from Trinity County just bought a parcel between here and Appleton. There are others, much to the chagrin of county government officials. There's a feeling that we have enough growers of our own without adding transplants from other parts of California."

Like Lanny Fitzpatrick, I thought. If Hallie had managed to get control over a portion of her mother's land at Lost Woman Creek, Lanny and Hallie might have joined the ranks of incomers who planned to start marijuana operations here in the county. Hallie's death had sounded the end of that proposal. Was the land, and Hallie's plans for it, a factor in her death?

A bell rang, signaling first call for the concert. People began moving toward the entrance to Bellweather Hall.

I downed the rest of my wine and set the glass on a nearby table. "We'd better find our seats."

Chapter 22

I WOKE UP AND stretched my hands over my head. Sam was on his side, his head propped up on the pillow. He smiled. "I've been watching you sleep. You snore. Not very loud. But a snore nonetheless."

"Thank you for that critique." I ran a hand over his bare chest, the red-brown hair tickling my fingers. Then I snuggled closer. He kissed me on the lips and then his mouth trailed down my throat to my breasts. One thing led to another and it was much later when he got out of bed. He pulled on a pair of shorts and padded barefoot to his kitchen. A short time later I heard the hiss of the coffee maker.

I propped myself higher on the pillows. Sam liked to read in bed of an evening, and he had several books stacked on his nightstand. Unlike the historical research books that crowded the shelves in his living room and office, these were mysteries and thrillers. His wire-rimmed reading glasses sat next to the stack. I picked up the first book, a historical mystery set in San Francisco, with a bookmark stuck midway between the pages. I glanced at the jacket copy. Did I want to borrow the novel when Sam was finished reading it? The jacket blurb caught my interest, so yes, I did.

I set down the book as Sam returned to the bedroom, bearing two mugs of coffee. He got back into bed and we talked a while longer as we drank that first mug of coffee. Later, we showered and dressed. I'd brought casual clothes to wear this morning. My concert clothes were stashed in an overnight bag.

Sam cooked breakfast—eggs scrambled with herbs

and goat cheese, accompanied by bacon and sourdough toast. We carried our plates out to the bistro table on the deck overlooking his small backyard.

I spooned plum preserves onto my toast. "Doing anything the rest of the day?"

He shrugged, reaching for a piece of bacon. "Puttering around the house. Always something to do around here, such as laundry. You?"

"I was going to work in the garden," I said. "But I've changed my mind. Let's go up to Lost Woman Creek and soak in the hot springs. Maybe we'll find out where your local outlaw had his hideout."

Besides, I thought, after finding out that Betty Garvin had inherited the property from her late sister, I wanted to take another look at the old resort hotel and the surrounding area.

"Great idea. It's been a while since I was up there."

We finished eating, lingering over more coffee. Sam stood and began gathering up the breakfast dishes.

I had driven my own Prius to Sam's house the night before. This morning, he followed me back to my house in his Honda. Though I'd left plenty of food out the night before, the cats rushed to the door with a chorus of meows and chirps, declaring how neglected they were. I mollified them with food and cuddles. In the bedroom, I stripped off my clothes and donned my teal blue tank suit. Over that, I put on a T-shirt and my hiking pants, the ones with lots of pockets, then rummaged in the closet for my hiking boots. That done, I stuck a large towel into my pack, along with a water bottle and snacks. I also took my binoculars and birding field guide. The basics, cell phone, keys, ID, went into my pockets.

Lost Woman Creek was midway between Rocoso and Jermyn, a distance of about twenty-four miles and another three thousand feet higher. Sam piloted his

Accord through the north side of town, heading out of Rocoso. Here the river curved, flowing through a broad, grassy meadow dotted with trees. A few miles on, the meadow gave way to a series of rolling hills. The highway twisted and curved as we headed into the mountains. Live oaks lined the road, along with stands of California buckeyes, showing clusters of white flowers amid the dark green leaves, their gray-green trunks covered with moss and lichen. At higher elevations, these trees gave way to black oaks, incense cedars, and pines of every variety—digger, knobcone, ponderosa. Higher still, up at Jermyn, were Jeffrey and sugar pines, the latter nearly as tall as sequoias. This late in May, the wildflowers were putting on a show. I spotted stands of purple lupine and yellow monkeyflower, brightening both sides of the road.

A sign up ahead told me we were nearing County Road 12, which meandered to the west, ultimately reaching Osprey Lake and the town of Lakeview, some twenty miles away. Sam signaled a left turn and slowed, waiting for an oncoming car to pass before he made the turn. A mile or so from the highway, we drove past what remained of the long-abandoned village of Creekside. In the years when the hot springs resort was a popular destination, this small community had businesses, a school, and a post office. Once the hotel burned, though, the town began to wither. The post office closed and the children who lived here were bused to Lakeview schools. What was left of Creekside was mostly building foundations, where bricks, stone, and wood had collapsed into holes in the ground.

Just past a derelict building, Sam made a right turn into a small parking lot. Here at the trailhead were a couple of picnic tables and a vault toilet, maintained by the county. There were other cars parked here, which meant we wouldn't be the only people on the fire trail, or down at the creek. Not surprising on this bright sunny morning in May.

The sky was a clear blue. When I looked to the north, I caught a glimpse of Mount Lassen, with its permanent patches of snow. The mountain had the highest annual snowfall in California. It was an active but dormant volcano at the end of the Cascade Range. It had last erupted from 1914 to 1917, and the mountain's May 1915 explosion had thrown boulders for miles and filled the air with ash that drifted over 250 miles.

Sam and I set out on the fire trail, which had once been an old railroad spur line. For the first mile or so it was straight and fairly level, then the trail twisted and turned through a canyon, ending in some six miles or so at a ghost town called Zena. Years ago there had been still-visible remnants of that old mining camp, with a few foundations here and there, boarded-up tunnels, rusted flumes and rockers, and a cemetery with weathered headstones dating back to the nineteenth century. I hadn't been up there in several years, but my last hike to the end of the trail revealed that vandals and the elements had done their work. There wasn't much left to show the place had ever been inhabited.

To our right, the woods were thick with pines and oaks. On our left was a meadow, mostly open but with stands of trees here and there. The meadow was bright with spring wildflowers—cows clover with reddish-purple flowers, wild hyacinth in pale blue, western columbines of deep orange hue, purple lupine, and pink-petaled fireweed.

Mountain lions and bears roamed the upper reaches of the canyon, but on this stretch, we were more likely to see deer and chipmunks. Last year there had been a sighting of a fisher, an elusive forest mammal that was in decline, due to hunting and habitat loss. There were isolated populations in the Northern Sierra Nevada, but this was the first time the creature had been seen in these parts. Wildlife biologists from all over the country had converged on the county.

I stopped walking as movement caught my eye in the meadow to our left. I raised my binoculars and focused. "White-tailed kite," I said.

"I see it." Sam had his binoculars to his eyes.

The small raptor, with its white body and darker wingtips, was hunting, hovering over the scrub at the end of the meadow. Suddenly it plunged toward the ground and came up a moment later, a small rodent in its claws.

I scanned the meadow again, looking for movement, and saw small birds flitting in and out of the vegetation. They moved fast, so it was hard to get them in view, but I finally determined that they were white-crowned sparrows. High above, an Anna's hummingbird swooped and chirruped, then landed on a bush, staying still long enough for me to focus on its iridescent green feathers and ruby throat.

"If you were an outlaw, where would you hide?" I asked.

Sam rubbed his unshaven chin. "I've been thinking about that. The hot springs resort was built in the 1890s, so it wasn't here during the local gold rush in the 1870s. This part of the county wasn't as productive as the mines up in Jermyn. The miners at Zena never pulled that much gold out of the ground." He pointed farther down the fire trail. "The canyon narrows between here and the old mining camp, about three miles on, I'd guess."

"Right. There are cliffs and crevices. And from what I hear, caves."

"A lot of them are on private property and fenced off. Too dangerous. I guess if I was an outlaw, that part of the canyon would be a great place to have a hideout."

"That's an exploration for another day. Today I want to soak."

We started walking again. To our right, a fence, overgrown with blackberry bushes, separated the fire trail from the old resort property. It was too early in the year for the thick, tangled vines to produce fruit, but in the late summer, the bushes would be loaded. I'd often seen hikers filling containers with the plump, juicy berries, their fingers stained purple. Of course, many of the berries were out of reach of the humans, leaving more of the bounty for the birds and animals.

A mile in, we reached a locked gate and a road that was more weeds than dirt, once used by guests to drive down to the hotel, on the south bank of Lost Woman Creek. Fifty feet past the gate, there was an opening in the fence. A footpath led down to the creek. The way I heard it, the county had come to some arrangement with the landowner, who was at that time Ruby Waldron, to allow hikers passage through the property to reach the hot springs pools that lined both sides of the creek.

The path, bordered by fiddleneck fern, zigzagged down the slope. We walked slowly, keeping an eye out for the poison oak that lurked in the shade of the trees. Above us, an acorn woodpecker, black and white with its distinctive red cap, landed on a snag, a low branch of a dead oak tree. It began tapping, using its beak to drive a hole into the trunk. The tree was already used as a woodpecker granary. Hundreds of holes had been driven into the trunk, and most of them held acorns. The woodpeckers had been known to use the sides of houses as granaries, much to the chagrin of homeowners here in the mountains.

Sam and I rounded a bend in the trail. The old hotel, once two stories high, came into view. The high chain-link fence surrounding the building had been erected several years before, when a bunch of high school kids had gone exploring. Several of them had climbed up what was left of the wide lobby staircase to the second floor. They were skylarking, as my mother would put it, and one of them fell, breaking a leg as he landed on the flagstone floor below.

Two-story wings with rooms for hotel guests had stretched on either side of the lobby, the second floor reached by the central staircase as well as other stairwells at the end of each wing. Now the second floor was gone. What remained of the burnt-out building had sheets of plywood covering the gaping spaces that had once been first-floor windows and doors.

In the old days, the hotel had been famous for the quality of its restaurant, located at the rear of the lobby, where a bow-shaped veranda loomed over the creek. Wide stone steps led down the bank to a bathhouse with changing rooms and a mineral pool. It was gone now, of course, the pool filled in. More steps descended to the creek, which was full of shallow pools where the hot spring water flowed into the cold water coming down the canyon.

Sam and I made our way down the footpath. As we walked, I looked with new eyes at the derelict hotel and the land that surrounded it. Betty's daughters had conflicting plans for this place. Sheryl wanted to rebuild the resort. She was already consulting with an architect. Never mind that she didn't at present have title to the land, unless she convinced her mother to sign it over to her. If Sheryl went ahead with the development, I suspected that would be the end of public access to the hot springs, at least for free. I could see a scenario where people would pay to spend a day at the resort.

According to Lanny Fitzpatrick, Hallie had proposed to use the land to cultivate marijuana. The creek certainly provided a water source, but as Lanny had told me the other day, pot was a thirsty crop. Legal marijuana cultivation in Rocoso County was just a few years old. There would be obstacles from those who didn't want to see a pot farm on this land. Hallie's murder meant that her plans for the pot farm were out of the picture. I wondered, though. Did Hallie have a will? If so, who were her heirs? Tamara, of course, since she was Hallie's daughter. But might Lanny also be an heir? He and Hallie had been together for three years.

When we reached the fence, we headed to the left, skirting around the building to the creek. As I suspected, we weren't the first people here. Several of the creek's pools were occupied. Some of the younger people were college students who greeted Sam as Professor Jermyn. Rocoso was a college town, so that happened wherever we went.

We found a spot farther upstream that offered a bit more privacy, though there were still people around. I sat down on a broad, flat rock and set the pack at my feet, then took off my boots and socks. I removed my T-shirt and unzipped my hiking pants, slipping out of the clothes to reveal my swimsuit. Next to me, Sam was doing the same, stripping down to a pair of dark blue trunks that hugged his hips. Sunlight glinted off the red-gold hair on his broad chest. A couple of younger women nearby eyed him with admiration.

I smiled, amused. "Middle-aged sexy."

He turned to me. "What?"

"Never mind."

The pool was about eighteen inches deep, warm with several spots where hot water seeped from the rocks. I immersed myself.

Sam stretched out beside me, most of his body submerged. "Ah, that feels good. I've been having some pain in my shoulder."

"The left one." That was the arm he'd injured in the motorcycle accident.

"Yeah. The doctor says it's arthritis."

"Welcome to the club." I too had some issues, involving my knee. Neither of us was getting any younger.

I leaned against him, my head pillowed on his shoulder. I felt his lips brush my temple. We talked, relishing the warmth of the sun and the water. Eventually, I found myself dozing off. What a pleasant way to spend a Sunday afternoon. Work seemed very far away.

Chapter 23

SO MUCH FOR ESCAPING work, I thought, as I set the phone on the end table. I'd just gotten a call from Sheryl Garvin.

It was the middle of the afternoon by the time Sam and I returned from our sojourn at the hot springs. He dropped me off at my house and headed home. As I unlocked the front door, I told myself I should work in my garden. But I felt more like taking a nap. I removed my hiking gear and swimsuit and put on shorts and a T-shirt. Outside, I hung my damp suit and towel to dry in the afternoon sunshine. I poured myself a tall glass of iced tea from the pitcher I kept in the refrigerator. Then I stretched out on the sofa with a book. The cats joined me, one on my lap and the others tucked in around me. I woke up when the phone rang.

Sheryl Garvin's voice sounded subdued. "Mother was released from the hospital this morning."

"That's good news."

"I think they should have kept her longer."

Was she saying that because of Betty's health? Or was it because she didn't want the police to talk with Betty about what she'd seen or heard the day Hallie died?

"Anyway, she's home now. I wanted to let you know." Sheryl paused. "That's not the only reason I called, though. Ethan and I have come up with a list of things we think are missing from the house. Can you come over?"

"Sure." I looked at my faded denim shorts, covered with cat hair. "I can be there in half an hour."

I dislodged the cats and headed for the bedroom. Then I put on slacks and a shirt and slipped my feet into a pair of low-heeled shoes. With my handbag on one shoulder and my keys dangling from my right hand, I locked the house and got into my Prius.

"Coffee?" Sheryl asked when she greeted me at the front door. "I just made a fresh pot."

"I'd like to see Betty first," I said.

Sheryl looked reluctant. "She's probably asleep, back in her bedroom."

"I'll just look in on her." I didn't wait for an answer. Sheryl was playing gatekeeper, but Betty was my client and I wanted to see how she was doing after her stay at the hospital. I went down the hall to the master bedroom.

Betty was stretched out on the bed, a light coverlet over her, two pillows propping her head. I stood in the doorway, thinking she was asleep, but her eyes fluttered and she looked at me. "Kay."

"Hi, Betty. How are you feeling? I didn't get much opportunity to talk with you while you were in the hospital."

"Better," she said. "I had a heart attack. A little one. But it sure got my attention. That, and . . ." A shadow passed over her face as her voice trailed off. I guessed she was thinking about Hallie.

"You rest and get stronger," I told her.

She nodded and her eyes closed again. As I watched, her breathing became slow and regular. She was asleep.

I went back to the living room, where Sheryl waited, an anxious expression on her face. "She was awake. I said hello. I think she's gone back to sleep now." I smiled. "I'll have that coffee now."

"Of course." Sheryl went through to the kitchen. As I followed her, I noticed the china cabinet looked bare. Several items that had been on the shelves had been removed and were now arrayed on one end of the dining table, along with a large wooden chest, the kind used to hold flatware.

The kitchen table held a square pan containing brownies and a platter with an assortment of cookies—chocolate chip, oatmeal raisin, and the cinnamon-dusted sugar variety known as Snickerdoodles. Someone had been making inroads on the chocolate chip cookies.

Sheryl took two mugs from the rack, poured coffee from the carafe on the counter, and handed a mug to me. "There's milk and half-and-half in the fridge."

I added milk to my coffee, then glanced out the window over the kitchen sink. Ethan and Richard were in the backyard, talking. Ethan looked relaxed, while Richard, in casual clothes, managed to look quite formal.

"Help yourself to cookies." Sheryl waved at the table. "Ever since Thursday, the neighbors have been bringing food. It was the same when Dad died."

"That's an old tradition, bringing food to the family so they won't have to cook."

I chose a Snickerdoodle from the platter and followed Sheryl into the family room. We sat on the sofa and Sheryl set her mug on the end table. "Now that the medical examiner has released Hallie's body, we're going ahead with a memorial service, later this week. We'll be having people over afterward, so I got out the good silverware."

"The box on the dining room table." I bit into the cookie, scattering crumbs down the front of my shirt.

Sheryl nodded. "Gorham Chantilly. It was a wedding gift, so Mother's had it for ages. A service for twelve, plus serving pieces. I just got it out and opened the box. I counted pieces and I think most of the flatware is there. But I'm sure several of the serving pieces are gone. It seems to me there was a carving knife that went with the set."

"Could I see a piece of the silverware?" I asked. "I'd

like to compare it with those photos I took at the antique store."

"Good idea." Sheryl got up and went through the kitchen to the dining room, returning a moment later with a knife, fork, and spoon. The silver pattern had a Rococo look, with a scroll design on the handles and fleur-de-lis accents at the end. I laid the silverware on the table, then pulled out my cell phone and looked at the photos I'd taken a few days earlier. The silver serving pieces I'd seen in the case consisted of two large serving spoons, a serving fork, a pie and cake server, a large ladle, and a carving knife. The ladle and serving fork were from a different pattern, but the serving spoons, pie and cake server, and carving knife looked like Chantilly.

"That's the carving knife, I'm sure of it," Sheryl said.

"Maybe. It's possible the dealer acquired the pieces through legitimate means. But I agree, it looks like the same silver pattern."

"I must confess, I don't know exactly how many serving pieces there were."

"That makes it hard to know what's missing. How long has it been since you used the silver service?"

Sheryl paused, thinking. "We used to get out the silver every year, at Thanksgiving and Christmas. But those family dinners were a long time ago. I think the last time we used the silver service was at my father's funeral, a few years ago. We had a reception here afterward."

Then the silver flatware and service pieces got packed away in the box, I thought, not seen again until now. "May I see the list you and Ethan came up with?"

Sheryl reached for a lined yellow pad on the end table, the top sheet covered with black ink scribbles. I brushed cookie crumbs from my hands and took the pad from her. The inventory was several pages long. The missing items, listed with brief descriptions, were small, easy to remove from the house.

"I went through Mother's jewelry and several items are missing. I wondered if Hallie and her friend were responsible."

Interesting that she was ready to accuse Hallie and Lanny of stealing. It spoke, once again, to the enmity between the sisters.

"I have a feeling these things have been disappearing for a long time. You said yourself that Hallie hadn't visited that often over the past couple of years."

Sheryl looked somewhat abashed. "Of course, you're right. A lot of this stuff must have gone missing before they showed up last week. That engraved bowl, for example."

For the most part, the thief had been careful, choosing items that were unlikely to be missed right away. Such as the serving pieces from the silver set, unused since the last Garvin funeral.

"You should report this to the police. That way it's on record that the items were stolen. They can talk with the antique dealer and find out who sold her the items I saw in her case. I'm sure they'll want proof that these things belonged to Betty."

"How do I do that?" Sheryl sounded exasperated.

"It's not as daunting as it sounds." I pointed at one item on the list, a brooch, described as a gold oval decorated with three small diamonds. It had come to Betty after the death of her mother. "You say this pin was a bequest from your maternal grandmother, I'm sure your cousin Tish could corroborate that. There must be family photos of Betty wearing the pin. Same situation with the other jewelry. And the silver pieces, such as the engraved bowl. Look through your photo albums and digital pictures to see if you have shots of Betty wearing the jewelry or holding the engraved bowl that the antique dealer now has. Check to see if you have pictures of the silver service, and of the china cabinet and its contents."

Sheryl had moved past annoyance and was now thinking along the same lines. She took the yellow pad from me. "We did some sort of inventory when my father died. I'll see if I can find that. As for pictures, I'm sure we have photos of the reception after Dad's funeral, which would show the silver pieces being used."

"Yeah, we have pictures," Ethan said as he and Richard came through the sliding door from the patio. "I remember shooting pictures on my cell phone. They're stored on the cloud. I'll look through them."

Sheryl's expression softened as she looked at her son. "That would be so helpful."

Ethan made a beeline for the kitchen. "Want coffee, Dad?"

"Yes, thanks." Richard looked at Sheryl and me as though he wanted to be included in the conversation. But Sheryl wasn't having any of it. She had difficulty hiding her disdain for him. Why was he here? I wondered. Other than being present for a family funeral, giving the outward appearance of support, was this a last hurrah, an attempt to save his marriage?

Ethan handed a mug to his father. Then he hovered over the platter, scooping up two chocolate chip cookies.

"How many of those have you had?" A faint smile lightened Richard's face.

Sheryl smiled, too. "He loves chocolate chip cookies. I think he's eaten half of them."

With a cheeky grin, Ethan said, "Hey, there's no such thing as too many chocolate chip cookies," He took a generous bite from one of the cookies. The doorbell rang. "I'll get it." He disappeared, a cookie in each hand, then called, "Mom? It's one of the neighbors."

Sheryl got up from the sofa and headed for the living

room, leaving me alone with Richard. He sipped coffee and looked me over as though he somehow found me wanting. "So you're the care manager. Just what is it that you do?"

I gave him the standard overview that I gave to prospective clients. He asked lots of questions, the way a lawyer would, which was not surprising, since he was an attorney. Initially, it seemed that he was probing to learn more about the business of being a care manager. But he wanted more specifics about the services I'd been performing for Betty and Sheryl.

"You've hired all these caregivers," he said.

I took a sip of coffee before answering. "I came up with a care plan based on my assessment of Betty's situation, reviewed it with Sheryl, and implemented it. I oversee the care, visiting Betty regularly, to see how she's doing. We had just started the relationship when—"

He finished my sentence. "When Hallie showed up. I gather she was like that, though Sheryl and I never had much contact with her."

I nodded, thinking about my short tenure as Betty's care manager. With everything that had happened, and Sheryl's plans to move back to Rocoso, would that business relationship continue after the dust had settled, after the furor and drama surrounding Hallie's death had died down? I wasn't sure. It was business, of course, but I had quickly developed a bond with Betty Garvin. It was like that with many of my clients.

Richard was talking again, and I got the distinct impression he was trying to find out how much I knew about Betty's financial situation—and whether I was involved.

"Not really," I said. "Sheryl's responsible for that. She's a signatory on Betty's bank account and she told me she has power of attorney, financially and for health care."

"Yes, of course." Richard raised his coffee mug to his lips as something resembling a smile briefly quirked his thin mouth. "I expect Sheryl will be taking a more active role in managing her mother's life."

Interesting that he should say that. Sheryl had told me the marriage was over. Did he know of her plans to move back to Rocoso?

"Betty is quite well off," he said. "Oh, her pension from teaching isn't that much. Nor is her Social Security. But she and her late husband had some decent-sized investments, mostly certificates of deposit. And there's the income from the rental properties."

Plus the potentially lucrative land up at Lost Woman Creek, which had been left to Betty alone. I had not been aware of that, or the extent of the rental property income, until Sheryl's cousin Tish Lehigh told me. "How many rentals does Betty own?"

"A dozen houses, I think. I understand they are all rented out, generating income every month. Of course, now that Hallie's out of the way, Sheryl will have complete control." Richard stopped, as though he realized just how mercenary that sounded.

I didn't respond. Richard's words hinted that Sheryl was planning to take over managing her mother's life—and her mother's assets. Was she? Now that Hallie was, as he put it, out of the way, there was no one to actively oppose Sheryl. Unless Tamara would, as Hallie's presumed heir. But Tamara gave all appearances of being uninterested in her grandmother's life.

"Complete control." That's what Richard said. What did that mean?

Sheryl wanted control of the land at Lost Woman Creek, so she could build the hot springs resort she was proposing. Lanny said Sheryl was trying to persuade Betty to sign over the land to her, and Hallie had objected strenuously to that.

Richard now looked as though he thought he'd said too much. He quickly amended his statement. "I meant that, with Hallie gone, Sheryl is the only one left to look after her mother. She can be her mother's guardian."

Guardian.

Interesting word choice. When it came to elderly people, "guardian" was a legal term. As an attorney, Richard surely knew that. If Sheryl was planning to become her mother's guardian, that meant far more than just looking after Betty. To become her mother's legal guardian, Sheryl would have to file a conservatorship motion in the Rocoso County Court. That would certainly give Sheryl the complete control her husband had mentioned.

However, getting herself designated as Betty's guardian would not be easy for Sheryl to do, nor should it be. I knew that from experience with past clients and their families. To make that happen, Betty would first have to be declared incompetent. Sheryl would have to file a petition listing all the reasons why a conservatorship of her mother was needed, provide the documentation, explain why various alternatives wouldn't work, thus making a conservatorship the only choice.

But the alternatives were working, in my opinion. The alternatives included me, as Betty's care manager, and the various caregivers like Louise Beltran and Bea Lovell, who helped with activities of daily living, cleaned her house and shopped for groceries, the Meals on Wheels volunteers who delivered prepared food, and Sheryl herself, who handled most of her mother's finances. Yes, Betty needed assistance. She needed caregivers. Certainly, she was forgetful. She had started some fires when attempting to cook for herself. And she had attempted to give jewelry to several people. But with the team I'd assembled, Betty had been doing well.

But incompetent? I didn't think she had crossed that line. There was no evidence that Betty wasn't paying her bills, because most of them were automatic payments, according to Sheryl. And Sheryl had the checkbook. I'd had elderly clients who'd been scammed by people on the Internet or the phone, but Sheryl said her mother had so far escaped such attempts to separate her from her money. Betty wasn't online, didn't have a computer or smartphone, and wasn't the least bit interested in email. She had Caller ID on her phone and her daughter had drummed into her head that she shouldn't answer the phone unless she recognized the number.

No, I didn't think there was enough evidence to convince a judge to declare Betty incompetent. And if Sheryl made such a move, I would have something to say about it.

Undue influence. That was a legal term. It meant one person was pressuring a vulnerable elder to do something. The person applying the pressure could be a family member, or someone else, convincing a person like Betty to think one way, or to act in what might not be her best interests.

Was Sheryl exerting undue influence over Betty, to convince her mother to sign over the property at Lost Woman Creek?

Complete control of the land would give Sheryl free rein for her plans to develop the area into a hot springs resort. That was the scenario Lanny had suggested during our conversation on Friday. His interpretation, colored by his association with Hallie, hinted that Sheryl was rapacious, emboldened, and only interested in money and property.

Still, if Betty signed over the land, I wasn't sure such a move would stand. Betty's will divided her assets equally between her daughters, as primary beneficiaries, Sheryl had told me. With Hallie dead, I wasn't sure what would happen. Tamara might inherit, as a secondary beneficiary. If Hallie had a will, and Lanny found it, we'd have to wait and see what it might say.

Sheryl walked into the kitchen carrying a covered Pyrex dish, followed by Ethan. She set it on the counter. "More food from the neighbors."

Ethan pulled off the lid and examined the contents. "It's a casserole, with green chiles and lots of cheese. Looks good. I'm going to do a taste test." He opened a cupboard and pulled out a plate, then rummaged in a drawer for cutlery. After putting a generous serving of the casserole on the plate, he raised a fork to his mouth. "Oh, wow. That's got some bite to it. You ought to try some, Dad."

"I believe I will." Richard took a plate from the cupboard.

I stood up, ready to leave. "Sheryl, can we talk in private?"

"Sure. Let's go outside."

We went through the living room and out the front door. Pausing on the porch, Sheryl leaned over the orange pot that held succulents and pulled out a stray weed.

"I saw you on Thursday, before Hallie died. You were outside the Marigold Cafe. With Alex Delattre."

Emotions flickered over Sheryl's face as she straightened. She sighed. "I told you my marriage was over. It's complicated."

That's what people usually say, in my experience.

"Richard and I have, well, I guess you could say we've outgrown each other. I've only stayed with him this long because of Ethan."

Essentially the same thing she'd told me a few days earlier at the bed and breakfast. I waited to see if she would provide more information.

She chose her words carefully. "It's awkward, Richard showing up here, right now. Ostensibly because of Hallie's death, and the funeral. It's not as though he had any sort of relationship with my sister. He barely saw her. I'm sure the last time was at Dad's funeral. I suppose he thinks he's being supportive. Or his version of supportive." She gazed at the rhododendron next to the porch, then turned back to me.

"I met Alex a few months ago. It was business at first. After Aunt Ruby died and left the land at Lost Woman Creek to Mother. I thought, why not resurrect the old hot springs resort? Mother seemed to be enthusiastic about the idea. She has all sorts of photos of the land and the old hotel, taken back in its heyday, before the fire. I thought it would be useful to consult with an architect here in town, kick around some ideas, show the pictures, and come up with a modern equivalent to the way the hotel looked back then. I searched online for architects here in Rocoso and found Marie Devorno."

"Whose office is near mine. I saw you leaving her office Wednesday afternoon." I wondered if it was Marie who'd steered Sheryl my way when she decided she needed help with her mother.

Sheryl nodded. "I looked at Marie's website and thought she might be a good choice, so I set up a meeting with her during one of my visits here. It was late afternoon and Marie was heading to a gallery opening after our appointment. She invited me to go with her. So I did. Alex was one of the artists exhibiting at the gallery. We got to talking and hit it off. I told him about my plans for the property. He seemed interested and the next day he went with me up to Lost Woman Creek. From there we went to his house in Lakeview. He cooked dinner for me and ..."

She paused. "One thing led to another. The

relationship has been going on since then. Alex is divorced and I'd been planning to leave Richard. I just hadn't decided where to go at that point. I didn't want to stay in Seattle, in Richard's orbit. Circumstances were drawing me back to California—my mother and her situation, Ethan going to school in Berkeley. Once I met Alex, things were a lot clearer. I'd come back to Rocoso."

"That's why you were thinking about buying the house next door to Betty."

"Living next door might be a little too close, I decided. Though it's a nice house. I just want to be somewhere here in Rocoso, close enough to check on Mother. And in my own place, so I'll have my privacy." Sheryl frowned. "I didn't plan on my sister showing up to muddy the waters. Much less her getting killed. And for what it's worth, I didn't kill her. It happened the way I said it did. I found her like that."

She sounded defensive now. I steered the conversation away from the subject of Hallie's death, at least temporarily. "I'm curious about something else. The same day I saw you with Alex," I said, "you came out of the bank and then you went back inside. It looked as though you wanted to avoid a man who was walking toward the bank. I didn't know who he was at the time. But now I do, because I met him yesterday at the farmers' market. It was Justin Brownlow, Hallie's ex-husband. Tamara's father."

"I didn't know Justin was in town," Sheryl said, tight-lipped. "I suppose he was here on business. He works for Caltrans. They have offices all over the state, probably here as well. I didn't want him to see me, because I didn't want to talk with him. For reasons that should be obvious."

Indeed they were, I thought. Sheryl was still angry at Justin. She'd been engaged to him, but he'd married

Hallie instead, because Hallie had been pregnant with Tamara. That had colored her relationship with her sister ever since, though it had never been easy.

But that wasn't the most important thing, as far as I was concerned. What interested me was the fact that Justin was in town the same day Hallie died. Yet he had not seen fit to share that information with anyone, especially the authorities. When I saw him yesterday, he claimed he'd just driven up from Sacramento. Why was he here on Thursday? Was it business, as Sheryl suggested? Was he here to see Tamara? But to hear Tamara tell it, she hadn't been in Rocoso when her mother died.

I would have to ask Justin, the next time I saw him.

Sheryl went back into the house and I walked out to the street, where I'd parked my car. The front door of the house across the street opened and someone came out. It was Ginny Cavalieri, the neighbor girl who'd been in the meadow behind the Garvin house at the time Hallie died. She stared at me, took a step, and hesitated. Then, as though she'd found her resolve, she crossed the street toward me. I waited next to my car, keys in hand.

"Hi, Ginny."

"Hi. Mrs. Garvin is out of the hospital. We were coming home from church and saw her with her daughter and grandson. They were getting her out of the car and into her house. Did you come over to visit her?"

"I did. I talked with her and she's feeling better. Having a heart attack, even a small one, is serious. Is there something you want, Ginny?"

She nodded. "It's about Thursday, the day that lady, Mrs. Garvin's other daughter, died."

"Yes, you told the detective you saw someone come out the back gate, someone wearing jeans and a T-shirt."

"I did," Ginny said. "But I was thinking about it this morning, after I saw Mrs. Garvin coming home. I remembered something that I didn't tell the detective. I'm pretty sure that person I saw coming out the gate had purple hair."

"I thought you said dark hair."

Ginny screwed up her face, her mouth turned down. "I know it sounds strange. It was dark hair, but it had some purple, too. You know, like people put colored streaks in their hair. Boys and girls. My cousin Bill did that, put red and green streaks in his hair, and my aunt and uncle freaked out."

"That's interesting," I said. "It's important. Detective Hamilton needs to know."

And I would call him as soon as possible. This could be a vital clue in finding Hallie's killer.

Chapter 24

"IT CERTAINLY LOOKS VALID."

I read through the will again. Three pages long, handwritten on lined yellow paper, it was signed by Hallie Garvin and witnessed by someone named Aviva Carlton. Both signatures were dated last November. Holographic wills in California didn't require a witness or notarization, but the fact that the will had been witnessed and dated underscored the document's provenance.

Lanny Fitzpatrick sat opposite me, his big body filling the chair next to my desk. He had returned to Arcata on Saturday, taking Hallie's dog with him. Now he was back in Rocoso, having left the coast early this Monday morning to make the long drive to the mountains. He'd called me en route, telling me he wanted to see me as soon as he got to town. I had time on my schedule at noon, so I gave him directions to my office.

Now he nodded, setting his coffee mug on the small round table next to the chair. "It is. The woman that witnessed it, Aviva, she owns the herb shop where Hallie worked. They've known each other ever since Hallie moved to Arcata. In fact, she's looking after Mitzi, Hallie's dog. I asked Aviva did she know if Hallie had a will. She said yeah, she witnessed it. When I got to our house, I went looking for it. Found it in a file box with Hallie's birth certificate and the title to her car."

"You read it, of course." I picked up my coffee mug, taking a sip of strong dark roast.

"Yeah. I knew she wanted to be cremated. She said that often enough and now I got it in writing, right there on the first page. As for the rest of it, that was a surprise.

I knew she'd leave her stuff to Tamara. But I didn't expect to see my name."

Hallie's will was straightforward. As Lanny pointed out, she had stipulated that she wanted her remains cremated. Sheryl had seemed resistant to the idea of cremation when the subject came up on Friday and when she and I had talked this weekend. She wanted to forge ahead with the plans she'd made for Hallie's funeral. There was an even bigger roadblock in front of Sheryl's long-term plans. Hallie left half her estate, such as it was, to her daughter Tamara—and the other half to Lanny. Betty's will divided her assets down the middle, with half to each daughter, according to Sheryl. This could mean that Lanny was in line to receive a portion of Betty Garvin's estate.

Lanny was thinking the same thing I was. "Sheryl's not gonna like that."

"You're right. I don't think she'll like it at all. But that's in the future. Right now we should focus on Hallie's wishes for cremation. You were there on Friday, when Sheryl said the medical examiner would probably release Hallie's body today. And this weekend, she told me she's planning a memorial service. That involves a casket and embalming. She needs to know about Hallie's plans for cremation, as soon as possible."

"I told her that on Friday. But she blew me off. Hallie's will should do it. I hope. I'll give her a copy."

I stood, the will in my hand. "We should also make a copy for the Garvin family lawyer, the one who drew up Betty's will. May I have one for my file as well?"

"Sure."

I opened the door and went out to the main office. I saw Gwen in the small conference room, talking with a prospective client. Carmen was out on her rounds, visiting clients. Our copier was on a table next to a bank of filing cabinets. I put the original will in the sheet feeder and pressed the appropriate buttons. The copier whirred and produced three copies of the will. I returned to my office, papers in hand. I handed the original and one copy to Lanny, setting the other ones on my desk. He folded the papers in half and put them into the small manila envelope that had held the original.

"Will you go with me to the house? Sheryl doesn't like me much and I'd feel better if you were there. Moral support, you know."

"I'd be happy to." I glanced at today's calendar. "But I can't do it right now. I have another appointment in half an hour and I need to get ready for that. And several other appointments after that. I'm free at two. I'll call Sheryl and ask if I can stop by then. You and I can meet at the house."

"That works for me. I'll go check into that same motel where I stayed before, on Main Street. I called ahead to make a reservation. I figure I'll stay in town until Hallie's service, then head back to Arcata. We're gonna have another service for her up there, when I get back."

After Lanny left my office, I called the Garvin house. Ethan answered. "Mom's not here. She had some errands to run."

"I'd like to stop by this afternoon. I have some time in my schedule at two."

"She'll be back by then," he said. "I'll let her know that you're coming."

No time for lunch, I thought. Not with my upcoming appointment. I ate a granola bar and chased that with a few bites of yogurt from the container in the office refrigerator.

While I ate, I thought about Lanny's new role as one of Hallie's heirs. How would that play out with Sheryl and her plans for Betty's estate, especially the land up at Lost

Woman Creek? Of course, if Sheryl could get control of the land before her mother died, that would be a different matter.

I recalled yesterday's conversation with Sheryl's husband. Richard Gillette hadn't come right out and said it, but he implied that Sheryl had designs on her mother's estate—the whole estate. How had he described it? He was an attorney, so it was natural that he'd couch the whole thing in lawyer language. Sheryl was planning a more active role in managing her mother's properties, he said. At first glance, that could very well mean that she was going to keep an eye on Betty's rental properties, which were providing Betty with income to supplement her pension and Social Security. But he'd also implied that Sheryl was considering a conservatorship, having Betty declared incompetent, with Sheryl designated as guardian. That would mean Sheryl would have control of the estate.

If what Richard said was true, Tamara and Lanny, as heirs to Hallie's estate, could very well put the brakes on Sheryl's plans. I didn't have a good feel for what Tamara might do, but Lanny genuinely liked Betty, and he didn't trust Sheryl at all. A family in conflict, and it could get worse before it got better.

I put the yogurt back in the fridge. Then I made a fresh pot of coffee, just in case. By the time the water finished trickling through the coffee grounds, the main office door opened. I greeted the people who'd made the appointment, ushered them into the conference room, and provided mugs of coffee. We spent the next hour discussing the assessment report and the care plan I'd developed.

When they left, I updated the file, then shut down my computer and left the office. Carmen was just outside, heading toward the door. "Ships passing in the night," she joked as she went inside.

In the next couple of hours, I visited several clients, including Fran Lomax, who was home now after rehab in the nursing home. From there, I drove to the Garvin house on Juniper Street, arriving a few minutes before two. Sheryl's rental car was in the driveway. Parked at the curb was Ethan's blue Toyota. I recognized the silver SUV across the street. It belonged to Tish Lehigh, Sheryl's cousin. In front of the house next door, the one that was for sale, was the rust-stained beige hatchback I'd seen drive past the house on Friday. I was guessing the hatchback, a Mazda, belonged to Tamara.

I parked at the curb behind Ethan's car and waited until I saw the dark green Jeep Wrangler, with Lanny Fitzpatrick at the wheel. He slotted the Jeep in behind the SUV, got out and stretched, then walked across the street to join me.

"Well, here goes," he said as we headed for the front porch. Tish answered the front door, beckoning us inside. I introduced her to Lanny.

"Oh, you're Hallie's friend." Tish smiled and took the big man's hand. "I'm so sorry for your loss. I know you two were together for a while."

"Three years," Lanny said.

"Well, have some coffee." Tish led the way through the empty living room to the kitchen. She headed for the coffee maker on the counter and grabbed a couple of mugs from the rack on the wall.

Since my last visit on Sunday afternoon, the amount of food spread out on the kitchen table and counters had grown. There were plates, platters, pans, and bowls, containing everything from cookies and fruit to sandwiches and casseroles. I was sure the refrigerator shelves were full as well.

Sheryl stood in front of the sink, rinsing a bunch of

grapes. She set them in a bowl and dried her hands on a dishtowel. "Tish, if that's a neighbor with another casserole, I am going to scream. We already have enough food to feed an army." She turned toward us with a rueful smile, one that froze into place when she saw us. "Oh. Kay. I wasn't expecting you." Ethan had neglected to tell her I was coming over. Now Sheryl paused and looked at Lanny. "Or you. Kay told me you'd gone back to Arcata."

Lanny was his usual patient and self-effacing self, smiling at Sheryl despite her obvious dislike of him. "Yeah, I did. I took the dog back, so's a friend can look after her."

Tish filled two mugs with coffee, handed one to Lanny and the other to me. Mine had the logo of the Rocoso & Jermyn Railroad. I reached for the small carton of milk next to the coffee maker. I poured a dollop into my mug. Lanny added milk and sugar to his. As he took a sip, he looked as though he was choosing his next words, and when to say them.

Just then, Ethan came into the family room from the patio, followed by Tamara. In one hand he carried a glass of water, in the other a plate holding a half-eaten sandwich and a pile of potato chips. He greeted us with a wave and a smile. "Are there any more chocolate chip cookies?"

"Hell, no, you scarfed all of them." Tamara glanced at Lanny and me but didn't acknowledge us. She leaned on the counter that separated the kitchen from the family room.

"I guess I'll have to start on the oatmeal raisin." Ethan lifted the foil cover on a pan. "Or brownies. That would be good."

"Maybe." Tamara examined the brownies, then moved to a pan containing apple pie. She picked up a fork and used it to transfer a wedge of pie to a paper plate.

"Kay, I have an update on that inventory," Sheryl said. "Ethan and I found more things missing."

Tish raised her eyebrows and gave her cousin a sharp glance. "What inventory?"

"Someone's been stealing from the house," Sheryl said. "Small things—jewelry, silver, and so forth. I thought Mom had been misplacing them or giving them away. But Kay found a few items at a local antique store and the dealer won't say where she got them. Ethan and I have been working on an inventory. As soon as we have a good idea of what's missing, I'll contact the police. I'm sure they can shake up the dealer and find out who's been selling those things to her."

I was across from Tamara, who had a bite of pie balanced on her fork, raising it to her mouth. She reacted briefly, cooked apples and flaky crust falling from the fork to the plate.

What was that about? Was Tamara the one who'd been helping herself to her grandmother's things?

Tamara saw me looking at her. She set the plate on the counter and crossed the kitchen to the rack that held coffee mugs, selecting one decorated with flowers. She turned to the coffee maker and filled the mug.

"Is there a lot of stuff missing?" Tish asked.

"Quite a bit. Small things. But when you add up the value, it works out to be a lot." Sheryl glanced at me. "Is that why you stopped by, Kay? The inventory?"

"Not really." I looked at Lanny.

He took a deep breath and pulled the folded pages from his pocket. "Taking the dog to Arcata wasn't the only reason I went home. I was looking for Hallie's will. And I found it. She wanted to be cremated." Lanny unfolded the will and held it out. "I brought you a copy. It's right there on the first page."

Sheryl reached for the pages and so did Tamara. But

Sheryl got there first. Her mouth tightened as she read the paragraph about cremation. Annoyance flickered over her face, then consternation as she read through the rest of the will, realizing that Lanny would get a portion of Hallie's estate. When she was done, she folded the pages and looked at me rather than Lanny. "I see. This is handwritten. Is that legal?"

Tish set her mug on the table. "Of course it is."

I nodded. "A handwritten will is legal in California. This one has been witnessed and dated, as you see. I'm sure if you have any questions, your attorney can confirm the legality. We've made an extra copy for him."

Tamara snatched the will from Sheryl's hands and read the first page, poking her finger at the paragraph where Hallie said she wanted to be cremated. She tossed the pages onto the kitchen table. "Okay, that's clear. We cremate Mom and have done with it. So much for your big funeral plans."

As she spoke, I thought of what Lanny had said earlier. Sheryl was all too quick to move in and take over. She'd done the same thing in planning Hallie's funeral. And Tamara didn't like that at all.

"That doesn't mean you don't have a service," Lanny said. "Hallie should have a good send-off. It's just that Sheryl was saying Hallie would be buried in the cemetery and I knew Hallie wouldn't want that. I just want to make sure her wishes about cremation are followed."

"They will be. I'm her daughter, and I get a say, too." Tamara turned to Sheryl and her mouth took on an ugly twist. "So screw your fancy funeral."

"How dare you— I should think you'd show some respect—"

"Respect? You hypocritical bitch." Tamara leaned toward her aunt. "You just want to make a big fucking deal out of Mom's funeral because you didn't have any use for her when she was alive. You hated her."

Sheryl recoiled, backing away from Tamara. Ethan tugged at Tamara's arm. Sheryl took a deep breath, opened her mouth, but before she could get any words out, Tish stepped between Sheryl and Tamara, her no-nonsense voice booming out. "All right, that's enough. You've been sniping at each other all day. You both need to go to your respective corners. You'll wake Aunt Betty and she doesn't need to hear any of this."

Tamara muttered a few curse words. She headed for the backyard. Ethan followed her.

Sheryl had retreated to the family room. With an effort, she composed herself. Tish shook her head, as though she'd had it with her battling relatives. She picked up the copy of Hallie's will and read through it. When she got to the part where Hallie divided her estate between Tamara and Lanny, she raised her eyebrows. She knew what it meant, too.

"This seems straightforward to me," Tish said. "The funeral home is picking up Hallie's body from the medical examiner this afternoon. We'll call right away and let them know about the cremation." She directed a pointed look at Sheryl, over the counter that separated the kitchen from the family room. Sheryl nodded. "We'll go ahead with the memorial service. That's planned for Friday. I'm not sure of the time yet. I will update you. Where can I reach you?"

"Here's my cell phone number." Lanny scribbled on a pad next to the kitchen phone, tore off the sheet, and gave it to Tish. "I'll be staying at a motel here in town until then. I appreciate all your help."

"I'll see you out." Tish shepherded us out of the kitchen, through the living room, and into the foyer.

"I'm sorry if things were—" Lanny began. "I didn't mean to cause a bunch of problems with the family. But

Hallie meant a lot to me. I've got no problem with her ashes being buried in the family plot. Thought it would be nice if I could take . . . Well, we're going to have a memorial for her in Arcata."

"I understand perfectly," Tish said. "There's no reason why there can't be two urns instead of one. I'm sorry about all this fuss. This nonsense has been going on for a long time. Far too long, in my opinion. Family's important. But I think— Well, who cares what I think. We'll make sure Hallie gets that good send-off."

"That's all I want," Lanny told her. "She'll get a good one up in Arcata, too, when I get back to the coast."

"I'm going to check on Betty before I leave," I said.

"Sure." Lanny left the house, heading for his Jeep.

Beside me, Tish sighed. "He seems like a nice man. I'm sorry for all of this family dirty laundry. It makes things tense and unpleasant."

"It does." I felt wrung out, from all the emotions ricocheting around the house. I could just imagine the effect this was having on Betty. All the tension, all the emotions, none of this was good for an elderly woman who'd just had a heart attack and experienced the loss of her daughter. "Now, I do need to see Betty."

"Of course. She's back in her bedroom. She was asleep the last time I looked in on her. But she's in and out."

I walked down the hall to the master bedroom. Betty was on the bed. Her eyes were open. She looked better than she had the day before. "How are you feeling?"

She smiled. "I'm okay. Everyone says I should rest, but I'm tired of it. Maybe I'll get up in a bit."

"I'm glad to hear it."

Betty reached out and took my hand. "I'm glad you came over. I want to talk—" She stopped and looked past me. I turned and saw Sheryl standing in the doorway.

"You're still here." Sheryl frowned. "I thought you'd left. Mother, you should be resting."

Betty's face took on a stubborn look. "I'm tired of resting. I want to get up."

Time for me to make my exit. "I should be going. I have other appointments. Betty, we'll talk again, soon."

As I made my way up the hall, heading for the front door, I wondered what Betty wanted to talk about. Whatever it was, she didn't want to say anything while Sheryl was in the room.

Outside, I paused next to my Prius, checking the messages on my phone. Then a Ford Focus pulled up to the curb and Justin Brownlow got out. He wore the same khaki slacks and green T-shirt he'd worn on Saturday. He looked at me and did a double-take. "Oh, hi. We met the other day at the farmers' market. You're Betty's caregiver, right?"

"Care manager. How are you, Mr. Brownlow?"

"Fine, fine. I'm looking for Tamara. Her car's here, so I guess she must be in the house."

I was just about to tell him she was in the backyard when Tamara and Ethan appeared, walking toward the street on the path that led from the meadow behind the houses. They must have gone out the back gate at Betty's house. After Tamara's blow-up at Sheryl, I wasn't surprised that she might wish to avoid going through the house again. When they reached the street, they headed for Tamara's beat-up Mazda.

Then Tamara spotted her father. She stopped and glared at him. "What are you doing here?"

Justin shrugged. "Trying to find you. I've called and texted. You don't answer my messages. I even went by the rafting company looking for you. I talked to your friend Crystal and she said she didn't know where you were. So I figured I'd come over here."

Tamara sneered. "Yeah, well, I'm busy. Better not go into the house. Sheryl the Bitch is on the warpath and I'm sure she doesn't want to see you. Besides, why bother to show up if you aren't going to help." She got into her car, started the engine, and drove away, tires squealing.

I stood on the sidewalk with Justin and Ethan, pondering the meaning of that last sentence. Tamara needed help? And Justin wasn't willing to provide it? Help with what?

"Well, that was awkward." Justin flashed a self-deprecating smile. Evidently, he was used to his daughter's disdain. That wasn't surprising if what I'd heard was true, that he hadn't been much of a presence in Tamara's life since he and Hallie had divorced. Still, why had he come to Rocoso? Why was he trying to reach out to his daughter? Was it because Hallie had been murdered? Was he trying to mend fences with Tamara?

"She's right. I shouldn't go in. Sheryl's still mad at me, after all this time. I just thought Tamara might be staying here."

"Sheryl's upset about a lot of things right now," I said.

"Tamara and Mom don't get along, so Tamara doesn't want to stay here." Ethan shrugged, the look on his face making it clear he found this meeting with his uncle difficult. "Tamara is staying with Crystal. I'm surprised Crystal didn't tell you that when you talked with her." He paused. "It's been rough these past few days. Things are crazy around here."

"Yeah, I'll bet," Justin said. "Tamara hasn't been responding to any of my messages, so I stopped by to see if I could find out anything about Hallie's funeral. I should be there. After all, we were married for nine years."

"Friday. At the same church where we had Grandpa Curtis's funeral. Don't know what time. We're still waiting to find out. I'll call and let you know for sure." The two men traded phone numbers, then Ethan added, "I guess I better get back to the house." He turned and headed for the front porch.

When he'd gone, I turned to Justin. "Will you stay in town?"

He shook his head. "I have to get back to Sacramento. That's where I live. But it's just a couple of hours away. I can drive up here for the funeral in a couple of hours. Like I did on Saturday, when you saw me at the farmers' market."

"I'm curious about something," I said. "When I met you on Saturday, you gave me the impression that you'd just arrived in town. But I'm sure I saw you on Thursday. The day Hallie died. It was around noon. You were crossing Main Street."

Justin looked taken aback. "Thursday? Thursday . . . Oh, yeah. I was in town. On business. I work for Caltrans. We have an office east of town. I come through here every few months. When I'm in town, I stop in and see Betty."

"That's interesting," I said. "She's never mentioned you."

He shrugged. "Well, she's getting a little vague, at her age."

There was some truth to that, but I had the distinct feeling that he was lying. He and Hallie had divorced when Tamara was in elementary school, nearly fifteen years ago, and I gathered from what I'd learned that Justin's contact with his ex, and his daughter, had been infrequent. I could be wrong, but I was sure there must be another reason why he was in town around the same time Hallie, his ex-wife, died.

"I guess I was on Main Street that day," he added. "I met some people for lunch."

"But you didn't see Hallie."

"No. Why would I? I didn't even know she was in town until Tamara told me."

"When did you see Tamara?"

He shrugged and looked for all the world like he wanted to avoid my questions. "Saturday. Tamara called me on Friday and told me about Hallie. I told her I'd come up on Saturday.

And when had Tamara arrived in town? She said she'd arrived on Friday, the day after her mother's death. I'd seen her outside this very house on Friday, after I met Tish Lehigh here, and again a short time later at the hospital. But I couldn't help thinking Tamara might have been in town earlier in the week. I remembered Betty's frequent questions, asking, "Where's Tamara?"

What if Tamara had been right here in Rocoso all last week?

Chapter 25

TUESDAY MORNING I WOKE feeling relaxed. My Monday evening tai chi class had put me in a good place, both physically and mentally. After a quiet evening spent reading, I had slept through the night, untroubled by interruptions from restless cats or dreams, pleasant or otherwise.

I got up and put on my bathrobe, then I stuck my feet into my slippers and headed for the kitchen. The cats had scampered ahead of me and waited patiently for food. I started the coffee maker. While water dripped through the French roast, I opened a can of fishy stuff and spooned it into their bowls.

I took my first mug of coffee out to my deck. Despite the early morning chill, the blue sky held the promise of a fine spring day. The bearded iris along the back fence were in full bloom, splashes of color ranging from deep purple and blue to bronze and bright yellow. I sat for a moment, drinking in the peaceful scene as I enjoyed my coffee. A California towhee in the flower bed to my left scuffed through the dirt and leaves as it looked for food. I'd hung a bird feeder from a low branch of the oak tree in the back corner of the yard. It was empty. I suspected that was due to the squirrels in my neighborhood, though the finches and sparrows were regular visitors. I'd have to refill the feeder later. For now, it was time to get started on my day.

I went back to the kitchen and left my coffee mug on the counter. I showered and dressed, putting on dark blue slacks and a light blue blouse over my white camisole, as well as a pair of low-heeled pumps. In the kitchen, I drank more coffee as I ate breakfast. Then I set out for the office, to start my day. After checking in with Gwen and Carmen, we left for our respective rounds of appointments.

Dolly Halstrom, feisty as ever, had won the argument with her children. She was out of the hospital and back at home in her cozy bungalow on the east side of town. She'd stood firm in her refusal to consider moving to an assisted living facility or a nursing home. But she would be receiving more in-home services. Her team of caregivers had increased by two, and the visiting nurse had upped the number of weekly visits. So had I.

"Paying for those caregivers is still less expensive than one of those places," Dolly told me when I stopped by that morning. "I'm feeling fine and those ladies are taking good care of me."

"Good. I'm glad to hear it."

Dolly was in her favorite reclining chair in the living room, feet in a pair of warm slippers with non-skid soles, a fleece blanket on her lap. Her expression turned serious. "I know I might have to consider going to one of those places, later on. If I fell and hurt myself or my health got real bad. But I don't think I'm there yet. Why do people automatically assume that just because I'm old I should go into one of those assisted living places? Warehouses for old people, that's what I call them."

I smiled, thinking Dolly would be just fine, for the time being. She was fiercely independent and had lived alone since her husband died several years before. She didn't like being told what to do and it didn't matter whether the person handing out the unsolicited advice was her own family, or me.

"I'm glad you're feeling better. You need to drink more water, though. Dehydration is a problem for people your age."

"I know, I know. That's how I wound up in the hospital this time." She waggled a metal water bottle, bright neon pink decorated with white daisies. "My granddaughter got this for me. She says I'm supposed to sip, several times an hour. I promised her I would."

Dolly and I chatted for a while longer. Before leaving, I checked her medication and looked at the caregiver schedule. Back in my car, I headed for The Pines, on the north end of town, where I saw the other side of the argument.

Earl Wendell had decided on his own to move into assisted living, rather than having the decision forced on him. He was now settling into life at The Pines. The facility was large and to my mind well-managed, offering a lot of amenities, as well as several options for seniors, including independent apartments, assisted living, and nursing home care.

Earl answered the door, pushing his three-wheeled walker, his little dog Jojo at his side. "Come in, come in and see my new digs," Earl said. He was in a one-bedroom unit, with a kitchenette and a large living room. He'd furnished the place with items from his house, including his favorite recliner and the wide-bottomed rocking chair where I now took a seat. Jojo woofed, his tail wagging. He presented his head for a scratch behind the ears and I obliged. He groaned with pleasure, then he stretched and jumped onto the sofa, curling up in a fleece dog bed at one end.

Earl piloted the walker toward his recliner, then sat down, raising the chair's footrest. He pointed at the tablet computer on the side table. "My grandson gave me that. At first, I said I didn't want one of those contraptions. But I'm getting the hang of it. He set it up so I can check those ebooks out of the library, which is handy. And he loaded on one of those bridge games, an app, he called it. You know how I like to play bridge. And Scrabble. This thing has a Scrabble app, too. My wife and I used to play

Scrabble all the time before she died. I miss playing with her. I used to play sometimes with people at the senior center. They've got a group of folks here at this place who play Scrabble, and bridge. And we have concerts, too. There's one coming up on Thursday, a fellow who plays the piano. That should be fun. They have exercise classes, too. My granddaughter says I should check out something called chair yoga."

"It sounds like you and Jojo are settling in just fine."

He nodded. "I am. You know, I was resisting it, for a long time. Determined to stay in my own home. But that fall took the wind out of my sails. So yes, I'm liking it so far. You know, at first, I was going to get one of the senior apartments and cook for myself. Then I thought, heck, I don't even like to cook that much. Might as well go with the assisted living and have my meals in the dining room. The food's pretty good and I'm eating regular. More than I was living in my old house. I usually sit at a table with two other guys. There's more women here than men."

Not surprising, I thought. Women tended to outlive men, so men who were Earl's age were in the minority.

"Jojo is good company." The dog perked up at the sound of his name. He left the dog bed on the sofa and jumped onto Earl's lap. "You like it here, too, don't you, fella?"

We talked a while longer, then I stood to leave. "Do check out the chair yoga class, Earl. You might like it."

"Anything to keep myself going."

It was just after ten when I left The Pines. I drove back toward downtown Rocoso and pulled over at a coffee shop. I had some time in the middle of my morning and I wanted a nosh. Car mug in hand, I went inside and ordered a latte, and a chocolate croissant to go with it. I had just finished the croissant when my cell phone rang. A glance at the screen told me the call came from Betty

Garvin, or at least from her home number. I wiped my hands on a napkin and touched the button to accept the call. "Hello."

No response.

"Hello? Betty?" I waited. "Is anyone there?"

Finally, I heard a voice. "Kay."

"Betty? Is that you? Is something wrong?"

"Come over. I want to talk with you. Sheryl says not to talk. But I have to. Please come over."

"I'll be right there."

I looked at my watch and my schedule. On my way out the door, I called and moved back an appointment. A chance to talk with Betty was an emergency, justifying jumping the queue.

When I arrived at the house on Juniper Street, Sheryl's rented Nissan was gone, but Ethan's car was in the drive. I rang the bell. Ethan answered the door, dressed casually in a pair of worn jeans and a Cal T-shirt. "Hi, Ms. Dexter. I wasn't expecting you."

Did Ethan know that Betty had called me? I decided to keep that information to myself, for now.

"Hi, Ethan. I dropped by to see your grandmother."

"Sure." He opened the screen door. "She's back in the family room."

"Is your mother here?"

He shook his head. "No. She has some errands to run. She took that inventory of stuff that's missing over to the police department, to report those things as stolen. Then she said she was going to the funeral home. I don't know when she'll be back."

We walked through the living room. He had been studying here, his laptop computer on the coffee table, along with a pile of papers. As we entered the kitchen, I saw Betty in the family room, tucked into her recliner, with a small lap quilt over her. The cordless phone she'd used to call me was in her lap, along with the TV remote. The television was on, Turner Classic Movies showing a trailer for *The Bad and the Beautiful*, with Lana Turner and Kirk Douglas on the screen.

Betty waved at me as she pressed a button on the remote, turning off the TV.

"Kay, it's nice to see you. Thanks for coming to check on me." She stole a glance at her grandson and I guessed that she didn't want him hearing our conversation. Her next words confirmed this. "Ethan, honey, you know what I would like?"

He stepped into the family room and leaned over her. "Anything you want, Grandma."

She gave him a sweet smile. "Strudel from Ludwig's Bakery. Ever since I got out of the hospital, I have just had a hankering for that strudel. Will you drive over to the bakery and get some? Get two, maybe. I really like the apple, and the one with cream cheese and blueberries. And I know you like the one with cherries and marzipan. Get all three. Kay can have a piece with us."

"Right now?"

I knew why he looked startled. Ludwig's Bakery was famous all over the county for its delectable pastries, cakes, and other delights. It was on the north side of town, though, and we were on the south side. It would take him a good half hour to get over there, park and purchase the strudels, with maybe another twenty minutes or so to get back to Betty's house. I masked a smile. Betty had planned this. Sheryl was out. Now she wanted her grandson to leave so that she and I could talk in private.

"Yes, please. Right now." Betty smiled up at her grandson. "There's some money in my purse. Take what you need."

Ethan reached into his pocket and pulled out his car keys. "Okay. Don't worry about money, Grandma. My treat. If you don't mind staying till I get back, Ms. Dexter. Mom doesn't want Grandma to be all alone right now. Strudel it is." He grinned. "Though I probably won't get out of Ludwig's with just that. Their chocolate eclairs are the bomb."

I gave him an encouraging smile. "That sounds good, too. I like the ones with the coffee custard. I'll have some coffee ready when you get back." Ethan left the family room. A moment later I heard the front door close as he left the house. I turned to Betty. "What's up? You want to talk with me?"

Betty spoke, slowly, hesitating. "Sheryl says I shouldn't talk to anyone but I have to. I owe it to Hallie."

"Did you see or hear something, Betty?" And if she had, why did Sheryl want her mother to keep her mouth shut? Why didn't she want her mother to tell the detectives what she knew? Was it strictly for Betty's welfare? Did she simply want to avoid public knowledge of the dispute roiling the family?

Betty nodded, her face somber. "But you have to promise not to tell anyone else. It's— What do you call it? Patient, client, whatever. Privacy. Confidential. You're my care person and I'm your client, so we have to keep it private, between the two of us."

"All right. What you tell me is confidential. I won't tell anyone else."

"Good. But I'll tell you. I have to tell someone, and I trust you." She stopped and took a deep breath before continuing. "That day, I was in the family room, like now. Hallie was out on the patio. She was doing something with the plants. Some of them were pot-bound, so she was moving them to bigger pots. I must have dozed off. When I woke up, I heard Hallie arguing with someone. It sounded like another woman. I thought it must be Hallie and Sheryl, going at each other like they always did. Then

I got up and went to the patio door."

Betty stopped and took a deep breath, fighting down emotions.

"What did you see?" I asked.

"Two people. I know one of them was Hallie. But the other, I didn't get a good look. They were fighting and it happened so fast." She gulped down a sob. "I'm not sure. I was afraid it was Sheryl. You saw how they were that day when you came over. Hissing and spitting at each other like a pair of cats. I thought they were going to come to blows then. And what I saw, it looked like they finally had. I think I yelled something, like, Stop it. Hallie turned a bit, like she was looking at me. And the other woman had something in her hand and hit Hallie on the head. Once, twice, maybe three times."

Betty shuddered and so did I, seeing the scene as she described it, a woman standing over Hallie. I knew the trowel was the murder weapon. In my mind's eye, I saw the rusty metal edge striking Hallie's head.

"Did you get a good look at the other woman?" I asked.

Tears trickled down Betty's wrinkled cheeks. "I think she had brown hair. And she was a little bit taller than Hallie. Just like—"

She stopped. I knew what she was thinking. Sheryl had brown hair. And she was taller, by a few inches. Suspicion washed over me like a wave, the same suspicions I'd had since the day Hallie died. Had Sheryl killed her sister?

"I'm so afraid," Betty said, her voice wavering. "What if Sheryl killed Hallie? I can't stop thinking about it."

"We don't know anything for sure." But I wondered.

"I don't think she meant to," Betty said. "But that must be what happened. They must have been fighting, like they always did."

"You didn't actually see—" I began.

Betty shook her head. "What I did see was just a few seconds. That's when I felt my heart, that squeezing, that must have been the heart attack the doctor says I had. It hurt so bad, I must have doubled over. When I looked up again, I saw Hallie lying there. She didn't move. And the other woman—" She stopped, as though she couldn't bring herself to name Sheryl. "The other woman was going out the back gate."

"You were at the patio door, but when I got here, you were in the recliner. I thought you were asleep."

Betty looked perplexed. "I remember the chest pains and feeling cold. Thinking if I could just sit down and catch my breath. I was just a few steps away. I must have sat down. And passed out. After that, I don't remember much. The dog barking. Someone calling to me. A lot of people. And then the hospital."

I sat back in the chair, considering what Betty had just told me. Raised voices, a struggle. One woman striking another.

Did Sheryl Garvin kill her sister? At the moment I didn't have another candidate for the role.

The killer had fled through the back gate out to the creek and the meadow, tossing the murder weapon at the creek, hoping that the water would hide it. Then she went to the pass-through that led from the meadow to Juniper Street. Sheryl—if it was Sheryl—then could have walked into the house through the front door, acting as though nothing had happened, finding Betty here in the family room and Hallie dying on the patio.

That's when I walked onto the scene to discover the chaos. Betty had been in the recliner. Hallie was on the patio, gasping her last. And Sheryl had been kneeling beside her sister. At the time, I'd wondered why she hadn't immediately called 911. Perhaps, having told me to meet her at the house, she'd waited so that I'd be the innocent bystander who made the call. And Sheryl was the one who was keeping the detectives away from her mother, even though Betty was a witness.

And yet— I didn't know what to think. What about Ginny, the middle-schooler from across the street? She had been out in the meadow with her school friends, just the other side of the creek. She told me this past weekend that she'd seen someone—a woman, though she wasn't sure—coming out the Garvins' back gate. That person had been wearing jeans and had dark hair. Sheryl had brown hair, dark enough, though it was threaded with gray. When I arrived at the house, she hadn't been wearing jeans. But her gray slacks could have been mistaken for denim.

Besides, Ginny was sure that she'd seen purple streaks in that dark hair. Or had it been a trick of the afternoon light?

"Thanks for telling me, Betty. I promise to keep this between the two of us, but I do think you should tell the detectives what you saw and heard. It's really important for all of us, especially for you, to find out who is responsible for Hallie's death."

Betty clasped her arms over her chest, as though protecting herself. Finally, she said, "I'll think about it."

I glanced at my watch. Ethan had been gone for nearly forty minutes. He would return from the bakery soon, and I'd promised to make coffee. I left Betty in her recliner, wiping tears from her face as she tried to compose herself, and headed into the kitchen. I filled the drip coffee maker with water and the filter basket with ground coffee and pressed the power button. As water dripped through the coffee grounds. I turned, intending to head back into the family room. Then I heard someone come through the front door. It was Sheryl.

"What are you doing here?" Suspicion colored her voice. "I saw your car. Where's Ethan?"

"Sheryl," I said, by way of warning Betty that her daughter had returned. "I stopped by to see Betty, to check on how she's doing. She wants strudel from Ludwig's Bakery, so Ethan went to get it."

Her eyebrows shot up. "Ludwig's? Well, yes, they do make the best strudel. But that's on the other side of town. I was out. She could have called me."

"Ethan wanted a break from his studies. And I was here. I told Ethan I'd make a pot of coffee. Do you want some?" I didn't wait for an answer. Instead, I took four mugs from the rack and set them on the counter. The coffee maker sputtered as it finished its cycle. I filled a mug and handed it to Sheryl.

"I went over to the antique store and had a look at that dealer's stall." Sheryl raised the mug and sipped the coffee. "Those things in the case are definitely Mother's. The dealer wasn't there, but I took more pictures. I had already printed out the photos you took. After I left the store, I went over to the police station and talked with an officer. He made a copy of the list of things that are missing from the house. He says he'll talk with the dealer. That's all I can do for now. Especially with getting ready for the memorial service."

The front door opened again. Ethan came in, carrying two pink bakery boxes. With a flourish, he transported them into the kitchen and put them on the counter next to the neighbors' offerings. "Hey, Mom." He leaned over and kissed her, then straightened and called to Betty. "Okay, Grandma, I got apple, blueberry with cream cheese, and my personal favorite, cherry with marzipan. Which one do you want?"

Betty, composed now, laughed. "Apple for me. With vanilla ice cream. There's a carton in the freezer."

Ethan turned to Sheryl. "Mom?"

"I had a big breakfast," she protested. Then she smiled. "But strudel. Yes, I have room for strudel. I do like the blueberry."

"And I'll try the cherry." I poured coffee for the four of us. "What about you, Ethan?"

He opened the boxes to reveal all three strudels, as well as an assortment of other goodies, including chocolate chip cookies and several eclairs. Ludwig's made eclairs with vanilla, chocolate, and coffee custard, and Ethan had gotten all three flavors. There had been a fourth eclair, but it was gone.

Ethan chuckled as he saw me examining the evidence. "Yes, I confess. I ate an eclair before I even left the parking lot."

"You're a bottomless pit," Sheryl told her son, her face warmed by an affectionate smile. "I remember that year I asked you what you wanted for your birthday, and you said, 'All the lobster I can eat.' Down I went to Pike Street Market and bought lobster tails."

"I ate three," Ethan took four plates from the cupboard and set them on the counter. Then he took a knife from a drawer and cut a slice from the apple strudel. "Hey, Grandma, you want me to nuke this in the microwave before I put ice cream on it?"

"Yes, that would be nice," Betty called.

While Ethan heated the strudel and dished up the ice cream, I took a mug of coffee to Betty. We moved to the family room and talked as we ate strudel and drank coffee, avoiding the specter of Hallie Garvin and her violent death out on the patio.

When I finished my strudel, I carried my plate and mug to the kitchen. Then I glanced at my watch. "I should go. Thanks for the strudel."

"I'll walk you out," Sheryl said.

I said good-bye to Betty and Ethan, then made my way through the living room, with Sheryl a pace behind me. Once we were outside, she said, "Why did you really come over?"

I turned to face her. "To see Betty, of course. Her welfare is my job."

And you haven't fired me, at least not yet, I thought.

"And Ethan was conveniently out. What did she tell you?" When I didn't answer, she added, "What are you thinking, Kay?"

I took my time answering her. "Why didn't you call 911 the minute you saw Betty? And Hallie?"

Sheryl gave me a long, measuring look. "In retrospect, I can see how you might take that the wrong way. But Mother was stretched out on her recliner. I thought she was asleep. And when I saw Hallie— At first I thought she'd fallen. Then I realized—" She stopped and shook her head. "All I can say is that I was stunned into inaction. So no, I didn't immediately whip out my cell phone and call for help. Then you came in. That's the way it happened. Are you saying you don't believe me?"

"I don't know what to think. You won't let Betty talk with the detectives. She could have important information about Hallie's death."

Sheryl shook her head. "No, I can't let anyone talk to Mother. I have to protect her."

"Protect her? Or yourself?"

Silence stretched between us. "You were alone with Mother when I got here," Sheryl said. "What did she tell you?"

"She told me what she saw and heard."

Sheryl clamped her mouth shut, her lips in a thin line. "Mother hasn't said anything to me. What did she see?"

"She insisted that our conversation be confidential. I

promised her I wouldn't discuss it with anyone."

"What could she possibly—?" A look of consternation passed over Sheryl's face. "She thinks I killed Hallie? You think I killed her? That's absurd. What reason could you possibly have for suspecting me of doing such a thing?"

"Besides finding you on the scene? You didn't get along with Hallie. I keep going back to that fight the two of you had when you got back to town. If Lanny hadn't intervened—"

Sheryl ran her hands through her hair. "I can't believe you suspect me of something like that. I had nothing to do with Hallie's death. Nothing. I swear it. Don't you believe me?"

"I don't know what to believe," I said. "When you and your sister were fighting, there was such venom. In the course of my career, working with families, I've seen my share of family disputes. But you and Hallie, that was nasty. When it comes to believing you, there's another problem, Sheryl. You've lied to me, several times. Right from the start, the day you hired me. You told me Hallie was not involved in your mother's life, that you didn't know where she lived. That wasn't true, in either account. You told me there was no one here in the area who could help you look after your mother. That wasn't true, either. Your cousin Tish had volunteered."

She swiped a hand over her lower jaw. "Not exactly lied. Stretched the truth, maybe."

"Regardless of what you call it, why should I trust what you say? Being able to trust is an important part of my relationships with my clients. And I'm not sure at this point that I do trust you."

"You can trust me to want what's best for my mother."

"I think what's best for your mother is finding out who killed your sister. I've urged her to talk with the detectives. She said she'd think about it."

Sheryl's voice flattened out, and her face was expressionless. "Mother thinks I did it, too."

"You're the one who hired me," I told her. "But my first responsibility is Betty, her welfare. If I thought—"

Now Sheryl's eyes blazed. "I am not going to do anything that puts Mother in jeopardy. How could you think that?"

"Mom?" Ethan stepped out onto the porch, a foil-wrapped package in his hand. "Grandma wants you."

Sheryl turned abruptly, without a word, and went back into the house.

Chapter 26

ETHAN STAYED ON THE porch, handing the package to me. "It's cherry strudel to take home."

"Thanks. It's delicious. I'll have it for a mid-afternoon snack."

He lingered, not saying anything. I was sure he wanted to talk with me privately, away from his mother and grandmother. But he was having trouble opening the conversation. I could get him talking about something else, though.

"You're in your second year at Cal, right? I gather finals are coming up."

He looked relieved at this detour from whatever was on his mind. "Yeah. Classes are over. This is what the university calls review week. Finals start next week, and my first one is on Tuesday, a week from today. I'll head back to Berkeley on Friday, after the memorial service."

"What are you studying?"

He pulled a spent pink blossom from the rhododendron next to the porch. "I'm in the College of Natural Resources. Now that I'm at the end of my second year, I have to declare a major. I was back and forth between several subjects, but I finally decided on conservation and resource studies. It's an interdisciplinary program and I'm excited about it. It focuses on things like natural resources and population, energy, tech, and cultural values."

"That sounds fascinating. Do you come to Rocoso often? I mean, since you started school at Berkeley?"

"Oh, yeah. I enjoy this place. There are some unique ecosystems here in the county. Like the apple-growing area farther down the canyon. The area up around Osprey Lake, too. And Lost Woman Creek. That's such an interesting place. Grandma's family used to own that hot springs resort up there."

"Yes, I know. I've seen pictures of the hotel, the way it looked before it burned down." I wondered if Ethan knew about his mother's plans to rebuild the resort.

"I enjoy coming to visit Grandma," he said. "She's a kick, when she's got all her marbles." He stopped, looking guilty for having said it. "I shouldn't put it that way. It's just that sometimes she's forgetful. It's gradual. I've noticed it a lot over the past couple of years. That's why Mom has been concerned about her." He paused for a sip of coffee. "Mom says you're a geriatric care manager, working with elderly people and their families. I'm sure you hear this a lot. That sounds like an interesting line of work. Tell me about it."

I did so, fielding his questions about my day-to-day routine. He was certainly personable and easy to talk with, unlike his parents. The conversation wound down and neither of us spoke.

"Maybe you'd better tell me whatever it is you want to talk about."

He sighed. "It's about Tamara."

"Tell me about her. Were she and her mother close?"

He shrugged. "Not particularly. At least that's my impression. I didn't know Tamara that well when we were kids. I was born and raised in Seattle. Tamara and Aunt Hallie were in California and I gather they moved around a lot, after her dad left and her parents got divorced. You see, Mom and Hallie were always . . . fighting, I guess. There was a lot of tension between them, growing up. Something about Mom being engaged to the guy Hallie married. Justin. Him, I don't know anything about. He left when Tamara was about nine. At least that's what she told me. She's not very close to him, either."

"It sounds like you know Tamara fairly well now."

"Not that well," he said. "Yeah, we've gotten to know each other, but I don't think anybody really knows Tamara. Not even her mother and father. Anyway, we connected about a year ago. I found out she was living in Oakland. I'm in Berkeley. We get together for coffee now and then."

"Did she go to college?"

He shook his head. "No. Well, I take that back. She and Hallie were living in Sonoma County when Tamara graduated from high school. She did a year at Santa Rosa Junior College. Then she dropped out and got a job. She's worked at a lot of jobs. In the time she's lived in Oakland, she's worked at a landscaping place and for a package delivery service. She likes being outdoors, doesn't want to be shut up in an office. We have that in common, me being at the College of Natural Resources."

"Outdoors, hmm? Your cousin Tish told me that Tamara enjoys river rafting."

He nodded. "Oh, yeah. Rafting is right up her alley. Tamara knows the river fairly well. She likes to go hiking, too. She comes up here a lot and stays with a friend—Crystal—who works for one of the rafting companies."

I nodded. "Is there something bothering you? About Tamara?"

"Yeah." He hesitated, then forged ahead. "I hear her telling people that she got to town on Friday, after Hallie died. I don't think that's true."

I'd had the same feeling, but at the time I'd had nothing to base it on. "What makes you think that?"

"Because I tried to get in touch with her," Ethan said. "Thursday, after Mom called me with the news about Hallie. I called Tamara's cell phone several times and left messages and she didn't get back to me. Then I called

Tamara's roommate. She shares an apartment in North Oakland, with a woman named Deanna. When I talked with Deanna, she told me Tamara had gone out of town for a few days. She didn't say when she'd left, but I got the feeling that it was earlier in the week. And I didn't ask where, either. But I was assuming it was here, to Rocoso."

I played devil's advocate. "That doesn't necessarily mean that Tamara was here. She could have gone somewhere else."

Ethan shrugged. "She's not close to her father at all, so she doesn't go visit him. And she hardly ever visited her mother up in Arcata. Besides, Hallie was here."

"Is there another reason you think Tamara was here?"

"The Indian casino," he said. "Whenever she comes up here, Tamara and Crystal spend a lot of time at the casino."

"Tamara likes to gamble?" The local Maidu band had built a casino on their property north of town. It was popular with locals as well as tourists.

Ethan nodded. "Yeah. A lot. Way too much. And not just here. She spends a lot of time in the card clubs in the East Bay and going to casinos in the Bay Area. Like San Pablo, and up in Napa and Rohnert Park. Tamara's always short of money. A couple of times she's asked me for money, because she was having trouble paying her share of the rent. I don't know why she goes to those places and throws it away on poker and blackjack. I guess she's got a gambling problem."

"It could be." In fact, it sounded very likely. How would Tamara get money if she needed it, without asking her mother or grandmother for cash?

I recalled the odd look on Tamara's face on Sunday afternoon, when Sheryl mentioned the inventory of items missing from Betty's house. And Betty's comments earlier, that implied Tamara had been to visit her. The valuables were portable, such as the silver from the china cabinet and the silver service, and from Betty's jewelry box as well.

Tamara must be the one who had been helping herself to her grandmother's valuables.

But how to prove it? I could show a photo to the antique dealer and hope that she would give me a straight answer about who had sold her the items. Of course, Sheryl had reported the thefts to the police this morning. It would be a better idea to talk with the investigating officer.

I left off turning the wheels in my mind and focused on what Ethan was saying. "I never know what Tamara's going to do. She's cut her hair. It looks like she did it herself. And she's changed the color, again."

"Tamara's not actually blond? I thought she might be. Hallie was."

"Blond? No." Ethan shook his head as he tugged at another rhododendron blossom. "Her natural color is dark brown, like her father. And she wore it long until just a few weeks ago. Last time we got together in Oakland, her hair was down past her shoulders. And she had all these streaks."

I frowned. "Streaks?"

"Yeah. Streaks. All different colors. Red, green, blue, purple, bright yellow." He laughed. "Last year she dyed her hair hot pink. Talk about a strange look."

I considered this. Ginny, the middle-schooler who lived across the street from Betty, told me—and the police—that she'd seen someone leaving the Garvin yard through the back gate, a short time before I arrived and found Sheryl on the patio, with Hallie's body. Ginny and her friends, walking home from school, had been on the other side of the creek. She hadn't been sure if the denim-clad figure she had seen slipping through the gate was a man or a woman. But she told me on Sunday that she thought that person's hair had a purple streak.

At the hospital, Tamara told me that she'd driven up to Rocoso from Oakland that same day, after finding out that her mother had died. But I only had her word for it. When I met Tamara on Friday, I had the feeling I'd seen her before. Indeed, she drove by Betty's house that morning, in her rust-bucket hatchback. But something else tugged at my mind.

Finally, I realized what it was.

Sunday, a week ago, the late afternoon when Sam and I were heading for the bluegrass concert at the county park. We had stopped at Rocky River Rafting to pick up Ed and Dina. There I saw two women I assumed to be employees, both wearing T-shirts with the rafting company logo. One had sandy hair peeking out from a red bandana. The other had long shoulder-length dark hair, streaked with color. I was sure one of those splashes of color had been purple.

Tamara? And her friend Crystal?

I reached for my cell phone. When we were at the rafting company, I'd snapped several photos of the green heron that had perched in the oak tree near the river. Then the bird had flown to the top of a shed. I was sure that one of my photos of the bird showed the two women in the background.

I would show that photo to Ethan, to see if he could confirm what I suspected, that the photo was of Tamara and Crystal.

As I unlocked the screen, the phone chimed, reminding me that I had an appointment at my office. I didn't have time to look for those photos now.

Chapter 27

I ARRIVED AT MY OFFICE in time to set up for my meeting. The woman was about my age, in her mid-fifties. Since her mother's death, two years ago, her elderly father had been living alone in the family home here in town. In his late eighties, he had resisted her suggestions that he leave Rocoso and move into her home in Citrus Heights, near Sacramento. As for assisted living, he wasn't having any of that. He figured he could do better living at home with caregivers, as needed. From what she'd told me, he was probably right. But I wouldn't know for sure until I'd had the chance to talk with him and do an assessment.

We sat, drank coffee, and talked. He didn't like asking for help. So many older people didn't. But it was clear that he did need some assistance. At least he was open to the possibility of hiring caregivers. And he liked the idea of having me oversee things. At the end of the meeting, he decided to go ahead and work with me. His daughter breathed a sigh of relief as I consulted my calendar. We made plans to meet at his house later this week, so I could do the assessment and plan his care.

By the time they left, my stomach was growling. It had been a while since I'd consumed cherry strudel at Betty's house. The strudel Ethan had given me was stashed in my little refrigerator. But I wanted something more savory than sweet. I didn't have much time for lunch, though. I had another appointment in less than an hour, with a married couple who were seeking some guidance on dealing with the husband's mother, who was showing increasing signs of dementia.

I closed the office and walked across Main Street to a

deli, where I got a ham sandwich on rye, with a couple of dill pickles. Back in the office, I spread my repast on my desk and ate as I prepared for the next meeting. Taking extra care to avoid dribbling mustard and pickle juice on the paper, I read through the notes and the assessment report I had created. Once I finished my lunch, I got ready for my client. She arrived and we reviewed the report and the care plan I'd created for her mother. When she left, I returned phone calls and responded to email messages. Now I was done for the day. No more appointments.

I took out my cell phone and touched the screen icon that led to the photographs. I scrolled up, looking at dates, finding the photos I'd taken a week ago Sunday. Several of them showed the four of us—Dina, Ed, Sam, and me—at the county park, where we'd eaten our picnic before the bluegrass concert. The earlier pictures were those I'd taken at the rafting company. There were four of them, images captured as I snapped photos of the green heron at the water's edge.

The first photo was blurry. The next two were better, showing the heron in clear detail. The fourth photo had been taken when the bird flew from the tree, landing on the roof of the storage shed. I'd gotten a good shot of the bird, but more importantly, the lower right corner of the photo showed the two women I'd seen at the site. Employees, I'd thought then, because both women wore rafting company T-shirts. They had been cleaning out one of the Jeeps used to transport customers and rafts to the put-ins upriver.

Sweeping my fingers across the screen, I enlarged the photograph and examined the two women. The blonde with the red bandanna must be Crystal. I'd caught the dark-haired woman's face. I compared it to the face I'd seen several days later, in the hospital, at the farmers' market, and Betty's house. Yes, the woman in the photo was Tamara. I was sure of it. But instead of the short blond hair she'd sported when I saw her this past weekend, in the picture she had wavy brown hair, tumbling down to her shoulders. And there were colorful streaks visible in her hair—red, green, blue. And purple.

Tamara was in town on that Sunday, four days before her mother was killed on Thursday.

What did that prove?

I considered different scenarios. Tamara could have gone back to Oakland. But Ethan said when he had called her apartment on Thursday, after getting news about Hallie's death, Tamara's roommate had told him that Tamara had gone out of town. But when? Ethan hadn't asked when.

I enlarged the photograph as much as I could without the image turning into grainy, unrecognizable mush.

Tamara had cut her hair and changed the color. Was this an attempt at disguise? But why?

When I'd seen Tamara at the hospital, she had been in Betty's room, leaning over her grandmother. Betty's eyes had been shut, but Tamara had been talking to her. And I'd heard her say, "Think about it." And her face and body language hadn't projected love and concern for the elderly woman in the hospital bed.

Had she been threatening Betty? Was Betty afraid of her granddaughter?

I needed to track down Tamara and ask some questions. Whether I'd get answers, I didn't know.

As I shut down my computer, my cell phone rang. The readout told me it was Sam, calling from his office at the college. "How about an early dinner?" he asked. "I have an appointment with a student at four, but I'm free after that. We can meet downtown, if that works for you."

"Dinner, yes. Downtown, no. I have some business to take care of on the north side of town." I paused. "Let's try

Santorini, that Greek restaurant, the one that opened last month. It's on the north side, just a block or so from Ed's rafting company."

"Good suggestion," he said. "I've been meaning to check out the place. The reviews have been positive. I think they open at five."

I glanced at my watch. It was about a quarter to four. That should give me time to locate Tamara at Rocky River Rafting and ask her a few questions.

"It's a weeknight," I said. "We shouldn't need reservations. I'll meet you in front of the restaurant, at five or a little before. I'll call you if I'm running late."

After Sam and I ended the call, I gathered my belongings. Gwen was out, but Carmen was at her desk, her fingers flying over her computer keyboard. She looked up as I paused in the doorway of her office.

"I'm leaving now," I told her. "Early dinner with Sam. We're going to try the new Greek restaurant."

"Rafe and I went there last week. We both liked it. I had the grilled fish with lemon and it was delicious."

"Sounds good. See you tomorrow morning."

As I drove through the downtown streets, my mind whirled with questions. What was the best way to approach Tamara? Was she the person with purple-streaked hair that Ginny had seen leaving Betty's backyard? I had no proof of that. Yes, I had a photo of Tamara with streaked hair, taken a week ago. But her hair was short and blond now.

Was it Tamara? And why?

I could think of several reasons for Tamara to be at her grandmother's house. She could simply have been visiting Betty or Hallie. After all, Betty's questions—asking "Where's Tamara?"—earlier that week led me to believe that she had been to the house.

But there was a less benign scenario. Given what her

cousin Ethan had told me about Tamara's propensity for gambling, it was possible she needed money. She could very well be the one who was stealing items from the house and selling them to the antique dealer. To me, it seemed an ineffective way to get money. Surely, she couldn't get that much cash selling a few pieces of silver. But someone having money troubles might not be thinking clearly. I could certainly see her approaching her mother for a loan. What if Tamara had asked Hallie for money? And Hallie refused? Then what?

Had Tamara been at the house the afternoon her mother had been murdered?

If so, had she seen something?

Or had she struck Hallie over the head with a trowel?

Proof. I didn't have any. That's why I needed to talk with Tamara.

I headed north, passing strip malls and motels. Then I passed the antique mall where I'd first seen the valuables that had disappeared from Betty's house and resurfaced at the dealer's stall. As I reached the outskirts of town, the gaps between the buildings widened. The river was to my right, meandering as it flowed through a wide meadow, with a forested hill on the far bank. I slowed the car as I neared Santorini, the Greek restaurant. The building had whitewashed stucco walls and a bright blue roof echoing the architecture of its namesake island. The covered patio in the back looked out onto the river.

Fifty yards beyond this was Rocky River Rafting, its gravel lot crowded with parked cars, including the rust-stained Mazda I'd seen Tamara driving. A slope on the south side of the office led down to the river. Two of the company's vans had trailers hitched to them. These were used to transport the rafts to a point on the upper Rocoso River, about a mile south of Jermyn, where the rafters began their journey downriver. It looked as though one such rafting trip had just finished. Several adults of varying ages milled in a group clustered near the shore, where a couple of employees were helping sort things out, collecting life jackets and other gear. Since it was nearly four, my guess was the rafters were done for the day. If Tamara had gone on a run with Ed or with her friend Crystal, she would be back by now.

I found a parking space and got out of my car, walking toward the office. As I neared the front door, Ed McGinty came out, dressed as usual in faded jeans and a company T-shirt. I called out to him.

He turned. "Hi, Kay. What brings you here?"

"I'm having an early dinner with Sam. At Santorini." I waved in the direction of the Greek restaurant.

"Oh, yeah, that's a good place. Dina and I have eaten there several times since it opened. Try the moussaka. It's great. You're early, though. The restaurant doesn't open till five."

"I know. I'm hoping to speak to Tamara Brownlow. I understand she works here sometimes, while she's in town."

Ed tilted his head to one side. "She does work here. I hired her about a month ago. With summer coming on and the rafting season picking up, I need the extra help." He paused, a questioning look on his face. "You said, 'while she's in town.' She lives here, shares an apartment with her friend Crystal, who also works for me."

"Really?" I chose my words carefully. "I thought she lived in Oakland and came to Rocoso just to visit Crystal."

Ed shook his head. "Tamara moved here about a month ago, to be closer to her grandmother." He frowned. "At least that's what she told me. Should I be worried about this?"

"No, I don't think so. I must have misunderstood."

But I hadn't. Tamara herself told me that she lived in

Oakland, when I'd first met her at the hospital on Friday. So had various members of her family—her mother, her aunt, her cousin.

What was the truth? And what was the lie?

Tamara said she'd driven up to Rocoso from Oakland the day after Hallie's death. If she was working for Ed and living with Crystal, she was already here in Rocoso the day her mother died.

I weighed asking the question, unsure about tipping off Ed to my concerns. "Was she working on Thursday?"

"No, she wasn't. She took a day off. Had to go down to Oakland to take care of some personal business. She said it couldn't wait."

That certainly muddied the waters. I had to figure out if Tamara was in town that day.

"I do need to talk with Tamara. It's important."

"Is this about her mother?" Ed asked. "I know she died. I heard that on the news."

"In a way. Is she here?"

He shook his head. "No. One of the rafters lost a day pack at the last pullout. She took the Jeep up there to look for it."

"Where's the last pullout?" I asked.

"It's that little picnic area below the tracks, where Lost Woman Creek runs into the river. A good place to stop before we shoot the Narrows," he added, referring to a series of rapids in the steep gorge, a stretch of the river where the canyon was constricted between high, rocky walls.

I knew the picnic area he was talking about. "Oh, yes. The turnoff is north of the bridge."

"Tamara left about twenty minutes ago," he said. "You're welcome to wait here till she gets back."

But I didn't want to wait. I had to talk with Tamara alone, without anyone else around, before she got back to the rafting company.

I thanked Ed without saying what I planned to do. He headed down to the river, and I returned to my car. Just as I reached the Prius, I stepped on an uneven portion of the gravel lot and felt something give way. I leaned on my car and lifted my left foot.

So much for that pair of shoes. The heel had pulled away from the sole. It looked like it could be repaired, though. Fortunately, I kept an extra pair of shoes in the car. I opened the rear hatch of the Prius and sat down, replacing the damaged pumps with a pair of well-used blue athletic shoes. I tied the laces with a double loop. That done, I shut the hatch and walked around to the driver's seat. Seat belt and harness fastened, I started the engine.

I drove north again, out of town and out of the valley where Rocoso sat, into the rolling hills, past a stand of California buckeyes, with their showy, six-inch blossoms, creamy white against dark green leaves. As I left the foothills and entered the mountains, the slopes became steeper, covered with oak and pine trees. By now it was after four. Though twilight and sundown were a couple of hours away, some of the canyons and slopes were already in shadow. I reached the turnoff to the county road that led to Creekside and Osprey Lake. Half a mile past this was the highway bridge that spanned Lost Woman Creek. I slowed, looking for the right turn that I knew was coming up, a hundred yards past the bridge.

I made the turn, onto a narrow, paved road that headed east and then curved a bit to the south. It wound down a steep slope for a mile or so, to an area where the terrain leveled out in a small clearing. I was familiar not only with the picnic spot on the river, but the railroad tracks that loomed ahead of me. Dad and the other volunteers on the Rocoso & Jermyn Railroad called this crossing Creek Station. It was the last point on the route where the narrow-gauge rails could be reached from the highway. North of here was a designated wilderness area, with no access to the tracks until the old mining town of Jermyn.

I stopped at the crossing, though I knew the afternoon train wasn't due through here yet. Stopping at railroad crossings was a habit my father had ingrained in me. As I drove on, wheels rumbling over the tracks, I thought about Greg Garvin, who had died so many years ago at a crossing. Suicide by train, according to Tish Lehigh.

Just past the tracks, the pavement ended. Now I was driving on gravel, my tires spitting up dust and rocks. The woods closed in on me again. Oaks and pines ranged along the road and blocked the sun in places or threw dappled shade on the road. Pine cones littered the sides of the road. Here and there, the road was rutted down to dried mud, in need of another layer of gravel.

Another mile or so and I neared the bottom of the canyon where the Rocoso River was visible from the top of a ridge. I drove down a couple of switchbacks to the small park. It was tucked on the riverbank, with a gravel parking lot. At one end of the lot were a vault toilet and a large bear-proof trash and recyclables container. Beyond the lot was a grassy oval containing a few picnic tables and fire rings.

The blue Jeep Wrangler with the Rocky River Rafting logo was parked here, but I didn't see Tamara. I pulled into the lot and got out of my car. Tucking my cell phone into one pocket and my keyring in the other, I walked past the tables to the water's edge and looked out at the river. Water rushed over the rocks, creating steady music that masked all other sounds. I stood on a small beach of sand and pebbles, about fifteen feet long, a good place for the rafts to pull out for a break. A jumble of boulders rose to my left. To my right, a narrow path led through a tangle of brush and white alder trees. As I knew from past visits to this place, the mouth of Lost Woman Creek was about fifty feet in that direction, gushing through rocks and past fallen trees as it emptied its waters into the river.

Tamara came into view, a pair of scuffed hiking boots kicking up dust as she made her way down the path. Today she wore a purple T-shirt and faded jeans, both tight on her lean body. She carried a bright yellow day pack, slung over one shoulder.

When she saw me, she stopped, her face wary. "What are you doing here?"

"I need to ask you some questions," I said.

"What about?" She began walking again, giving me a wide berth as she headed toward the Jeep. She opened the rear hatch and set the pack next to a plastic crate in the cargo area. Then she reached into the crate and pulled out a bottle of water. She took a swig and recapped the bottle, tossing it back into the crate. She perched on the tailboard, arms crossed over her chest.

"Where do you live?" When she didn't answer, I pressed on. "Your family says you live in Oakland. That's what Ethan says. In fact, on Friday, you told me that you lived in North Oakland. But I was just at the rafting company. Ed McGinty says you moved to Rocoso a few weeks ago and that you're living with Crystal. Which is it?"

Tamara shrugged and brushed one hand through her short blond hair. "You heard me wrong."

No, I hadn't, I thought. And I said as much. "Oakland or Rocoso. Which is it?"

She gave me a withering look. It was clear she didn't like my questions. She spoke like she was explaining something to a child. "I used to live in Oakland. Now I live in Rocoso. What's so hard to understand about that?"

"Where were you on Thursday? Ed said you took the day off."

She fixed me with a steady gaze from her light blue eyes, so much like her mother's. "What business is it of yours?"

"I'm the one who found Hallie's body. I'm just trying to fill in a few gaps."

She reached for the water bottle again, taking another swig. "I drove down to Oakland, to pick up the check for the returned deposit on the Oakland apartment. I didn't want to wait for them to mail it. I need the money. I've got to pay Crystal for my share of the rent, since I'm bunking at her place."

"So you gave up the apartment?" Another lie, I thought. Ethan had called the apartment in Oakland and talked with Tamara's roommate, who'd told him that Tamara was out of town, temporarily.

"Yeah. What's the big deal?" She leaned to her left and set the water bottle in the crate.

I walked toward her. "Your hair's different."

She stared at me. "What do you mean?"

"I saw you at the rafting company," I said. "A week ago Sunday. My friend and I stopped there to pick up Ed and Dina to go to a concert. You and Crystal were there, cleaning out one of the Jeeps. I wasn't sure at first that it was you, but I was down by the water, taking pictures of a heron. I looked at the pictures again today and I recognized you. Your hair was brown, all the way down to your shoulders. And it had streaks of color, red, green, and purple. When I saw you at the hospital on Friday, you'd cut and dyed your hair."

Her lips thinned and she narrowed her eyes, shrugging off my comment. "So what? I change my hair all the time. That's what people my age do. I dye it, I cut it off. It grows back and I do something different."

"Or maybe you had a reason." She didn't say anything. I went on. "Purple hair. A witness saw someone with dark hair and purple streaks leaving Betty's backyard on Thursday, about the same time your mother died. Was that you?"

Tamara's eyes shifted, looking at the river, the trees, anywhere but at me. I had seen that look before, when someone was about to lie to me. She shrugged. "Okay, I came over to see Mom. We talked. Then I left."

"Through the back gate?" My skepticism showed in my voice.

"She said something about Sheryl coming over. I didn't want to see her. I don't have much use for Sheryl."

I could believe that, having witnessed her earlier interactions with her aunt. But I didn't believe her story about why she left the house that way. According to what she'd told me on the phone that afternoon, Sheryl hadn't given Hallie any warning that she was on her way to Betty's house.

"Come on, Tamara," I said. "Level with me. Why did you want to talk with your mother?" She didn't say anything and I pressed on. "Is it about money? Ethan implied that you have a gambling problem."

At this, emotion flickered on her face. "Ethan talks too damn much. It's not a problem. It's just . . . Sometimes I'm a little short of cash."

A classic case of denial, I thought. I pushed harder. "It's tempting, I know. With all the card clubs in the Bay Area. And the Indian casino near Rocoso." I paused. "Those things that have gone missing from your grandmother's house, the ones I saw at the antique mall. You took them, didn't you? You need the money."

Her gaze was steady, calculating. "Okay, fine. I need money." She stood and put her hands on her hips. "I'm in hock to a loan shark. I'll be up shit creek if I don't get the money to pay him off."

"How much money do you owe?"

She hesitated, then named a figure that took me aback.

"That's a lot of money," I said.

"No shit. I figured I'd buy some time by coming up here. I'd already asked my father." Her mouth twisted in anger. "He's the one with the steady paycheck, working for the state. But no, he put me off. Said he couldn't come up with that kind of dough. Which is bullshit."

I'd already witnessed two encounters between Tamara and her father, Saturday at the farmers' market and again on Monday, at Betty's house. Both times I'd seen the tension between the two. If she'd been asking for money, that would explain it. I also noticed that Tamara was avoiding the topic I was most interested in.

"What happened Thursday, when you talked with Hallie?"

Tamara hesitated, her face taking on a look of sullen resentment. "She said she didn't have it. Said she's always living close to the edge. But she could get it from Lanny. With his pot business, he's got plenty of money."

"Maybe she didn't want to ask him."

She lashed out. "What about me? What about letting some damn loan shark break my legs?"

"What did you do, Tamara?" I kept my voice even, thinking that yes, it was Tamara who picked up the trowel and struck down her mother. Maybe I could convince her to come with me to the police.

"Never mind," she snapped. "I don't have time to listen to this nonsense."

She turned, as though ready to shut the Jeep's rear hatch. Then she moved toward me. A flash of sunlight on metal told me she had something in her hand. It was an X-shaped lug wrench. She swung it at my head.

Janet Dawson

Chapter 28

I THREW UP MY ARMS and turned to my right, trying to get away from Tamara. But she hit me on the left side of my head. I stumbled and fell to my knees. I'd deflected the worst of the blow. I was stunned and shocked, but still conscious, as I struggled to stand. Then Tamara kicked me, her heavy hiking boot connecting with my hip. I fell onto my side and rolled into a ball, my hands over my head, waiting for the next blow. But it didn't come.

She tossed the wrench into the plastic crate on the Jeep's tailboard. Then she leaned over, her hands moving over me. I pushed her hands away, but she slapped me. Then she rifled the pockets of my slacks. She took my phone and my keyring and shoved them into her pockets. I balled my hands into fists and struck at her. She kicked me in the side. As I reeled from the pain, she grabbed me by the arms. She dragged me toward the river, then into the water, then gave me a shove like I was nothing more than a raft.

I landed face down in the ice-cold water, gasping at the shock. I scrabbled at the nearby rocks, hoping to get a firm grip. The current tugged at me and I went under. I surfaced, gasping, and grabbed at a tree limb that had lodged between two rocks. It broke. The current carried me farther. I looked at the riverbank and saw Tamara closing the Jeep's rear hatch. She opened the driver's side door and slipped into the vehicle. Then she gunned the engine. The Jeep's wheels spun on the gravel as she sped up the slope, heading toward the highway.

I went under again and struggled to surface. The lace-up shoes I'd put on before leaving town were dragging me down. Should I take them off? A second later, the current hurled me into a pile of rocks. Here was another tree limb. I grabbed it and pulled myself closer to the rocks, buffeted by the cold water that numbed my body.

Hypothermia, that was the danger here. Already my hands were stiff with cold and my teeth chattered. I was shivering, and that was the first stage. The next would be a slowed pulse and a lack of coordination. And I needed all my resources to get out of this.

The limb I held shifted and twisted, the rocks loosening their grip on the wood. I managed to pull myself onto the larger of the two rocks. Then something hit me. It was a tree branch, a rough-barked pine, six or more feet long. It thudded against the rocks and moved on, pulled by the current. And it took me with it, past the creek's mouth and into the middle of the river.

The canyon wall rose to my left, steeper and more forbidding as the river rushed downstream. On the right, the river shore was lined with boulders and fallen trees. I was above the Narrows. I had been through there once before, on a rafting excursion with Sam, Dina, and Ed. I remembered that stretch of the river, with sheer rock walls on either side, water churning as it funneled between huge boulders. I had been glad that Ed, with his experience and savvy, was piloting the raft. Later I told Sam that once was enough. Shooting the rapids of the Rocoso River just wasn't my thing. Yes, the scenery was terrific, but I preferred to see it during a sedate meander down one of the many local hiking trails, without fear of being tossed from a raft into the swift, icy water.

Now here I was, clinging to a branch as the river, running full, fast, and icy cold because of the spring snowmelt, carried me toward the Narrows.

Cold, so cold. My hands, my arms, my legs felt like

blocks of ice. Shivering overtook me, overwhelmed me. Was I going into shock? The cold water was winning. I had to get out. But how?

Think, think. The log that was carrying me downriver had several smaller branches protruding from it. I inched forward, grasping the one nearest me with fingers that felt like useless icicles. This wasn't a long-dead log. It looked as though it had been recently torn from a digger pine, recognizable by the gray-green needles and the heavy seed cones, several of which were still attached. I slowly bent the branch, hoping the needles and cones would act as a drag, slowing the log as it went downstream.

It seemed to work. At least I thought the log's momentum had slowed a bit. I moved forward again, reaching for another branch. This one was smaller, but it too had thick clumps of needles and a few seed cones. I couldn't get my hands to work. I was so tired of fighting the water, the current. No, I couldn't give in. I bent the branch as much as I could, hoping it wouldn't break. Yes, that helped.

I glanced behind me, looking for other branches, and spotted a good-sized one floating toward me. With leaden hands, I reached for it. Maybe I could use it as a makeshift paddle to steer my way out of the current, closer to the shore. The branch snagged on a boulder. Then it pulled free and veered my way. I stretched out my left arm as far as I could reach. The branch was heavier than I expected and I had a time wrestling it toward me, tearing skin off my palms in the process. But I had it, finally. If I were on land, my heart would be beating with exertion. But the hypothermia was overtaking me. My pulse had slowed. I felt weak, ready to let the river take me.

I heard it. Up ahead, the rush and roar of water. I looked downriver, knowing that I was approaching the Narrows.

I grasped the branch with both my hands, mottled white from the cold and torn from the branch. Up ahead I saw a tree that had toppled. The upended roots lay between rocks on the shore, and the trunk protruded at an angle into the river. My shoulders ached as I fought the current, using the branch to steer myself. Slowly, gradually I neared the downed tree. Finally, I was close enough. I launched myself at the tree, feeling the rough bark abrade my hand as I pulled myself from the river onto the tree.

Out of the water. I lay there for a moment, panting and shivering. It would be so easy just to lie here. But I couldn't. Not out of trouble yet. Move, move.

I crawled along the log, heading to the shore. I fell rather than climbed off the log, onto the rocky verge of the river. I forced my frozen, unwieldy body to crawl farther up the bank. Then I moved with agonizing slowness, dragging myself upright. Kneeling, then standing. I moved a few feet to my left, away from the shade and into the sun, relishing the warmth. As I stood there, I blew on my hands and rubbed them together, then rubbed my hands on my arms, hoping to restore some circulation. As my skin began to warm, the scratches on my hands and arms bled. I used the tail of my shirt to stanch the blood.

Where was I? Ahead of me was a steep slope paved with rocks of all sizes, a gully on the right offering a possible route out.

Somewhere above me were the railroad tracks. Had the last train gone by, returning from Jermyn to Rocoso? I didn't remember hearing a train whistle, which the engineer would have sounded as he approached the crossing at Creek Station. Even if I missed the train, I knew that if I walked north, I'd eventually reach the crossing. From there it was a mile up to the highway, where I could flag down a car. But I didn't relish doing any of this in the dark. I looked at my left wrist and discovered my watch was gone. No doubt it had been torn off during my struggle to get out of the water. The slant of light in the canyon told me the sun was lowering in the west. It must be after five by now, twilight coming on.

I reached up and felt the spot where the wrench had connected with my head. It was on my temple, just above my left ear, tender as I probed it with my fingers. I looked at my hand. No blood. It must be water, then. Or, if there had been blood, it had washed away. But maybe the wrench hadn't broken the skin.

Thank God I had exchanged those pumps for these athletic shoes, still laced tight on my stumbling feet. How else would I climb out of the canyon?

Sam. I was supposed to meet Sam for dinner at five. When I didn't show up, he'd start wondering. He'd call my cell phone, to see where I was. Maybe he'd go over to the nearby rafting company to ask if Ed had seen me. Sam would start looking for me.

But how would he know where to look? Where was I? How far had the water carried me? Half a mile? A mile? Even more?

I had to move, to climb. There was just an hour or so of daylight left in this canyon. And the temperature was already dropping. I would be even colder than I already was. Again I rubbed my hands over my arms and shoulders, then my legs. I had to get moving. I had to get out of here before it got dark.

I approached the gully, limping as my knees protested. From a tangle of fallen wood at the base of the tree, I found a sturdy branch that would serve as a hiking pole. Then I began to climb. It was slow going, but at least the exertion was raising my body temperature. I can do this, I told myself, as I tackled a particularly steep and rocky section.

Overconfidence. I twisted my ankle, gasping with pain. Keep going. I winced as I put weight on the ankle, but I kept going.

It seemed to take forever. Inching upward, stumbling. But moving. I was midway up the slope when I heard the train whistle. It was the Rocoso & Jermyn narrow gauge, the last train of the day, heading back to Rocoso. How far away was it? Some distance yet, I thought, approaching Creek Station. The train's route wound along the river, and it never traveled fast through these mountains. But I had to get up to the tracks, and soon. I ignored the shivering, my clumsy body, the pain in my ankle, and pushed forward. Finally, I scrambled the last few feet up to the railbed. How far away was the train? Now I heard it, the locomotive puffing and chugging. Ahead of me the tracks curved. The locomotive came into view.

I quickly unbuttoned my blouse, the blue fabric still damp, that and the camisole underneath now stained with dirt and blood. With my cold fingers, I tied both of the sleeves of the blouse to the limb I had been using as a walking stick. I raised my makeshift flag and began to wave it back and forth. The engineer responded with two short bursts on the signals. In whistle code, that meant an acknowledgment. The train began to slow.

Chapter 29

THE EXAMINING TABLE WAS tilted at one end, propping me into a half-sitting position. I was covered with a thermal blanket, used by the hospital to raise my body temperature. I savored the heat. It felt so good after that ice-cold river. The warmth was making me drowsy.

An emergency room nurse stood nearby, holding a mug of hot tea. She handed it to me. "Drink more of this. As much as you can."

I held the mug with both hands, sipping the tea. Warmth trickled down my throat. This was my third cup since I'd arrived at the ER several hours ago. I finished the tea and handed the mug back to the nurse.

The doctor entered the examining room, white coat over gray slacks and shirt, a stethoscope draped around her neck. "How are you feeling now?" She touched my forehead and peered at the bump on my temple.

"Much better. Nice and warm."

"Good. You don't have a concussion, fortunately. Just a bad whack on the head. And we've got your body temperature back up where it should be. Rest should do it. Drink lots of fluids. And take a mild pain reliever. Acetaminophen would be good. Not just for the headache but the bruises on your arms and legs." Her smile was reassuring. "I know you don't want to be cold again, especially after what happened, but cold compresses will help with those bruises. You should be fine. See your own doctor to follow up."

The warming-up process had started as soon as I flagged down the train. The conductor and brakeman had climbed down to the tracks, listening to my garbled plea, and helped me to board the train. The brakeman wrapped me in a blanket as the conductor got out his cell phone and called the depot in Rocoso. They'd put me in the first car, where a woman zipped me into her down jacket and others piled on their coats and jackets. A man had a thermos that was half-full of coffee, still warm, and I sipped that, shivering. I borrowed a phone to call Sam and asked him to call my mother.

The ambulance was at the depot when the train arrived. Sam and Mom were waiting at the emergency room. That was hours ago and I was exhausted. The burst of adrenaline that had helped me get out of the swiftly flowing water and propelled me up the steep climb to the tracks had dissipated. All I wanted now was to go home and sleep in my own warm, comfortable bed.

The doctor excused herself and left the room, then the nurse helped me dress. My skin was covered with blue-black splotches, where my body had banged against the rocks while I was being carried downriver. I felt a twinge in my ankle, the one I'd twisted while climbing up from the river. Everything was sore now and would be worse in the morning.

The clothes I had been wearing were now stained and dirty, torn in several places. I put on those old athletic shoes, wincing as I propped my feet up so I could tie them. On my feet now, I stood for a moment, checking my balance.

"Okay?" the nurse asked.

I nodded. "I'll be fine."

I sat down again, this time in a wheelchair. The nurse wheeled me to the waiting room. Sam sat in the nearest row of chairs, my mother next to him. Ed and Dina were there as well. So was my cousin Riley, the detective from the Rocoso County Sheriff's Department. They all stood and converged on me.

I'd already talked with Riley. Cop that he was, he'd followed me into the examining room, refusing to be put off by the emergency room staff. I gave him a brief statement. He had a grim look on his face as I informed him that it was Tamara who had attacked me. "I think she killed Hallie," I added, outlining my reasons for coming to that conclusion.

"Why didn't you tell me your suspicions earlier? Instead of playing detective on your own." He frowned. I could feel the lecture coming. Before he could launch into it, the nurse told him to leave. "I'll talk with you later," he said as he headed out to the corridor, his phone already deployed.

Now I greeted Mom and the others, giving them an update on my condition. "I'm finally warm. No concussion. Just a bad whack on the head, the doctor said. And lots of bruises."

Mom put her arms around me. "I'm so glad you're all right."

"A quick follow-up," Riley said. "We have Tamara Brownlow in custody. I'd like a more detailed statement from you. Tomorrow's fine. First thing in the morning?"

"Let's see how I feel when I get up." The thought of doing anything first thing in the morning was daunting.

Riley nodded and headed out the door. So did Dina and Ed, after both gave me hugs.

"I've already talked with Gwen and Carmen," Sam said. "They're canceling and rescheduling your appointments for tomorrow."

I nodded. "I'll call them in the morning."

Sam fetched his Honda from the garage and pulled up in front of the ER a few minutes later. He helped Mom and me into his car. At Mom's house, he walked her to the door and made sure she was inside. Then he headed for my house a few blocks away. The LED readout on the dashboard told me that it was nearly midnight. He parked in my driveway and got out, quickly moving around the car to open the door for me. Then he helped me up the steps to the porch. He had a key to the house, which was good because Tamara had taken my keyring. And I was without transportation. My car was still up at the pullout near Lost Woman Creek.

The cats met us at the living room door, meowing their usual concerns about having no food. Sam switched on lights as he led me from the living room to the bedroom. I bent over and untied my shoes, kicking them off. Then I reached for the buttons on my shirt.

"Let me do that." Sam's fingers pushed my hands away. He unbuttoned the shirt and slid it from my shoulders. The camisole came next.

"Will you feed the cats before you go?"

"I'm spending the night." His no-nonsense voice brooked no argument. "I'm staying here, to keep an eye on you."

"Ordinarily, I would say you don't need to and I'm fine and all that. But . . . Yes."

Sam unhooked my bra and removed it. He shook his head. "Those bruises on your arms look bad."

"I have more on my legs. I got banged up bouncing through those rocks."

His fingers moved to my waist. He unzipped my slacks and pushed them down, along with my panties. I tossed the discarded clothing into the laundry basket visible in my closet. Sam surveyed the black splotches on my body. "Those will be purple in the morning. What did the doctor recommend?"

"Acetaminophen." I pointed a thumb at the bathroom door. "There's a bottle in the medicine cabinet. Extra strength. Two should do it."

"Take more if you need to."

Sam retrieved my sleep shirt from the hook in the closet, where it hung next to my robe. I held up my arms, wincing with the pain of pulled muscles. He slipped the shirt over my head. Then he steered me to the bed and pulled down the comforter. I settled into bed, propped against the pillows as he pivoted and went into my bathroom. He opened the cabinet, taking out the familiar bottle. He ran some water into the glass that sat on the counter. He carried these to the bed and set them on the nightstand. I opened the bottle, shook out a couple of pills, and swallowed them, washing them down with water.

Sam sat down on the chair next to the dresser and removed his shoes. As he stood up, he pulled his T-shirt over his head, unzipped his jeans, and let them drop to the floor. Wearing only his shorts, he got into bed beside me. He put his arms around me and I leaned into his furry chest. Sam was something of a furnace and I was enjoying his body heat.

"Oh, that feels good." I snuggled deeper into his arms. "I get cold thinking about being in that water."

"You've had a rough day." He kissed me on the side of the head, careful to avoid the sore spot. Then his lips moved down my neck, brushed my shoulder, and moved to my mouth.

I kissed him back. Then I saw the cats hovering in the bedroom doorway. "You were going to feed the cats."

"It will keep for a while."

"Not to hear them tell it. But I don't want you to get out of bed just yet."

I thought back to what Sam had told me during my hectic arrival at the hospital between the time they'd taken me out of the ambulance and rushed me into the examining room. It was about my phone, and how he and Ed had figured out that Tamara had something to do with my disappearance.

When I asked him, he nodded. "I wasn't sure you'd heard me."

"Tell me again." I snuggled closer, enveloped in the warmth of his arms, inhaling his scent. "Now that you have my full attention."

"I got to the restaurant at five," he said. "You weren't there, so I figured you were running late. I sat outside, waiting for you. After fifteen minutes or so, I called your cell phone. Several times. It kept going to voice mail.

"Because Tamara took my phone."

"Yes. And that backfired on her," Sam said. "Around five-thirty, I saw Ed come out of his office, so I walked over to talk with him. When I said I was waiting for you, he told me that he'd seen you earlier, that you'd gone up to the pullout to look for Tamara. Ed had just called her to find out if she'd located the day pack, because the customer was getting antsy and wanted to leave. So she had to get back in a hurry. She drove in a short time after I walked over from the restaurant. When Ed and I asked about you, she said she hadn't seen you. She was nervous, handed over the day pack, said she had to finish up here and get going, because she had to be someplace. By then I was really worried. I decided to call your cell phone again. It started ringing. It was coming from the Jeep."

I nodded. "I saw her throw the phone and my keyring into the back cargo area. I'm surprised she didn't silence it. Or get rid of the phone."

"She was going to," he said. "When it started ringing because of my earlier calls, she pulled over on the highway, planning to find it and pitch it. But while she was driving, the phone slid around in the cargo area and slipped under one of the seats. She couldn't find it. Then her own phone rang, because Ed was calling her. She must have gotten rattled from all those calls. When Ed and I found your phone and your keyring in the back of the Jeep, Tamara couldn't, or wouldn't, tell us why she had them. And she wouldn't give us a straight answer about where you were. She kept giving us conflicting information. Ed called the sheriff's office and kept her there while I drove up to the pullout. Your car was there, but you weren't. I called out, thinking you might be somewhere nearby, but you didn't answer."

"She shoved me in the river. She tried to kill me." I shivered again, remember the cold, rushing water.

Sam pulled me closer. "I drove back up the road, slowly, calling out in case you were walking near the road. I had to stop at the crossing, because the train was going by. The same train you flagged down."

"I'm glad I did. That was the last train of the day. If I hadn't gotten up to the tracks when I did, I would have had to walk back to Creek Station."

"I was on my way back to Rocoso when you called. I was so relieved." Sam pushed back the covers on his side of the bed and swung his legs to the floor. "Now, get some sleep. I'll go feed those voracious cats."

WEDNESDAY MORNING, MY HEAD didn't hurt as much. I'd had a much needed and undisturbed night's sleep. I sat up in bed and reached for the bottle of acetaminophen on the nightstand, washing down two more tablets with the last of the water in the glass.

Beside me, Sam plumped his pillow, then leaned back and stretched his arms over his head. Then he slipped out of bed. "I'll make coffee."

The cats, who'd spent the night curled at the foot of the bed, got up with him, eager for breakfast. Barefoot, in his shorts, he headed for the kitchen, followed by the cats, who were now vocalizing their desire for food. Sam answered back. "I'll feed you as soon as I make coffee. First things first. Coffee. No? Well, none of you look like you've missed any meals." The coffee maker hissed, followed by the sound of Sam opening and closing a cupboard. Then a lid came off a can and a spoon clinked against the ceramic cat bowls.

"Thanks for feeding the cats," I said as he returned to the bedroom with two large mugs of freshly brewed coffee. I took one from him and had my first restorative sip of caffeine.

"I was afraid I'd get mugged if I didn't. Those fat cats of yours look capable of it." Sam slipped back into bed. We sat, chatting as we drank our coffee. "Want a warm-up?"

I shook my head, gently so it wouldn't hurt. "I'd better get up. A lot to do. I'll need to check in with Gwen and Carmen. Though I'm sure they have everything under control at the office. Will you take me to see Riley? My car is still up at that park on the river."

"Of course. Riley first, then I'll take you up there to get the car."

I threw back the covers, wincing a bit as I got up. I pulled my sleep shirt over my head and stood at the mirror, examining the bruises and scratches on my arms and legs. The bruises were an alarming shade of black and purple.

"You're quite colorful," Sam said.

"I won't be wearing short sleeves for a while."

"Breakfast coming up. Scrambled eggs okay?"

"Sure."

Sam pulled on his T-shirt and jeans and went back to the kitchen. I headed for the bathroom and took a long hot shower. That helped work out some of the kinks. I belted my robe around me and joined Sam at the kitchen table. He had scrambled the eggs with grated cheddar and was just taking English muffins out of the toaster. He buttered them and set the plate on the table, along with a jar of raspberry jam.

Once we'd eaten, I called my colleagues. We had a three-way conversation, with Gwen and Carmen outlining what they'd already done to rejigger my schedule. "You don't need to rush back to work," Carmen added. "We've got everything covered. And I'm coming over later, with a pan of homemade enchiladas."

"That sounds great. I love your enchiladas. I'll talk with you later." I hung up.

A few minutes later, I got calls from both Mom and Dina. Then they came over, bringing food and conversation. "I baked," Mom said. "Chocolate chip bundt cake."

"I don't bake," Dina chimed in. "But I'm great when it comes to ordering food. You just say the word and pizza will be on its way."

I dressed, finally, wearing a loose-fitting shirt and slacks. Then Sam drove me to the sheriff's office, where I sat down with Riley and another detective, giving the detailed statement that they wanted.

"The photos. Tamara took the phone for two reasons. She didn't want me calling for help and she wanted those photos I'd taken at the rafting company. I'm surprised she didn't delete them."

Riley nodded. "She was planning to. When she got back to Rocoso. But Sam and Ed grabbed her first."

"It wouldn't have done her any good. I back up everything to the cloud."

Sam waited for me in the station lobby. We headed out to his car and he pointed the Honda north on the highway. Our destination was the pullout, to retrieve my Prius. It was a beautiful spring day and I was all right for most of the trip. But when we turned off the highway and onto the narrow road leading down to the river, the feelings washed over me. At the park, we got out of his car. I heard the swift water rushing over and through the rocks. It brought back the fear of yesterday's ordeal.

"You okay?" Sam stood close, his arm around my shoulder.

I drew in a breath. "I'm fine." And I would be. I took a long look at the river and thought, as I had many times since yesterday afternoon, how bad it could have been.

Spare key in hand, I turned toward my car. I drove up the gravel road, with Sam in my wake.

It was early afternoon when I got home. There were lots of messages on my home phone as well as my cell phone. I dialed in to check the messages on my office phone. But I only returned those calls that were urgent. The day's activities left me exhausted. I took off my clothes and got into bed. Time for a nap. The cats concurred, wedging themselves close to me.

I WAS BACK TO WORK on Thursday, feeling much better. My head was still tender. The bruises were indeed colorful.

I spent the day playing catch-up—visiting clients, rescheduling appointments, returning phone calls. One of those appointments was with Sheryl Garvin.

It was mid-afternoon when I drove over to Betty's house. Sheryl met me at the door and ushered me into the living room. "Will you have some coffee?"

I smiled. "Yes, thanks. I could use the caffeine boost to get me through the rest of the day."

I followed her to the back of the house. On the counter that separated the kitchen from the family room, I saw a plate of cookies and a pan of brownies.

"Help yourself," she said with a wave. "The neighbors keep bringing over food. I'm trying not to eat so much, but Ethan is making inroads on the baked goods."

I selected a large oatmeal raisin cookie. "Is Ethan still here? I didn't see his car in the driveway."

"He's having a late lunch with his father." Something flickered over Sheryl's face, as though mentioning her estranged husband annoyed her. "Ethan's going back to Berkeley as soon as the funeral is over. He has finals next week and I don't know that's he's been able to get much studying done this week."

She filled two mugs with coffee from the carafe. Then, remembering that I took milk in mine, she pulled a quart from the refrigerator. I poured in a splash of milk and put the carton back in the fridge. I took a sip of coffee, then bit into the cookie. Ah, yes, that was the pick-me-up that I needed.

In the family room, Betty sat in her recliner, a colorful crocheted afghan tucked around her. She looked frail after everything that had happened—her daughter's death, her granddaughter's arrest, and her heart attack. She had been reading, but now she was asleep, her eyes closed and her head tilted to one side. The book was about to slip off her lap. I left the mug and cookie on the counter and stepped over to the recliner to steady the book.

She woke with a start and looked at me, confusion in her blue eyes. "Who's that?"

"It's Kay Dexter," I said.

Recognition dawned. "Oh, yes. Kay. You're Rose's daughter. It's nice of you to come over."

"How are you feeling, Betty?"

The old woman mustered a thin smile. "Well, I'm still under the weather, you know. After the hospital. And . . ." She stopped, sadness turning the smile into a frown. "Everything piling up. It's just too much to deal with."

I squeezed her hand, wondering how much she knew about Tamara's involvement in Hallie's death. "I know. We can talk about that later, if you want."

"That would be nice." Her gnarled fingers returned the squeeze.

I straightened and stepped back to the kitchen to retrieve my coffee and cookie.

"Let's talk in the living room." Sheryl glanced at Betty, who was nodding off again. "I don't want to disturb Mother. She needs all the rest she can get before the funeral. You got the message I left about the time?"

I nodded as Sheryl and I went to the living room. "Yes, I did. Eleven o'clock tomorrow morning." The service would be held at a church that Betty had attended in the past.

I took a seat in the armchair near the front window, finishing off the cookie. Then I sipped coffee and cradled the mug in my hands.

Sheryl sat down on the sofa and put her mug on the coffee table. "Good, we'll see you there. By the way, we got Mother's things from that antique dealer."

I looked over at the china cabinet, but I didn't see the silver bowls and other items I'd found in the stall at the antique mall. Perhaps they were put away for the time being. "I'm glad you got them back. Was it difficult?"

Sheryl flashed a smile. "A deputy talked with the dealer. That got her attention. She handed them over. But they're still at the sheriff's office. Evidence, they tell me. I gather they are going to charge Tamara with theft."

"She's going to be charged with murder, so I don't know that the theft charge matters."

"It does to me," Sheryl said, her mouth hard. "After everything she's put us through. And attacking you the way she did. She could have killed you."

She could have indeed, I thought. But somehow, I didn't feel as vindictive about it as Sheryl seemed to. The family had been through a lot in the past couple of weeks. Would there ever be a time for healing? Maybe not. I'd seen families pick at wounds for years.

"When are you going back to Seattle?" I asked.

"I'm not going back. Not for a few weeks, anyway." She reached for her coffee. "I've told Richard it's over. He wasn't surprised. At some point, I'll go up to Seattle to pack up my things and arrange to have them shipped here to Rocoso. I'm living here with Mother, for the time being. I'll look for a place of my own, of course. I saw a condo I liked yesterday, a few miles north of town."

She smiled now, and I knew she was thinking about her relationship with Alex Delattre. Living on the north side of Rocoso would put Sheryl that much closer to the artist, who lived in Lakeview.

"Closer to Lost Woman Creek," I said. "Is your hot springs resort project on hold?"

"Not at all," she said, with a toss of her head. "I'm moving forward with the plans."

"That's a bit difficult. I mean, Betty has title to the land, not you."

"I'm sure I can get Mother to agree to the project." She shot me a narrow look that invited me to butt out.

Now that Hallie was dead, there was no one to oppose Sheryl. She would make every effort to persuade her mother to sign over the land. It was another example of what Lanny had described as her tendency to take over and run roughshod over everyone else. This was especially true since Hallie's will had split her estate between Tamara and Lanny. Tamara had killed her mother, which meant that she wouldn't receive her portion of the estate. Sheryl didn't want Lanny in the mix at all. She'd take the first opportunity to cut him out.

I was concerned about Sheryl putting undue influence on her mother. Since I was Betty's geriatric care manager, I'd have to walk a tightrope to make sure Sheryl didn't take advantage of Betty.

As it turned out, I wouldn't get the chance.

"We won't need your services any longer," she said. "Since I'm living with Mother now, I can look after her needs, make sure she's getting proper nutrition, take her to the doctor. And once I move back to Rocoso, even though I'll have my own place, we'll manage."

There was nothing for me to do but make the best of it. After all, it wasn't the first time a client had dispensed with my services. Sheryl was free to hire the caregivers I'd recommended, and she probably would.

However, whether I was her care manager or not, I worried about Betty Garvin and what lay ahead for her.

I kept my face neutral and set aside my mug, telling Sheryl I had another appointment. Which was true. We talked briefly about transitions and then I made my exit.

HALLIE GARVIN'S MEMORIAL SERVICE was a subdued affair.

The mood inside the small church on the south side of town contrasted with the sunny day outside. May had erupted in all its glory, showing off this Friday morning with a blue cloudless sky. The houses near the church displayed everything from roses and lilacs to flower beds full of bright, colorful petunias, pansies, and freesia. Farther down the street, an orchard full of apple trees was covered with pink-tinged white blossoms, promising a bountiful crop in the fall.

Large ceramic pots of red and pink geraniums sat on either side of the church's double doors. The riot of color didn't extend to the foyer. It was bland and institutional, carpeted in utilitarian beige that extended into the sanctuary.

A long table covered with a white cloth had been set up in the foyer. It held a small vase of pink carnations as well as a guest book. I signed the book, then entered the sanctuary. The pews on either side of a central aisle were made of varnished pine, with no cushions. The same wood was repeated in the altar and pulpit. Behind the pulpit were several rows of empty chairs that would seat the choir on Sunday morning. A door led to the back of the church. To the left of the altar were several chairs, one of them occupied by a white-haired man in a dark blue suit. He held a Bible and a few index cards. I assumed he was the minister, waiting to start the service. To the right of the altar were a piano and an organ. A woman in a navy-blue dress sat at the piano, playing hymns. As she segued from one tune to another, I recognized one of them, "Abide with Me." It had been my father's favorite, played at his funeral.

I walked up the aisle, looking at the assembled mourners. There were about two dozen people in the pews. I recognized a few family members and guessed that the others were neighbors and friends.

Betty sat in the first pew on the right. She wore a black dress and clutched a white handkerchief, using the cloth to dab tears from her face, weighed down by all the drama and turmoil of the last week. Sheryl sat next to her mother. On her other side was her son, Ethan, and, next to him, Sheryl's estranged husband, Richard.

In another pew, I saw Tish Lehigh, the cousin from Appleton. She was accompanied by two younger women. They looked so much like her that I guessed they were her daughters.

Justin Brownlow, Hallie's ex and Tamara's father, sat alone at the back of the church. He looked down, as though staring at the carpet beneath his feet. I wondered what was going through his mind.

I walked up to the altar, which held a pewter urn decorated at the bottom and top with a pattern of leaves. According to her wishes, Hallie had been cremated. There were half a dozen floral offerings grouped around the urn. I glanced at the cards accompanying the flowers. Sheryl and her family had sent the huge arrangement that dwarfed all the other offerings, a tall, wide concoction of yellow roses, white chrysanthemums, and pale pink lilies. Next to this were several smaller displays, including a bouquet of pink and yellow roses from Lanny Fitzpatrick.

Lanny was there, of course, sitting in a pew on the left of the aisle. He beckoned me to join him, sliding over to make room, and I sat down. The big man with the long gray ponytail had dressed up for the occasion, though he looked as though he would be more comfortable in the denim shorts and T-shirt he'd been wearing the first time I met him. Today he wore a pair of neatly pressed gray slacks, with a dark blue blazer over a lighter blue shirt. He'd shaved, but he was one of those men with a heavy beard. The lower half of his face was covered with bristles, white in the sunlight on this morning in late May.

He shifted, glancing first at the front of the church, then back at me. "When I get back to Arcata, Hallie's gonna have a good sendoff. I've lined up a place. It's a club we liked to go to. She loved bluegrass music. I got her favorite local band lined up to play at the service. Me and a bunch of her friends, we're going to put up all sorts of pictures. I'll say a few words and so will her friend Aviva. Then we'll have an open mike, you know. Do it so people can get up and talk about Hallie. She had lots of friends."

"She had you," I said. "I know you loved her."

I took his big hand in mine and squeezed it, feeling his answering pressure.

"She was so full of life." His voice was sad and wistful.

And opinions, I thought, remembering that first time I'd met Hallie.

"Sheryl has dispensed with my services as Betty's care manager," I said, keeping my voice low. "Of course, I saw that coming."

"I figured she would," he said. "Now that she's moved back here."

"You should be aware that she's planning to go ahead with the hot springs resort."

He looked at me. "She doesn't own the land. Betty does. But I guess I shouldn't be surprised. She's gonna try to convince Betty to give her the land. She might even persuade Betty to change her will. That way it would cut me out. You just wait. That will be what happens."

I agreed with him and I wasn't sure how I could prevent it from happening. "I'd consult an attorney, if I were you."

He flashed me a smile and a sidelong glance. "I already have. A guy here in town. Benny Ma. He says he knows you."

"We go way back, and he's a good lawyer."

The pianist stopped playing and the minister got up, walking over to the pulpit. The service itself was short and prosaic. It was clear the man had never met Hallie and was operating from information given to him by her sister.

After the service was over, the mourners filed out of the church, some gathering in the foyer, where they spoke with Betty and the others, paying their respects. Other people moved out to the lawn in front of the church, some clustering in groups, others heading for their cars. Lanny and I went outside, in time to see Justin Brownlow get into his car and drive away. As far as I could see, he hadn't spoken to anyone.

Ethan walked up beside Sheryl, holding a cardboard carton. After glancing at his mother, he held it out to Lanny. The big man took the carton and opened the flap, revealing a small urn that looked similar to the one on the altar. He looked up at Sheryl, a question in his eyes.

"This urn has some of Hallie's ashes," Sheryl said. "I know you're planning a memorial service up in Humboldt County, with all her friends there. I thought that . . ." Her voice trailed off.

"Thanks," he said with a nod. "I really appreciate it."

"We're going to bury the other urn in the family plot. You're welcome to join us at the gravesite."

"I think I'll head on back to Arcata." Lanny shut the flap on the carton. "It's a long drive."

Sheryl nodded. Lanny and I watched as she and Ethan walked away, joining Betty and the other family members at the church entrance.

"That was a nice thing for her to do," Lanny said.

"It was." I walked with him to his Jeep.

He opened the rear hatch and tucked the carton into a safe place, protected by his duffel bag. Next to this was a canvas tote. I saw a T-shirt and a pair of denim shorts and smiled.

He laughed, removing his blazer. "Yeah, I'm getting out of these clothes as soon as I get out of town." He shut the hatch.

"I hope you'll stay in touch." I held out my hand to Lanny.

"None of that handshake stuff." Instead, he leaned over and hugged me, drawing me to his chest with his big, powerful arms. "Yeah, I got your number and you've got mine. I know you stay busy, but if you ever get up to Humboldt County, call me."

I hugged him back and then he released me. He got into the car and buckled his seat belt, then he started the engine and backed out of the space. I watched him drive away, then headed for my car. The funeral was over, time to move on. I had an appointment with another client in half an hour, and if I didn't leave now, I'd be late.

Acknowledgments

The idea for *The Sacrificial Daughter* came to me several years ago as I dealt with aging parents, something common with many people of my age. Many of the incidents described came from real life—my own experiences with my parents as well as the experiences of relatives and friends.

Many thanks to Robin Burcell, who not only writes terrific novels but also has thirty years of experience as a police officer, detective, hostage negotiator, and forensic artist. I appreciate her generosity in sharing information about police procedure. I appreciate the information obtained from Robin Sanow, R.N., who has a long career as a medical social worker, first at a Bay Area hospital and then for Alameda County, and now as a care manager for Senior Alternatives in Oakland, California. Susan Russell provided information on Meals on Wheels and Roger Dawson added information on river rafting.

Many thanks to fellow mystery writers D. Z. Church and Margaret Lucke, always willing to answer questions, who assisted me and answered many questions as I wrote this book and brought it through to publication.

If you enjoyed this book, please leave a short review on Amazon, Goodreads and/or BookBub, to help other readers discover it. Just a few lines would be fine. Thank you.

About the Author

Janet Dawson writes the series featuring Oakland private investigator Jeri Howard. Jeri has sleuthed her way through thirteen books, beginning with *Kindred Crimes*. The most recent book is *The Devil Close Behind*.

She also writes the California Zephyr historical mysteries, with Zephyrette Jill McLeod, who solves mysteries aboard the historic train in the 1950s. The series stars with *Death Rides the Zephyr* and the most recent book is *Death Above the Line*.

Dawson's other fiction includes a suspense novel, *What You Wish For*, and a novella, *But Not Forgotten*, as well as a dozen short stories.

In the past, Dawson was a newspaper reporter in Colorado. Her stint as a Navy journalist took her to Guam and Florida. As a Navy officer, she was stationed in the San Francisco Bay Area. After leaving the service, she worked in the legal field and at the University of California.

She is a long-time member of Mystery Writers of America and Sisters in Crime. She enjoys birding, riding on trains, gardening, going to the theater and museums, and thinks afternoon tea is a most civilized English tradition. She loves cats but denies being a crazy cat lady.

For more news about Janet Dawson and to sign up for the Bodie Blue Books newsletter, go to: www.janetdawson.com

Facebook:
https://www.facebook.com/Mysteries.PrivateEyes.Trains/

Bodie Blue Books: bodiebluebooks@gmail.com

Latest Books by Janet Dawson

The Jeri Howard Series

The Devil Close Behind

Oakland PI Jeri Howard is on vacation in New Orleans. A friend asks a favor: her sister has disappeared with a boyfriend, a mercurial musician. Jeri's trip turns into a case, taking her from French Quarter clubs to workaday NOLA, then back to California, where she finds jeopardy and an explosive conclusion.

The California Zephyr Series

Death Above the Line

Travel back in time—to the 1950s—with Zephyrette Jill McLeod, aboard the train called the California Zephyr. Jill takes care of passengers' needs and keeps an eye out for trouble. That includes murder. In her latest adventure, the train has been replaced by a movie set. When someone winds up dead, Jill uses her sleuthing skills to find the killer.